SON OF
FLAME

SON OF FLAME

BOOK ONE

J. J. Hutto

Podium

To my wife, whose trust is the greatest treasure I have ever won & to my daughters, who begged me for the next chapter long before anyone else knew who Tilly was.

Copyright © 2025 by Joshua James Hutto

Cover design by Mario Teodosio

ISBN: 978-1-0394-7978-4

Published in 2025 by Podium Publishing
www.podiumentertainment.com

Podium

SON OF FLAME

CHAPTER ONE

Regrets

Fifteen minutes before Transference

There is nothing like being in a burning building. Flames roll overhead, and you descend into the eerie calmness that waits for all those who walk the knife's edge between life and death. Even after all his years in the service, Tilly still felt most like himself in this place. Doing what few others could.

They were on a primary search of the building, and his rookie had just cleared the last room in the basement when a terrible moan reverberated through the joists above. The "Orange Shield" froze in a doorway, looking up at the growing flames in confusion. He had probably never heard the sound of a building collapsing from the inside. This is where he would either fall in love with this job, or quit.

Tilly remembered his first fire, the feeling of stepping into a new world, one painted in orange and red. He had forced himself to move one step at a time in the pitch-black smoke as they searched for, and eventually found, the seat of the fire. Every man or woman in this profession faces a moment like this. All the noise, all the talk burns up in that flame, and all that is left is your training and discipline. Everything you think you know about yourself is tested, and you find out who you are when your choices can kill one of your brothers or sisters on the line next to you.

Tilly gave the rookie one more second, waiting for him to conquer his fear and remember his training . . . but he just stood there, filling the doorway like a mannequin masquerading as a firefighter, as he continued to look up at the groaning ceiling.

That's it, time's up.

Tilly grabbed him roughly by the strap of his Air-Pak, and pulled him close, facepiece to facepiece.

"Get moving, kid," Tilly growled. He shoved the panicked rookie toward the stairs leading up from the basement and out of the collapsing building.

The moaning from above crescendoed into a terrible splintering sound like a man with pneumonia finally coughing up his last breath. Both men were now rushing toward the stairs in a crouch to keep the heat off their heads as they covered the distance as fast as possible.

The rookie made it to the stairs and scaled them in a few bounds, showing none of his previous hesitation. But Tilly stopped short, some niggling feeling tugged at his subconscious, and he turned to take one last look down the darkening hallway. Then he saw it, ten feet down the hall to the right. A small side door, probably a closet they had missed, opened on its own, and a terrified, tear-stained face peeked out from the bottom of the opening.

Tilly's stomach turned to stone, and his limbs went heavy as the ceiling slowly collapsed under the weight of the collapsing timbers above it.

It's already too late . . .

Even if I get to her, she wouldn't survive the smoke and flames on the way out.

While his mind struggled to process through his lack of options, his body was already moving. At this point, he was limited to a crawl toward the closet to keep the heat off him. He reached the door as the sounds of the building's collapse thundered to a conclusion of shattered drywall and splintered joists. In a flash decision, he pushed her back from the door and dived in, jamming the door shut behind him.

In the dark cramped space, he could barely hear her coughing between weakening sobs, and then the staticky crackle of his radio blared into their flimsy haven.

"I repeat, all crews evacuate. There has been a collapse in the primary fire floor," the radio droned.

Yeah, I noticed, Tilly thought wryly to himself as he took a deep breath and keyed up his radio.

"Mayday, mayday, mayday. Command, this is Firefighter Tillman, I have a victim in the basement near the A side of the building. We are sheltering in place, and will be conserving oxygen."

He turned, and his jacket light lit up her face. She was staring at the heated door in shock, her eyes slowly glazing over. Tilly knew she was probably experiencing CO poisoning and made another flash decision. He was bigger and had breathed clean air more recently, so if anyone had a chance to survive the exposure . . . it was him.

He took a few last deep breaths into his mask, before taking it off and putting it over her face. It only took seconds for the cloying smoke that was seeping through the cracks in the doorway to invade his unprotected airway.

"It's okay, sweetie." *cough*

"This"—*cough*—"will help you feel better." *cough*

He tightened the straps around the back of her head on either side of her little ponytail.

When he turned her now-limp head back toward his light, he saw that she had passed out under the mask and he figured it was for the best. He coughed a few more times, and fogginess began to set in. His thoughts came to him more slowly, as if billowing through his mind on a lazy cloud of smoke.

Why did it have to be a little girl?

His mind began to wander, and he was taken back unwillingly to that flat, gray Wednesday afternoon when he had finally said goodbye to his daughter after her long fight in the hospital. He could still feel her small, cold hand going limp in his.

It isn't going to be enough . . . I'm failing all over again.

The lines between past and present slowly blurred along with his vision, and there was suddenly no difference for him between that sad Wednesday so many years ago, and this one.

"It's okay, Emma." *cough* "It's okay," he mumbled as he took off his jacket in the growing heat and draped it over her curled-up form. His arms felt like they had been filled with cement, and he distantly heard his radio crackling. Little cinders fell from above to sear his shoulders, but the sharp pain felt distant and unimportant for some reason.

"Tilly! . . . five minu . . . old on!"

. . .

CHAPTER TWO

Transference

He awoke to a strange light that seemed to have no source but filled the space all around him with a soft, golden warmth. He felt almost weightless and was having difficulty looking around. In fact, he couldn't even look down at his own body. Everything felt distant and disjointed, the soft warmth glowing around and through him.

He didn't know how long he floated there bathing in that light. The movement of time seemed hard to comprehend in this space. Even the flow of his thoughts seemed hazy and sluggish, the linear nature of logic having difficulty establishing any momentum in this place. What might have been minutes or years passed until a sound like the ringing of bells reverberated all around Tilly.

Transference complete, uploading Administrator . . .

Then the light bloomed in front of him, and rich hues of purple, blue, and red burst forth in front of him as a figure emerged, breathing up the endless nothingness that had been the light. Each of its features seemed painfully real in this place of softness. The figure had a royal cast to its bearing that was neither masculine nor feminine. They wore a laurel of light on their brow and wore a robe slightly reminiscent of a Roman senator.

"It has been quite some time since one from the Middle Realm was bumped up to me. Most simply move on to the appropriate option, but you are an interesting case, aren't you?"

Words emanating from this figure seemed to echo from all around Tilly, and it felt like each sentence imposed itself on his fragile thought process, bringing pain, and with it greater cognizance. Its mouth didn't move at all as it spoke, but nonetheless, its words echoed around and through Tilly, inviting some response.

"Hmmm." Tilly tried to speak but all that emerged was a low hum. One that did not originate from his mouth, or any place at all, for that matter.

Despite that, the figure had no difficulty understanding the intention of Tilly's inquiry,

"Yes, you have left behind your corporeal form, but I would not call this 'death.' Do not bother trying to speak. I can understand your thoughts plainly, Jonathan Luke Tillman," the figure stated, a small comforting smile softening its otherwise statuesque face. Those instructions sunk into Tilly's being slowly, and in response, he strung together a full sentence in his mind,

Where am I if I'm not dead?

"You are nowhere and everywhere," the figure said, leaning forward before continuing.

"Perhaps *the Infinite* would convey it best in your language. And before you ask, this is not the afterlife. You are here to make some decisions that will impact your future greatly. In a moment, I will return you to your full emotional and intellectual capacity, but before I do that you need to listen, so for now you will feel . . . muted."

Muted?

His head felt like it was full of wool, and the concerns of his past life had been reduced to faint shadows of memories . . . *Who are you?*

"I am a System Administrator. I work for a being far beyond your scope of understanding, who created all known and unknown realities bound by time. The Origin.

"You have some understanding of him from your world as God, but very few understand his goals. In the beginning, he gave all his creation true freedom in the hope that one day it will return to him as wholly unique and new. You are a soul, one small piece of this incomprehensibly large work, but significant all the same.

"At this point in your existence, you would typically either move from the middle plane to a higher one and come closer to him, or you would move down into the lower planes, having dedicated yourself to the pursuit of goals outside his intent. While power is abundant in the many Realms, complete freedom of choice is reserved for those few he placed in the Middle Realm. And make no mistake, *everyone chooses*."

At this, the figure paused, and its eyes took on a very peculiar focus. Wells of deep liquid light flowed from them and moved through Tilly, and he felt a deep, instinctual fear take hold even in his detached state.

"I am only called in when one has given up a life of extraordinary potential to save another soul, yet is not an obvious candidate to move up or down in the Realms . . . And in you, I find a very interesting case. Get ready. I am removing the *Mute*, and the shock of your situation will hit you. This effect

would be far more powerful in a physical body, but it will be significant all the same."

Then the figure gestured with its hand, which released a flash of . . . something. Along with the flash came the immense weight of Tilly's past, his few triumphs, and his many failings. Memory after memory flooded him, lending cadence to the high and low notes of his forty-six years on the planet.

His daughter, Emma, sick on her hospital bed.

His ex-wife, Laura, looking up at him with guilt and accusation mingling like poison in her eyes.

Drink after drink trying to forget but never quite able to.

Endless nights spent trying to escape his reality through any kind of fantasy or game he could get his hands on.

Decades on the job passing up promotions, and staying out in the streets as long as possible. Avoiding the responsibility of leadership at all costs.

Catching a fire call on his last shift of work.

. . . that little girl.

If he had a throat, he would have screamed as the reality of his entire life was summed up in one eternal moment. Instead, he felt the insubstantial substance of his being begin to tremble as regret racked his soul. He had been weighed and measured and found that his whole life with all of its struggle and pain had barely made a drop of meaningful impact in the grand scheme of things. Only in his last reckless minutes of life had he truly moved and lived entirely for the benefit of another, his decisions motivated more by sorrow and loss than any sort of hero complex.

Did she make it? he thought toward the Administrator, shakily pulling himself back from the deep abyss that was his past.

At Tilly's question, the Administrator's small smile grew.

"Yes, Tilly, she lost some lung capacity and her only parent in that fire. But she will go on to live an amazing life, one made no more or less precious by her accomplishments. She will find a new family and burn with a bright joy for the rest of her days."

Then it paused, leaning back as if pondering something. Tilly sagged in relief at the news, knowing at least something good came out of the complex shades of escapism and self-punishment that had made up his life. Too many thought being in his profession made him inherently less selfish than others. The sad truth was he had spent the last decade of his life distant and disinterested in anything but his next paycheck and the future distractions it would buy him.

"This is where we come to the conundrum. You see you are not actually dead; you are moments away from death in your world, lingering on the brink. Before today, your self-pity and bitterness would have sent you to a lower realm. The life you lived had the potential for far more nobility than

you realized, and you squandered it in fear and bitterness. Many who moved through your life were made less for having spent their time with you . . .

"That is until your very last moments when you chose to become something much greater. The man you were always meant to be. This qualified you to move up. Yet, I have been sent to evaluate you because in your case there is another option. You represent almost perfect balance on the cosmic scale, and with your great potential, it can be moved in either direction. Because of this, I am empowered to make you an offer.

"There is another Realm, one that is neither closer nor further from Origin. One that touches on the hearts and minds of each soul in the cycle. This realm is called *Nephesh*. It is the realm of myth and legend and the place where all of the stories of mankind come together to do battle for the minds and hearts of the collective psyche of creation."

So I can go "up" to heaven or go to this place Nephesh? Why wouldn't I take my ticket up?

"Good question, Tilly. The answer is quite complex, and due to the rules, I can not influence your decision one way or another . . . But I can say that Nephesh represents more *opportunity* to make a difference, than your standard path toward Origin. Think of it this way: you have won money at the casino, and you can take your winnings and leave . . . or you can put it all on the table for one more roll."

CHAPTER THREE

Decisions, Decisions

All of this new information washed over Tilly like a raging river, both overwhelming him with its implications and somehow calming him with the cold shock of truth. His life, the summation of all his decisions, had equaled out to barely anything. One child lost to cancer, one wife whom he had pushed away as he slowly closed in on himself in the pain. No lasting impact in the fire department, no continuous group of friends. It was only because of his last few moments that he even had the option to go "up."

Here, faced with some sort of higher power, he couldn't muster up the strength to feel bitter. He just felt acceptance. There was no one else to blame or reward for his circumstances. Life had dealt him a mixed hand, and he had chosen to barely play it.

But in this cosmic moment, face-to-face with an agent of the Divine, one concept appealed to him like a life raft to a drowning man.

This is another chance?

"That is correct, Jonathan Tillman. You, with all of your faults and strengths, have the potential for greatness. Whether great evil or great good is up to you. I will not lie to you—to choose Nephesh is to choose a path of suffering. This is not a kind world. It has been formed of the dreams and myths of men, and I fear lately that those dreams have grown into nightmares more often than not."

The fact that trying again would be hard didn't even faze him. If there was anything Tilly had going for him after decades in the fire service, it was the ability to make a choice quickly and stick to it.

Alright, I'm ready, give me a second chance, he thought, his essence slowly firming under the weight of a new purpose for his being. This time would be different. He would be what he had failed to be in his first life.

The Administrator nodded, still smiling, and that same voice from before spoke.

. . . Accord Acknowledged . . .
Uploading available paths of ascension.

Then light bloomed behind the Administrator again, and they started to fade into it.

"It was a pleasure meeting you, Jonathan Tillman. Good luck out there, and remember, it's not about how much power you have . . . It's what you do with it."

With those words, the figure was gone, leaving behind only the soft light of its immense power, which slowly thickened into four outlines of the same figure. As the light finished coalescing, Tilly found himself looking at different versions of his old corporeal body. They all had the same blunt features. His overhanging brow and too-hairy face. His dark, strong features, on top of a dad bod that did a great job hiding the deceptive physicality of the man underneath. But that was where the familiarity ended.

Soul-scan complete, four possible paths to power available. . . .

Tilly noticed medieval weaponry and robes on the first two figures, and he felt an incorporeal grin form on whatever passed for a face in this form.

Something he had almost never spread around the department was his obsession with all things fantasy and gaming. For him, it had been a greater escape than alcohol and women combined. Almost no one knew the extent of Tilly's passion for the nerdier side of life, and he had kept it that way through his decades in the fire service. Now it seemed like he was being offered a new life that in some way would involve swords and sorcery. To see something that he had always thought a distraction become so useful confirmed his choice to go for this second chance.

He had no clue what life in a world full of walking myths and dreams would be like, but he guessed he was about to find out. Starting with the four options standing in front of him. As he studied the first figure, a flicker of blue light caught the corner of his vision. He focused in that direction, but all he saw were four other figures of himself.

He shrugged his nonexistent shoulders and looked back at the first option. The figure was armored in plate mail and had an oversized ax in his hand.

Knight of the Eternal Flame

Your past life experience qualifies you to enter into the Brotherhood of the Eternal Flame as a Knight. + 3 Endurance, Strength, and Constitution every third level. Starting Abilities: Weak Flame Manipulation, Flame Blade, and Fiery Rush.

Tilly frowned. He had a good idea of what each of these values meant theoretically but had no clue how many points he would get per level, or what the other values would be. He decided to keep looking to see if that would clear anything up.

The second figure showed a younger version of Tilly wearing a robe and cackling as his hands burned with a crimson flame.

Pyromancer of the Sixth Circle

You have spent more time watching the destructive effects of fire than almost any other ascension aspirant. For this, you qualify to walk the path of a Pyromancer. You will forsake all other magic for a supreme affinity for fire. Any fire damage dealt to you will be added to your health instead. +4 intelligence at every level. Starting Abilities: Flame Mastery, Pyrokinesis.

As attractive as that +4 was to intelligence, something about seeing his face filled with such an unbridled glee gave Tilly the heebie-jeebies. He didn't want to go for a full mage class anyway. It had never been his style. He had always leaned more toward the more well-rounded classes, like ranger or bard. So he moved on.

The next figure had a bow on his back and was covered in tan leathers that seemed to meld into each other. His face was determined, and he seemed to be searching for something.

Dune Ranger of the Sand Seas

Your survival instinct and basic medical knowledge qualify you for entry into the clandestine order of sand rangers. Roaming the endless sands, this order originated from the sand elves. Part ranger, part treasure hunter, these masters of survival are known to be difficult to find and even more difficult to kill. +1 to Endurance, Wisdom, and Dexterity at every level. Starting Abilities and skills: Basic First Aid, Piercing Shot, Concussive Shot, Stealth, Long Walker, and Last Legs.

Now, this was more his style! Although he didn't like the idea of the endless sands . . .

Well, he wasn't sure if there was a requirement for him to stay in his starting area or not, but the prospect of living in a sandy desert was a huge deterrent for him. He was the kind of guy who spent his beach vacation poolside. He never cared what other people thought; there was nothing pleasant about covering yourself in an abrasive, impossible-to-remove substance. Tilly eagerly focused on the next figure. This one showed him wearing a dirty chef's hat stirring a caldron with a cheerful look on his face.

> ### Line Cook for the Thousand Phalanx Legion
>
> *You have spent much of your life cooking for a crew of rowdy rough men. They weren't always grateful, but you kept them full and ready to face the challenges of the day. Go out into the wild and find rare delicacies to push your comrades to new heights. +1 to Constitution, Wisdom, and Strength at every level.*

As much as I liked cooking for the guys at the station, I'm going to go with "no" for this one, Tilly grumbled to himself. Well, he would have if he could grumble. With a silent sigh, he moved on to the fifth figure . . . Wait didn't that voice say there would only be four choices?

This figure showed him wearing a collection of skins that were arranged in a way that was vaguely reminiscent of his firefighting gear. Hooked through leather loops on his hips were two large hatchets that were similar to his favorite spike-headed fireman's ax.

> ### Son of Flame
>
> *Fire destroys, renews, and purifies. It is time for Nephesh to feel the Wrath and Renewal of **Origin's** Flame.*

That was it . . . No other details about stats or any abilities. Something about this whole option seemed off, and it left Tilly with the feeling that it was by far the riskiest choice.

Yet, something about this display of a possible ascension path spoke to him. The cast of the figure's face seemed fierce, and his body was postured with its arms spread wide like it was protecting something behind it. Before he could think about his options any further, that same voice rang out.

Survey of available paths to power complete. Selection required in three seconds.

What? Just like that, he had to choose?

Two

Well, what the heck, if he was going to roll the dice, he might as well roll big.

One
Son of Flame path selected. Initializing transference . . .

Tilly felt the space he had been occupying grow brighter as his soul self was fused with the selected image. As he became one with the figure, he felt his sense of place rush back to him as he dropped out of that plane of nonexistence and into a new place. His five senses returned to him with a roaring rush as he found himself once again in possession of a physical form. The experience was so intense that before he could take in any of the sights or sounds around him, his mind put his body through a full reboot, and he collapsed unconscious.

As the brightness died back down, the space was filled with two figures sitting in comfortable chairs overlooking the vast cosmos.

"Don't you think that was a little on the nose, sir? What if he is used to weigh the scales of free will further in **Corruption's** favor? There is far too much bitterness and selfishness for me to be comfortable with this."

"Addy, I think you have been with me long enough to know that I care little for what Corruption will or won't do. I care for my people, and I think this man is the perfect Catalyst. For far too long many have believed they are stuck in the systems those with some modicum of power have set forth. The truth is coming for them, whether they are ready or not."

CHAPTER FOUR

Hardcore Mode

Tilly felt something digging into his back. He groaned and rolled over, groggily coming to his senses. He was in some sort of forest. He looked down at the rock-strewn dark soil and realized he had been lying on one of the plentiful small half-buried rocks that filled the areas between shrubs and tall trees. He stared down at the ground, taking some time to reconcile the radical turn his life had just taken.

Everything he knew was gone. The life he had lived and the choices he had made were gone. Now he was in some sort of new world that was at least in part governed by a system that somehow managed and defined all of the legends and dreams of mankind.

It was a lot to take in. A burgeoning panic started to well up in his psyche in a delayed reaction to his recent radical shift in existence. He tamped it down in frustration and did what he always did with an overwhelming problem: he broke it down one piece at a time. He couldn't do anything about the vast majority of his circumstances. So start small.

Where had he been sent?

Tilly lifted his head from his downward musings and took in his surroundings. Aside from the dark soil, he found a forest not that different from any temperate climate on Earth. While the flora wasn't exactly identifiable, it was at least familiar. He got up from his knees and found himself facing up a slope in a small clearing surrounded by foliage.

He heard crickets chirping, and a bird in the distance and started to relax a little. He still seemed to have the body of a man moderately fit in his forties. He had never slacked when it came to staying fit for the job, but a lifetime of gaming and alcohol with a moderate amount of exercise hadn't exactly made him a male model. None of that stood out to him nearly as much as what he was wearing.

"UGH, this is not at all what I was shown!" he choked out in frustration.

Instead of the well-stitched quality padded leather outfit and twin hatchets he had seen on the figure, he was wearing a rough-stitched, animal-skin coat with stiff matching pants. The pants seemed to be held up with some leather thong suspenders over his shoulders and had two loops built into the waist that held two stone-headed hatchets. Moccasins that could have been made by a child hung loosely around his feet, and to top it all off, he felt absolutely no undergarments between him and the scratchy material.

"Chafing is going to be a nightmare," he muttered darkly as he scowled down at his starter gear.

Congratulations! *You have learned the skill, Identify. You can intuit basic facts about the things and people in the world around you.*

"What the—" Tilly started, while flinching back at the glowing screen that popped into view with the sound of fanfare. He swiped at the screen, and it disappeared from view before quickly being replaced by others.

---

*You have identified **Origin's** primitive leather armor: +10% to Endurance.*

*You have identified **Origin's** primitive stone hatchets: +10% to Dexterity.*

***Caution!** This is a Legendary Soul Bound set of equipment, and cannot be discarded or replaced.*

Tilly again swiped at the front of his face as if trying to get rid of an annoying insect.

"How do I get these to stop exploding in my face!" he yelped desperately, a life of endless phone notifications rearing its menacing head in his already bruised psyche.

System messages are set to silent. All new updates will be cached behind an update icon.

The boxes stopped appearing, and instead, he found a blinking icon flashing at the top right of his peripheral vision. He tried to focus on it to see what the icon was, and instead, a new screen popped up in his field of view.

> *Transference complete.*
>
> *Status debuff Unconscious removed.*
>
> *0.005% of health damage taken by small forest rock.*
>
> **Congratulations!** *You have learned the skill, Identify. You can intuit basic facts about the things and people in the world around you.*
>
> *You have identified primitive leather armor: +10% to Endurance.*
>
> *You have identified primitive stone hatchets: +10% to Dexterity.*
>
> **Caution!** *This is a Legendary Soul Bound set of equipment, and cannot be discarded or replaced.*

Tilly absently thought about swiping away the screen, and it minimized on its own.

"That's a relief. I don't think I could have survived here for five minutes with those things popping up all . . . wait a second, 'Legendary Soul Bound'?" Tilly looked down at his gear incredulously.

"You have got to be kidding me!" he griped, holding up one sleeve of his jacket for closer inspection. It seemed to be an amalgamation of several different patches of animal fur stitched together. But something seemed off with the fur. It went in and out of focus when he tried to look at the individual hairs on the animal-skin patches.

Then the blurring snapped into clarity, and Tilly saw minute glowing symbols crawling over and between the sewn-together animal skins.

"Huh," he said, seeing his gear in a new light. Then the icon started blinking again, and he focused on it curiously.

> *Identify level up! Level 1*
>
> *Identify level up! Level 2 . . .*
>
> *Identify level up! Level 15*
>
> **Congratulations!** *By taking time to analyze a Legendary set of gear you have greatly advanced your skill! Study new and interesting things to level up this skill even further.*

"Oooh, that's more like it!"

An idea struck him, and he reached down toward one of his hatchets and tugged it free from its loop. Before he could pull it up to his face to try to study it, he heard a rustling from a nearby bush.

Tilly's grip on his weapon tightened, and he crouched down, suddenly alert. A bush about ten yards up rustled again, and a creature that looked a lot like a desert hare with antlers hopped into view.

"It can't be . . . is that a—" Tilly whispered, bringing up his once again flashing notification log.

You have identified a level 2 ***Juvenile Jakalope!***

At first, the Jakalope just sniffed at the air, looking in a different direction, and Tilly slowly took a step back, before snapping a twig under his foot and cursing softly. The Jakalope's head whipped around and focused on Tilly.

It was then that Tilly saw the blackened veiny pattern fanning out from the creature's mouth into its eyes and antlers. It looked like it had caught a serious bug, like "zombie apocalypse" serious, and did not look friendly.

"Nice bunny . . ." Tilly said lamely, gesturing the universal calm-down motion with his hands, and trying to pretend that he wasn't holding a weapon.

"Ggrrruuuggg," the creature gurgled in reply, a frothy black substance foaming at the corners of its mouth as its bloodshot eyes quivered in its sockets.

Tilly slowly tried to take another step back, his hands upright, palms out. The Jakalope took in his posture and then snapped forward in a springing charge, its head tilted down with its antlers thrust forward.

Tilly tried to swing his hatchet in some sort of defensive block and failed miserably as the sharpened tips of the antlers pierced his forearm and bicep in several places.

"ARRGGG." Several points of pain bloomed on his blocking arm, but Tilly was no stranger to pain and the need for quick decision-making in the face of danger.

The thing shook its head back and forth, trying to free itself for another attack, but Tilly took the opportunity it had presented by getting lodged in his arm to hook his leg around the dog-sized creature. He locked it in place and grabbed his hatchet from his pinned arm before bringing it down furiously on the creature's neck.

The creature gurgled again and redoubled its effort to get free even as Tilly brought the hatchet down over and over, turning its neck into a bloody mess. With a final jerking motion, the Jakalope stopped moving.

"Holy crap . . . that sucked." Tilly gasped as he looked down at the corpse of the creature he held to the ground with his leg, even as it still pinned his arm in place on its antlers. Its dark red blood had stained the whole front of his patchwork leather gear, and his arm was on fire with the pain of being shallowly impaled in several places.

"Okay, just rip off a Band-Aid . . ." he muttered to himself, and then before he could think about it more, he yanked his arm free from the antlers.

"JESUS CHRIST!" he yelled before collapsing to the ground gasping as he attempted to distract himself from the pain.

He should have gone for the "Cook" class . . . Tilly was willing to bet that guy wouldn't have had antler bunnies trying to stab him as soon as he woke up in a new world. And what was with that black stuff going on around the bunny's mouth and under its eyes?

He tried to ignore the blinking icon at the edge of his vision and pulled his arm out of his jacket gingerly to look at the stab wounds. They were painful, but not very deep. The two on his forearm were barely bleeding, while the one on his bicep was releasing a small trickle. The bleeding would resolve on its own with pressure, but what he was most concerned with was infection.

Wait, does infection even happen in this world? How does the health system even work? He forcibly took his mind out of EMT mode and looked up at the blinking icon, sending it a mental command.

You are now in combat.

*You suffer 5% damage from a piercing attack. You are **Partially Restrained**. You cannot move your right arm.*

*You have successfully pinned a Juvenile Jakalope. It is **Fully Restrained**.*

*You suffer 1% damage from a **Continuing Pierce** attack.*

*You attack the Juvenile Jakalope for 25% of its health. Bonus x2 damage from striking a critical area. You have inflicted **Major Bleeding** on your opponent. They will suffer 5% damage per second until resolved.*

You attack the Juvenile Jakalope for 25% of its health. Bonus x2 damage from striking a critical area.

Juvenile Jakalope is defeated. You have now exited combat.

Congratulations! *You have defeated your first creature with a martial weapon. You have learned the skill, **Beginner Hatchet**.*

Beginner Hatchet level up! *Adjusting for previous experience . . .*

Beginner Hatchet *level up! Level 1*

Beginner Hatchet *level up! Level 2 . . .*

Beginner Hatchet *level up! Level 9*

You have earned 200 exp

> **Congratulations!** *You are now level 2. 500 exp until the next level.*
>
> *You have earned 5 stat points to distribute plus 2 points in Endurance and 1 in Dexterity from the class* **Son of Flame.**

Even after the traumatic encounter he just had with the horned bunny from hell, Tilly was excited to see that some of his experience from his previous life would be quantified by this world.

Suddenly, a full career of shoving his personal ax into his belt before every fire call didn't seem so pointless, no matter how many times he got written up for improper PPE.

"Take that, Captain Burnard!" He growled in triumph at the memory of his many pointless write-ups. He squinted at that last line of his notifications, trying to ground himself in what was most important about this world first.

Okay, what am I learning here? There are stats issued to me at every level, and health is measured in percentage points instead of some arbitrary numeric . . . is there some sort of status screen I can—

As soon as he thought to look for one, it popped up in front of him like a glaring beacon of numeric certainty.

Jonathan Luke Tillman

Level: 2 *(500 experience to next level)*

Display Name: *Tilly*

Race: *Human*

Class: *Son of Flame*

Titles: *[Harbinger]*

Stats:	**Abilities:**
Health: *93.95% (+0.8% per minute)*	*-None.*
Mana: *100% (+0.7% per minute)*	
Constitution: *8*	
Endurance: *12 (13.2)*	
Dexterity: *8 (8.8)*	
Strength: *9*	
Wisdom: *7*	
Intelligence: *5*	

Skills:

-Identify level 15

-Beginner Hatchet level 9

Equipment:

-Origin's primitive stone hatchets: +10% to Dexterity.
(Legendary, growth type)

-Origin's primitive leather armor set: +10% to Endurance.
(Legendary, growth type)

Everything more or less made sense to Tilly from his previous experience in gaming. He had a level that increased any time he gained enough *experience*. His skills could also level with use, **Identify** had gone crazy high the moment he tried to puzzle out his gear, which was one thing he had going for him.

He looked down at his patchwork leather and fur pants and shrugged. Legendary sounded pretty good, even though he had nothing to compare it to at the moment. He did love the wording, "growth type." If he understood that right, then for better or worse he would never need another set of gear. No *Abilities* though . . . all the other classes had come with *Abilities*. Maybe it was a trade-off for starting with Legendary gear. The one thing he completely didn't understand was the *Title*. What was a [Harbinger]?

Almost in reply to his question, another screen popped up.

[Harbinger]

One touched by **Origin** to bring about change. *"None may interfere."* This and all other **Origin**-related Titles, Abilities, and items will be changed and seen as unremarkable by any deity or deity-aligned faction.

---

*Huh, there is that **Origin** guy again, I guess he is like God with a big "G" but seems to have some sort of non-interference thing going . . . well kinda, or else I wouldn't be here with some strange class with zero explanation. Speaking of explanations—*

"Can I get details on stat breakdowns or how health is calculated?" Tilly asked in the open air.

Nothing.

"Well, any explanation on my class?"

The annoying "pop in your face any time you have a thought" system was again, completely silent.

"Well isn't that great!" Tilly snarked while taking his hand off his wound. Insanely, it had already stopped bleeding. He quickly checked the other two and saw that they had already scabbed over.

"Okay, well can I at least have my health and mana show above my line of sight?"

Instantly his configuration changed, and he had his health and mana showing at the top of his vision opposite the notification icon.

Health: 96%
Mana: 100%

"Now we are talking. Well while we are at it, show me any active status effects when they happen." Tilly breathed out in exasperation. Nothing changed, but Tilly hoped that was because he didn't have any effects at the moment.

Then a thought struck him like lightning.

"Inventory!" he declared triumphantly.

Nothing.

Tilly's dreams of an endless magic storage space were dashed. No carrying around tons of rocks that he could just drop from a high overlook and defeat his enemies. That also meant he couldn't just steal everything in sight and save it for a rainy day.

"I guess this is the hardcore, 'bring camping equipment and rope or else' kind of world." He huffed, his shoulders dropping in disappointment. The motion brought his attention to his now completely clean gear. He examined the sleeve that had just been covered in blood and pierced through a few times. Nothing, completely restored to its previous state, which juxtaposed annoyingly with his arm, which was still covered in a mixture of blood and dirt.

"Legendary huh? Well if you are going to do that magic clean-up thing, why don't you share the love?" he said as he rubbed off as much of the drying filth as possible in the dark, loamy dirt.

". . . grruugg . . ." Tilly instantly froze, picking up a faint but now dreadfully familiar gurgle. His head snapped up, and he saw some movement behind a distant tree. He looped his hatchet and turned to flee, before looking back at the dead Jakalope with a grunt of frustration.

"I hope you aren't poisonous . . ." He growled as he hefted the surprisingly light creature over his shoulder and made his way as quickly and quietly as he could through the forest in the opposite direction of the noise.

He was all for leveling, but survival came first. It was time to go full man versus wild.

CHAPTER FIVE

No One Likes Camping

Tilly moved at a decent pace for a while, until he had put enough distance between him and the possible danger that he felt good about coming up with a plan. With the dead Jakalope over his shoulder, he knew his first priority was water, then food, then shelter. So he decided to make his way through the forest going perpendicular to the slope at an easy and cautious pace. He hoped to find a stream or river at some point if he kept circumnavigating the mountain he was on.

If Bear Grylls had taught him anything it was that water liked to flow downhill. Plus, moving water meant the ability to clean, and whatever infection this Jakalope had, he really didn't want to catch it. Hopefully, after butchering and washing the edible parts of the animal, it would be safe.

He continued to distract himself with practical and goal-oriented thoughts as he walked for a few hours over rough terrain. He would be lying if that first encounter had not stirred an acidic anxiety that churned his stomach. Had he made the right choice coming to this world? He knew he had banked some stat points, but until he had taken care of the basics, he wasn't ready to start working on his "build."

Every rustle of a bush froze him in his tracks and set his heart racing. Despite all this, he thought he was coping with his new circumstances surprisingly well. He had always been pragmatic. You needed some sort of go-with-it attitude to last any period of time in the fire department. Need a guy to keep calm and carry on, no matter how crazy things got? Tilly was your man. He swallowed down the churning worry and kept hoofing it.

He was on foreign soil with little to no knowledge of this world or its inhabitants. He had left behind a life spent ignoring the pain in front of him by coping with alcohol and escapism. He had run a few tabletop games as a DM and had read every kind of fantasy there was. That experience was already helping him to cope, but he had no clue how the concepts in those games and books would play out here.

Luckily even with his nerdy hobbies, he had spent enough time camping with crazy family and coworkers to have some common sense out in the wild. He wouldn't exactly call himself a wilderness expert, but he wasn't going to die from exposure if he could help it.

As he walked, he kept trying to **Identify** things, but none of the trees and rocks seemed to want to activate the skill. Looking at them closely didn't pop up any new notifications, nor did looking at his gear give him anything new.

He needed to find a way to gain some sort of advantage, or he wouldn't last long. Sighing to himself he shifted the weight of the dead Jakalope. He had exhausted all of the normal concerns he would have, being lost out in the woods . . . so his mind reluctantly turned back to the words the Administrator had used when describing this place.

"This is the world of the dreams and myths of men, and I fear lately that the dreams have grown quite dark."

He really hoped they didn't include *everyone's* dreams . . . if his coworkers were anything to go by, things were going to get gross, fast.

His thoughts were interrupted by a faint rushing sound at the edge of his hearing, and he smiled to himself and picked up the pace.

"Where there are mountains there is water," he whispered with a smile.

He finally broke through the tree line and found a large stream. It looked to be a few feet deep and had a rocky pebble-strewn shore, like something you might find on the Appalachian Trail. The canopy was fairly thick but not tropical, and one or two of the trees nearby were climbable. What made it perfect was the large rock outcropping that jutted out of the shore making it a passable place to set up a fire and protect his back from any encroaching dangers. Tilly looked around suspiciously for a second before making his decision.

He would make camp on this side of the brook, but ford it and find a tree to climb before dark to sleep and hang his stuff. It would be rough, restless sleep, but it is not like he would sleep any better on the hard ground, completely defenseless.

He couldn't be sure, but this didn't seem like an environment with many predators that prowled the tree canopy. The temperature was temperate, and as long as this world followed some loose ecological rules, this place probably wouldn't have a bunch of monkeys or crazy insects. There was no way his campsite would be safe, but hopefully, any potential threats would pass him by once they lost his scent in the water.

He dropped the Jakalope near the stream and knelt down to drink and wash off some of his accumulated grime. While he reveled in the icy cold running water he pulled up his notifications, which had started flashing the moment he had decided to make camp.

Congratulations! *You have found a moderately safe place to camp! You have learned the skill* **Forestcraft**.

Forestcraft - *You are at home in the wilds. Many fumble through this environment, but you have committed to blending into it and folding yourself into its ecosystem.*

Your **Forestcraft** *level has increased. Adjusting for previous experience . . .*

Forestcraft *level up! Level 1*

Forestcraft *level up! Level 2 . . .*

Forestcraft *level up! Level 5*

Okay, so skills are a thing I can learn by demonstrating any beginner level of competence. Then once I demonstrate a skill somehow, the system seems to factor in my past knowledge and calculate a level based on the combination of the two. Whereas Abilities seem to only be gained through other means, like class-level rewards or something.

So far the **Son of Flame** class seemed like a real mixed bag. Supposedly amazing gear but no starting *Abilities* to speak of, and the same average three assigned stat points that his other class options had—that is of course assuming they would have all gotten the base five points to assign at every level.

Now that he had a seemingly system-approved place to camp, he got to setting up the basics. Tilly worked with enough "country" firefighters in his time to know the basics of processing an animal. That, plus his general medical knowledge and comfort with the natural mechanics of a living being, made figuring out how to strip the animal of skin, head, and organs moderately painless. While crude, his two primitive hatchets were plenty sharp and made decent forestry tools. He made a pretty good mess of it, but in the end, he had a skin lying over a nearby bush drying, and a mostly cleaned animal ready to cook and run through a spit.

He then arranged some of the larger rocks into a fire pit on the side of the rock outcropping and gathered some fallen wood from the surrounding area, before starting a fire. He had only ever watched the friction fire-starting method on TV, but he could feel the influence of his **Forestcraft** skill kicking in as he rubbed the dry stick between his fingers into a pile of fat lighter, over and over until smoke started to show. He enthusiastically blew on the little pile of dry kindling. and it caught, all in a few minutes.

That was way easier than it should have been.

That wasn't the only way his new skill was making itself known. Other things, like how to find and burn a strong-smelling plant from near camp to disguise the presence of his cooking, also just came to him.

He set up the cooking spit over the coals with the smoldering fragrant herbs off to the side and finished up by washing off in the stream and hunkering down near his fire with his hatchets out, in case something wandered across him even with his meager precautions.

He was also rewarded with another skill as he finished processing and skinning his kill.

Congratulations! *You have skinned and processed your first animal. You have learned the skill* **Animal Processing.**

Animal Processing *- You know your way around the creatures of this world, and you honor them by taking all they have to offer upon their deaths.*

Your **Animal Processing** *level has increased. Adjusting for previous experience . . .*

Animal Processing *level up! Level 1*

Animal Processing *level up! Level 2 . . .*

Animal Processing *level up! Level 5*

"Four skills, and I'm not dead yet . . . not a bad day, I guess," he grumbled as he hunkered closer to the fire.

Night was beginning to fall, and in the distance, Tilly heard a howl, answered by others even farther away. A shiver ran down his spine, and he hoped he was right about his tree idea. Before any creature came calling, Tilly wanted to have the meat cooked and packed away. He eyed the haunch that was slowly beginning to brown and willed it to hurry.

"Okay, this isn't going to happen any faster for me by worrying. Let's assign these five stat points," he said, rubbing his hands together. He wordlessly called up just his basic stats to give them another look.

Stats:

Health: *100% (+0.8% per minute)*

Mana: *100% (+0.7% per minute)*

Constitution: 8

Endurance: 12 (13.2)

Dexterity: 8 (8.8)

Strength: 9

Wisdom: 7

Intelligence: 5

Huh, so no charisma or stamina . . . He didn't really know what that would signify for this world. What exactly was *Endurance*? Was *Dexterity* the same as in DnD? Did *Strength* make him hit harder or do more damage in general?

Not for the first time Tilly wished there was some sort of basic primer or description that came with all these new terms. Even the descriptions of skills were more flavor than help.

Well, nothing to it but to take what he had been given and min-max the hell out of it.

He saw that his class heavily favored *Endurance* with an additional emphasis on *Dexterity,* especially with that percentage increase on the weapons. As a DM he had hated when players tried to play too balanced in their stats, trying to avoid paying the cost of power that any game offered to those who were willing to work around the drawbacks. He resolved to lean in to whatever benefits *Endurance* would give him, betting that his emphasis on *Dexterity* would somehow end up working well with the weapons that came with this class.

Alright. 1 point in *Constitution* to get himself to 9, health was health after all. Then 4 points in *Dexterity* to match it to *Endurance* and get the most out of his percentage increase. The strategy wouldn't do much for him now, but if he kept it up, he would hopefully see some crazy gains in the future. He just had to live long enough to see them.

The Jakalope had just begun to sizzle, clear juices emerging from the haunches.

Congratulations! You have cooked your first meal. You have learned the skill **Cooking***.*

Your **Cooking** *level has increased. Adjusting for previous experience . . .*

Cooking *level up! Level 1*

Cooking *level up! Level 2 . . .*

Cooking *level up! Level 12*

Twenty years of coming up with meals out of whatever was in the firehouse fridge had paid off. Tilly smiled. No salt, no tent, and surrounded by a forest filled with creatures that probably wanted to kill him.

Hell of a way to start his new life.

CHAPTER SIX

Axing the Right Questions

To say Tilly had slept would be a vast overstatement. He spent the night wedged between two tree limbs with the burnt Jakalope meat wrapped in a bundle of fat leaves he had pulled from a nearby tree. The night had passed fretfully as he shifted from one extremely uncomfortable position to another.

He had managed to doze off a few times but was frequently awoken by pain from his sleeping position, or the sound of different creatures moving through the forest below him.

He finally "awoke" to 100 percent health 100 percent mana and a **Minor Exhaustion** debuff.

- After sleeping in an environment not conducive to rest, you are afflicted with **Minor Exhaustion**. *-10% Endurance, Dexterity, and Intelligence for 10 hours.*

Caution! *If you are afflicted with* **Minor Exhaustion** *debuff three nights in a row it will be upgraded to* **Exhaustion**.

He mentally pinged the debuff and was surprised at an actual explanation.

Well, he added better sleeping arrangements to his growing mental to-do list and absently reached for his burnt-meat bundle.

After choking down a few mouthfuls of the Jakalope meat, he gingerly climbed down from his perch and looked around warily to make sure the area was clear. Something he hadn't noticed last night in his rush was how easy it was to scale the tree. While the night had passed painfully and slowly, he hardly needed to stretch before he felt the lingering effects of the terrible sleeping surface recede.

Looks like my health regen will take care of small aches and pains as long as I don't have too many debuffs.

He dropped from the final limb with something that could have been mistaken for catlike grace. In a fit of inspiration, he decided to draw both his hatchets at the same time with a flourish, and they pulled from their loops smoothly. He hadn't had time last night, but his extra points in *Dexterity* were really showing.

"Well hello future superpowers . . ." he said as he flipped one of his weapons and caught it deftly. The motion seemed trivial, and he repeated it with both hands, unable to keep a smile from blooming on his face.

He wouldn't have called himself uncoordinated in his past life, but he was now certainly displaying abilities beyond what he could do even in the prime of his youth. He looped both hatchets back into his pants and lifted his leather jacket excitedly to see if the new changes had included abs.

Nope.

The same disappointing dad-bod paunch looked back up at him, exuding a comfortable level of sluggishness, even in the face of Tilly's burgeoning superpowers.

"I guess it's gonna be a few weeks of the carnivore diet before I say goodbye to you, old friend," he said, patting his jiggly abdomen like a favored pet.

He then crossed over the stream to his "camp," which for now was just a ring of rocks, and looked around, finding it pretty much undisturbed. He knew he was going to have to level if he was going to stay alive long enough to worry about things like real shelter and finding the actual inhabitants of this plane. He leaned against his big rock and took some time to think through his situation.

Just because he had survived the night didn't mean he was ready to rush off and go full murder-hobo. He didn't have much to show from his last life, but he sure as hell knew how to manage time and resources when it came to gaming.

First, he needed to know exactly what he was capable of with his weapons. Hopefully, he could unlock one or two other useful skills in the process. He had **Beginner Hatchet** at level 9, and he wondered if that just represented his current skill or if it was augmenting what he could already do like his **Forestcraft** had last night.

Then he had to find some of these other weird dream creatures and hope they were edible. That way he could kill two birds with one stone when it came to leveling and building up his food supply. The Jakalope would probably last him two more meals . . . It had been pretty lean, but on the plus side with the head gone, none of that black stuff had been present in the rest of the meat.

Finally, he had to find some sort of high point and get his bearings. If he could spot some sign of civilization, he would happily stop being survivor-man and head toward whatever passed as people in this place.

Dwarves . . . I hope it's Dwarves.

Something about the accents, the drinking, and the axes had always spoken to him. But all of that was in the future. First, he had to make sure he lived long enough to get there. He took a deep breath and reached down to draw his weapons and get started.

He was about to start practicing when his blinking icon finally got his attention. It had been flashing away merrily all night, and Tilly had just given up looking at it. It was insane how fast that thing had become background noise when it blinked at him all the time, especially when most of the notifications were details he didn't need in the moment. He might have to set up a new method for notifications in the future, but for now, it was too dangerous to leave them to pop up whenever something happened with the system. Which seemed to be all the time.

He mentally opened the notification log and was surprised and annoyed by how the game quantified his attempted night's sleep.

> *-0.02% of health damage taken from a large tree limb.*
> *-0.02% of health damage taken from a large tree limb.*
> *-0.02% of health damage taken from a large tree limb. . .*

It went on and on like that, and he assumed that he had taken damage all night, but it had not been enough to outpace his passive regeneration. There had to be a way to filter out some of this detail. Having this notification show up every time he stubbed a toe or something would be unbelievably annoying, and it would keep him from finding the stuff that actually mattered.

"System, can you remove any damage notifications that don't result in a net loss to my health?"

The log instantly shortened, and he was left with a very pleasant surprise.

> ***Congratulations!*** *You have survived your first night in the wilderness!*
> ***Forestcraft*** *level up! Level 8.*
> *Congratulations! You have learned the skill* ***Stealth***.
> ***Stealth*** *- Discretion is the better part of valor. Your attempts to avoid detection are more successful than most.*
> *-You have successfully avoided detection by a very dangerous hostile creature.*
> *-You have successfully avoided detection by a dangerous hostile creature.*
> *-You have successfully avoided detection by a hostile creature. . .*

Notifications like the last three had come disconcertingly frequently through the night, and Tilly's only solace was that he had received some great leveling for **Stealth** out of the crazy dangerous environment.

> **Stealth** *level up! Level 1*
>
> **Stealth** *level up! Level 2 . . .*
>
> **Stealth** *level up! Level 6*

It looked like this forest was much more active at night . . . That did not bode well for his future in these woods. Tilly shrugged off the dread that wanted to encroach on his happy moment. Instead, he decided he was on a roll and drew a hatchet. He wasn't ashamed to admit that the motion had a few needless flourishes; the *Dexterity* boost was just too fun to ignore.

He stepped forward gracefully and chopped the weapon down diagonally across his body. The motion felt good. Not quite the same as forcing entry on a door or chopping through walls to find possible fire extensions. But near enough that the motion felt at home in his body. Like sitting in your favorite chair in the living room. He tried a few more moves and found that the hatchet felt exceedingly comfortable in his hand as he moved through imaginary enemies.

The weapon was only slightly smaller than the ax he had carried on his belt for decades, and he had used that thing for all kinds of interior work over the years. Whatever else was true about this class, the starting weapons were perfect.

Feeling confident, he went ahead and drew his second weapon and started trying to chain attacks. He immediately found the motions awkward, even with his newly improved *Dexterity*. It felt like all of his skill-assisted grace had drained away, now that he held a second weapon. He disappointedly popped open his merrily blinking notification screen.

> **Caution!** *You do not meet the prerequisite skill to wield two small weapons at once. -50% penalty to Dexterity while wielding two weapons at once.*

"Of course, **Dual Wielding** is a thing here! And it is very much a skill I don't have from my previous life." He grunted.

Nonetheless, he continued to step forward and hack down at an angle, alternating each arm in a motion that felt awkward as hell with a hatchet in each hand. It was extremely frustrating that something that had felt so natural just a moment before could be nerfed down by such an arbitrary change.

He went on like that for fifteen minutes and built up a deep burn in his fore-arms and wrists from the repetitive motions. Finally, he stopped. He was panting and felt the familiar sensation of being drenched with sweat under thick clothing.

He glanced hopefully at his notification icon and saw it just sitting there smugly staring back at him with unblinking eyes . . . or eye. Or whatever.

Looks like he would have to do more than just repetitive swings to learn a new skill. The others seemed to have been awarded to him after he accomplished some sort of feat with the skill. Unfortunately, that probably meant he was going to have to learn this one in real combat . . .

Tilly cringed at the thought, but before he let his anxiety begin to spiral, he hardened his expression and tamped down any thoughts of complaint or worry. This was his new life, and he was going to try his damndest to make it count. There was no escaping this reality. No video game to go veg out and play, or bar top to stare at over cheap whiskey . . . This time it was nut up or shut up, and unlike the fire department, there was no end of shift.

Before he could find any reasons not to, he took a long drink of water and started moving upstream hoping to stumble across something that he could level against without being outright killed.

He cautiously followed the tree line ready to hightail it across the stream or up some tree if he had to.

Identify still wasn't working for him as he tried to look deeply at different plants and natural features. He sighed. He knew from **Forestcraft** that the fra-grant herb growing around the stream bed was good to burn along with food to hide its scent, but it would be nice to know other information about it . . . like if it was edible or poisonous.

As he continued to move upstream his stomach grumbled, and he grimaced in consternation as the urge to have a bowel movement started building in his lower abdomen.

"Guess these haven't been magicked away either," he grumbled to himself, looking down at his abdomen in accusation.

One thing he had definitely learned at the fire station was to always go when you have the urge. Nothing was worse than being on scene, fighting fire, and all you were thinking about was finding a place to take a dump. Many foolish fire-fighters had been known to search out a bathroom in a burning building and drop trou right there, consequences be damned.

With that sage wisdom in mind, he moved into the tree line and found some fat tan leaves hanging from a shorter tree. He plucked one from the dwarf tree and rubbed it between his fingers. He was pleased to find the leaf to have a supple feel, yet a soft strong surface that didn't break or tear as he rubbed it against itself.

He sighed and looked around for a place to do the deed. Moving next to some nearby bushes, he dropped his pants and squatted down. Everything came out okay, and nothing jumped out of the forest to attack him in his moment of vulnerability. He used a few of the leaves to clean up, then awkwardly kicked some dirt over the evidence of his humanity.

He grinned up at the short tree that had made what was usually a miserable experience much more bearable.

"I dub you Charmin Leaf Tree," he said, taking a moment to nod to the sapling.

Then he noticed that his notification icon had started blinking and he opened his log in surprise.

Congratulations! You have discovered a new valid entry into the Herb Lore Codex. Notify any qualified Alchemist or Herbalist to add it to the Codex.

Congratulations! You have learned the skill **Herb Lore** by discovering a new previously unknown use for a piece of flora on Nephesh.

Herb Lore - Mana infuses everything on Nephesh. You have become a student of the unique effects this has on its plant life.

Herb Lore level up! Level 1

Herb Lore level up! Level 2

Tilly barked out a laugh at finally figuring out how to **Identify** plants. He couldn't wait to find some herbalist somewhere and inform them of his discovery. He excitedly reached to pluck some more leaves from the tan tree but froze as several gurgling yips sounded from deeper in the forest, answered by a loud snort and the clickety-clack of hard objects colliding.

Tilly's hands immediately dropped the leaves and found his hatchets, clutching the handles tightly. This was it . . . he would have to try himself against the inhabitants of this forest eventually, and it sounded like there was already a conflict playing out nearby. He wouldn't get a better chance than this.

Putting any doubts aside, he took a deep breath and drew one of his weapons, moving cautiously through the undergrowth toward the sound of combat, leaving the Charmin Tree behind, forgotten and alone.

CHAPTER SEVEN

A Noble Gift

Tilly crept through the trees, noticing that his ability to move silently had increased significantly with his **Stealth** skill and improved *Dexterity* stat. He wouldn't say he was undetectable by any means, but it no longer seemed like he was tromping through the woods on a weekend hike. The sounds of combat grew as he drew closer and stopped short of entering the clearing where the snarls and yips originated. He double-checked his notifications to make sure he hadn't been noticed in his approach.

> *You have entered into **Stealth**.*
>
> *You have avoided detection by several hostile creatures.*

Something about the scene in the clearing struck Tilly as wrong. Despite his unfamiliarity with the ways of this world, he knew what he was witnessing was not an occurrence in the natural order of things around here. Four skinny hyena-like creatures with bulbous heads surrounded a majestic white stag-like creature with a set of antlers so thick they resembled brambles. Scattered around the clearing were numerous gored bodies of the hyena creatures.

All of their bodies, including the four still alive, were riddled with the same veiny black affliction that had marred the face of the Jakalope. They had obviously been harrying the stag with attacks for a long while, and Tilly noted that it alone was free of the infections that had marked every other creature Tilly had seen in this forest so far.

While the stag had held its own against many opponents, it was clearly on its last legs. Its beautiful white coat was covered in an oozing network of cuts and teeth marks. Tilly called up his log for more information on what he was seeing.

> *You have identified a level 4* **Corrupted Crocotta***.*
>
> *You have identified a level 4* **Corrupted Crocotta***.*
>
> *You have identified a level 4* **Corrupted Crocotta***.*
>
> *You have identified a level 5* **Corrupted Crocotta***.*
>
> *You have identified Level 47* **Carnonos***.*
>
> **Caution!** *This is a Local Forest Spirit and holds sway over this Domain.*

As he was reading, two of the Crocottas rushed toward the Carnonos's front with gurgling yips and snaps of their black, frothing jaws. The Carnonos lowered its antlers to meet the charge, but their attack was a feint, and a third Crocotta lunged from behind, latching its teeth on to the Carnonos's bloody flank like a yellow-and-black stained vise.

The Carnonos's antlers glowed bright green as he thrust them forward, and Tilly was surprised to see some of the antler tips vanish and appear to stab into the opponents who had feinted ten feet away. The glow faded, and the antler tips returned, leaving gaping holes with rivulets of dark blood pouring from the hyenas' sides. The move had depleted whatever remaining energy the Carnonos had, and it drunkenly swayed from side to side, trying to dislodge the Crocotta from its hindquarters.

Tilly ground his teeth as he watched the stag fighting to its last breath even though it was outnumbered and surrounded. A burning sensation started to build in the pit of his stomach, almost like his anger at the sight had manifested a physical sensation, giving weight to the dissatisfaction he felt at the injustice playing out in front of him. The black substance, or **Corruption** as the system called it, was clearly attempting to infect everything in this forest. The idea of this stuff spreading through the local wildlife evoked memories of all sorts of movies and books that told him this kind of thing, if left unchecked, would quickly become a calamity for everyone in this region.

He didn't know what he could do against such a huge problem, but a long time ago he had learned to follow the tug in his guts. He once again found himself moving before he had consciously thought through his actions. He needed to level, and these assholes seemed like a great place to start. He lifted his right hatchet above his head and let it fly at the Crocotta still flanking the stag and charged one of the two in front with the fresh wounds.

While the infected creatures were slow on the uptake, the Carnonos's eyes lit up with renewed energy as it spotted him. It suddenly leapt back, ramming its unwelcomed rider against a tree.

That was all he was able to take in before Tilly's entire attention was taken by the enemy in front of him. The creature had begun to turn its head, but it was too late, Tilly had it. He arrived at its side in a full sprint and brought his hatchet down in a crossbody chop that eviscerated the already wounded torso and knocked the Crocotta flat, exposing the interior of its infected and nearly liquified chest cavity.

A vicious gurgling snarl sounded to his right as he regained his balance from the half-tackle, half-chop. He stumbled back to his feet from what was a much more effective attack than he had anticipated and instinctively threw up his right arm to shield his body, as foaming jaws chomped at him.

In a sickeningly familiar twist of fate, his right arm had been pierced again in several places under the creature's chomping onslaught. Yelling in defiance at the shock of being mauled, Tilly brought around his hatchet in an overhand strike. The head of his weapon lodged in the creature's neck even as the creature began to try to rag-doll him in the grip of its jaws.

Tilly planted his feet and ripped the head of his hatchet free in a spurt of dark blood. The creature weakly swiped at his leather-clad legs with its front paws before falling completely still. Tilly quickly worked his arm free of its jaws and looked up to try to locate the other two. He shook out his injured arm and was surprised to find that while the sleeve had holes in it, the armor had held up fairly well, keeping the wounds superficial.

The Crocotta that had clamped on to the Carnonos's hind leg was in a bone-less heap on the ground, with a possible broken neck, and the other was pinned against a tree by several ethereal antler tips. Surprisingly it also had Tilly's other hatchet lodged in its back.

Score one for ax throwing at the county fair!

The Carnonos, however, was barely any better off. Its sides were covered in weeping gashes that seemed inflamed even from a distance, and worse, the Crocotta it had managed to dislodge from its back had taken a significant chunk of its flank with it. It was now free-flowing with bright arterial blood.

The creature's features, however, seemed calm. It settled down into the grass of the clearing as if to rest and stared at Tilly.

Tilly was at a loss for what to do. It was clearly beyond help, yet his heart went out to the thing. He moved slowly with deliberate steps toward the Crocotta pinned to the tree, and with a quick jerk, he pulled his weapon free. He then turned to look at the Carnonos, once again at a loss for what to do.

You may approach, Son of Flame. A bass voice resounded in Tilly's thoughts.

Tilly stood stock-still for a second, completely shocked to hear a voice in his head.

CAN YOU HEAR MY THOUGHTS? Tilly shouted in his head like a senior citizen using speakerphone.

The creature just looked at him placidly.

Guess that's a no, Tilly thought with a shrug, before approaching slowly.

"Uh, you're the first thing I have officially met . . ." Tilly began, lamely trying to find what would pass for small talk with the Forest Spirit.

I was once the Elder Spirit of this area, but my authority has been usurped, and what you see now is a result. I am a shadow of my former self, and even that shadow now fades.

Tilly slowly closed the distance between them until they were just a few feet apart, keeping his movements calm and measured. It didn't seem like it held any animosity against him, but just to be safe he made sure to appear unthreatening.

"Is that how you know my class name?"

It is how I know many things, none of which can help me now. But perhaps I can help you, the Carnonos answered tiredly, its large eyes beginning to droop.

Tilly almost sagged with relief. The unnoticed feeling of being abandoned had been subtly grinding down any hope he had of actually surviving such a hostile environment. To find someone even slightly sympathetic to his plight was a huge relief. Even if that someone was a giant magical deer-thing.

"That would be incredible! I could use any help you can give me. They kind of dropped me off here yesterday without a tutorial or guide or anything . . ." Tilly's ramblings were cut short as he saw the creature's head begin to dip as if finally succumbing to the weight of its numerous antlers.

"Wait. Is there anything I can do to help you? Those wounds don't look too good."

My time has passed. If I linger too much longer, I will become like one of them . . . No, I would rather give up the rest of my power to one who will fight, it said, some ferocity entering back into its voice as it thrust its head upright by sheer force of will.

Tilly felt that same strange burning stir behind his navel at the sound of those last words of defiance. The fire there churned and intensified, and he could feel the slight nausea of doubt and anxiousness begin to burn away.

This isn't a game, and I will survive! I can't let this thing go without getting some information.

"What is infecting the forest? How is it getting into the creatures around here?"

It is not just here. It is many places across the Land. The time for choosing sides has come, and I realized it far too late. It has taken root in the temple dedicated to the old one, not far up the mountain from here. There it is attempting to claim a place of power and grow unstoppable. Hold out your weapons to me. My time comes to an end, and if I am to give my gift, it must be now, the voice finished urgently in his head, as the Spirit dipped its antlers forward again.

Well, whatever this thing wanted to do, Tilly was pretty sure it wouldn't hurt his chances at survival. He wasn't so sure about getting caught up in this conflict, but as things stood, he didn't think he had much of a choice. The infection was raging all around him, and he would need every resource he could get to survive. He slowly lifted his two hatchets before the Carnonos. As he did, the new fire at his center roared in approval, and he realized it was tied to the part of him that was tired of running. It might have been reckless to choose another life on this plane and risk whatever reward he had earned. But he had done it. He had rolled the dice, and now it was time to see just what he could do in this new world.

No more running from pain, or other people's problems. Tilly didn't know exactly what he could do against something like this. He was used to simple problems. Someone in front of you is dying? *Save them.* You pull up to a burning building? *Put it out.*

But this? An infection growing to threaten all of the "*Land*"? He didn't know if he would be able to do anything about it, but he was going to try. He was done quitting on life before he even tried.

The Carnonos nodded to him as if it could sense his decision and lowered its head until his huge brambly rack of antlers touched the ends of his weapons. As they made contact, the handles of the hatchets and the antlers began to glow.

The light grew brighter and brighter until, in a flash, Tilly was blinded. He tried not to panic and continued to hold up the weapons, but his world had become a blueish-white haze. With the light came heat, and that heat grew until even Tilly couldn't stand to hold on to them any longer. He dropped them with a grunt and shook out his hands while blinking rapidly to try to gain back his vision.

He squeezed his eyes shut and rubbed them with the heels of his hands for a few long moments and then opened them again.

As soon as he did, he found the Carnonos was gone. Lying on the grass in front of him were his two hatchets with completely new handles. They now seemed to be made out of an antler-like material and were covered in indecipherable markings.

Tilly began to reach for them, and they popped out of existence before his eyes, reappearing in his hand instantaneously. He stood there marveling at them when **Identify** triggered.

> *Origin's* primitive stone hatchets: +10% to Dexterity.
> **(Legendary, growth type)**
> +*Imbued Ability: Recall*

"Oh, hell yes!" Tilly exclaimed loudly to himself. Without another thought, he wound back his arm and threw one away, sending it soaring through the trees. Then he made a grasping motion with his hand, and it reappeared back in his grip.

"Hello, very exploitable power!" he said in triumph as his DM mind started furiously processing the possibilities of such an *Ability*.

He did note that the two recalls had depleted his mana by 2 percent each, which, while negligible, was still something to keep in mind. He was about to throw both off into the distance to further test his new power when more of the gurgling barks sounded from outside the clearing.

"Shit, I guess they are still looking for this guy!" exclaimed Tilly as he realized he was already caught in the crossfire of this conflict. Hoping to evade pursuit, he tucked his hatchets through the loops on his belt and dashed in the opposite direction from the sounds.

This time, as he moved, he prioritized speed over stealth. He needed to find a way out of their reach, and none of the thin, pine-like trees surrounding the clearing were going to work. He leaped over bushes and swiped away branches as his eyes roamed his surroundings looking for something climbable and tall.

The gurgling barks had grown more aggressive as they entered the clearing he was just in, before pausing and then continuing on in his direction.

Tilly spotted what he needed up ahead and took a running leap to catch on the lowest hanging branch before hauling himself up. The whole action might not have been quite to Spiderman level yet, but it definitely would have been impossible for him just yesterday.

He continued to climb until he was comfortably two stories off the ground. He then turned back toward the ground and found a brand-new pack of Crocottas milling around the bottom of his tree. There looked to be about eight of them, and just as Tilly started to wonder what he was going to do now, one of them looked up and started to bark manically.

CHAPTER EIGHT

Fish in a Barrel

Tilly was alone in a tree, surrounded by big-headed hyena things. The only plus was that the crazed creatures didn't seem to be able to get to him. They just crowded the base of the tree, yipping madly at him. A few of them jumped up to try to grab the lowest branch in their oversized jaws, but they clearly weren't built to climb.

For a few moments, Tilly just crouched on his perch, catching his breath, while the Crocottas jumped and snarled and barked to no avail. As the flight instinct slowly subsided, a smile crept up the edges of his lips.

"I would have been in a real pickle if this had happened half an hour ago . . . but now, you guys just became free levels. Let the grinding begin."

Tilly quickly pulled up his notification log and scrolled it back to the fight in the clearing to confirm what he had been hoping for.

Congratulations! You have struck down your first creature from a distance with your ax. You have learned the skill **Ax Throwing**.

Ax Throwing level up! Level 1

Congratulations! You are now Level 3. 500 experience to next level.

You have earned 5 stat points to distribute plus 2 points in Endurance and 1 in Dexterity from the class **Son of Flame**.

Tilly's smirk turned into a full-on grin, and he threw three of his available points into *Dexterity*, and one into *Constitution*, because he didn't seem to be able to avoid getting hit just yet. And finally, one into *Endurance* to stay focused on his build. He then took in all his stats, ignoring the sound of furious barking in the background.

Health: *95% (+1% per minute)*
Mana: *100% (+0.7% per minute)*

Status Effects:
Minor Exhaustion *-10% Endurance, Dexterity, and Intelligence for 10 hours. (7 hours remaining)*

Stats:
Constitution: 10
Endurance: 15
Dexterity: 16
Strength: 9
Wisdom: 7
Intelligence: 5 (4.5)

He didn't love the debuff, but at least it was mostly offset by the bonuses his gear gave. He hoped he was doing the right thing by leaning in to the build his class seemed to want from him. In the short term, he knew the increase in *Dexterity* was going to help him make full use of his hatchet's new abilities. In the long term, he knew he couldn't leave things like his *Intelligence* at 5.

Tilly looked back down at the creatures driven almost insane with anger. They were still stuck in the cycle of snarling and barking without displaying any of the animal cunning they had shown on the ground against the Carnonos. Tilly's smile fell.

"Yep, I need to put some points in *Intelligence*."

He wedged his thigh in between two sturdy branches and launched one of his hatchets down at the abundance of enemies. This time, he missed fantastically, but he also noticed that besides continuing to rage up in their infection-addled delirium, they didn't react at all to him throwing the hatchet or it reappearing back in his hand.

Looks like live target practice it is . . . This might take a while.

He then tried a throw with his off hand, missing again. Part of him knew that if his build was going to work, he was going to have to become ambidextrous, and while such movements felt more natural than ever with his 16 in *Dexterity*, there was still the trick of getting the ax to rotate the right amount of times before it hit the target.

After seven or eight attempts, Tilly was finally rewarded with a hit, a rather spectacular one at that. From his safe perch, he turned on battle notifications to learn a little more about how the damage was quantified, and what influenced those numbers.

His hatchet tumbled through the air before rotating into a perfect downward chop onto the bulbous black-veined head of one of the Crocottas. It shattered the fragile skull and lodged into the brain. The Crocotta collapsed bonelessly to the ground like a puppet with its strings cut.

Tilly scanned his notifications to catch what had happened on the system's side while continuing to throw, his motions becoming rote as he took aim, threw, and recalled the weapon.

You attack the Crocotta for 50% of its health. *Bonus x4 damage from striking a critical area.*

You have earned 75 Exp.

Ax Throwing *level up! Level 2*

That was the second time he had seen that critical strike multiplier. He knew that his hatchets were never going to be devastating damage dealers per strike, but if he could develop a fighting style that incorporated many quick strikes at critical areas, he felt like he could stack some significant DPS for his build.

He also saw that while two of the creatures had earned him the 200 exp to get him to level 2, now they were each only giving him 75 exp a piece. Which followed game logic comfortably and let Tilly know that there was very much going to be grinding in his future. That said, he had not given up his dreams of finding some ways to cheat the system and gain some sort of unfair advantage that would increase his survivability significantly.

He kept throwing for the next few minutes, the motion beginning to burn as he tried aiming from different angles and postures to make sure his hatchet throwing became as dynamic and useful as possible.

After what seemed like fifty to sixty throws, he finally killed the last of the creatures. He found himself unsurprised that through the entire process, they had not tried to leave or even dodge for the most part. They had just kept snarling and barking up the tree as he picked them off one by one.

Not that he was complaining. The last few minutes had been immensely profitable for him, and he spent a moment silently thanking the Carnonos for its gift. With the ability to almost instantaneously recall his axes, he had been able to make some serious gains in levels and *Abilities*.

-Ax Throwing level up! Level 3

-Ax Throwing level up! Level 5 . . .

-Ax Throwing level up! Level 6

You have earned 75 exp for defeating a level 4 Crocotta

You have earned 75 exp for defeating a level 4 Crocotta . . .

Congratulations! You are now level 4. 950 exp until the next level.

You have earned 5 stat points to distribute plus 2 points in Endurance and 1 in Dexterity from the class **Son of Flame.**

Tilly thought about it for a moment, before deciding, to leave his *Endurance* and *Dexterity* at their normal increases for this level, and put the rest of his points to balance out some of his glaringly low points in his stat build. He put 3 points in *Intelligence* and 1 in *Wisdom* before throwing the last one in *Strength* to get it to 10.

His low *Intelligence* stat hadn't bothered him before, thinking it only affected his mana total, but after basically killing the Crocottas like fish in a barrel, he decided it was better to be safe than sorry and make sure there was at least a healthy presence of points in each stat, while still leaning in to the strengths of his build.

He then pulled up his full character sheet to take stock of where he was at.

Jonathan Luke Tillman

Level: 4 *(950 exp to next level)*

Display Name: *Tilly*

Race: *Human*

Class: *Son of Flame*

Titles: *Harbinger*

Health: *100% (+1% per minute)*

Mana: *38% (+0.8% per minute)*

Status Effects:

-*Minor Exhaustion* -10% *Endurance, Dexterity and Intelligence for 10 hours. (7 hours remaining)*

Stats:	**Abilities:**
Constitution: 10	-None.
Endurance: 17	
Dexterity: 17	
Strength: 10	
Wisdom: 8	
Intelligence: 8 (7.2)	

Items

Origin's *primitive stone hatchets: +10% to Dexterity.*
(Legendary, growth type)

+Imbued Ability: Recall

Origin's *primitive leather armor: +10% to Endurance.*

(Legendary, growth type)

Skills:

-**Forestcraft** *level 8*

-**Identify** *level 15*

-**Cooking** *level 12*

-**Beginner Hatchet** *level 9*

-**Animal Processing** *level 9*

-**Stealth** *level 6*

-**Herb Lore** *level 2*

-**Ax Throwing** *level 6*

He still found the *Abilities* section of his character sheet to be depressing when he thought about some of the starting *Abilities* he had read about on the other Paths to Power, but at the end of the day, he did have Legendary gear. Sure its bonuses didn't do much for him now, but he imagined that as he continued to invest in his build's stat superiority, 10 percent would pay out more and more dividends, plus whatever increases they would show from their **growth** characteristic.

As he climbed down through the tree, he looked up at the sky through the canopy, noting that even though it felt like hours had passed since his encounter in the clearing it had probably been less than one. The sun was reaching its apex, and he still had plenty of time to look around before trying to make it back to camp.

The Carnonos had asked him to look into the temple farther up the mountain, and it was the least he could do while keeping an eye out for more food. He was starting to get freaking hungry. Plus, he still wanted to find a vantage point above these trees to get a feel for the surrounding area.

He climbed down and took in the emaciated bodies of the Crocottas and briefly considered them as food, before gagging at the thought. The search for food continued, and he moved on, holding his conspicuously clean sleeve over his nose as he moved past the carnage of his recent leveling.

He made his way back toward the general direction of the stream, knowing it was his most dependable landmark for navigating this area. Whilst moving in more or less open underbrush of the forest, he continued to try to train his Stealth skill, but it was becoming more and more apparent that the sorts of skills involving interaction with hostile creatures could only be trained in a live-combat environment. Maybe more target practice with his hatchets wouldn't be remiss, but it was obvious that he had only made gains in these areas while in actual danger.

That didn't mean he couldn't train any of his other skills. Every time he passed by a plant that seemed to have some specific characteristic that set it apart from the rest of the forest he would try to activate **Herb Lore**.

*You have successfully used **Herb Lore** to identify Goose Grass. This long, lush greenery is found in virgin forests and can be used for bedding for all sorts of domesticated fowl. It helps with egg production and fertility.*

Hmm, interesting, but useless.

*You have successfully used **Herb Lore** to identify Maiden's Kiss. This flowering bush is known for its small white blooms, the scent of which can cause lightheadedness and a persistent flush to the blood vessels around the nose. For additional information, level up your **Herb Lore**.*

The **Herb Lore** skill continued to supply him with interesting but unhelpful bits of knowledge. He didn't have a way to store any of the things he was finding and didn't know if there would be any benefit to doing so anyway. He wondered what the **Herb Lore Codex** was and if his discovery being added to it would let the world know about the wonders of the Charmin Tree.

Finally, he came around to something edible, and while he was hungry enough to eat them despite the consequences, he didn't think he would be making them a regular snack.

---

*You have successfully used **Herb Lore** to identify Fingle's Flatulence berries. These pleasant-tasting yellow berries are filling and energizing, but are also known to cause gas in any of the taller humanoids. They are however a beloved snack of gnome kind. For additional information, level up your **Herb Lore**.*

Tilly's stomach growled insistently, and with a grimace, he reached over and plucked a berry, before popping it in his mouth.

The supple skin burst with bright, tangy juice that tingled as he chewed. His grimace melted away, and he figured he was alone in the woods anyway, consequences be damned. He quickly grabbed a few handfuls of the stuff and started eating them en masse.

With great satisfaction, he satiated the hunger that had already become his constant companion in his short time on Nephesh. After making a sizable dent in his hunger he grabbed a handful for the road and sighed in contentment.

"*Ppppffftt.*" His anal sphincter happily agreed.

CHAPTER NINE

Can You Take Me Higher

After maybe an hour or two of traveling along the stream uphill, Tilly found the landscape growing more sparse and rocky. The sound of wildlife also faded, leaving only the occasional snap of a twig and puff of escaped berry gas to mark his passing. He tried to move forward as cautiously as possible, depending on his nascent skills in stealth to keep from being too obvious. He was only level 4, and it seemed like this area didn't have too much for him to worry about so far, but then again, he was hardly going to bet his life on an unconfirmed starting area theory.

Anything in this forest could kill him as far as he was concerned. Until he identified it, it was deadly and should be avoided. Apart from avoiding the local fauna, Tilly kept his eyes out for anything that seemed climbable and would let him see over the canopy to get his bearings. The mountain itself was pretty standard, with occasional interesting plants, a hoot or a chuff in the distance, and rock formations that kept getting bigger and bigger. This point was driven home by the fact that his way upstream was anything but clear. It was marred by the fact that he had to scale several waterfalls and small cliff faces to keep next to the stream. And even this was only possible because of his growing *Dexterity* and *Endurance*.

One thing that was showing up more frequently the farther up he went up the mountain was evidence of the **Corruption's** growing influence. Sometimes it was a long scar like a gash on a tree, oozing darkly infected sap. Other times it was a sludge-like puddle that collected in the natural dips of stone and smelled like a mixture of rotting flesh and sulfur. These signs were accentuated by the absence of any of the smaller wildlife he could at least hear in the distance farther down the mountain.

This whole world was new to Tilly, but even he could tell that what was going on here was deeply wrong. Each time he came across some new sign of the natural landscape becoming twisted into something nightmarish it set his teeth on edge, like the visual version of nails on a chalkboard.

By the time he found an immense tree that had a trunk as thick as a car that seemed climbable, Tilly was seriously considering giving up on his favor to the Carnonos. It was too early to take on something that was so obviously above his pay grade.

> *You have successfully used* **Herb Lore** *to identify a Sentinel Oak. These trees are known to grow in deeper parts of the wilderness, and if left undisturbed they can grow to three or four times the size of their surrounding counterparts. Sentinel Oak is a much-sought lumber, known for its strength and supernatural durability.*

"This will work . . . Spiderman powers, activate," he mumbled to himself as he started to scale the tree, his new *Dexterity* making equal use of tree limbs and cracks in the old, gnarled bark. His nominal *Strength* was more than enough to lift his body weight, and his growing *Endurance* made the repetitive pull-up motion possible if not yet easy.

He went up and up and up until he must have been six or seven stories in the air and could clearly see far over the natural canopy. He first scanned the rest of the way to the top of the mountain to see if he could catch a glimpse of his target destination.

Near the peak, several hundred yards up, was some sort of structure. It was carved into the mountainside itself with columns, crumbling statues, and a large relief of a burning flame above a relatively small opening. This itself was extremely impressive, considering the logistics of building something like that this far up the mountain.

But Tilly hardly noticed the crumbling majesty of the architecture, because snaking out of the entrance were dark, thick growths that stretched into the surrounding forest and brought desolation wherever they touched. Tilly had to squint to make it out, but it seemed like these things were reaching into the local plant life and robbing it of vitality. This produced a semicircle of fallen trees and blackened bushes that were slowly advancing down the mountain. The sight again set his insides buzzing, and the burning reignited in his stomach.

It was probably early afternoon by this point, and Tilly couldn't spot anything moving up there, so he decided he would at least give it a closer look before returning to camp. He owed the Carnonos that much for its final gift, and he felt an unexplained animosity at the **Corruption's** continuing subversion of the area.

Tilly shuffled around the huge diameter of the tree to face down the mountain and saw a sea of trees covering thick mountains reaching to the horizon.

Nestled in a valley perhaps two or three miles past the base of his mountain, plumes of lazy gray smoke were visible. He also saw the curved impression of a mountain river snaking past the area and figured that even without frequent climbs to catch his bearing, he would be able to follow his stream down until it met up with the larger body of water and let it lead him to the point of his interest.

Tilly couldn't see their origin from his angle, but he knew smoke. That was not the smoke from a burning forest fire; it was the simple, sedate smoke trail that would climb up from a campfire or even better, a chimney. There were enough of them that they had to represent a significant gathering of people or creatures or whatever.

Whatever they were, they weren't too concerned with hiding, and Tilly hoped that meant they were settled. The seductive call of possible civilization reorganized Tilly's goals. He would check out the cave-temple to see what he was up against and then make his way toward the smoke. With a set of clear goals in mind, he scampered down the tree back to its base and continued his cautious trek upstream. After another hour of rough hiking upward, the trees had almost completely cleared out, and he had made it to a sheer cliff face marred by a huge crack. His stream had shrunk to a trickle and seemed to originate from the mountain face.

At this point, Tilly was on high alert. The sun was three-quarters of the way through the sky, and he knew he would have to make his inspection quick if he wanted to put any distance between this place and himself before nightfall. As quickly and quietly as he could, he followed the sparse tree line around the mountain until the temple came in sight. Its front would have seemed noble and ancient, if not for the thick, ropy tendrils that choked the bottom half of the entrance, reaching greedily out into the surrounding forest and spreading death.

Even though he was almost a hundred yards away, one of the things was rooted into the ground at the base of a tree nearby, and Tilly could see the veiny black protrusion spidering up the trunk. As he followed the path of the root back to the temple entrance, he found a history of infection and death, marked by fallen logs and bushes turned into dry skeletal structures. The roots not only were infecting these plants, they were robbing them of their water and life.

The whole scene sent goosebumps running along his arms under his jacket. It was one thing to see it from hundreds of yards away; it was a magnitude more intimidating to witness the effects up close.

Thankfully, as Tilly continued to scan the unnatural clearing, he saw no sign of movement. He even held his breath for a while and heard no evidence of other creatures near his location. The only sound was the gusty breeze that one finds in all mountain ranges near the peaks. No birds, no squirrels, nothing. The absence of living things was eerie, but Tilly figured that whatever was going on here had probably either chased off the locals or infected them already.

He followed the line of a nearby root back to the temple complex. The heart of what was happening here hid much deeper in the temple complex. Tilly sighed deeply as he realized that a quick peek at the entrance wasn't going to tell him anything useful.

So far he had learned nothing besides that plants and animals were being infected and that the infection originated from this temple, which is exactly as much as he knew after he had spoken to the Carnonos. If he wanted any new information, he would have to see what was going on inside.

He really didn't want to go inside.

He looked around again, indecision tugging him in multiple directions. The place seemed empty, and he could always run at the first sight of . . . well anything. So much of him wanted to turn back right now and try to find some semblance of shelter. Forget all about everything he had seen and just try to survive. The logic of it whispered convincingly at the back of his mind.

You've gone far enough. Don't be an idiot. Run, get stronger, then you can come back.

This line of thinking was achingly familiar to Tilly. It had been by his side, offering counsel since he was little. It had encouraged him to hang back as he saw others get bullied in school. It had told him not to bother trying to change the hazing and abuse he had found in the fire department. It was there when his marriage got rocky and when his daughter got sick . . . it had whispered to him his whole life, inviting him to take care of himself, come back later, *run*.

This is the moment . . . The moment where I choose to be something different.

Something deep inside shouted in defiance, raging against the complacency that had grown to mark his previous life. The warm, unnoticed burning behind his navel bloomed into a full and complete heat, radiating up his torso and into his extremities.

"I'm going in . . ." he whispered to himself, surprised.

CHAPTER TEN

NO Lions, NO Tigers . . . Just a Freaking Bear

He moved over to the nearest "root of all evil" in a crouching walk, attempting to keep his presence out in the open as subtle as possible. Once he arrived at the gnarled and organic appendage, he slowly put the weight of his foot down, wincing in anticipation of some nightmarish reaction. He strained to hear any new disturbance in the terrain as he ever so gently set his weight down on his foot.

Nothing happened.

He didn't hear any reaction and couldn't feel or see the roots moving in response to his weight. Maybe it *was* just a mindless plant?

That would be a huge relief! Even if it was evil, all he had to do was go in and chop it down at the base . . .

That's typically how these things go right?

He continued toward the entrance in a crouch, hoping that if he just kept moving, the idiocy of what he was doing wouldn't overwhelm him and lock up his extremities. If there was one thing Tilly could do, it was move first, and ask questions later. He ignored the weathered and crumbling statues that flanked the approach to the temple and kept moving. Dirt gave way to ancient paving stones, and he found himself before the entrance to the temple.

The ground he walked upon was now covered in layers of roots, and the opening to the desecrated temple yawned before him, choking on the mass of plant matter that filled its bottom third and dived deeper into the complex. Tilly couldn't see any windows, and the roots didn't seem to be coming from any other part of the mountain. Just this one, towering, dark, entrance.

One way in, one way out . . . a firefighter favorite, he mentally quipped as he moved into the large entrance, trying to take up as little space as possible.

The light from outside faded the farther in he went, and the roots got thicker. He walked for a while until the passageway opened into some sort of large entryway chamber, where none of the light from outside could reach. But to his surprise, Tilly could still see a decent distance in front of him, and he looked around trying to discern the source of this new subtle light.

After a while, he realized that the whole interior was covered over with different stones of natural shapes and sizes, and the places where they met had no gaps. It seemed like each was fitted uniquely with the ones around it, making the walls and ceiling feel almost like a natural occurrence, even though they must have been painstakingly placed by hand. Even though there was no gap, the joint was easy to see because it showed a very faint radiance. The light was subtle, but the fact that the whole of the structure shone with it kept the interior from feeling dark. But the fact that it had taken Tilly minutes to figure out where the light was coming from gave the whole place an eerie feeling, not to mention what was carpeting the floor.

The first room he came to was still covered in thick roots, which formed a strange sort of depression as the layers lost some of their height and fanned out to spread across the wider footprint, before gathering together again and leading even further into the structure. The walls had unlit torches at regular intervals, calling back to a time when the temple wasn't some sort of living nightmare.

As Tilly crept forward, he belatedly drew both hatchets and continued on with a hunched gait. The presence of the place seemed to weigh heavier on his psyche with each step deeper into the structure as if every foot forward was another strike against his chances to make it out again.

I'm just going to get a look . . . if I can take this thing out, I will, he repeated to himself for the thousandth time as the space in the temple seemed to stretch, making his progress seem almost comically slow. The next doorway was not as big as the front entrance, and the roots had only increased in size, crowding the bottom half of the walkway and leaving significantly less room above Tilly's head. While he hadn't seen so much as a twitch from the roots, he couldn't shake the malevolent feeling that emanated from them. He couldn't stop picturing them suddenly rearing sinuously up and looping around his extremities.

An eternity of achingly slow steps later, he reached an opening into a natural-looking cavern. Before clearing the doorway, he strained one more time to hear even the slightest sound, holding his breath.

Still nothing.

He sighed subvocally and crept forward the last few steps. The same dim light subtly shone from the walls and ceiling of this room, revealing a scene of brutal contest.

At the center of the auditorium-sized room was what seemed to be a simple altar of unhewn stone, with an intense blue flame flickering on its top surface. The flame radiated an electric blue light and flickered wildly, hovering just above the altar. It would have been mesmerizing if it wasn't for what filled the rest of the room. Behind the altar was the source of the seemingly endless, rootlike appendages.

It looked like a cross between a tumor and a dead oak tree, and it expanded to fill the entire back of the room. Podlike growths marked each new expansion the tree had made, fanning out from the center trunk in concentric circles. The newest growths were closest to the altar, with rows and rows of pods filling the room as far as Tilly could see in the dim light. Each pod hung from a thick vine that led up into the branches of the tree, like a corpse hanging in a noose.

These background details filtered in slowly as horrific context to the main contest playing out around the altar. The roots all ran around the altar as if held back by some invisible barrier, but three appendages thicker than any other growth on the tree seemed to be straining toward the flame from different directions. Each one ended in an impossibly sharp point, oozing the same ghastly black substance Tilly had seen plaguing the forest.

Nearer to the walls, far away from the altar, were all sorts of creatures in varying states of infection and decay slowly being subsumed by the roots. Tilly saw that many were still breathing, but had entered into some sort of extreme stupor and had each found places to lie against the roots or bark. To his horror, Tilly saw small fresh root growths reaching out and burrowing into the creatures at the places where their bodies touched the tree.

Tilly barely registered his notification icon blinking at him, as he just stood there in shock. His mind reeled at what he was seeing, torn between immediately fleeing and attempting to do something. He couldn't even imagine where to begin, but someone had to stop this thing from growing any further.

There had been no reaction to his presence so far. Not from the creatures slowly being eaten alive or from the tree itself, and he desperately clung to the fact that he had gone unnoticed. Maybe he could do something after all.

He took a deep panic-averting breath and stepped inside, fighting every instinct to flee while trying to come up with some sort of plan. There had to be something he could do to change what seemed to be an inevitable victory by this creepy tree and the **Corruption** it was spreading through the forest.

Could he kill all the creatures it was eating? Would that wake them up? Could he even cut one of these creepy roots with his *Strength* stat where it was? Tilly hesitated. Each of these ideas seemed to be futile, but he also couldn't face the crushing hopelessness that came with doing nothing in the face of such evil. Maybe he would find some hint of what he was supposed to do if he could make it to the altar.

He took a few more crouched steps into the chamber when he suddenly retched. As he closed the distance to the newest pods, he saw that the barklike skin covering them was thin, almost transparent. Floating in coffin-sized pods were emaciated humanoid bodies infested with the smaller root feelers. The sight hit Tilly on such a visceral level, that his stomach clenched in rejection, and attempted to empty itself.

All reason left him, strategy forgotten as he lurched into a run at the nearest pod, desperate to free the thing trapped inside or end its nightmare of an existence. The fire at his center roared in approval, and he felt something building within him as he rushed forward, his face drawn in a rictus of pain and terror. Then the root-covered floor in front of the altar started to shift, and a small mountain of patchy infected fur and dirty yellowed claws rose from the ground.

It was a *giant* freaking bear.

One the size of a minivan, trailing root appendages like power cords hanging from a VCR.

Tilly had never frozen in a fire during his decades-long career. He knew good men and women who had, describing the moment as so overwhelming that all thoughts shut down and you were left blank, unable to do anything but stare. While he understood how that could happen to someone it had never happened to him. No matter the danger, he would always find that his body would move according to his training, and his mind would catch up later.

But this was different. He had never trained on how to fight a giant bear from hell. His body locked up, and his grip on his weapons grew so weak that he was afraid he would drop them. He just stood there, arms out as if welcoming his inevitably grizzly end. But his impending death never came. Well, *it was coming*, but seemed to be moving at a glacial pace.

The snarl painting its already horrific features seemed to be locked in place as it moved toward Tilly in slow motion. Tilly couldn't help but watch, mystified at its approach.

Some part of his mind noted that as the bear moved away from the flickering flame, its movements were incrementally speeding up. Then it clicked for Tilly: the roots reaching for the flame were not being blocked by a barrier; they had been immensely slowed. The flame was slowing time around it to a monumental degree, with an effect that grew weaker the farther from the altar you were. This immediately sent his mind whirling.

The barrier that the corrupted tree was pushing against wasn't some kind of force field, it was a time-dilation field. Something about the analytical nature of his conclusions was enough to break through his fear, and he found his hand whipping forward, launching one of his hatchets at the bear's slowly opening maw.

Tilly watched for one more fascinating second, as his weapon slowed on its rotational path, also affected by the time dilation. The sight fully snapped Tilly out of his shock. His NOPE threshold reasserted itself, and he turned and sprinted for the exit.

The journey to the entrance passed by in a blur as a roar of fury washed over him from behind. He didn't know if the time dilation was gradual or had a fixed boundary of effect, but he went ahead and called back his other hatchet as he burst through the entry door.

He immediately slid to a halt, stopping himself before an environment that was completely different from the sunny afternoon he had left behind just a few minutes ago. It was fully dark now, and the radius of destruction wrought by the corrupted roots had doubled in size. Not only that but the clearing that had been empty during the day was now filled with different creatures, all showing signs of infection.

Tilly had just a moment to process his increased danger before the dark, glazed look that clouded their eyes transformed into bloodshot fury.

"Shit, shit, shit," he stuttered to himself, diving into a roll as several of the closest creatures lunged at him with tooth and claw. He came up from his roll surrounded on all sides, with another furious roar emerging from the entrance behind him, sounding much closer.

CHAPTER ELEVEN

Rafting, I'll Show You Rafting

From the moment he exited the cave, Tilly's world became one of exhaustion and pain. He sprinted through the surrounding creatures, taking advantage of their momentary confusion to push, hack, and dodge past any in his way. His recent increases in *Dexterity* allowed him to survive the manic sprint through his surrounding foes, but he certainly didn't get away unscathed.

He dodged, ducked, dipped, dived, and dodged, avoiding getting pinned down or tangled. But every movement brought with it a new wound or near-death miss.

> *You suffer 3% damage from a slashing attack.*
>
> *You suffer 7% damage from a crushing blow.*
>
> *You suffer 2% damage from a piercing attack . . .*

By the time he had broken through the gauntlet of tooth and claw, he was gasping in a wobbling sprint, barely propped up by his *Endurance* and *Dexterity*. His body was covered in bloody gashes and bruises.

> ***Warning!*** *You have been inflicted with the debuff **Minor Bleeding**. (-1.2% per minute.)*

> ***Warning!*** *Your debuff **Minor Exhaustion** has been upgraded to **Moderate Exhaustion**. (-20% Endurance, Dexterity, and Intelligence for 10 hours.)*

> ***Health:*** *65% (-0.2% per minute)*

The notifications came and went, and some part of Tilly dimly recognized that despite the discomfort with his new body, he should be able to keep moving as long as he didn't damage either of his legs too badly.

The combination of snarls, snaps, and growls that followed his mad retreat mixed into an audiological soup that ultimately shouted the same thing.

As soon as we catch you, we will rend your flesh from bone.

Not that Tilly needed the encouragement. He continued to push his injured body, his lopsided gait staying just ahead of the furious pursuit until he reached the stream that had guided him up the mountain. He jumped into the shallow path and started making his way down the slope, squeezing every bit of juice out of his newly enhanced body as possible.

Many of the smaller infected had less of a problem keeping up once he was moving over rougher terrain, and he had to bat away or dislodge several infected squirrel and birdlike creatures. While they didn't do much to slow his momentum, they threw themselves at his legs and face to try to slow him down, or trip him so that the other hobbled creatures could catch him.

He exhaustedly fended them off as he focused almost all his remaining energy on moving as fast as possible down the mountain without breaking something important. He half-jumped, half-climbed down the first small waterfall, narrowly avoiding the grasping claws and teeth of his pursuers. The infected animals hesitated only a second before jumping down after him with little to no regard for their own bodies.

He heard several jarring cracks and whimpers as he stumbled through his landing, turning his own ankle in the impact. Unfortunately, he could hear even more unimpeded splashes of pursuit behind him as he kept up his best speed downhill. New body or not, the near-death encounter, and now the injured flight down the mountain had ground his reserves to nothing, and a deep burning began to set into his lungs on top of the pain shooting through his body from multiple injuries.

The wounds that covered his body continued to burn like lines of fire in the wind, slowly being covered in his salty sweat, introducing a new ecstasy of pain. His whole left side felt like a bruise at this point, and he was losing the ability to take a deep breath as something in his ribs grated painfully.

Then he felt something click into place, and his breathing became slightly less difficult. He quickly threw up his most recent notification, shooting it a glance as he splashed down the stream in the low light of the evening.

Congratulations! You are now level 5. 9000 experience
until the next level.

*You have earned 5 stat points to distribute plus 2 points in Endurance and 1 in Dexterity from the class **Son of Flame**.*

Tilly didn't let the surprise distract him, and he quickly spread his new stat points out, distributing them to the places he needed them most. He put 2 points in *Constitution* to mitigate the loss from bleeding, one in *Endurance* and two in *Dexterity* on top of the automatic point allocations that came with his class. In his desperation he even found he was able to assign the points without pulling up the screen, willing them to the right places and feeling his body respond with a rush of endorphins and adrenaline.

He felt something snap at the back of his coat, attempting to rip it free. Tilly blindly swung one of his hatchets back and knocked the attacker loose before turning to throw both his hatchets at his closest pursuers, missing one, but nailing the other in the head. Spinning to throw while on the run was something that was just on the edge of his ability, even with all the recent dumping he had done in *Dexterity.*

The distraction of a successful attack pulled his attention from the route just long enough that he didn't notice the next drop-off down the stream. He ran straight off the edge, falling and rolling down the mountain for twenty to thirty feet, hitting every rock in the stream bed.

You suffer 10% damage from falling.

You suffer 7% damage from a crushing blow to the chest.

You suffer 3% damage from straining your ankle.

Health: 45%

Tilly groaned as he stumbled to his feet, and grinned manically as he heard several more of his pursuers miss the same drop and land badly. The crunch of their bones resounded in a symphony of vindication.

He struggled forward for a few more stumbling steps before croaking out a yell and forcing his body back into an asymmetrical jog. His ligaments and muscles strained at the continued pace through all the abuse, and knives of pain plunged deeper as he poured everything he had into continuing his all-or-nothing flight.

After several gasping minutes, he looked back and was surprised to see that he had put some distance between himself and the much-diminished crowd of infected forest pursuers. If they had not already been weakened by infection, they probably would have never let him escape. There was no way he should have been able to stay ahead of animals in their natural habitat, but Tilly had begun to notice a pattern with how the **Corruption** affected the body of its host. Their ferocity increased, even as the physical vessel was weakened and drained of life.

While they were still very much deadly, their movements were all character-ized by a sort of twitchy ferocity, reminding Tilly of some of the more intense zombie movies he had seen. This difference showed in the shambling run they used to pursue him, instead of the more natural animalistic movements that they probably normally had.

That didn't mean he was out of the woods yet. He was barely moving faster than a shuffling jog himself, and he had no clue how long his pursuers would be able to go at this pace. It had become a war of attrition. They would catch him if he stopped or passed out, and it would all be over.

I just have to keep going.

His journey down the mountain became a never-ending slog of gasping breath, soaked leather, and wounds that didn't seem to be healing. At least the pain had dulled to a deep ache the longer he stumble-ran down the mountain.

His legs were lead, and every breath sent a knife deeper into his chest, but he couldn't stop. The disjointed rhythm of his shuffling gait clashed with the harsh, regular sound of his shallow breaths as his mind narrowed down to a singular focus.

Keep moving.

The snarls and splashes continued after him, constantly pushing him to keep moving. At some point, he dropped both his weapons, as the drive to take another step gained precedence over all other worries. Time faded, and even his reason for running was ground out of his mind, one exhausted step after another.

The excruciating chase went on until the stream deepened enough that he could no longer cross it without wading up to his waist. The sound of his pursuit had fallen far behind as the terrain became even more difficult, but things like strategy or hiding had slipped from Tilly's exhaustion-addled mind.

Warning! *Your debuff* **Moderate Exhaustion** *has been upgraded to* **Major Exhaustion**. *(-50% Endurance, Dexterity, and Intelligence for 10 hours.)*

At this point, his legs had turned to stone, and every step was a monumental act of will. His mind had been reduced to simple, stubborn self-talk, descending into an exhaustion-induced fugue.

Just another step.

He didn't notice as the horizon above the tree line began to lighten with dawn's glow, and he missed it as the stream connected with the river. He just kept mov-ing until he was up to his chest in water and started treading water. Some deep-seated instinct prioritized air and kept him kicking even as he struggled to stay conscious. His new reality became one of slowly waving arms and occasionally kicking feet, his light armor proving to be slightly buoyant.

The light brightened the surrounding forest, and if he had the presence of mind to take it in, he would have seen a healthier and more populated temperate valley. The birds could be heard greeting the morning, and some deer watched from the shore as he passed by, his stubbornness as much a part of his survival as any conviction.

The river current had carried him along a fair distance when his path was intersected by a large line of logs floating along the middle of the river. He numbly pulled himself up on two logs floating side by side and let the sweet soundless embrace of unconsciousness take him.

Jonathan Luke Tillman

Level: 5 (9000 experience to next level)

Display Name: Tilly

Race: Human

Class: Son of Flame

Titles: Harbinger

Health: 45% (+1.2% per minute)
Mana: 87% (+0.8% per minute)

Status Effects:

-Major Exhaustion -50% Endurance, Dexterity, and Intelligence for 10 hours. (5 hours remaining)

-Minor Bleeding - 1% to health per minute.

-Unconscious - You are not alert or oriented to your surroundings. Lasts until well rested or you receive medical intervention.

Stats:	Abilities:
Constitution: 12	-None.
Endurance: 20 (12)	
Dexterity: 20 (12)	
Strength: 10	
Wisdom: 8	
Intelligence: 8 (4)	

Items

Origin's primitive stone hatchets: +10% to Dexterity. **(Legendary, growth type) +Imbued Ability: Recall.**

Origin's primitive leather armor: +10% to Endurance. **(Legendary, growth type)**

Skills:

-*Forestcraft* level 10

-*Identify* level 16

-*Cooking* level 12

-*Beginner Hatchet* level 9

-*Animal Processing* level 9

-*Stealth* level 6

-*Herb Lore* level 2

-*Ax Throwing* level 7

CHAPTER TWELVE

What's Up, Doc?

K uro . . . what's that on the logs?"

"Well, Nyuk, how am I supposed to know? Looks like another one of those washed-up dead animals."

"I don't think so. It's something else wearing furs . . . Hold on, I'll hook that bunch and pull it in."

"Gods above and below! It's a pit-cursed human!"

"AYAH! What do we do?! Should we just dump it in the river? It's obviously dead."

The back-and-forth conversation slowly dug deeper into Tilly's consciousness, and he was able to rouse just enough to mumble.

"Please . . . don't."

"Ugh, did you hear that, it said something!"

"Kuro, you need to calm down. Pull him in, and I'll go tell Lord Hiro about this."

Tilly came to consciousness feeling warm and weak. He was lying on a bed of scratchy fabric that felt like a memory-foam king after his past two nights in the forest. He looked around at his one-room abode and saw a small window and sliding shoji-style door opposite a river-stone fireplace and a hewn plank floor. His patchwork leather jacket, pants, and moccasins were folded neatly next to the bed with his two hatchets lying on the floor next to them.

He attempted to sit up and found it very difficult. He reflexively pulled up his notification log to catch up with what had happened during his escape. He scrolled through the numerous damage notifications, trying to find an explanation for his leveling during the escape.

> *A creature that you are in combat with has taken environmental damage.*
>
> *A creature that you are in combat with has been defeated due to environmental damage.*
>
> *You have earned 75 Exp.*

Tilly guessed that the system counted any damage they took trying to follow him as if it was partially dealt by him. It hadn't led to a ton of *experience*, but at least he gained a level, which had probably been the difference between life and death for him.

He also learned that his **Identify** skill had picked up some of the insane things he had seen yesterday.

> **You have identified a Corrupted Ancient Cave Bear level 38.**
>
> *You have failed to Identify the source of the corruption.*
>
> *Con~~g~~ratulations! You have found a **Place of Power**. These are the source of all life and growth across Nephesh and can be used for great and terrible purposes.*

Aside from that, he had leveled **Forestcraft** for his "Successful Night Hike" and had gained one more level in *Ax Throwing*. Probably from the few lucky shots he had managed to get off while on the run.

His health was at 100 percent, and his debuffs were gone. All that was left was a status effect called **Recovery**.

> *You are in a state of **Recovery**. You have experienced extreme emotional and physical trauma over the last 24 hours, and your need for healing goes deeper than just your body. -50% Strength and +50% Wisdom while in **Recovery**.*

He was wearing some bandages with old bloodstains on them, and his ankle and the right side of his chest had some sort of poultice pressed against them. Pleasantly, neither of them even showed a twinge of pain as he gingerly attempted to move those parts of his body.

Feeling encouraged, he unwrapped one of his bandages and found that they only covered areas of faint scarring. Despite everything he had just been through, Tilly found himself smiling. This world certainly had its drawbacks, but he could get used to the insane healing factor he already had with a *Constitution* of just 12.

Just as he was about to struggle into his clothing, the sliding door whispered open. Standing in the doorway was a full-on rabbit person holding a tray.

The figure was feminine and had on a distinctly Japanese-style kimono. She took his level of consciousness in stride and firmed the lines of her mouth before removing her sandals and moving into the space. She put the tray down on the floor next to his clothing, smoothly moving into a seated position on her knees.

Tilly didn't know what he was expecting when he had awoken in this mysterious village . . . but it wasn't this.

"Please eat," she said in a voice barely above a whisper, looking down to avoid eye contact.

"Uh . . . can you tell me . . . where I am?" Tilly stumbled over his words, not sure where to even begin when it came to resolving his ignorance of this new world.

Her face was covered in a light fur that only slightly changed her mostly human features and her long rabbitlike ears were laid flat, falling behind her head and lying over her bun. She just shook her head at his question and bowed again, before rising and backing out of the room.

"Lord Hiro will answer your questions. So sorry." She then stepped back out and gracefully slid the door closed.

Tilly was left there with his mouth hanging open. He had been expecting something weird . . . but Japanese rabbit people took the cake. *I guess this won't just be bread and butter Middle Earth–style myth and legend.* If this was any representation of the population of this place, things were only going to get stranger.

A loud growl from his stomach interrupted his musings, and he looked back down at the tray, now noticing the generous bowl of rice, some grilled fish, and a glazed mixture of carrots. The bowl was of course accompanied by chopsticks and tea. Any of the shock he felt at his first civilized interaction faded before the all-powerful call of hunger.

Sometime later, a burp sounded out through the room, signaling man's triumph over food once again. Tilly could feel strength returning to his limbs and happily noted that the **Recovery** effect cleared once he had eaten and gotten dressed. He was glad they had left him his hatchets; hopefully, this meant he wasn't seen as a threat to these people.

Not knowing what else to do, he hesitantly moved toward the door, and just as he was reaching for it, it seemed to open of its own accord, revealing two rabbit men armed with spears. The one on the left flinched in surprise, while the one on the right nodded at the sight of him standing and dressed.

It was difficult for Tilly to tell them apart.

"Lord Hiro said you would be up. Come with us please." After the request they simply turned and walked away, leaving Tilly to follow.

Both rabbit men wore simple peasant clothes in the Japanese style and had their ears tied behind their heads with thongs of leather.

He tried to keep up with their odd hopping gait, and did his best to take in the village that surrounded the small house he had woken up in. It was every bit feudal Japan, except with rabbit people instead of Japanese. For some reason, the strangeness of it all was already wearing off on him. Maybe it was the monsters or his afterlife experience, but his pragmatism kicked into overdrive, and he quickly adjusted to the reality of the people in this new world.

Underneath the strangeness, Tilly couldn't help but notice other things. The few children he saw were somber; the people, worn down and dirty, even as they went about their tasks with an aloof dignity that spoke of deep cultural pride. They quickly made their way through the village of simple but well-built wooden houses with sliding doors and opaque white-grid siding. Before them reared a tightly built palisade of logs with an inner platform that seemed to circle the whole circumference of the town.

The front gate was a large, counterbalanced affair, rigged to collapse down if its tightly bound winch was disturbed, and it was manned by guards in well-worn clothing either holding spears or longbows in hand. Their vigilance outward remained unchanged by Tilly's approach.

There were several ladders up the lookout walkway but no stairs, and as his escort reached the base of the one nearest the gate they turned and posted up on either side of it. The one on the right jerked his head up, toward the top.

With a small smile for the ease with which he could now scale vertical surfaces, Tilly climbed up the ladder and found himself facing the back of an actual samurai in full armor. Tilly could see from the ears pulled back and held by a thong that this was another rabbit-man, but that did nothing to ease the air of controlled death that emanated from the warrior. Something about his posture spoke of a profound readiness for violence as he stood facing the distant line of trees.

"When I heard my people had found you, my first thought was of killing you, just to save my people the grief you will inevitably bring if left alive." His voice rumbled in a deep bass, every bit a match for his intimidating aura.

This sudden threat to his person instantly put Tilly into a surly mood.

"I'm sorry, I don't understand what you mean. I just got to your world and barely lived through a couple of nights in those woods over there. You have a serious problem brewing at the top of that mountain. What do you mean, 'save my people grief'?"

At that the rabbit-man, who could only be Lord Hiro, turned and revealed a profoundly careworn face, weathered by time, but unbowed before its relentless passage. His eyes were hard and carried a deep sorrow.

"I should have known one of your kind would come. You always do in times of great change, and change is seldom kind to its victims," he said, looking over Tilly as if searching for something. Something about Tilly's presence seemed to set off an internal conflict in him, and suspicion warred with a flicker of hope on his heavily lined face.

"Look, uhh . . . Sir, I don't know what you think you know about me, but I have barely survived my first few days here, and while I appreciate your hospitality, you need to get over your prejudices and send people to stop what is happening up in that mountain," Tilly said with a forceful gesture toward the looming mountain at the head of the valley.

"Some evil has taken over a temple up there, and it is spreading all throughout these lands!"

Nothing in Lord Hiro's countenance changed at his gesturing, but Tilly couldn't help but notice the nearest guard tighten his grip on his spear shaft as he struggled to not look like he was listening. His words seemed to strike some deep chord of worry in these people . . .

*They already knew about the **Corruption**.*

The pieces he had seen on his way over to the wall fell into place. These were a people under attack. They had probably already lost friends and family, and here he was mouthing off. The angles of Tilly's self-righteous scowl softened, and in a lower voice he said, "I can see that things have not gone easily here, but whatever is growing at the heart of that mountain is only getting stronger. I think that whatever forces you have seen are only a small portion of what will be brought to bear if it goes unchecked."

Shadows deepened across Hiro's features as Tilly's simple statements hit him one by one.

"Do you think we are ignorant of this, human? We have already gambled our future to see this threat eradicated, and we lost," he replied, a dark stormy fury settling over his expression.

"We sent our best, and the attacks have not ceased. Every night they come, and with me, we stand with few losses. But without me, my people would be overrun before I reached the source and attempted to stop them. Our loggers are good men, but they have to sleep in the middle of the river on rafts to stay safe from attack at night. We simply have no one left to spend on this mission. We have lived with this burden for many days. Now tell me, human, have you come to defeat this abomination, or are you simply a fresh harbinger of our doom?"

Something about Hiro using the same word as the [Title] he had below his name struck Tilly. He had been content with just warning the people after his narrow escape, but try as he might, he could not shake the feeling that there was still something he could do. This couldn't all just be an accident, his starting point in this world, his only Title, even these people, locked in a struggle for their lives. These were all variables stacked next to each other like dominos, in the hope that one would impact the other in a cascading effect that led to some unseen outcome.

This line of thinking and its implications played out in conflict openly visible on Tilly's face. Hiro watched the human struggle to answer his question, his own face inscrutable. Tilly was vastly underpowered when considering the challenges these faced, and the idea of heading up that mountain to try to fight the bear again caused a surge of panic to rush up his throat from the pit of his stomach. A desperate thought crossed his mind, and he flicked open his notification log to see just how powerful Hiro was.

Level 52, Samurai Lord

The idea of this guy asking him to solve a problem so far above his ability filled him with bitterness. This guy could snap him in half, and yet here they were, in the classic, "send the new guy to fix all of our problems" situation.

"There must be something you can do. I know you said you can't leave, but . . . for God's sake, it's feeding off of people up there," Tilly uttered, trying to keep down his growing panic. The gut-level horror at what he had faced in the temple caused his voice to crack, and he looked down to cover the naked fear in his eyes.

But even looking down, he felt the air around him change, growing heavier. Then he heard the creak of armor in front of him as if it was straining to hold back the taut body beneath.

"Human . . . answer me carefully. You said it is feeding off people. Did you see any alive?"

CHAPTER THIRTEEN

Voluntold

Tilly was suddenly deeply aware of how close he was standing to the samurai with a death grip on his sword. The warrior's proximity was beyond intimidating, but the memory of the man-sized fleshy pods had been burned into his psyche. However dangerous Lord Hiro was, it was nothing compared to the room full of nightmare fuel at the top of that mountain. He pushed through his warring fears and the pressure of Hiro's presence to carefully answer the question.

"Look, from what I saw, the thing causing this **Corruption** is some sort of demonic, subterranean tree. Around its base, there are these podlike things with shapes inside them. I think it has been capturing things for a long time and sets them up as some sort of energy source to maintain its growth. The pods nearest to the entrance looked like the newest growths and had some figures in them that were already husks, but one particular pod near the altar at the center of the room seemed to still have an intact figure within. It might have something to do with how time works in the chamber. Whatever is in that pod, there is only a small chance it could still be alive. It's suspended in liquid, and I have no idea how it could still be breathing, but it did not have the sucked-dry look the other bodies had."

Tilly tore his mind away from the memory to find a new, wild hope burning in the samurai's eyes. He looked like a man on death row given a fresh appeal. Tilly was suddenly concerned that he was giving the wrong impression.

"Look, I'm saying I don't know . . . and even if that someone is still alive, there is no way they are not totally infected with **Corruption**."

Lord Hiro's eyes had already lost focus in thought, and Tilly could tell he had lost the man to whatever machinations his news had aroused. Finally, Hiro looked back at Tilly, his eyes focused again with determination.

"It will have to be enough. *They* have abandoned us here to die a slow death . . . Well if death comes, let it be by our own choosing."

Then as if his decision came with a jolt of electricity, he jerked his head to the side and called down to Tilly's escort.

"Take him to Shuji. Make sure he has whatever he needs that we can spare, and bring me Kuro and Nyuk. They will leave with him at dusk," he said, his authority ringing out across the wall and into the village. Its effect was impossible to miss, as people stopped what they were doing and looked up at their leader, hope dawning on their faces. One of the guards rushed off, while the other waited at the bottom of the ladder.

"Um . . . am I leading you guys up there or something?" Tilly asked lamely, hoping against hope that he misunderstood the events unfolding before him.

"No. Your words have spurred me to one final gamble. The walls are as good as they can be for now; I will send my logging team scouts with you, and you will do whatever you can to free anyone alive in that place and end this threat."

His words landed on Tilly like an avalanche, crushing him with their implications. The fear and panic that he had barely been holding in check slipped from his control.

"You have got to be kidding me, man . . . That tree is guarded by all kinds of monsters, and a level 38 Corrupted Ancient Cave Bear! I don't know if you noticed, but I'm only level 5! You're level 52; it's gotta be you!"

At his words, the Samurai Lord slowly turned his head away from the conversation and back toward the forest boundary, flat dismissal showing in his posture.

"You know nothing of the obligations I am under. I would like nothing more than to go off on this quest, but to leave my people is to condemn them to certain death. This I cannot do as their lord. I will risk some of my few remaining men, and I will spend precious resources on you, *human*. That is all.

"There is a chance that some god looks down on you with favor. I see a divine mark on you. There is little possibility that you will succeed, but I have precious few options left to me. It will be you, and if you fail, we are doomed to continue our slow march to oblivion."

Tilly stood floored, his mouth opening then closing as he failed to come up with a response. He didn't want to die if he could help it, and he was sure these people felt the same way . . . But the panic that his traumatic experiences had seared into him raged against the thought of doing anything but running away. As if sensing this, Lord Hiro looked at Tilly. "If you do not go, I will kill you myself," Hiro stated simply before turning completely away from Tilly and putting the final nail in the coffin of his dismissal.

Here he was again . . . getting shit on by life, with no way out. His feelings roiled and churned within him and threatened to overwhelm him. Then he thought of the person who was trapped in that pod one more time. Maybe he felt trapped, but anything still alive in the clutches of that tree had to be living in hell . . . The heat started to bloom behind his navel once again, as his world expanded beyond his own fears.

How many times had he run into burning buildings when others were running out? This was no different. It was who he was. Idiotic or not, he got people out. It was what he had built the best parts of his old life around. If he ran now, he would always be running. Either he manned up and figured out how to fight back against this fantasy-horror bullshit or he might as well let Hiro kill him.

He wasn't perfect, but he knew enough about himself to know that if he didn't tighten up now, the rest of his short life here would be on the back foot, always reacting, never taking any initiative. Wasting his second chance at life . . .

Something in him settled, then firmed, and Tilly realized it was resolve. Resolve to draw the line here, and either fight back or die trying. His conflicted expression relaxed, and a small self-deprecating smirk formed at the corner of his mouth.

How do you eat an elephant? One bite at a time.

Without wasting any time in further pointless conversation with the desperate leader, Tilly turned and climbed down the ladder. The remaining guard stared at him, seeming to be just as amazed by his leader's decision as Tilly was. Under his scrutiny, Tilly awkwardly put his hands on his weapons, attempting to appear far more confident than he was.

"Nothing to it but to do it . . . Let's get going," he said, lifting one of his hands from his stance and waving vaguely back down the street. The motion seemed to wake the guard from his stupor, and he nodded quickly before turning around and jogging off, not saying a word.

Tilly blinked in surprise before lurching to follow.

"Um, do you have a name?" Tilly called to the guard's back.

No answer.

Hopefully, Shuji is a little more talkative than the rest of these guys.

Shuji, as it turned out, was part logistics officer, part general store manager, and part crazy librarian. He presided over the only completely stone building in the village. As they approached the squat structure, the door banged open, and by far the largest rabbit-man Tilly had seen thrust himself out of the entryway, followed belatedly by the other guard.

Tilly immediately pulled his notification log, wanting to find out as much about his lifeline as possible.

Level 39, Librarian

"So this is the human I have heard so much about! I, of course, have never seen one of your kind in person, but I can't help but confess a burning curiosity," the rotund rabbit-man boomed as he approached with a strange sort of jiggly grace.

He was wearing a robe slightly more ornate than the others, and besides his girth, his features were set apart by an impressive Fu Manchu mustache and a pair of spectacles sitting on top of his flat, rough nose. Before Tilly fully understood what was happening, Shuji slid into his personal space and began manipulating his extremities and tutting to himself.

"Hmmm yes, similar to most nonbestial bipeds . . ."

Tilly coughed and stepped back, trying to find a way to gain back the space he had lost along with any possible initiative in the conversation.

"Um, I just got here . . . the world, I mean, not the village. Although that too . . . Lord Hiro sent me to you for supplies," Tilly said, stumbling over his words as he was completely thrown off by the out-of-place gregarious mannerisms Shuji displayed, along with his complete lack of social awareness.

"Oh yes, of course! You showing up now can only mean one thing," Shuji said, nodding to himself, while once again stepping into Tilly's space and reaching to feel the sleeve of his jacket, making interested humming sounds.

Tilly gently pulled his arm away and tried to keep the conversation going.

"Would you mind explaining what that means? Hiro said something similar, and I would really like to know what being human implies in this place."

"Ah! Yes." Shuji clucked.

"Your coming signifies that things are about to change! If we were happy, and we lived in a stable society, a human showing up could mean calamity. But lucky for us, we seemed to be doomed, so change is most welcome!" he replied enthusiastically.

"Well that's good, I guess . . . Look, man, I have been here for barely three days. I don't even know what you are. I'm willing to try to help, but I am going to need some sort of baseline of information."

"Why yes! Of course, where are my manners? Come in, come in," he said, his wide cheerful face not at all dimmed by the grim context of his existence.

He moved adroitly through the doorway into a large well-lit room covered with trinkets, candles, and scrolls. At the back of the room was a large iron-banded door, guarded by a counter that gave this place the barest appearance of a shop. It reminded Tilly of a disorganized fantasy Goodwill.

"Please sit, sit!" Shuji said, gesturing at a bench adjoining the cluttered table. It was, of course, also covered in stuff, and Tilly hesitantly stacked as many things as he could to one side, making enough space for him to set himself down without knocking anything over.

Meanwhile, Shuji had seemed to pick two cups from the mess at random and produced a steaming teapot from god knows where. He poured both of them a cup and handed one to Tilly.

"Tea?"

"Thanks . . ." Tully said, accepting the steaming cup.

"First off, please tell me, what do I call your people? I mean, you know I am a human, but I have no clue what you are."

"We are called lapins," he said with an indulgent smile and in a tone that would have been at home in a kindergarten classroom. Then he took a loud sip of his tea and gestured for the human to continue.

Tilly felt torn between the tension of being somewhat safe for the first time in a few days and the grim reality of having to go back up the mountain in a few hours. He had so many questions, but he had no clue where to begin. Any line of information could be superfluous or it could save his life . . .

Noting the conflict on the human's face, Shuji interrupted.

"Look, I can understand you are in an impossible situation. It seems we share that fate. But seldom does one of your kind show up with no way forward. Many of you die, of course, but the ones who live almost always end up as the monarchs and emperors of this world. In fact, I believe it was a human thousands of generations back that had a hand in the beginning of our race . . . although it is that belief that got me sent here in the first place."

Something in that statement poked out at Tilly, not the puzzle of how to make a human-rabbit hybrid. Something else.

"Lord Hiro said something about being abandoned. Why is no one coming to help?"

"I am afraid that is perhaps a longer story than you have time for on the eve of your departure . . . Rather I think we should focus on what abilities and talents you have, and how I can supplement them with our meager supplies to give you the best chance at success."

Tilly got back on track, focusing on the immediate future. The problem was he literally didn't know anything, and the questions that had come up over the last couple of days about stat distribution and class progression probably wouldn't make a single difference in his coming fight with the ancient cave bear. So he started by sharing everything he knew could bring to the fight. Except for his strange [Title]—something about its language hinted that it was best to keep it close to the chest until he knew more about what was going on.

"Well, as you can probably see, I'm level 5, and I have zero *Abilities*. The only thing I have going for me is that when I throw these, I can make them appear back in my hand."

To emphasize his point, Tilly caused one of his hatchets to appear from his belt loop into his waiting palm. He decided to also keep the fact that they were Legendary to himself until he knew more about what that meant too. All in all, he had zero idea of the role his class was meant to fill and no hints at what *Abilities* if any would appear as he grew stronger.

"Yes, yes. I see . . . very rare not to have a single *Ability* at your level, but not unheard of. And a soul-bound set of equipment is nothing to sniff at either . . . but it won't help you much at this stage."

Tilly's poker face broke as he realized if he could identify his gear as Legendary, then of course someone else in this village would have been able to! Shuji missed none of this and waved Tilly down as if it wasn't a big deal.

"Do not worry, human, you are right to keep such things hidden from strangers. Part of the nature of soul-bound equipment is it is very difficult to detect much about it unless you are the owner. We would not have known except that every time we confiscated your gear while you were unconscious, it kept appearing next to you neatly folded. We are not in the habit of letting armed strangers walk through our village, especially not one of your kind."

"Huh, that makes sense . . . Well, now that you know what I am working with, any ideas? Because I am pretty sure I could hit that bear a thousand times, and it could still rip me in half."

"Yes, that does pose a significant problem. The two Lapins Hiro has ordered to accompany you are talented loggers, but they will not be much help against such an enemy. There must be something. Some strange outworld knowledge or magic that can even the odds in your favor. If there was not, I doubt you would have been thrust into such a precarious situation. The gods can be mysterious and inscrutable, but they are hardly ever frivolous when it comes to expending their power."

Tilly raked his mind, reviewing all the information he had on the terrain he was returning to. Dead plant life everywhere, a cave with only one entrance, and an enemy that was far beyond his ability to fight . . .

"Shuji, how much do you know about what **Corruption** does to these creatures? Do they become some sort of undead . . . Wait, even more importantly, do they still breathe?"

CHAPTER FOURTEEN

Mission Impossible, Literally

"This is the best I can do," Shuji said with a grimace as he produced something that looked suspiciously like Chinese fireworks covered in arcane symbols.

"It is meant for celebrations, and we were saving it for when the village became fully self-sufficient . . . but this is the closest thing I have in our current stock. I can think of several things back in the capital that would serve you much better, but this will have to do. I am fascinated by your theory, and hope you live to tell me if it works."

"Yeah, me too, Shuji . . . Me too," Tilly replied distractedly as he adjusted the tight-fitting satchel designed to sit on the small of his back over his jacket. In it were two health potions, some bandages, flint, and tinder, along with some simple rations and water.

"I wish we had more for you, but our stock is dangerously low, and we have no healer here. Just a few farmers with some poor medicine skills, and these last potions. It says much that Lord Hiro is issuing them to you . . . they are the only thing that can save a dying man on the walls."

Tilly nodded slowly in understanding as he looped the satchel around his back and let it settle in place. It may have been his imagination, but he thought he felt his jacket shifting for a second. But then the sensation passed, and Tilly found the storage item sitting snuggly but not uncomfortably on his lower back.

"Don't worry Shuji, I get it. No one wants this, but we all have to do what we have to do . . . Your village is in trouble, and Hiro is risking some of his most precious remaining resources in a last-ditch effort to change the situation. Another potion or better fire starter won't make much of a difference. Either my plan works, or it doesn't."

With those words, the door opened, and one of the escort lapins grunted in Shuji's direction. Through the open door, Tilly heard a loud, nasally voice complaining.

"Nyuk, are you sure we can't just raft him to the bottom of the mountain and wait to see if he comes back?"

"Kuro, you idiot, you heard Lord Hiro. If he doesn't stop whatever is up there, we all die anyway. Your wife and son included! Now, if you don't shut up, I will shove—" He stopped talking as he noticed the guard had opened the door, and both Shuji and Tilly were watching the pair.

"It was just a joke, you don't have to be so harsh," replied Kuro in a low, petulant voice.

Well, looks like it's time to go.

Tilly looked back at Shuji and gave him a small bow.

"Thanks for your help, Shuji. I hope I see you again. I would love to be able to ask other questions."

"Good providence, human. I too look forward to your triumphant return," the lapin replied with just a hint of worry coloring his cheerful tone.

With that, Tilly brushed past the guard and stood before two particularly muscular lapin males with felling axes strung behind their backs. The sun was beginning to set, and the rest of the village had taken on a hushed, defeated tone. Women were shooing children toward homes and sharply shutting doors. The men not already on the wall were moving in that direction. The gurgling calls of the **Corrupted** began to ring out from the surrounding forest.

All the energy seemed to go out of the loggers as they turned to look at the gate. Tilly emerged from the squat building, and the pair looked back at him with their faces set in grim lines. The two guard lapins checked that the trio was set and then hurried off to join the others at the wall.

"So, Kuro, Nyuk. My name is Tilly. Nice to meet you, did you say something about rafting?" Tilly started, not exactly knowing how to begin with the reluctant duo.

"That is correct, human. We typically lash our logs together upriver and ride them downstream to the mill. Instead, tonight we will take some of the logs and use them to pole upstream and ride out the night on the river. Tomorrow morning we will hike up the mountain and face whatever we find there, likely our deaths. These creatures seem most active at night, so we plan to arrive at our target around noon tomorrow," Nyuk answered solemnly.

"Huh, well I can't say I like the death part, but everything else sounds good. I want you guys to know, I do have a plan, and if it works, none of us will die tomorrow."

"I have already kissed my son goodbye, human. Don't ruin my mood with false hope," Kuro stated dismissively before turning and walking toward the small dock on the riverbank.

Well, so much for team building, Tilly thought wryly as he and Nyuk followed after the sullen lapin.

They marched through the village, toward the area where the wall met the river. When they arrived a few minutes later, Tilly was interested to see that they had built the palisade a good distance into the river. This created a small harbor that sheltered a small dock leading out into the water. At the edge of the platform rested a crude but sturdy-looking raft of eight large logs.

The trip upriver was uneventful. There were a few **Corrupted** creatures on the banks of the river, but they mostly headed back toward the village for what Tilly learned was a nightly battle.

They would spend twilight crowding the forest around the village and then throw themselves at the wall until their numbers were spent. For some reason, they only attacked at night, and did so in a steady stream, almost as if they didn't want to take the village, but rather exhaust its inhabitants night after night. The tactic was disturbingly sophisticated for something Tilly still hoped was not sapient.

He spent the ride taking throws at the passing creatures. He only managed to wound a few and didn't get any *experience* for his efforts. The two loggers just ignored the creatures as they steadily poled up the river. For them, this was business as usual.

"How long have these attacks been happening?" Tilly asked one of the stoic lapins after missing another impossible throw at a creature moving through the dark forest.

The one called Kuro looked over at him, almost surprised he wanted to talk as they set out on such a grim task. He looked over at Nyuk incredulously, and the other lapin just pretended not to have heard. With a wearied sigh, Kuro answered.

"First our hunters started discovering creatures slain in the forest by unnatural means. They were killed but not eaten, and the killing was uncommonly savage. Then attacks began to happen at the logging camp. We always posted a guard and were able to fight off the creatures, but Lord Hiro grew concerned. He sent our hunters to follow the creatures' trail during the day and find their source." At this point, Kuro slowed in his story and watched another creature stumble by on the riverbank, clearly ravaged by corruption.

"Only one hunter returned from the mission. He was wounded and severely poisoned by the **Corruption**. Before he died, he spoke of an evil spreading at the top of the mountain and reaching down toward the valley."

At this, Nyuk lifted one of his hands from the pole and made a sign to ward off evil. Kuro looked over at the motion and narrowed his eyes in annoyance.

"At this point, Ichiro, our lord's son, and our last true warriors formed a party and went to stop this threat before it grew too great for our village to overcome . . . they failed.

"They have not been seen since that day, and the attacks on the village started a week later. With Lord Hiro on the wall, we have held."

"In no small part because we finished the palisade far ahead of schedule," Nyuk grumbled.

Kuro just ignored him and continued. "But our supplies run low. Our rice fields and gardens have gone untouched so far, but the game we used to subsist from the forest is all but gone. We fish the river for now, but even that has its limits. If the attacks intensify, there will be too many for Lord Hiro to handle with only our militia to assist. Even if they merely continue as they are, we will flag and fail eventually."

"Can't you run? Or at least send your women and children to safety?" Tilly asked quietly, the weight of the villagers' plight weighing down on him.

Kuro's sneer returned with a vengeance.

"Our teleport platform is inactive, and our messages go unanswered. They told us we were being sent to 'subdue this area of the frontier for the glory of the empire . . .' What a load of pit-cursed shit," Kuro finished before spitting vehemently over the side of the raft.

That answer only produced another round of questions in Tilly's mind, but he saw the flat look of fury burning in the lapin's eyes and decided to hold back for now. It wasn't too much longer before the lapins seemed to notice some landmark that was invisible to Tilly's eyes in the dark. They moved the raft closer to the bank and lodged the poles deep in the silty riverbed through two holes in the middle of the raft that seemed to be made for this purpose.

Tilly looked around and saw that the eddy they were in was produced by a small but familiar stream flowing down into the river from the nearby shore. The poles seemed to be able to anchor the raft well enough in the reduced current near the mouth of the stream, and Tilly noted that they were still far enough away from shore that any creatures would have a difficult time approaching the raft without making a lot of noise.

Without a word, both lapins settled down and reached into their packs to produce some of the rice ball and fish rations that each of them had been issued. Tilly followed suit and hunkered down on the unsteady raft, reaching into his satchel for his own rations. He felt sick to his stomach when he thought about what they would be attempting tomorrow, but he knew he had to eat, so eat he did, with mechanical efficiency.

"We will get what rest we can here until dawn. Then Kuro and I will go with you up the mountain to this 'temple,' and we shall see if this plan of yours works," Nyuk said with finality. Kuro just let out a quiet burp before curling up on his side of the raft, and almost instantly began snoring.

"Wow, he doesn't waste time, does he?" Tilly wondered, unable to keep the awe from his voice.

"Kuro is only really good at two things. That lapin can fell and haul more trees than any other two put together, and he can sleep through anything," Nyuk said looking over at his companion with something other than the hard expressions he had worn for the whole of the trip.

Tilly simply nodded, wondering if he would be able to sleep at all with the horrors he planned to face tomorrow. Nyuk laid down himself, but surprisingly continued in a voice just loud enough for Tilly to hear.

"Kuro *likes* to say that he is only really good at three things . . . But don't ask him what the third thing is."

Tilly snorted and almost choked on the last of his rice ball, shooting a glance at the more serious lapin, but he was already snoring. Looked like they both were no slouches when it came to that second skill.

Tilly gingerly followed suit, lying back and looking up at the sky visible through the overhanging branches.

He hadn't gotten a chance to do so during his last two harrowing nights, and what he saw hit him in the chest with the force of its beauty. It was like one of those special Hubble images that NASA used to raise money. Instead of shining from a computer screen, the incredible sight spanned the night sky. There were uncountable stars, intermingling with nebulae and something resembling the northern lights dancing beyond the mountaintops.

It was truly incredible, and Tilly idly started to wonder just how many of the dreams of men were nightmares, and how many were things like this. Sometime during his reverie, he fell asleep to the sound of the quiet rush of the river.

CHAPTER FIFTEEN

The Plan

Tilly awoke to a not-so-gentle kick in the leg.

"Ouch, man!"

"Come on, human, dawn is in an hour, and we have a long way to hike before getting to work," Nyuk replied dryly, not looking away at all from Tilly's glare.

Kuro stood to the side, chuckling as he used his pole to push the raft up on the bank of the river. Tilly took a few quick drinks from the river before splashing some on his face to help wake himself up. By the time he was done, the lapins had already hopped onto shore and were looking back at him, with longsuffering frowns.

Tilly sheepishly wiped his hands on his leather armor and leaped to shore next to them, almost slipping as the soft sand gave way under his feet. Nyuk turned and started moving uphill, while Kuro took the time to slowly shake his head at Tilly before turning and moving uphill as well. They did not set an easy pace . . .

Something about the obvious teasing set Tilly at ease. He had spent his whole life around salt of the earth, manual labor types. In those kinds of groups, if you weren't being made fun of, you weren't accepted. They might not be an elite team, but Tilly was beginning to think these guys wouldn't be so bad . . . if they lived through the day.

They forged ahead, not waiting for him as they moved easily through the undergrowth, up the mountain.

"So, that's how it's gonna be, is it?" Tilly growled, ready to show these two the power of his 20 *Endurance.*

Turns out these particular lapins ate 20 *Endurance* losers like Tilly for breakfast and asked for seconds.

Tilly barely managed to keep up. Each time they would pull too far ahead, they would turn and look back at him, faces oozing disappointment. At this point, Tilly couldn't tell if these two were sent to help, or torture him.

Whatever the case, it was clear they spent a lot of time moving through these mountains. They moved with an almost mechanical consistency, seeming to effortlessly avoid obstacles that continued to catch Tilly unaware. Like hidden roots, low-hanging branches, or the occasionally ankle-breaking rock. In exasperation, Tilly realized he had never even checked his log to see what level his merciless companions even were. He spent a few moments trying to jog and scroll through his log before he finally found them.

Level 28, Logger
Level 23, Logger

I totally forgot to check their actual levels when I met them, he thought as he continued to huff up the hill.

He had just assumed that they would just be typical lower-level NPC-type characters when they had been assigned to this mission . . . and here they were making him look like a bumbling idiot.

"System, can you float identifiers over any sentients I meet showing me whatever information **Identify** can produce?" he whispered between breaths.

As if in response, he saw his notification icon begin to blink, and he opened it curiously.

Congratulations! *You have found a new way to utilize your existing skill.*
Identify *level up!*
Identify *level 17*

He was so busy fiddling with his screens while trying not to trip that he almost missed it when they arrived at the temporary camp he had made a few days ago. The lapins had found it easily, following a stream up the mountain, just like he had on the way down. He stumbled to a halt next to the pair as they examined the campfire and the skin he had left to dry near the stones.

The Jakalope hide just lay there, splayed out in all of its incriminating glory. He hadn't even thought of the implications of what he had killed in the forest being so anatomically similar to the people he had found in the village.

"This your camp?" Nyuk asked with a blank face.

"Uh . . . yep." Tilly gasped out between breaths.

"You do that?" Kuro said, gesturing at the hide with a nod of his head.

"Yeah . . ." he answered, looking back and forth between their rabbitlike faces. They stared back at him impassively.

"It was corrupted . . . and it attacked me first!" he blurted out, feeling immensely uncomfortable, not for the first time wishing he had some guidebook to this crazy world.

They gave him a flat stare for another few seconds before Kuro busted out laughing. Nyuk allowed his lips to twitch upward.

"It's all good. Next time we see a monkey, we will make sure to murder it," Kuro said in between laughing breaths.

"Hope that doesn't bother you too much monkey-man."

"Ha. Ha. Ha . . ." Tilly scowled back.

"You should consider trying out for an amateur hour at the local comedy club. You guys would kill," he shot back, giving them a taste of their own sarcastic medicine.

Both of their expressions instantly turned serious.

"What club?"

"Who would we have to kill?"

Tilly choked down his frustration and stomped past them, not quite yelling back, "Let's keep moving! We have a demon-bear to kill."

The desolate clearing surrounding the temple was just as he remembered it. Veinlike roots stretched into the forest in all directions sucking the life out of anything they touched. The sun had fully cleared the tree line and hung high in the air as they emerged into the open. There wasn't a **Corrupted** creature in sight.

Tilly slowed his breathing and listened, making sure they weren't missing anything . . . but absolutely no life could be heard anywhere nearby. Just like last time. Whatever happened here, it seemed to stay pretty dormant during the day. The only sound he could hear was the steady breeze blowing against the side of the mountain. Whoever had built this entrance knew exactly where the prevailing winds were and had planned for them to ventilate the structure. The persistent wind pressed against his back as he looked at the entrance again, reviewing its size and shape.

"Okay, so last time I was here, nothing was guarding this place until the final chamber, which is a straight shot once inside. I'm going to scout and make sure there is nothing active inside the first chamber, and then we will start."

"I still don't understand. How will starting a fire that far away from the bear burn it?" Kuro asked, dropping his pack, and detaching his ax from its cord over his shoulder.

"We are not trying to burn it. We are creating a fire hot enough to consume all of the oxygen in the chambers," Tilly explained again.

"What is oxygen?"

"Yeah, never mind, just set up the logs to cover the entrance like we talked about. I'll scout and then set up the fire."

"Yes, Yes. We are clear on our part, get moving before something shows up to kill us." Nyuk grunted, moving toward the nearest fallen tree.

Tilly hurried toward the entrance and only hesitated at the stone arch for a moment before grimacing and ducking inside. Once again, he moved toward the first chamber, his eyes taking a moment to adjust to the strange light faintly showing between the rocks.

He moved down the hallway with furtive steps, trying to keep his breathing under control. After a minute or two, he made it to the first chamber where the floor of roots thinned and fanned out. Nothing was waiting for him there, and he eyed the next doorway.

Here's to hoping you don't have a fire-science degree, Mr. Zombie Bear.

He waited for one moment more, making sure he couldn't hear any response from deeper in the chamber, before legging it back to the entrance. As he emerged into the bright day, he saw that the lapins had already cut one log into two pieces just higher than the entrance and were hauling it to the door.

They didn't even spare him a glance as he signaled them to continue. All was clear for now. He sighed and moved away from the ancient statues. It wasn't far before he reached the beginning of the deadened clearing and began gathering as many small husk-like bushes as he could carry.

He then crept back to the first room and placed them in the center, before exiting to find slightly larger fuel to surround his first pile. He took these back-and-forth trips for over an hour until he was hauling anything he could find that would burn to the perfectly engineered pile of fuel.

This thing will make one hell of a bonfire, he thought to himself as he wiped his hands free of the dust and sweat that covered them. He had left himself a small pathway to the center with the smallest brush lightly packed together into a sort of nest, surrounded by the rest of the dead wood.

The whole time he worked, his nerves had tweaked his senses to the edge of sensitivity. He had found himself frequently stopping at some imagined sound or distant movement. But by the time noon came around, the lapins were done and ready to seal the entrance with a reinforced log barrier, and Tilly was standing at the center of his creation.

He could no longer see the far doorway, but he looked in its direction nonetheless, trying not to think about the horrors that lay deeper in the temple. He shook his head once to clear it and pulled out the final item Shuji had secured for him. It was a deep-red paper construct with a simple fuse on the end. He gently nestled it at the center of the small dried-out twig nest he had carefully created.

"God, if you are out there, I need this thing to burn hot and fast," he whispered to himself, beads of sweat dripping down his forehead, and he once again looked up in the direction of the doorway.

He then took out his flint and began to strike it with the head of one of his hatchets. The impacts echoed through the room, and Tilly winced each time the sharp noise rang out through the structure. His motions became more panicked as he silently willed the emerging sparks to catch.

Finally, a perfect, beautiful spark landed right in the nest under the fuse and began to smoke. Tilly immediately leaned forward and blew on it, giving it the gentle constant stream of oxygen it needed to live and grow.

Then, suddenly, a flame sprang up, and soon after the sparkler-like burning of a fuse followed. Tilly didn't need to see anything else. He sprang up from his crouch and ran out of the room, not bothering with stealth any longer. He ran down the hallway, passing the neat rows of thick branches, placed against the walls on either side. This place had become a death trap . . . hopefully.

Just as he cleared the entrance, the blood-curdling sound of a roar emerged from the depths of the temple, like whatever intelligence the **Corruption** possessed had finally noted that there was something wrong.

"Close it up?" Nyuk asked, desperation coloring his voice.

"Not yet. We need to see smoke billowing out first, or else the fire won't have grown past its incipient stage."

"It doesn't sound like we have much time," Kuro answered tensely, staring at the entryway.

Just then, the high-pitched whine of a firework went off and echoed through to the entrance.

"Look, I told you, there is a time dilation. It will take longer than you think for the bear to emerge from the central room, plus who knows what it will do when it comes to the fire room."

The lapins hunched their shoulders against the noise and waited.

A minute passed, then two, and Tilly was beyond tense. Every muscle in his body seemed to be trying to twist him in knots. Finally, what started as a light stream of smoke began to thicken and push out of the entrance faster, matched by the constant stream of air that rushed through the bottom of the entryway, feeding the growing conflagration.

There was another furious roar, this time sounding much closer, followed by sudden silence as something ended the high-pitched squeal of the firework.

"Now!" Tilly yelled.

CHAPTER SIXTEEN

Plan B

Showing a strength far beyond what their frames should have been capable of, both lapins deftly hefted the logs into place, rolling them over the entrance, and shoving them together so closely that hardly any gaps remained. Then they wedged logs in at an angle to brace the whole structure. Tilly then rushed forward and started shoving dirt and leaves in any opening larger than an inch. Soon they had the entrance completely barred, with lazy streams of smoke escaping through any crack it could find.

Another roar sounded from within the temple. This time, it was more muffled. The two loggers had taken up their positions on either side of the door, and both stiffened, adjusting their grips on the shafts of their axes nervously at the terrifying noise.

"That one sounded a lot closer," Nyuk muttered through gritted teeth.

"Roars are good. The more oxygen it uses, the better for us. We gave the fire all the oxygen it needed to grow into a real monster of a burn. Now we have cut it off. The fire will consume all the oxygen in the structure at an enormous rate, while at the same time, filling the space with toxic smoke. At least that's the plan . . ." Tilly shouted, rushing through an explanation, more for himself than for his science-averse companions.

The reality was, just because he hadn't seen any other openings, didn't mean there weren't any, and then there was always the possibility of some magic bullshit exception throwing a wrench in the plan. He just had to hope that the conditions would deteriorate rapidly enough to take out the beast.

But for better or worse, this was the best they could do. Tilly's notification log was flashing like crazy, so he took two more steps back from the barricade and pulled it up.

You have entered Combat with a Level 38 **Corrupted Ancient Cave Bear.**

You have poisoned your opponent with . . . Error . . .

Your opponent is suffocating.

Your opponent takes 0.5% radiant heat damage

Your opponent takes 0.5% radiant heat damage

Your opponent takes 0.5% radiant heat damage . . .

There were a lot of those, but not enough to take more than half the thing's health.

Your opponent is suffocating. Without access to a fresh air supply, it will lose consciousness in 30 seconds.

"Holy hell guys, I think it's working," Tilly exclaimed, eyes wild with excitement at the sight of the notifications continuing to pour in real-time.

"Human . . ."

"No seriously, check your notification logs!"

"Human Tilly!" Kuro said, his voice strained.

Tilly looked up from his notification screen in confusion. His face fell as he saw Kuro and Nyuk looking not at him, or the entrance, but out into the surrounding forest.

Tilly whipped his head around in dismay.

Corrupted animals and mythological creatures emerged from the tree line all around the clearing, moving toward the temple in their twitchy uncoordinated manner. They still had about a hundred and fifty yards before they reached the temple, but that wouldn't add up to much time.

"It must have called for reinforcements. SHIT! How smart is this thing?" Tilly snarled, looking down at the swollen dark roots he was standing on in accusation.

Just then, another roar demanded their attention from just inside the structure, followed by a huge thump that caused every log in the barrier to jump. Tilly's head whipped back around to his notification log. The timer till unconsciousness was still ticking down.

---

7 seconds until loss of consciousness.

Another thump, this time causing a few logs in the barrier to teeter away from the wall, before miraculously falling back into place.

The knuckles on Tilly's hands turned white from how hard he was gripping his weapons. It wasn't going to be enough . . .

He looked over at the two lapins, and a sardonic smile cracked his anxious features.

Time for plan B. I hope this shit works . . .

"Alright, you guys take the infected monster army. I'll take the bear! Make sure to stay clear of the entrance when it opens up."

Kuro's eyes widened, and he nodded, moving past Tilly to stand between him and the oncoming wave. Nyuk quickly formed that same warding sign with his hand, before stepping up beside Kuro, and Tilly took one last steadying breath before hunkering down just outside the falling radius of the logs.

A final terrible impact sounded against the log barrier, flinging them in all directions. Air was immediately sucked into the void created by the escaping plume of thick smoke.

The corrupted bear loomed in the midst of the vortex; its already grotesque appearance had not improved under the deadly conditions inside the temple. Its matted, dirty fur had become a nightmare landscape of melted hair and burned flesh. Its front forepaws and head were charred so badly that Tilly could see bone, but none of that compared to the sound of its breathing. A deep crackling gurgle sounded from its throat, revealing what should have been life-ending burns in its lungs from attempting to breathe superheated gasses.

Yet still, it stumbled forward, its forepaws barely able to hold its weight, the furious hatred in its eyes undimmed by the damage it had endured. The air rushing back into the temple had not been lost on Tilly. Plan A had failed. It was time to bet it all on Plan B. In this case, "B" stood for *Backdraft*. Tilly's mind had gone so far past panic at this point, that he had nothing left but stupid snarky lines and movie references. The words of his captain after Tilly's first fire filtered up through the chaos that was his internal environment,

"Rookie, I don't give two shits if you are nervous. Process that shit later. When you are on scene, it's go time. However you feel on the inside, all I want to see out here is a Salty Jake, unimpressed by the shitstorm unfolding before you. I want you to look like you see this shit every day."

Just another fire . . . another day at work . . . His mind spun on manic wheels, beating down the animalistic fear that closed in on his chest like a vise. *It's just a giant bear trying to claw my face off. No big deal.*

"Wow, you don't go down easy, do you?" Tilly shouted, his voice full of false bravado. He then stepped right into the bear's face, pouring it on thick.

"Did you hurt your little pawsies in the fire?" he asked in a shout, his voice rising several octaves as if addressing a toddler.

For just a moment, the bear's charred face froze in incomprehension, and then its eyes glazed over in fury again, and it stood up to its full height, ready to squash another pitiful annoyance. Its immense size filled the entrance as it squared up against its challenger. With its full attention on Tilly, it completely missed the wall of flame now rushing up the hall, greedily following the flow path of fresh air right up to its source, consuming all of the fuel Tilly had laid in its path like a train on tracks.

"Kurt Russell sends his regards," Tilly snarled before diving to the side under the bear's furious swing.

It turned its head sluggishly to follow where the prey had landed and was engulfed in an explosion of flame. The heat was so intense that it burnt the skin on the back of Tilly's legs under his leather pants as he crouched in a protective huddle at the side of the entrance.

The fire almost immediately burned through the fuel Tilly had left near the entrance. As it died down, nothing remained of the corrupted bear other than a charred husk.

Tilly had no time to gloat as the sounds of a fresh conflict started to build behind him. Gurgling barks and snarls approached the entrance, and Nyuk and Kuro stepped up to the tide and began to swing their simple but effective axes in wide, sweeping arcs. This fazed the creatures for all of two seconds before they began to try to flank the pair, and Tilly leaped to his feet to join the fray.

He started throwing his hatchets one after another trying to take the pressure off the two lapins as they continued their fighting retreat. They carefully moved backward until they came up against the charred bear husk, lying half in the temple and half outside.

The **Corrupted** seemed to hesitate at the heat. That or the sight of their huge immolated ally.

Whatever the reason, the lapins and Tilly took their chance and leapt around the bear's corpse, using it as a macabre barricade, and took up new positions just inside the temple. The heat had reduced to bearable levels, as fresh air continued to vent the structure, leaving the entrance full of thin, lingering smoke. They fought through coughing fits and reengaged the infected creatures, who in turn moved forward with renewed ferocity.

This new position limited the creatures' possible approaches to over the corpse or around one side, the other being completely blocked by the corpse. This created a bottleneck that reduced the attack from overwhelming to barely manageable. Tilly felt something changing in his Legendary primitive armor, as he continued to fight in the unbelievably hot conditions.

"You will go now, and we will hold them off!" Kuro grunted through a cough while absolutely demolishing what once might have been the face of a cute forest deer.

"I can't leave you guys to fight all these alone!" Tilly replied between racking coughs, continuing to fling his weapons at anything that appeared over the top of the body.

"We did not come here to slay its minions . . ." Nyuk said, pausing to plant a vicious kick on some poor jungle cat's head.

"You will find a way to kill the abomination, or you will die trying. *This* is our duty," he finished, shoving Tilly out of the way, and moving shoulder-to-shoulder with Kuro.

Kuro didn't add anything else, but Tilly saw him nod fiercely along with Nyuk's statement.

Tilly took one long look at the struggling loggers bravely holding the line and felt a burning heat begin to build in his torso, mirroring his environment in its intensity.

He turned and laid a critical eye on the path forward. The thick roots covering the ground seemed burnt on top but by no means destroyed. Tilly had built his trap to draw the fire toward the entrance, so the deepest chamber would have gone untouched by flame. That didn't mean it wouldn't be hot. He doubted he would even survive the environment he was about to enter without some sort of a crazy resilient body.

Just then, Tilly heard Nyuk grunt in pain, and he stopped thinking and sprang into action. He didn't bother looking at how many levels he had gotten from the battle with the bear. He had felt something change as he received the automatic *Dexterity* and *Endurance* that came with each level, but he didn't have time to check on exactly what he had gained.

He just mentally dumped all of his free stat points into *Endurance*. This time the effect was impossible to ignore. The pain in his lungs from his wracking cough was numbed down to a mild dryness, and the fiery pricking sensation covering his exposed skin felt like it had been covered by a cool blanket. Even the weariness that had been weighing down his body from the long day of strenuous physical activity had lightened.

He reached around for his satchel and pulled out his water container and bandaging. He took a quick drink to wet his throat and then used the water to completely soak the bandaging through. Then he wrapped the soaked gauzy cloth around his mouth and nose several times until it felt slightly difficult to breathe through.

Slinging his satchel back over his shoulder, he started moving down the hall in a low crouch, toward the superheated epicenter of the fire. The sounds of the two lapins fighting faded as Tilly moved quickly but carefully, controlling his breathing in anticipation of what he would find in the center room. The bear was only the beginning of his problems. A prologue to the hellscape that was the tree's *Domain*.

Tilly fought through his instinct to stop moving forward, even as the heat on the front of his face built to unimaginable levels. He arrived at the entryway to the first room and found that while the flames had died down, it still felt like his skin was about to melt off in the face of the heat radiating off the smoldering embers that filled the room, turning it into a giant oven. A path stretched out before him through the burning wreckage, left by the giant bear's rampaging charge out of the inner sanctum. If he was ever going to stop this thing, he had to make it through the rest of this blaze before the two behind him were overwhelmed.

Tilly didn't hesitate. It was too late to turn back now. He lowered himself face down on the ground and took a few short breaths of the best available oxygen in the room, fighting down an almost irresistible need to cough. As he filled up his lungs with hot, dry air, he rose up like a sprinter on blocks.

He then locked down his desire to breathe, and before he could rethink his cobbled-together idiotic plan, he leaped forward into a sprint.

CHAPTER SEVENTEEN

Getting to the Root of the Problem

Tilly's world was fire.

Some part of him registered that he was running through actual flames, but something seemed wrong with the sensation. He could feel burning distantly, but it was nothing like being exposed to fire back on Earth. The heat was there, and so was the pain, but some part of him recognized that he wasn't taking any actual damage from the contact.

His lungs had begun to spasm after the first few steps, and he continued to run forward blindly, despite the pain. He had squeezed his eyes shut in order to save his sight when he had begun his sprint, and the desire to open them to make sure he wasn't off course was almost overwhelming. But he pushed onward through the fire, trying to keep as straight a course as possible to stay on the cleared path.

Then as suddenly as it began, it was over. The unimaginable heat abated, and he slid to a halt in the noticeably cooler hall. He took a slow breath in through his improvised mask and found the air to be hot and thin . . . but not deadly.

He tried cracking his eyes next and saw everything painted by the orange glow of the blaze behind him. The path deeper into the temple had a downward slope, and this actually helped with pulling the smoke up and out in the other direction. Tilly wondered if his plan would have succeeded at all if the bear had not come charging out of the inner chamber.

He took the time to pull in another couple of shallow breaths, attempting to slow his racing heart. He could not believe that he had actually lived through that. He looked down at his body, to check for burns and was surprised to find his armor completely changed.

Earlier that day, it had appeared to be made up of different patches of the fur-covered hide. Now it looked like it was cut from some sort of yellowish leather, and Tilly noted the presence of soft leather gloves and a deep hood now hanging over his head.

As he felt the material in wonder, it slowly changed back to its earlier form. Tilly shot a curious glance at the blinking icon in the corner of his vision but shook the thought from his mind. Now he understood how he had managed to withstand the blaze . . .

"I don't have time to mess around with blue screens," he said, sparing a glance back the way he came.

He swallowed down on his sandpaper-coated throat and turned back toward the path deeper into the temple. He put min-maxing and nerdy upgrades out of his mind and moved forward in a crouched jog. He would have time to mull over his gains later. Now, he had a tree to kill . . .

Or not. It was pretty likely that even with the guardian gone, he wouldn't stand a chance against such a creature. He found himself wondering about that brief time he had spent in the infinite. He was beginning to think that no matter what the Administrator had said, he had died that day on Earth. That life and its regrets were over.

He had another chance, and he would be damned if he wasn't going to lay it all on the line and actually try to do something from the start with this one. If he was going to go down, he wanted to show back up in that stupid glowing room, with a goofy smile on his face, knowing he had gone out doing everything he could to do what was right. He moved through the last hall and out into the final chamber.

The emotions now burning in his chest continued to give strength to his limbs even as they grew heavy with doubt at the sight of the overwhelming scene before him.

There again, was the altar of uncut stone with a flickering blue flame above it. Looming behind it was the bulbous, disfigured trunk of a tree, its roots and branches filling three-quarters of the chamber. Hanging everywhere were coffin-like pods that for the most part had hardened and become opaque, with the exception of one or two near the altar, holding the remains of some poor soul.

Tilly did a quick scan of the room and found none of the previously living creatures had made it through the temporary removal of oxygen, each one lying in its place against the roots, unmoving.

He really hadn't thought about what he would do when he got here, but he knew he couldn't hesitate for long. Every second spent closer to the time dilation equaled some exponential amount of time that his two companions had to hold on.

His eyes were drawn back to the flickering flame, being pressed in by the three thickest roots in the room. Each one straining toward it, attempting to pierce it with a jagged, sharpened tip. The tree clearly wanted that flame, and it was only inches away from achieving its goal.

Fuck that.

Tilly threw himself forward with a yell, determined to thwart the **Corruption** any way he could. The fire in his chest roared in agreement, and Tilly felt the heat start to move in a completely new way, flowing down his arms into his weapons.

This sensation fell to the back of Tilly's mind as he approached the center of the chamber at a dead sprint and felt the roots under him begin to writhe. Each step toward the altar pulled Tilly deeper into the time dilation, and as a result, what had initially appeared relatively frozen, began to move.

Tilly realized that the flame had not just been protecting itself, but locking down the core of the source of **Corruption** with its time dilation. As he entered deeper into the effect, he saw the three roots begin to creep toward the flame, and he felt the roots under him reach up to try to snare his legs.

Squeezing every drop of improved agility from his *Dexterity,* he turned the snaring motion of the floor roots into a springboard and leapt the remaining yards toward the altar.

He swung each of his hatchets at one of the straining roots, and while his previously slow-moving targets had sped up in his perception, they weren't quite fast enough to avoid the blades of his weapons cleaving into their fleshy bark.

The heat that had begun free-flowing from his chest exploded out from the head of each weapon, leaving a blazing trail of fire in their wake.

When the blades met the body of each root, they moved like a hot knife through butter, making a meaty sizzling sound. Each of these things seemed to be playing out in slow motion, and Tilly strangely found himself able to comprehend and think through it all as he moved through the air on a collision course with the top of the altar and the flame that rested there.

Every part of Tilly's body was committed to the momentum of his attack, and there was no way he was going to avoid crashing into the stone structure. Just as he was closing his eyes in anticipation of the impact, he saw the third root snaking around the flame and reaching eagerly to pierce his side as he slammed into the altar. On the tip of its spearlike appendage was some sort of fleshy seed, and Tilly felt the entire thing stab into him just above his right hip.

The horror of this sensation was oddly not drowned out by the jarring impact of his body on the altar, which hurt, but was nothing compared to the roiling acidic sensation that was shooting out from the root lodged in his side.

The momentum of his tumbling crash was immediately halted as his body reached the flame. As soon as he came in contact with it, his vision flashed white, and he found himself completely frozen in place midroll over the stone top of the altar with one of **Corruption's** roots lodged deeply in his torso.

His perception, however, was not at all frozen, and the acidic burning from the root tip continued to radiate agony. It no longer seemed to be spreading, but it hurt like hell, and he was having trouble with the mounting panic that felt like it would explode through his mind at any moment.

The flame stopped flickering and grew brighter.

Sacrifice acknowledged and accepted.
One Major Boon granted to Jonathan Tillman.
Eligible candidate for Origin's Champion detected . . .
Do you accept the Mantle of Champion?
Y/N

The words each hovered in the air before him, similar to the system's blue screen, but at the same time different, more primitive. Tilly was having trouble thinking through the feeling of panic at his body being violated by something so disturbing.

What was that thing that had been thrust into his body?

What was it doing to him?

He couldn't take a deep breath to steady himself; he was just stuck, and it seemed like he would be until he made a decision. Time itself took on a sort of ephemeral, dreamlike quality, and he couldn't really tell how long he had been locked in place by the temporal blast. He only knew that everything was being held in place until he made his decision.

He wondered if he was allowed to choose his boon before answering the flame's question about accepting the Mantle of Champion, whatever that meant.

Major Boon is available in two different forms at this point in the
Temporal Spiral.

It was difficult to understand how he was receiving this information because the flame's text wasn't just appearing out of nowhere. It was just there, like it had always been there, and he was only now just noticing each new word. His mind began to bend as he tried to comprehend it, and he decided instead to just keep reading.

Option 1:
You have been infected with Mythic-level artifact, Seed of Corruption. You may
*choose to destroy the Seed, removing any of **Corruption's** influence on your soul*
and suffering no ill effects.

Option 2:
This temple and surrounding area is suffused with Corrupted Growth. You may
choose to purify this growth and anything this growth has infected, leaving the Seed
within you intact.

Tilly took that in for a moment before silently asking if he could get any more information on the **Mantle of Champion.**

Mantle confers all rights and responsibilities of a Champion of Origin, and cannot be removed or changed until the eligible soul has ascended or descended from the Conflict Plane of Nephesh.

Seemed like legal jargon was all he was going to get there. At this point, the vise of pain in his side had become an almost familiar companion to his frozen existence, and he pondered his dilemma.

On one hand, the ability to just end the infection in this area would be extraordinary. He hoped his boys at the entrance were still alive, not to mention the village. To be able to choose a boon to instantly wipe out the infection was incredible. It should have been easy for him to choose the area purification.

But it wasn't, Tilly was frozen in the middle of a hellscape of gnarled life-stealing bark and flesh-invading plant appendages. The thought of something like this growing inside him filled his mind and heart with such abject terror that he just blanked out a couple of times that he actually came near to deciding.

The other notification held even more unanswered questions. He had no idea what the **Mantle of Champion** would do to him, and maybe if he was free of this seed, he could use it to do a lot of good for this area and its people . . . Of course, that was gambling with an awful lot of lives.

Not to mention, he was sure if he chose this option, the lapins with him at the entrance would die.

Maybe he could fight free of this chamber, and maybe he could make it back to the village to make a difference for the people there.

But something about this option struck him as cowardly.

He just couldn't choose the death of the lapins over himself, and he couldn't choose whatever life of horror keeping that seed inside himself might lead to. So he stayed there, literally frozen in indecision for an indefinable amount of time.

Then a question broke through his gridlocked thinking.

What would old Tilly have done?

He would have chosen to purify himself, and played the decision as if it was all about helping others.

"There were no good options," he would tell himself, and then he would have reluctantly chosen to free himself and fight clear of this chamber, all the while, griping about what a load of shit life had thrown at him again.

That same sector of regret rose up in him again, and for the first time in that frozen eternity, he felt the heat return to his body, roiling up and crashing against the wound in his side.

He was terrified of what keeping this thing inside of him would do, but something deeper than his fear compelled him to risk it for the chance of saving everyone he possibly could. He was still a firefighter at heart, and it wasn't in him to leave someone else in the building so he could get out himself.

He mentally flipped the bird at the tree of **Corruption** and chose the area purification boon before choosing "Yes" to the mantle. That last one didn't feel like much of a choice. He was going to need all the power he could get.

CHAPTER EIGHTEEN

Finally, Real Superpowers!

The beachball-size flame that had been hovering on the altar exploded outward in all directions, and Tilly lost all ability to hear or see. Fortunately, even though the flames were washing over him like the incoming tide, they didn't seem to be doing him any damage.

Well, that wasn't entirely true. His side and the point of entry for the seed were still agony, and he felt the flame cauterizing all of the flesh surrounding the wound. Tilly thought for a brief dark moment about cutting through the cauterized flesh to get the thing out . . . but if the God power blue flame thing couldn't do it easily, he probably wouldn't be able to manage with a primitive weapon.

The roar of the explosion filled the rest of the chamber, and Tilly was finally able to move, which he promptly did, falling over the back edge of the altar onto his head. The feeling of fire and acid seemed to be swirling in conflict in his wound, and he found himself in a new ecstasy of pain. A scream tore itself from his mouth as he ripped the now-shriveled root end from his side.

Even as his vision doubled from the pain, the brightness faded, and Tilly was able to see again. Blue flames were eating through almost every inch of twisted vegetation in the chamber. The tree and its roots shuddered while being consumed by the blaze, and a mind-shattering screech emerged from the trunk. The idle question of what unseen part of this creature had been able to emit such a sound just added to Tilly's already full stock of nightmare fuel.

The fire continued its work, hungrily consuming. It didn't release any smoke and seemed to exude much lower heat than a normal flame, or maybe he was just getting really used to being surrounded by fire.

As Tilly watched, the nearest pod split open in the flames and disgorged its occupant, covered in some disgusting fluid that the flame eagerly consumed like gasoline.

The pitiful corpse was totally covered in flames, but they soon dissipated, leaving behind an emaciated male lapin clutching a beautiful sword in both hands. His face showed an oddly peaceful expression in death. Tilly was going to crawl forward to see if there were any other identifiers on the body when the lapin's eyes popped open, and he vomited bile and pod fluid all over the charred floor.

A signifier popped up above his head.

> *Level 42 (25) Samurai Hatamoto*

"Holy hell!" Tilly flinched back before reaching behind him to pull out his satchel.

It, unfortunately, hadn't endured his fiery dash as well as he had and was barely hanging together. The two potions inside had fared just as poorly, both blackened, with only powder as their contents.

He looked up from his rummaging to find the lapin sitting up on his knees, serenity returning to his features. He was clearly barely strong enough to move, but he slowly put his sword to the side before looking Tilly in the eyes and making a shallow bow.

As he came back up, his eyes glazed, and he fell over, completely unconscious. His breathing was rapid and shallow, and Tilly recognized signs of some sort of internal trauma at work. Tilly clutched at his cauterized side and let out a pained gasp as he began to move toward the lapin.

His side wouldn't stop cramping in torment, but even still, he crawled over to the lapin and began to search his body for any signs of injury. Typically, in the ambulance, he would just cut off his patient's clothing and make sure he didn't miss any major wounds or breaks. But with the regeneration available to anyone with a decent constitution, he figured he was more looking for some sort of obvious ongoing physical problem that might be leading to an internal debuff.

The lapin's head didn't seem to be bruised or swollen, and his ribs and extremities were all unbroken. In fact, Tilly could find nothing wrong with his physical body, besides the fact that he seemed unnaturally thin.

Yet, while feeling around for breaks, Tilly did make a lucky discovery. Wrapped tightly on the inside of his left forearm was a small vial, filled with a bright liquid that showed with a faint red light.

"Yahtzee! Years of medical training down the drain, how about a health potion instead," he muttered to himself dryly as he unstopped the vial and tipped it down the lapin's throat.

Having done all he could for his surprising companion, he finally glanced up at his HUD and was pleasantly surprised to find his health and mana in good straits.

Health: 72%
Mana: 56%

Seeing that he wasn't about to die from whatever was happening with the **Seed**, he looked around at the scattered remnants of the **Corrupted** tree slowly being completely consumed by beautiful, blue flames.

"How about them apples!" he triumphantly declared at the burning remains.

Then he lifted his jacket and took another look at the wound. It had closed up with a disturbingly barklike scab, which was surrounded by what appeared to be burn scars. Tilly bent down as far as he could and saw that all around the scab were tiny spiky growths that were already attempting to burrow deeper into his burned flesh.

At least the pain was finally starting to ease up . . .

He let out a weary sigh and put down his jacket. Now that the mad dash of the last hour was over, Tilly decided to try to sort out any important information he could pick out from his notification log.

First, he found where he had leveled up after taking out the **Corrupted** bear.

Congratulations! You have defeated a level 38 Corrupted Ancient Cave Bear.

For defeating an opponent over 9x your level you have earned a 9x multiplier on awarded experience.

You are now level 6. 15000 exp until the next level.

*You have earned 5 stat points to distribute plus 2 points in Endurance and 1 in Dexterity from the class **Son of Flame**.*

You are now level 7. 20000 exp until the next level.

*You have earned 5 stat points to distribute plus 2 points in Endurance and 1 in Dexterity from the class **Son of Flame** . . .*

You are now level 11. 55000 exp until the next level.

*You have earned 5 stat points to distribute plus 2 points in Endurance and 1 in Dexterity from the class **Son of Flame**.*

Woah . . . that was a lot of stat points he had just dumped into *Endurance*. Of course, he doubted he would have survived the fire, let alone the invasion of corruption into his body without truly monstrous *Endurance* for his level.

Before he could pull up his character sheet, he saw the next line on the log after he had mentally assigned his points.

Congratulations! You have earned the Title:
[Resolute].

[Resolute]: *Your Endurance stat is higher than all of your other stats combined. As long as this remains true, you may completely negate one fatal blow per day.*

"Hell yes!" Tilly exclaimed out loud. This was exactly the type of game-breaking nonsense he had been waiting for.

Then he took a closer look.

Shit, I have to keep Endurance *ridiculously high if I want to keep this Title active. Well, beggars can't be choosers.*

He moved through the rest of the procedurally generated fluff until he got to something else really good. His yellow, Mighty Morphin Power Ranger suit!

Congratulations! *You have been subjected to an extreme environment while wearing* **Origin's** *primitive leather armor, activating a hidden growth prerequisite. In the presence of fire or extreme heat, your armor takes on the characteristic of Sun Salamander hide and alters to protect you from heat. -75% to any heat-based damage.*

"I'll never doubt you again," he whispered in awe to his now favorite jacket.

Then the sound of some distant shouting reached his ears,

". . . Man Tilly . . . you . . . alive?"

"I'm in the inner chamber with another survivor!" Tilly yelled with a fierce grin. "Looks like at least one of those tough bastards made it!"

Running out of time, Tilly quickly scrolled through the rest of his log to find the moment when his hatchets had erupted in badass flames—

"Oooh, here we are. My first *Ability!*"

"Human Tilly!" one of the lapins called as they entered the chamber.

Flame Strike: *Channel the fire within you to strike at your opponents. Each strike leaves a smoldering ember at the point of impact and does damage over time. Ember damage is stackable.*

Tilly looked up from behind the altar and saw Nyuk limping in, supporting Kuro, who was absolutely covered in gore and seemed to be walking in an exhausted haze.

"Over here!" Tilly yelled, before looking over to find the unconscious lapin stirring.

"One of your guys made it!"

"Master Ichiro!" Kuro gasped as he came around the altar. His daze faded as he sank to his knees. Tears streamed through blood-matted fur as he beheld the still-living scion of his lord's house.

At his words, the lapin came to consciousness and opened his eyes to behold the three battered warriors before him.

Ichiro - 20 minutes earlier

Something had broken through Ichiro's Level 30 **Meditation,** and instantly his sanity was once again hanging by a thread. He did not know how long he had been here in this waking nightmare, but everything in him howled in animalistic horror at what was being done to his body.

The abomination had been draining his levels and stats for what seemed like years, and the feeling of it reached into his very soul, evoking such a deep terror that Ichiro had barely been able to enter a meditative trance and shield his mind from the consequences. When he had failed to defeat the **Corrupted** guardian of this place, it had simply knocked him unconscious, and he had woken up in this torturous prison of liquid and needles. His body was unable to move, but his eyes were locked open, watching as the abomination's appendages strained toward the defiant flame flickering on the shrine's surface.

It was this act of defiance that gave Ichiro the strength to beat down the madness bubbling up from his subconscious and activate his meditative trance in the beginning. He had drifted there, encasing his psyche and soul in a protective shell of *Will.* He was unaware of how long he had been captured, losing himself in the meager protections of **Meditative Trance,** but something had changed. Some part of him emerged from his spiritual protections, even as all of his senses screamed at him in fresh denial of his circumstances. He channeled his *Will* and focused on the pink-tinged world outside his prison.

There, amidst all of the abomination's apogees was a human moving impossibly fast. He seemed to be charging right at the center of this desecrated shrine, yet his movements slowed as he approached the altar. Then he activated some sort of *Ability,* unleashing flame from his weapons and cutting through two of the abomination's appendages before crashing into the shrine's core.

A flash of white and blue light. The flash brought a fresh wave of intense pain, starting with his eyes. They had watched the flame for so long that the sudden flash ripped through his vision, leaving a deep darkness, faintly hued with dark dancing patterns.

This was followed by a brief but terrible burning sensation, that cut through the terrible numbness that had pervaded his whole body as the Abomination had turned him into another of its energy sources. His prison became unbearably hot, and the burning sensation flooded his body, sinking deeply into his core.

> *You have been cleansed from all* **Corruption**. *Your mind and body have been shattered and reformed, and you have earned a* **Title: Reforged Enlightenment**.

CHAPTER NINETEEN

Intermission

Stephen Brightborn - Level 152 Champion of Light

"You must be mistaken! If this affliction is from the Pits, then at least some of our people must be able to cure it," Stephen said, slowly rubbing his temples.

His strong features and brilliant armor all seemed diminished in that sun-bathed office at the top of the Tower of Light. Many beings of great power had cowed before his presence, and he was a living legend in this Epoch. Even on Nephesh, where myths were common, the name of Stephen Brightborn evoked deep respect in his allies or shuddering fear in his enemies. He was the Champion of Light, and his was the voice of the Church. Despite all this power, something deep within him quavered at the incoming reports.

This was one enemy he could not face. There was no army to fight, no great villain to slay.

"I'm sorry, sir. We now have multiple reports across several principalities. Even our spies in the more infernal-aligned territories are sending in similar reports."

"Light dammit!" Stephen cried, his fist slamming against his exquisite desk of divine marble. The spymaster did his best not to flinch as the impact was felt throughout the entire structure of the Great Tower.

"How is it that not even our High Priestesses can cure this affliction!?" he demanded, unable to understand what he was hearing.

The spymaster grimaced and did his best to take a different tack.

"Your Radiance, they can cure it in its first form, one that sometimes presents as poison or plague. The vectors it travels are very diverse and difficult to track in this regard. Nevertheless, it is curable at that stage, just very resistant to our abilities. But at some point, as it advances within a host's body, those with high enough stats can partner with the invader and form some sort of covenant. They receive an increase in various stats, typically in exchange for a reduction in *Wisdom*. We believe it begins to behave something like an inborn ability at this point, entangling itself in the mana pathways of its host. Once such a level of bonding is achieved, it is only removable by the system or the gods," he reported quickly, hoping that in the continuous retelling, he was not earning the wrath of one of the most powerful unascended beings on *Nephesh*.

Stephen's cloudy expression of anger faded.

"Yes, I have spoken with Lady Light. Disturbingly, not only does she not have any guidance for us in this regard, but she hinted that they are experiencing a similar incursion in the divine and infernal spheres."

This news came as a shock to the forgettable-looking man in servants' clothes.

"How can it be! Surely something like this is unable to threaten the combined powers of the heavens!"

"That is just it, Reginald . . . I believe that as more and more followers come under the sway of this **Corruption**, the gods themselves are beginning to be influenced by its presence."

"Gods above . . ." Reginald whispered, cowed by a threat so grand that it beggared any thought of defense or reprisal.

"Yes . . . Gods help us all."

Tim, Level ??? Chronomancer

"Curious, very curious . . ." the Time Lord muttered to himself as he stood hovering above the mountain that had been radiating so much temporal dilation just minutes before.

The **Weave** running through the fabric of reality here was fascinating. At first glance, it was another incursion of this new extraplanar influence. Its rotting and breaking of the **Weave**, while unpleasant, was nothing new to Tim who had been observing it with mild disgust for decades.

He had always found the **Weave** to be astonishingly beautiful. The first time it had been revealed to him, he had lost years to its mesmerizing pattern. Yet this new influence, whatever it was, seemed to be intrinsically contrary to the nature of reality, twisting, breaking, and undoing the pattern wherever it appeared. While this did not yet affect Tim, he found it prudent to keep an eye on all new influences on the plane. All of this, while important, was not what tickled the back of Tim's awareness. Something else was going on here, something even deeper.

It wasn't the temporal energies, which while rare, were not unheard of. No, this incursion seemed to have met its end, something rarely accomplished in any of the other iterations. A force had opposed this **Corruption** with such subtlety that Tim had trouble identifying any traces of its presence at all.

The Time Lord adjusted his optic nerve through several spectrums of light and took another deep breath through his considerable nose. There it was again! Flickering just outside of his awareness.

This was something old, older even than Tim, which was quite a feat. If he wasn't mistaken, this was the scent of the First Epoch. Its earthy, primordial odor harked back to a time of predator and prey when the only **Concepts** on the plane embodied ideas like *Fear*, *Rage*, and *Authority*.

It had been a truly long time since he had detected any of the First Epoch's influence in this Realm, and he was beginning to see the evidence of its working in the *underlayer* of the **Weave.** Only a handful of beings even knew the underlayer existed, let alone had the power and deftness to influence the plane through such an abstract vector.

Yet here it was, subtly pulling the underlayer in the places where it had been destroyed into a new and more solid structure. This new pattern astonishingly seemed to reinvigorate the original **Weave**, producing even greater beauty and complexity. The effect of such subtle interference was a considerable strengthening of this area's Fate.

Tim rotated through several optical-based *Abilities* before shifting his observation to the interior of the mountain, where a human knelt beside three primitive crossbred figments. Hardly any weight on the fabric at all. Truly distasteful creatures in Tim's opinion.

Then, to Tim's astonishment, a foreign energy signature revealed itself in their midst! A frown creased the Time Lord's forehead as he flexed his will. The **Weave** of reality itself, marching forward inexorably toward some unknown conclusion, shuddered to a halt and then reversed under the influence of the Epoch Traveler. He then scanned the area again, this time replaying time slowly to watch the changes in the **Weave**, and the underlayer.

The center of all that subtle change was this altar and its flame. That temporal spike was more than just a cleansing and reworking of **Corruption's** influence. Something was altering the very destiny of the Concepts these inconsequential creatures represented. Tim hesitated to approach a force outside of his understanding. He had not survived the last three Epoch Upheavals by being rash.

He flexed the interchange between time and space and was suddenly gone. Off to re-examine some of the other incursions to see if he could spot this other force at work there as well.

Change was coming.

And for the first time in a thousand years . . . Tim wasn't sure he knew what that meant.

Titus Janus Marcellus - Level 38 Quaestor

Titus flicked his hand in disgust, trying to remove the glob of spit mingled with blood that had lodged between his rings. When it would not immediately come free, he snapped his hand in irritation, and one of his attendants leapt forward to offer a silk cloth in a trembling hand.

"Why must my family be plagued by weaklings!" he bemoaned, once again laying his spiteful gaze on the creature before him.

There, tied to a chair was a bloody and bruised lapin, its head lolling from the force of the backhand that had just shattered its jaw.

"Evander!" the young Quaestor snapped.

"Yes, your eminence!" a sharply dressed man stated crisply, stepping up from the crowd of attendants who had been made to watch the "educational session" the young master had chosen to display.

"This weakling obviously had no clue why his partner failed to send in reports for the last two weeks, and the distasteful problem of these creatures falls on me once again. My father is not to hear of this . . . am I clear?" he finished, his voice taking on such a sharp edge that the washerwoman in the back almost fainted.

"Perfectly, your eminence," Evander answered smoothly. His frozen expression of disinterest was not shaken in the least by the display of cruelty being played out before him.

"The responsibility of teaching these pests their place has once again fallen to me, and everything was going perfectly well until we lost what I was told was a very reliable asset . . ." he said, leveling his gaze at Evander with enough petty cruelty that it would have broken a lesser servant.

"Sir, even the best of these creatures is but a pale and sickly shadow of one of our people. They can never be relied upon for any length of time," Evander answered cooly, looking down but not cowed before his master's displeasure.

"Yes, well, as with anything of import, it seems I will have to go and handle this myself. Draft the papers for a teleport, and draw up some sort of grievance that will force that wrinkled old fool to return to the capital and give account. If the last reports are at all to be believed, his absence will spell an end to this farce, and we can throw him in jail along with the other upstarts."

"Right away, sir," Evander pronounced with a perfectly monotone inflection, before turning and moving through the crowd.

Titus simply stared down at his captive, not seeming to notice the departure of his chief servant. Every other servant in the room stood frozen, hoping against hope that he would not notice them.

Suddenly, faster than a striking snake, his hand was around the unconscious lapin's neck, slowly constricting the airway until their chest began to spasm and their lidded eyes fluttered in a weak attempt to regain consciousness. The audience of servants averted their eyes in horror, trying their best to be as small as possible. At that moment, if any had looked, they would have seen a manic gleam in the young man's eyes. Under the sleeve of the exquisitely trimmed jacket, something writhed in glee as the helpless captive weakly jerked a final time before going completely still.

Then as if coming to himself, Titus Janus Marcellus stood straight and pulled down his jacket cuffs fixing some invisible wrinkle.

"For Pit's sake, someone remove this trash." He sighed wearily to himself and walked calmly out of the room, the crowd parting before him with unconscious cattle-like motions.

Hiro - Level 52 Samurai Lord

He stood sentinel at the wall this evening, just as he had for the past several weeks. His *Endurance* and *Constitution* made sleep all but unnecessary. Not that he would have slept, even if he had been able.

Last night, the infected beasts had not come. He had ridden out himself after several hours of waiting and found many bodies in varying states of death, all of them displaying very peculiar burn marks as if a fire had risen from inside their forms and vented through any opening it could find.

Upon his return, he had learned that the twenty-three villagers that had been afflicted with varying states of infection had all almost spontaneously recovered, after an intense period of fever and shaking.

Something had changed. His choice, made almost in anger at the plight of his people, had borne surprising fruit, but none of this gave him comfort. He had still lost his son, his last living link to his dear wife, and the legacy of his people. He had counseled caution when the reports had started coming in, but after losing the hunters, Ichiro had been beside himself with anger.

"We have run too many times. Our backs are against the wall. We can hide no longer," he had whispered in fury in the council chamber in a rare show of lost self-control. Then Ichiro had left with his two retainers, some the last of their warriors . . .

Hiro had thought it was just to patrol, something to do to work through some of the frustrations of their seemingly hopeless situation. But they did not return from that outing. He sent people out the next day to search the lower reaches of the forest, even running a quick patrol himself in a large circle around the village . . .

They had found *nothing*.

He was the last of his line now, and the fate of his people had withered in his hands. He had hoped his son would be the one to deliver them out of these many centuries of bondage. The boy had all of his mother's wisdom and all his father's strength, his only failing being an anger that led to rash action. Yes, he had been their hope, but in the end, Hiro lost him too.

This did not change the sudden upswing of his people's fate. The Abomination's influence had seemed to have been burned away. The attacks had stopped, and the people, especially those who had received revived loved ones could not help but rejoice. They held a small but earnest celebration within the wall of the village, sensing their lord's mood, but unable to contain the joy of surviving such a calamity.

Hiro alone stood vigil on the wall as the others left to celebrate. Their plans, carefully laid over generations, had taken a major blow, and with none to carry on the work, Hiro was, for the first time, unsure how to proceed. Most of his people did not know the details, but without strong leadership in the days to come, he was not sure they would survive the transition.

And so, he stood watch, wondering if the human had survived and if his son had found rest.

Then in the distance, his supernaturally sharp hearing picked up a familiar drawling accent.

"Hey, Nyuk, it sounds like they are having a party in the village . . . doesn't seem right to start without us."

CHAPTER TWENTY

Rabbit Reunions

Ichiro - Level 42 (25) Samurai Hatamoto

Something was wrong with his sight.

As Ichiro tried to focus in on the three before him their forms began to swim in such a swirling riot of color that it made him dizzy. He closed his eyes, and the dizziness slightly lessened, the complex vortex of color still dancing before him even with his eyes closed. He tried opening them again and now saw a shifting sea of interwoven energies flowing through the entirety of the cleansed shrine. The strands of energy were so tightly packed and varied that it was impossible to pick one out from the complex movement that danced before him hypnotically.

Braided cords of these strands formed ever-changing patterns that wove in and through every physical object in the room. Yet, as he stared, he began to understand that what he was seeing was only loosely tied to the physical realm. Reality bloomed and intertwined before him, carrying in its movements a deep conceptual meaning that linked this place and time with . . . *everything*.

As his awareness expanded, the barest hints of temporal meaning began to rise to the surface of his mind as he watched one movement, then another, in this ever-changing tapestry of color and light. It occurred to him then that what he was seeing was the very language with which Nephesh was written: past, present, and future.

Dreamily, he watched as a specific knot formed around Kuro's mind, and a second later the lapin asked, "Lord, are you well? Is it some debuff from your time held captive by the Abomination?" As he said the words, Kuro looked around at the husk of the dead tree in disgust, even as many of its forms collapsed into ash.

Ichiro watched in fascination as the pattern accompanying those words moved through each of those who heard and produced different effects. He was speechless at the beauty he was beholding; every interaction was a work of art, a dance of sublime grace, and it was all connected.

In his daze, he did not notice the others trade anxious glances before the human spoke up.

"Come on guys, let's help him up and get out of here. I know this place has been cleansed, but honestly, it still gives me the creeps. And if you don't mind, there is one stop I want to make on our way down to the village."

His words vibrated through the incomprehensibly complex sea of colorful threads in a much more significant manner than the previous speaker's had, and even Ichiro felt their tug on his soul. The human's soul was a dense network of cords and braids of varying diameters running out from his center, reaching in all directions.

Kuro and Nyuk came over and gently lifted him to his feet, each of them taking position under his arms as they guarded their still-healing injuries.

His mind was still reeling, overloaded by information, but he knew that he was no longer damaged . . . just overwhelmed. Some part of him finally came to himself, and he began partially cycling his **Meditative Trance**.

He *inhaled*, centered his breath deep in his core, then *expelled* it, dragging distraction out along with his spent breath.

He was able to vaguely recognize the transition from darkness to light as they finally emerged out of the temple, but almost all of his augmented meditative focus was bent toward regaining some measure of function, despite the exponential increase in information he was taking in.

At some point on the journey, they stopped moving, and Ichiro discovered that in a meditative state, he could cut off information from his optic meridians completely. The moment he did this, his mind was vastly more able to produce chains of logical thought, and he found himself suddenly much more grounded in the present and his physical surroundings.

While he was unable to converse normally while holding on to basic meditation, he slowly shifted into his **Battle Trance**, allowing himself to time movements with his breathing. He took another serene breath in, held it, and then released, producing a calm monotone statement along with his breath.

"I need something to wrap around my eyes."

Then he breathed in again calmly, careful to maintain the concentration needed to completely cut off input from his primary perception sense.

His three companions froze. Ichiro was still being supported by Kuro and Nyuk, and at some point, the human had obtained a large armful of unfamiliar leaves. None of this information was seen. Rather, it was absorbed through a strange new passive meditative osmosis.

Inhale . . .

Exhale.

"I think he is coming out of it!" the human exclaimed in excitement. The lapins, however, said nothing. One shifted to bear the majority of his weight, while the other made quick jerky movements accompanied by the sound of ripping cloth.

Inhale . . .

Exhale.

"It must be wrapped around my eyes thick enough to block out all light," he continued, in his deep droning monotone.

Kuro began wrapping his torn clothing around Ichiro's eyes and continued until a thick, awkward wad covered his head above his nose.

Ichiro began to relax the meditative restriction on his optical input and once again was rocked by the information he received even as his eyes no longer took in any light.

Cutting off any physical input did successfully lessen the load on his mind, and he found that he was able to stand on his own, even if he swayed like a drunkard.

"My lord, is there anything else we can do to help? How are you afflicted? Are you still somehow marked by the Abomination?" Nyuk asked with concern.

His words floated to Ichiro on the vibration of many different strands of the . . . **Weave**. That is what it was called, the name settling down deep in his soul as if acknowledging what it was slightly solidified the fragile, shifting state of his mind.

This realization took him hours, and his three companions started leading him slowly down the mountain again. Then his answer came, responding to a question that he was unaware had been posed hours ago.

"The Abomination stole much from me. Many of my levels and stats have been taken, but it was unsuccessful in taking my mind. It is because of this that I was able to witness your honorable attack against its base of power, human. While I do not understand what happened in the end, I do know that its branching taint in my mind and soul was cleansed, and in the cleansing, I was remade. Unfortunately, I believe I am greatly handicapped by my much-reduced *Wisdom* and *Intelligence*. I believe this results in my being unable to handle the majority of this gift. Even now, if I relax my focus for just an instant, I will be lost in the flow of my surroundings once again."

He felt the three around him freeze as he began giving words to the thoughts he had been stringing together for hours, and they stood stunned as they processed the information. Well, the two lapins stood stunned, and the human simply muttered under his breath,

". . . a blind samurai? Finally, something cool."

He seemed unaware that each of the lapins was more than capable of hearing such a low-volume utterance at such a close distance. His insensitivity to Ichiro's condition came as a shock to the two loggers, but Ichiro's mouth quirked upward at the words.

"You are mistaken, human. I am not blind. Rather, I have been given access to a level of awareness that is too great for my present mental abilities . . . I will need time and practice to adjust."

The human's body tensed as he realized that he had just been overheard, and then he relaxed. Ichiro could not see his posture but was able to passively absorb both his physical and emotional stance through the shifting pattern before him. The human was desperately troubled but seemed to be trying to deflect himself from some deep worry. The **Weave** around him was vibrant and energetic, but Ichiro was beginning to notice a fraying or breaking in the pattern near his center.

"Oh, uh, sorry about that. You are Lord Hiro's son, right? I wonder if he knows we are still alive. I doubt he will be expecting us to return . . . unharmed. Especially you," the human answered, his tone choppy and distracted.

"What is your name, human?" Ichiro asked, stopping his assisted walk and standing up straight.

"Jonathan Tillman . . . uh, Lord Ichiro," he answered haltingly. His posture reeked of self-doubt and confusion of what was expected of him. It would be dishonorable to allow him to continue in such a state.

"Jonathan Tillman, I name you [Trusted Gaijin]." The other two lapins marked his statement with sharp intakes of breath. Ichiro simply continued droning in his meditative monotone, despite the unprecedented nature of his decision.

"You have given our people hope again, and in so doing, you have tied your fate to ours. It is because of this I give you the highest honor I am able. Each of our people will see part of this Title displayed over your name, and it will mark you as a friend to all lapins."

"Wow, uh . . . thank you, lord, or my lord . . . uh can I ask you a question? What do I call you?" Jonathan Tillman responded, clearly distracted by the notification he had just received.

Ichiro's small smile deepened,

"I have marked you as a friend, so you may simply refer to me as Ichiro. With my father, however, it is probably best to continue to offer him the title of Lord for now. Although with what I have just done, it is also no longer required."

Both of the lapins stood stiffly under his arms as he offered levels of privilege to an outsider not seen in their generation. Ichiro then slowly turned his blindfolded face toward his two faithful companions, holding his focus tightly in order not to lose his place in the present,

"And to you, I command that you keep half of the *experience* that you undoubtedly earned on this quest. The other half you may give to the *Promise*, but no more. In my foolishness, I lost our two remaining warriors. You have shown more than enough heart to be raised to that station, should that joyful day come."

The stiffness in their forms only increased, and at once they carefully stepped out from under him and offered deep bows of respect. Ichiro could sense Jonathan Tillman as he followed the conversation with interest, but chose not to speak. Ichiro marked his patience in this and inwardly nodded in approval.

None could know just how many of the strands of his people's fate now ran through the soul of this human. For better or worse, Nephesh had tied them together, and Ichiro would have him as a friend if at all possible. For his sake and theirs.

"Now I will relax my hold on the present. This will allow me to move easier as you guide me, but I will lose my ability to converse until I have a better command of this power," he intoned, letting some of his iron control on his will loosen.

"We will see you safely to the village, my lord," Nyuk intoned.

"We are probably pretty safe here anyway. The whole forest seems to be dead after what the human . . . I mean Jonathan Tillman did," Kuro continued, again coming under one of Ichiro's arms as he felt the rigid fluidity of his lord's concentration begin to lapse.

"Guys . . . I told you. Call me Tilly, please. It's gonna take forever to talk to you if you keep saying, Jonathan Tillman all the ti—"

Then Ichiro was gone, lost again to the moment, floating along on the sea of destiny that was the infinite strands of the **Weave**.

"Hey, Nyuk, it sounds like they are having a party down there . . . doesn't seem right that they started without us," Kuro said teasingly, happy to finally be within the sight of the village.

The knot formed by Kuro's decision to speak met a far more complex piece of the pattern in the distance which reacted with such violence and speed that Ichiro was jolted from his daze and found himself reentering into his **Battle Trance**.

With a boom of displaced air, his father had appeared before them. Ichiro felt an immense welling of emotion at the presence of his father. One that threatened to break his concentration as no other kind of pain or attack could.

He immediately tightened his focus to its maximum and disentangled himself from the two lapins before prostrating himself. What Ichiro did not realize is that he had begun moving even before Nyuk had finished speaking, and the three looked at him in confusion, completely taken by surprise at the boom of his father's approach.

From his bowed position, Ichiro declared formally.

"Father, in my arrogance, I have failed you and our people. I formally offer you my life for bringing such disgrace to our family."

His father's face was stone, and each of his companions around him froze, not able to recognize the deep interplay of desires and fate being played out in this exchange.

Instead of answering, his father drew his sword in a smooth and dangerous motion.

CHAPTER TWENTY-ONE

That Escalated Quickly!

Tilly

It had been a long walk . . .

But with Ichiro acting all loopy, both Kuro and Nyuk wanted to see him back to the village as fast as possible. So they had hiked all through the afternoon and part of the night, forgoing the raft in favor of the overland route due to the newly depopulated forest actually being faster than the stream and river route.

The upside of this was that Tilly was able to collect an armful of the Charmin Tree leaves on their way down. He hadn't had to "go" since before his treacherous flight down the mountain, but now that the near-death adrenaline had started to fade, he expected that to change.

He really didn't trust whatever would pass for toilet paper in this world, so he had decided to take matters into his own hands . . . or arm.

The downside was that without a bag, or a break, he still hadn't gotten a chance to take a deep dive into his character sheet. The two times he had tried, he had fallen, the grating sound of snickering from the other two lapins heaping coals on the fires of his embarrassment. But he needed to find out what happened to him in that temple.

As soon as the forest started to thin out near the village, they transitioned from thin, winding game trails to a nice footpath leading deeper into the valley. Tilly was ready to try his luck again.

He readjusted his armload of precious cargo and shot a glance at his traveling companions. Both lapins were still leading Ichiro over and around any obstacles that came up, and the lapin himself was occasionally muttering under his breath. Tilly took his chance and called up his character screen again.

Jonathan Luke Tillman
Level: *11 (15500 exp to next level)*
Display Name: *Tilly*
Race: *Human*
Class: *Son of Flame*
Titles: *[Harbinger]*
Health: *100% (+1.2% per minute)*
Mana: *100% (+0.8% per minute)*
Status Effects: *Minor Corruption [Hidden]*

Stats:
Constitution: 12
Endurance: 69 (75.9)
Dexterity: 27 (29.7)
Strength: 10
Wisdom: 8
Intelligence: 8

Equipment:
Origin's primitive stone hatchets: +10% to Dexterity. **(Legendary, growth type)**
+Imbued Ability: Recall.
Origin's primitive leather armor: +10% to Endurance. **(Legendary, growth type)**
+Imbued Form: Sun Salamander leather.

Skills:
-Forestcraft level 12
-Identify level 17
-Cooking level 12
-Beginner Hatchet level 10
-Animal Processing level 9
-Stealth level 7
-Herb Lore level 2
-Ax Throwing level 8

He immediately focused on the **Minor Corruption** debuff, but all that came up was,

---

Minor Corruption:

Effects: N/A {Nascent stage}

He didn't like the sound of that at all, but at least the pain had settled down. He would just have to wait and watch while he kept an eye out for any way to get rid of it. The rest of his sheet was about par for the course. He saw that he had some great gains across his skills with **Forestcraft** and his hatchet-associated skills having seen the most growth over the twenty-four-hour gauntlet he had just run.

The real surprise came next when he saw his lonely, but awesome *Ability* had changed!

Abilities:

-*[Blue] Flame Strike: Channel the fire within you to strike at your opponents. Each strike leaves a smoldering ember at the point of impact and does damage over time. Ember damage is stackable. This Ability has been augmented by your Mantle and does 200% more damage to Corruption.*

How had that happened? He thought about it for a moment and realized he had read about the *Ability* before he had touched the flame and that this change probably came from his new Mantle.

Well, he was happy with it! No downsides, and a huge bonus against any future **Corrupted** creatures he would face. Then his face fell as he realized that this was clear evidence that he was being set up as opposition to a much larger problem than just a local infestation . . .

He ground his teeth for a moment before continuing down to the descriptions of the three Titles he hadn't gotten a chance to read yet.

Titles:

*[Origin's Champion]: You have accepted the mantle of champion from **Origin**. This will augment your skills and Abilities over time to reflect your new nature.*

*[Corruption's Host]: You hold within your body a **Seed of Corruption**. This entity's progress has been slowed by divine interference, but it will take every opportunity to grow until it has subsumed your will. **Seed's influence: 3%***

[Trusted Gaijin]: The highest honor that can be bestowed on a nonlapin by the ruling class. It marks you as a friend to all lapinkind, and they will be immediately predisposed toward offering you any help they may have.

He unconsciously scratched at the scabbed wound in his side as he read the second Title.

He winced as he reread the consequences of the **Seed** growing. He wished he knew how to stop it, or better yet how to get it the hell out of his body. It did look like he was going to be able to keep track of its progress through the Title though, so at least the eventual crushing of his will wouldn't come as a surprise. Then he heard Kuro say something about a party, and he looked up from his brooding, dismissing the screen in front of him.

Two things seemed to happen at once. Ichiro removed himself from the grip of his guides' hands and bowed to the ground while something that sounded like a sonic boom echoed from the distant village, and suddenly, Lord Hiro was standing before their little group.

Tilly was so shocked at the sudden change of events that he missed what Ichiro said from his bowing position, but he did not miss the bowel-liquifying sight of a stone-cold Lord Hiro drawing his sword in a smooth motion.

Tilly was unable to do anything but drop his armful of leaves, as the samurai swept his gaze over the four companions, stopping as his red eyes met Tilly's with bloodshot intensity. The other two lapins simply bowed their heads, and for a moment Tilly thought it was all over.

Then Lord Hiro stepped up to the space before him and bowed deeply, offering his sword up in both hands. It was hauntingly beautiful, the handle wrapped in fine white leather, and the blade itself a matte black, seeming to have been forged from the darkness of an empty night sky. It thrummed with power, and Tilly knew he was in the presence of something truly powerful.

"My son, our future, has returned to us," he announced gravely, his head held low.

"I see he has already awarded you the Title that is your right amongst our people. Know that I and Tsugomori owe you a debt. There will come a time when this world comes to strike you down. When that day comes, you will have us by your side. Until that time, we call you *friend*," he finished, his bass growl of a voice going up a single octave at the end as he choked back some of the emotion he had held so rigidly in check for the entire encounter. He took one final moment in the bowing position, then he stood up and sheathed his sword before turning back toward his son.

"Your life is not yours to give . . . it is your people's. Get up and tell me what has happened since I last saw you."

Ichiro's portion of the story was related before they started walking again, with his current state explained in as much detail as he was able. Then as he entered into his semi-meditative state to continue walking, the rest of the group spent time answering the lord's questions. He showed himself a sharp interrogator, asking for multiple viewpoints at the same moment, trying to grasp details that Tilly could barely comprehend.

The final hour of walking to the village passed quickly, and before Tilly knew it, he was entering back through the same gate he had stood over the day before, and continuing to the small but neat village square.

The party Kuro had apparently been able to hear almost an hour's walk away was still going by the time they arrived. It was past midnight, and Tilly could tell that many of the villagers had already returned home. The ones who were left had been deep in their sake cups for a while.

"Look, it's Lord Hiro down from the wall!"

"Wait . . . is that human back from banishment already?"

"Shut up, you fool, it's young Lord Ichiro!"

The whispers and gasps washed over them as they entered the center square. Ichiro was still being led by the two loggers, and Tilly followed behind, not exactly sure what was expected from him as a "friend of the people."

Lord Hiro led them to the center of the square and looked around at the remainder of the people still in attendance.

"Listen to me carefully. I want everyone here to pass on my words to the rest of the village by morning," he announced in a deep voice that easily suffused the surrounding square and crowd.

"My son has returned, and the abomination poisoning these lands has been defeated. For his part in this, the human Jonathan Tillman is owed a debt, one that perhaps our people are unable to repay."

At these words, many of the eyes turned from the speaker to the level 11 human standing in mismatched furs to the left of their lord. Standing there, next to the last of the noble family of their race, his presence seemed somehow thin. But they had all heard stories of what humans were capable of: toppling empires, establishing dynasties, even ascending to the heavens. Perhaps this was one such human, and if he had agreed to a bond with their people, maybe the great dishonor of their past would finally be expunged.

Tilly knew none of these things, but he did feel the weight of their expectations settle uncomfortably on his shoulders, along with every eye in the village. He really didn't like the sound of debts or obligations owed either way. Sure, he had been pretty much forced into the confrontation, but it didn't matter, at this point. He had figured out that something like that would have happened no matter where he had shown up in this world.

Something big was happening on Nephesh, and whether he wanted to be or not, Tilly was involved.

I just had to pick that fifth class . . . didn't I? he thought mockingly to himself as he considered the people looking upon him with wide eyes.

Whoever this **Origin** was, he was probably laughing his ass off right now.

The small crowd dispersed after the announcement to go and spread the word of Ichiro's return and the official confirmation that the threat was over. Lord Hiro moved to quietly speak to the two loggers, who bowed their heads and moved off, leading Ichiro somewhere. Then the lord turned to Tilly, taking in his humble form once again.

"Our fates are now tied together. You will not survive long if you remain such as you are."

Tilly looked down at himself, hugging his armful of leaves closer to his chest. The lapin's words struck him as ungrateful, and he immediately found himself fighting back a sarcastic reply.

"Uh, I am definitely interested in getting stronger, but do you mind if I get a little sleep first? Also, where exactly is your bathroom? I'm not sure what the correct etiquette is, but I need to take care of something . . ." he finished, trailing off as the stonelike visage of Hiro's expression didn't crack in the slightest.

"You will stay in the same home you did your first night here. Unfortunately, it belongs to one of the warriors we lost and it is now free. Look slightly beyond that building toward the wall, and you will find the facility you need. Tomorrow, we will sit down with Shuji and come up with a plan to balance out your deficiencies and plot a course for your growth," he answered, his eyes not wavering for a second.

He then turned and left, leaving Tilly to fend for himself.

It was actually kind of nice to no longer be escorted through the streets, although he couldn't quite remember where his one-room house was. He took another look around the square, noting a large stone slab that seemed to be a stage of some sort. It sat at the end of the square opposite the street to the front gate. To the right of that was a street leading off to the river, and to the left was the street that Tilly thought might lead to Shuji's shop. He shrugged to himself and wandered over to the river street. He thought he remembered his little house being pretty close to the dock.

Unnoticed by Tilly or any of the other lapins present at the celebrations, a small, glowing arcane mark flashed to life on the corner of the teleport platform. The one that confirmed the platform was clear and still in working order.

CHAPTER TWENTY-TWO

The Empire Strikes Back

It turned out the village had some rudimentary plumbing in the form of a simple aqueduct that led under a small but neat outhouse. In the dark, Tilly didn't find anything they could possibly be using for wiping. But the Boy Scout in him smiled as he grabbed a couple of choice leaves from his pile and took care of business. Soon after, he found his little house marked by an open sliding door and a small fire going in the fireplace.

Despite the initial hostility of the villagers, Hiro's radical turnaround and now the simple care they took in preparing a place for him touched Tilly in a way he was not prepared for. He felt some of the stony pragmatism that had been forcing him forward start to crumble. Its strength had been essential in keeping him going, but he knew from experience, it was a brittle thing. Now that he was back down in the now-quiet village, and the threat to the people had ended, the iron tension in his shoulders slowly started to ease, and he looked down at his side in renewed concern.

Lowering his nose to his chest turned out to be a mistake. While his armor remained smugly clean, the body underneath had become ripe with sweat, grime, and the acrid scent of an adrenaline detox. He thought about finding some way to clean himself for a moment and then yawned. That and any other thoughts quickly died as he plopped down on the bed. The cool night air mingled with the warmth emanating from the coals glowing merrily near his bed, and he sighed, letting the simple sensations wash through his senses.

He hadn't realized what a heavy toll the constant fight or flight had taken on his mind. Now that he was finally done moving from one near-death experience to another, the urgency driving his every step had run out, and his body felt like an engine coughing on the fumes of an empty gas tank.

He tried to think about a plan for tomorrow or even questions he could ask Shuji now that he was finally going to have some time to get this place figured out. Those thoughts and others flared up eagerly in his too-tired mind, before fizzling out just as fast. His mind spent a few minutes trying to ratchet down the near-panic state he had lived in for the last couple of days, running itself ragged without producing any meaningful progress.

Finally, with the hypnotic sound of the crackle and pop of the hearth playing in the background, he fell into the deep dreamless sleep of exhaustion. He didn't even think to slide the door closed.

"Human! I mean, Mr. Tillman!"

The voice came to him in the deep blackness of unconsciousness, its tone urgent.

"Uggh . . . wah?" Tilly replied, trying to form some sort of coherent understanding of where he was.

"Please, you must come! They have sent a Quaestor, and Lord Hiro's presence has been demanded in the capital."

The words "they" and "capital" cut through his too-little sleep fog. Whatever that meant, he was sure the best-laid plans of mice and men were now crumbling around him. With a groan, he pushed himself up from the bed and looked over to the militia spearman standing at the open entrance of his temporary house. He was hopping back and forth on his feet.

"Hurry, please. Shuji sent for you the moment the platform activated, but the empire will care little for our timing."

"Alright, let's go," he said, patting his side to find his only two possessions still looped into his belt. The spearman turned around and rushed down the street, with Tilly running to follow.

He hardly had time to compute that the sun was just rising over the industrious Japan-inspired village when they arrived at the center square and the small crowd that had gathered there. It looked like Hiro and Ichiro had only arrived seconds before Tilly, and everyone gawked, facing the group standing on top of the still-glowing platform.

There were four . . . goat-men? The two in front wore more ornate clothing reminiscent of ancient Greece and seemed to be mostly human, with normal legs showing through purposeful slits in the bottom of their robes. They had large horns jutting through their dark, curly hair with wiry goatees. One seemed to be wearing a uniform, while the other flaunted an immense wealth with his clothing and jewelry. Tilly guessed they must be some sort of race of satyrs. The two in the rear had much more animalistic traits and were far more muscular. They wore what looked to be bronze cuirasses and had cloven hooves instead of normal human legs.

The front two were identified as a level 38 **Quaestor** and a level 45 **Steward**. The two behind were both level 48 **Emperor's Bastions**.

The one in the uniform was reading from an ornate scroll.

". . . of treason against the *Thousand Phalanx Empire*. His royal majesty and the noble senate have subpoenaed you for trial under the charges of gross misuse of imperial resources and negligence in fulfilling your mandate to subdue and conquer this frontier territory for the glory of the empire. You are to report to the Imperial Cura immediately to stand trial," the satyr announced, reading out the edict like some sort of herald.

He then rolled it up and smartly stowed it away, stepping back from the front of the platform. The more ornately dressed satyr to his right snorted, before adding in a dismissive tone, "You have failed. Just like your kind always does. Come with us, you old hare, and we will settle things in the capital once and for all."

His words moved through the surrounding lapins like a wave, each one stiffening, and any who had weapons tightened their grips visibly. At the front of the crowd stood Hiro and Ichiro. Ichiro's face showed a placid empty expression that Tilly had begun to associate with his meditation, while the Samurai Lord's face was set in a granite, longsuffering frown.

This can't be right. Are these guys from the same empire that had abandoned the village in the fight against **Corruption***?* Tilly looked around at the worn but proud people filling the square. He saw anger, fear . . . but no surprise. This was not the first time something like this had happened to the lapin people.

Then, from off to his right, Shuji appeared, huffing as if he had just run over.

"We will, of course, comply with the emperor's command!" he gasped out.

"Lord Hiro will return with you, along with a small honor guard, as is due to his rank."

At these words, the younger satyr scowled and leaned over to the smartly dressed servant and muttered something. The servant just shook his head once and said something back.

"Yes, of course, but no delays. He is to come immediately," the Quaestor turned and answered curtly. His eyes had been absently scanning the crowd as he spoke and froze once they found Tilly. The uncomfortably oblong irises narrowed at the sight of the human, and he looked like he was about to say something else before Hiro spoke up, responding for the first time with a slow, thoughtful acquiescence.

"My son will stay and lead the outpost in my stead, and my logistics officer will accompany me to answer any questions about misuse of resources. Otherwise, I have recently lost any others who could serve as capable guards, so in their place, I choose to bring a *friend* of our people."

Tilly tore his eyes away from the group of satyrs to look over at Lord Hiro in shock. Lord Hiro in turn was looking at Shuji. His halting declaration was juxtaposed by a rapid series of hand signs that he flashed subtly behind his back.

Through these, he relayed far more information to those around him than his forward-facing manner had shown. While Tilly had no idea what they meant, he saw several lapins rush off in response.

The ornately dressed satyr, however, seemed to allow himself a satisfied grin, picking up on who Hiro was referring to immediately.

"Very well. I'm sure this *friend* of yours is dying to see some actual civilization. Time is up, come with us now while the spell is still active, or face immediate arrest."

At this, Hiro turned and placed his hand on his son's shoulder.

"Prepare what you must," he said cryptically before turning to look over at Tilly, the barest hint of a question hidden behind his hard eyes.

Tilly only hesitated a moment, his mind whirling before the rapid change in his circumstances. As the pieces fell into place, it all came down to one simple thing. Despite their rough start, these people had decided to trust him. He wasn't going to back out on them now.

He nodded and hurried forward, joining a still-panting Shuji, and a stoic Hiro at the base of the platform.

The two armored satyrs came down and formed up to either side of the trio as they moved toward the platform, which had begun to glow brighter. Right before the steps, Shuji seemed to stumble, and a few lapins rushed to his side to help him up.

"Very sorry, sirs. I find myself quite out of sorts at your early call. Thank you for your patience," he poured out profusely to the hard-faced guards and sneering Quaestor. From his position just behind the lapin, Tilly saw Shuji pocket several things that he hadn't been holding a moment before.

The three made it up to the top of the platform and this close to the satyrs, Tilly felt a fiery itch build in his side around the new scar. The glow of the platform increased into a searing light, and the ornately dressed satyr issued a command.

"Evander, break it." To which Tilly heard a snapping sound in response. Then the world went black, and his stomach felt like it had flipped inside out. Light once again bloomed all around them, and Tilly found himself at the center of what seemed to be a huge ancient metropolis.

The ornately dressed satyrs brushed past them with his entourage.

"You are to report to the Cura immediately. You cannot hide here, and don't even think about running," he spat back at them, shaking out his right arm in apparent discomfort. Then strangely he hurried off with his attendants in tow, not even leaving the guards behind.

The metropolis was reminiscent of something Tilly imagined you might have found in Italy thousands of years ago. Except for the fantastic creatures moving around and through the open area before him. Tilly stood on a platform that was part of a grid of similar stone structures situated at the center of the wide, multi-block area in the middle of the city. Some sort of turtle-human hybrid was walking away from their platform with a crooked staff glowing the same hue as the arcane symbols on the floor around Tilly's feet. The creature moved slowly but smoothly, knocking his staff against the cobblestones every other step.

Level 32, Tidal Mage

"We are undoubtedly being watched. Shuji, tell me you got off those messages," Hiro whispered in a low voice as he put a hand on Tilly's shoulder and moved him forward off the platform, not giving him much time to gawk.

"Yes, sir. We got back two responses. The Cura is meeting in an hour, giving us barely enough time to do anything but arrive and defend our cause."

"Damn that Marcellus brat," Hiro snarled fiercely, showing emotion for the first time that day.

"Anyone want to let me in on what is going on?" Tilly cut in, keeping his voice at the same level as theirs.

"I am afraid things continue to move at an unfortunate pace for our people, although our position is not without opportunities," Shuji answered excitedly, his voice creeping up in volume.

They had begun moving through some of the traffic surrounding the platforms even in the early hour. There were several other variants of human and animal hybrids from myths and legends, as well as a few of the classic fantasy interspersed through the crowd. Tilly almost stopped in his tracks at the sight of his first dwarf.

"These things are best discussed in private. Jonathan Tillman, please stay close and stay quiet." Hiro turned and spoke in a low voice before leading them farther away from the platforms. Many of the creatures seemed busy with their own business, but several stopped and stared at the group as they passed. Tilly even saw a couple of minotaurs point to him with animated gestures from across the square.

Then Hiro led them to one of the huge streets leading from the teleport hub, and Tilly saw his first guards, all of whom seemed to be satyrs. They stood at the corner of the square, overlooking the traffic flowing in and out of the huge square. They frowned at the group as they passed but otherwise did nothing as they turned onto a huge promenade leading through the center of the city.

The road was the size of a four-lane highway back home, and the center had statues of different satyrs posing triumphantly every fifty feet or so. The street went on for hundreds of yards, ending in a truly monstrous blocky building built on top of enormous columns. Even from this distance, Tilly could tell it was huge beyond belief.

But despite its initial powerful impression, Tilly couldn't help but see the filth caked on the surfaces of the city. The promenade was bordered by different ornate structures, all gated and surrounded by tall marble walls. And against those walls were endless stalls and tents. Some housed businesses selling things to the growing throng, while others sheltered grimy groups of what looked like beggars or refugees.

Worse of all were the children. They were everywhere, sleeping in the shadow of the tall statues, roving on the outskirts of the light crowd or just staring list-lessly at nothing. They came in all shapes and sizes but universally had the look of the abandoned. The sight of so much hopelessness weighed on Tilly's soul.

Lord Hiro's figure cut through the thickening soup of misery like the bow of a ship parting the waves with Shuji and Tilly hurrying to keep up in his wake.

"Truly sorry for all of this, my friend," Shuji said once again huffing along-side Tilly, making some attempt at reassurance.

"Stay close, and I will endeavor to explain everything to you after the trial . . . as long as they don't arrest us," he said conspiratorially with a grin.

"Arrest us for wh—" Tilly began, but was interrupted by a crash of a cart up ahead.

"My cabbages!" the wagon driver yelled in dismay.

His cart had been overturned by a huge rolling barrel that seemed to have rolled free from one of the tent shops.

"Sorry, mate!" an honest-to-God gnome shouted up to the cart driver.

As the whole street watched the exchange, Shuji suddenly shoved Tilly into a barely noticeable break in between two stalls, causing him to stumble forward into a claustrophobic alley.

"Quickly now," he breathed out harshly, shooing Tilly further down the alley. Tilly only then noticed Hiro already disappearing into a doorway deeper in the shadows.

Tilly rushed after, with Shuji right behind. As they turned into the doorway, they found a female lapin waiting for them dressed in washerwoman clothes.

"Gods, what a mess. At least I got your message," she exclaimed without preamble.

They had entered some sort of storeroom with several lanterns burning, illu-minating dusty shelves, and old wooden crates. Shuji quietly shut the door behind him and let out a sigh of relief.

"We have precious few minutes. Who do we have with us in the senate, and how do the charges sit with the emperor?"

The washerwoman barely spared Tilly a glance, her gaze fixed on Hiro with an unparalleled intensity.

"First, my lord, I must know. Is this it? Is it time?"

CHAPTER TWENTY-THREE

The Plot Gets Thicc

Lord Hiro considered her words and their implications for a long moment, the muscle on his lower jaw working overtime as he slowly weighed out an answer.

"Mochizuki. I cannot give you an answer that I do not yet know. Much has changed in the past week, and while we have not lost all hope, I am going to trial today. They will force me into a *Truth Domain*. We have planned for something like this, but everything depends on our ability to stay mobile. I promise you, I will get our people out or die trying. This is my pledge to you. But you must wait for my signal."

At those words, the intensity drained from her face, and she bowed deeply, "My apologies, lord, I never doubted. It can be . . . difficult here, watching our people suffer and knowing that salvation is such a close possibility." She came up from her bow and shifted to look at Tilly. Looking him up and down, she wiped her hands on her apron in a businesslike manner.

"I see that we now have a human and that you even named him *friend* . . . Your choices are your own, but is it really wise to have him with you before trial? They could try to surprise you by calling him up for questioning instead."

Hiro nodded thoughtfully. "For now, answer my questions as directly as possible. As long as you do not stray, he will remain mostly ignorant. This will both protect him and keep him from unknowingly becoming a source of information for our enemies."

"You can say that again . . ." Tilly mumbled, unable to keep the surliness out of his voice as they talked about him like he wasn't even there. He didn't relish the idea of spending even more time in forced ignorance. But Shuji winced in sympathy at him from behind Lord Hiro, and Tilly bit back any more complaints. Whatever *Truth Domain* was, he had to admit that continuing to be oblivious to the intrigue unraveling before him was as good a defense as he could hope for. In fact . . .

"Wait, I know we don't have a lot of time, but if I might be questioned, shouldn't I leave? Or cover my ears? Or something?"

Shuji's ever-present smile broke into a small guffaw.

"Ha! Yes, that is very kind of you, but we have already taken this possibility into account, and our enemies do not know enough to ask you the right kind of questions. If questioned about anything you don't understand, respond truthfully that you do not know what the questioner means. This will be sufficient for anything they have to ask you. They did not know of your existence until this morning, so their advocates have had no time to plan for your inclusion."

Mochizuki nodded along with Shuji's words before continuing with the report Hiro had requested on the disposition of the senate.

"Now that we have settled that, here is what we know about the senate as it stands today. Obviously, the Purist Party is responsible for this injunction. We have recent intel to suggest that the elder Marcellus is very busy with some sort of treason himself. He has been spotted leaving the walls several times in the last months by discreet means. It looks like he has left the majority of this particular grudge in the hands of his youngest . . . and cruelest son."

"Yes, the boy came himself to insult our people and lay his eyes on our operation so far. Let us hope he is only half so cunning as the father. We are fairly sure he only saw what we wanted him to see," Hiro replied shortly, waving for her to continue.

"The honu and Asterion minorities will generally oppose anything the Purists put forward. That leaves the dwindling Economic Party and the Loyalist Party. The Economics are currently leaning with the Purists on grounds of how tight the imperial coffers are. In their eyes any misuse of funds in this time of geopolitical pressure is treasonous. The Loyalists are a complete mystery . . . No one has seen the emperor since you got approval for the venture into the unclaimed lands. In light of this, his party has remained largely silent, choosing to abstain from the most recent senate votes."

Tilly followed the conversation with fascination, despite having little or no context for the information. Hiro grunted in interest and thanked her for the report before following up.

"Invaluable as always, Mochizuki. You are a treasure to our people. What changes on the frontlines?"

"The empire's last satellite city has been lost, and the Asterion tribes are all but scattered. Almost none remain loyal to the empire, most choosing to sell abroad as mercenary clans or return to the caravans. This has led to a significant change in the Asterion party's voting block. They have now shifted focus to primarily representing the empire's mercenary forces. Their position is now either weaker or stronger, depending on the vote in question. The seat numbers have not changed since my last report."

"Gods above . . . I thought we had concentrated the majority of our last expeditionary Phalanxes in defense of Lograth?" Shuji broke in, his customary smile flattening.

"We had," Mochizuki whispered with finality, the shadows in the small storeroom dancing across her features ominously.

"The Cult of the Serpent has become ravenous, and they bear some strange new berserking power that broke the empire's defenses outside the gates of Filaresh," she continued in a defeated tone.

Unlike Shuji, Hiro did not bat an eye at this news. His face remained drawn in grim resolve as he slowly brought forward some steadying words.

"We are citizens of a dying empire. None of this is new. We will just have to adjust our timetable and make do with what we have. Now come. We will have to run part of the way as it is, and I will not be seen sprinting up to the Cura's halls," he said before offering a bow of respect to the informant. Then before he turned to the door he added, "Hold on a little bit longer, Mochizuki. Keep our people together, and if the gods are kind, we will see you tomorrow." He finished with a small smirk. Then he turned and nodded to both Tilly and Shuji before stealthily opening the door and moving out into the shadow of the alley.

Shuji performed a small bow himself before following, leaving Tilly with Mochizuki.

"My name is Tilly by the way . . . uh, thanks for everything," he said, awkwardly trying for a bow himself.

She smiled in response to his attempt, no doubt due to his Title more than any sort of innate friendliness.

"Yes, I can see your name, Jonathan Tillman, but you cannot see mine, and if you do see me in public here, we do not know each other, and you must not speak to me. Now hurry, time is short!" she said, making a shooing motion with both her hands.

Out of reflex, Tilly tried to pull up her identifier and all that came up was:

Level 13, Household Servant

He nodded to her again and moved through the still-open door, her voice following after him.

"Oh, and most people will feel when you try to **Identify** them if their *Wisdom* is higher than yours. It can be considered quite rude in certain situations."

Tilly grimaced as he ducked through the door. That was one more thing he had probably been messing up since he first got here. Tilly rushed out into the alley while trying not to kick over the piles of trash, catching up with Shuji and Hiro at the mouth of the narrow passage. They held back in the shadows of the tall, windowless walls to either side and observed the passing traffic. Then Shuji whispered something into what looked like an origami bird in his hand, and it flared briefly before flying off.

"Just a moment. We will know when to move," he whispered.

The throng of people on the main street had grown much more crowded, and it seemed like it would be slightly easier to move through unnoticed. As he silently watched the things that made up the crowd he began to notice a rough ratio of the citizens present. About three-quarters were some form of satyr, although many of the common-looking folk had more in common with an upright goat than the humans that supposedly existed in their heritage.

The rest of the crowd was broken by occasionally towering minotaurs, stocky dwarves, gnomes, elves, and other humanoids that were supernatural in nature. Many of the bypassers seemed overburdened by numerous possessions, some pulling hand carts, others weighed down by huge packs. Then it hit Tilly. These people knew what was happening, and those that could were getting out.

Then a familiar voice rang out over the murmuring roar of the city.

"Welp, looks like no one is gonna buy from a damaged barrel anyway! Alright, I'm draining this thing, one penny per pour. Get it while it's flowing! Genuine Gnomish Hard Seltzer!" The crowd immediately reacted, moving toward the stall about thirty feet ahead of the alley that had been the site of the accident earlier.

Without hesitation, Shuji and Hiro entered the throng of unwashed bodies suddenly heading for the stall, all shouting excitedly at the deal. "One at a time! One at a time!" the gnome called out, trying in vain to bring order to the sudden rush.

Hiro led them deftly through the press until they were beyond it on the other side of the promenade and then he turned back toward them. "Now we must pick up the pace significantly until we are close to the Cura," he said in a low voice, while his eyes roamed the crowd.

"Do not worry about being spotted. They will expect us to have spoken to someone, and that we need to come in a rush. We are just protecting our source."

Then he turned and jogged forward, clearly expecting to be followed. With his newly increased *Endurance* Tilly wasn't bothered by the pace, but that was clearly not the case for Shuji, who was panting and out of breath after just a minute or two. Tilly couldn't begin to guess what his *Endurance* was, but he bet it was probably pretty low. That said, Shuji did not falter or complain as they continued forward at a brisk pace, cutting through the crowd with a focused urgency.

It probably took another twenty minutes before they arrived near the steps of the giant blocky building that stood above the surrounding structures on a foundation of columns. They slowed to a walk the last few hundred feet, and Shuji pulled out a small vial of something, downing it in one go, before sighing in relief.

The marble steps were flanked on both sides by the **Imperial Guards** standing every third step at attention and watching the crowds below with practiced scowls.

At the center of the wide stairway was an ornate table manned by several bored-looking officials and another ten guards. Hiro turned to give his companions a quick inspection. Tilly was more or less the same dirty-looking wild man he had been this morning, and Shuji had managed to catch his breath and even wipe the sweat from his lightly furred brow before Hiro turned back to look at him.

"Now we test ourselves against the slow grinding weight of bureaucracy," he muttered darkly before allowing himself a slight smirk at their appearance. He then schooled his expression and moved to approach the officials at the table.

Tilly tried to straighten his patched fur jacket, and Shuji put on his biggest smile, his large front teeth on full display. Tilly followed after the grizzled Samurai Lord, trying to look like he was supposed to be there.

"Names . . ." the official satyr droned, not bothering to look up from his stack of papers.

Shuji stepped forward. "Lord Hiro Matsumoto. Last living lord to the lapin people. Hero of the tragic western retreat and once honored chair of the minority party in the senate. He is here on charges to stand trial, and we are his escort."

When the official looked up, the practiced look of indifference may as well have been a work of art for all the care he took in confirming the lapin in question was in front of him.

"Very wel—" He started looking back down to mark something on his form when his head snapped back up in a double-take. His eyes drilled into Tilly, practically oozing curiosity.

"My, my . . ." he said, his double chin wiggling under his oily goatee.

"How did your kind get its grubby mitts on a human?"

"I'm right here . . ." Tilly sighed. At this point, he was very tired of being treated like he couldn't speak for himself.

"And, just for the record, my name is Jonathan Tillman. I'm here as a *friend* of Lord Hiro. No one has 'gotten their mitts' on me."

"Yes, well, my apologies, Mr. Tillman," the official stated, continuing to look at Tilly like he was some sort of exotic animal at the zoo. Then Tilly felt a slight tingling in the back of his mind, like the brush of an unexpected hand.

At that, the face of the official fell in disappointment. "Oh, another dud. Two humans in the last decade, and both turn out to be utter bores." At his words, the other officials at the table tittered annoyingly.

Did this guy just identify me? Tilly marveled in frustration at the satyr's manners. He looked the official dead in the eye and activated **Identify** right back.

Level 15, Bureaucrat

"Well, your 'empire' doesn't seem to be doing too hot either!" Tilly growled in frustration, literally going so far as to make air quotes around the word "empire."

At this, several of the guards who had been successfully holding a statuesque attention looked over at Tilly sharply.

Then Lord Hiro spoke for the first time in the conversation, letting his killing intent pour out of his aura. Tilly immediately felt a cold sweat break out under his jacket, and he barely kept himself from unconsciously whimpering.

"We have been held up long enough. I will not be late due to the incompetence of a nobody," he declared in a dangerous voice under a flat-eyed expression that spoke far more than an elevated tone ever could.

The bureaucrat and his several silent associates simultaneously choked on the deadly aura. He waved them past the guards while covering a whimper of his own with a cough and reaching for a nearby goblet of water.

CHAPTER TWENTY-FOUR

A Few Good Lapins

Tilly was not prepared for the grandeur that unfolded before him as he moved up the steps, passing through the front row of columns. Both of his companions didn't look up at the tree-sized columns as they walked by, but Tilly couldn't help but pause for a moment and take it in. If the city below was a clear display of an empire crumbling at the edges, this was its proud gilded heart, seemingly untouched by the squalor unfolding in its surroundings. Many figures scurried to and fro, dwarfed by the forest of immense marble supports. Each of the hundreds of columns was in itself a work of art, ridged and shaped to be uniquely beautiful.

Soft light shone from the ceiling four stories above. It bathed everything in a glow that felt a little bit like a sunny afternoon with an occasional cloud providing pleasant and intermittent shade. In the midst of all this, Tilly couldn't help but admit a grudging respect for the empire and its citizens. Sure, some of them were obviously racist pricks . . . but here, standing in such a feat of supernatural architecture, Tilly saw something different in these people. A determination to leave their mark, to build something that endured.

Yet, as is often the case of true civilizational glory, this sight was undercut by the innumerous cogs of bureaucracy spinning purposelessly. There were hundreds of open-office-style stations set up all around the plaza, distracting from its elegance and beauty. Each station held a table filled with paperwork being attended by multiple aides. They buzzed around the piles like flies, occasionally shifting a stack of paper from one table to another. He could almost hear them excitedly babbling about this sort of achievement with other functionaries. In their minds, this was probably the most important work happening in the empire. The sounds of thousands of minor functionaries creating what, in all likelihood, was more work for the rest of the empire's citizens grated on Tilly like nails on a chalkboard.

The two lapins cut through the hive of activity toward the center of the gargantuan plaza which held a spiral staircase the size of a city block, and Tilly rushed to follow, leaving behind the philosophical thoughts that the scene had evoked in him, and turning his mind back to the trial. He needed to focus on not going to fantasy jail. He could think about empires and governments later.

Near the foot of the huge staircase stood another contingent of guards. They stood radiating a casual air of violent competence, and Tilly saw that they had the same class as the two who had accompanied the young aristocrat that morning. Each of these satyrs stood at attention in gleaming perfect armor, juxtaposed by bodies covered in scars and corded with thick muscle.

Level 50, Empire's Bastion

When Hiro arrived at the base, he moved to stand before the first guard at attention, this time announcing himself.

"Lord Hiro Matsumoto, here to stand before the Cura and the empire, accused of treason," he rumbled in a bold but steady voice.

The guard nodded once, his facial expression unchanging as he stepped to the side. Hiro bowed once in return, his manner the complete opposite of the one that he had adopted in the face of the officials outside. Then he moved up the steps, eating up the oversized treads with long strides. Again Shuji and Tilly hurried to follow. Tilly was beginning to feel a little like a lap dog, always pitter-pattering after his master. He scratched at an annoying itch under his jacket as he practically had to leap from step to step to keep up.

For some reason, he started thinking about the life-or-death ultimatum that Hiro had forced on him at their first meeting. At first, he had let it roll off his back as he realized what an impossible situation the leader had been in. But now, irrationally, he was starting to question why he had even come.

Why had Hiro brought him? To show him off for political points?

The stated reason for "protection" was laughable. The stairs went on for a frustratingly long time, during which Tilly decided that even if they ended up in prison, he was going to get some answers tonight. No more being jerked around. He kept his head down as he concentrated on keeping his pace and not tripping on the awkwardly large steps when he heard the boom of an announcement from above them.

"Thus concludes the presentation of the children's refuge bill by the human, Amelia. As the bill stands, the vote is 33 nays, 24 ayes, and 8 abstained. The bill is floored at this time."

They had arrived at an intricate arched opening at the top of the spiral stairs, and the glare of the naked sun almost blinded Tilly's eyes. They adjusted painfully, with spots dancing in his vision as a form emerged, moving quickly through the dancing spots.

Then the words from above hit Tilly. *Another human?*

She was wearing a simple brown overcoat that was flying open with the force of her red-faced exit, revealing hundreds of pockets. Under the coat was a neat, practical blouse over tan safari-looking pants. She wore her hair in a pixie cut of auburn brown, framing a pair of angry tear-filled eyes that didn't register their group as she stormed past. Tilly was so shocked at the sudden appearance of another one of his kind that he almost turned around and followed her down the stairs.

"Now the assembly will hear the emergency charges leveled against one of its previous members, and vote on judgment thereafter," the voice boomed again from beyond the light.

He looked down the stairs for one agonizing second before turning back to the opening with a sigh. Hiro and Shuji were already moving through the relief-carved marble and gold arch, and Tilly ran up the last few steps to emerge with them into the light. The brightness of the full morning sun illuminated the basin of an open-air amphitheater. On the floor were several sectioned-off areas with their own seating, and surrounding the basin was a tiered arena with stadium-style seating.

The first level of the stadium seemed to be reserved for a large empty throne, and the rest of the low levels were filled with groups of figures dressed in white, formal-looking togas fringed with various colors. This lower group of formally dressed officials was made up of mostly satyrs with about a sixth of those in attendance being creatures of other heritages. Above this group in the higher seats of the stadium were many more spectators, all finely dressed, although not in any sort of robes of office. There was a murmur of excitement building up in those seats, and Tilly got the feeling that politics was a national sport to these people. The recent sight of the woman rushing from this place flashed back in Tilly's mind, and he felt the slow building burn of indignation smolder in his chest.

The upper audience cheered and hooted at the announcement, all while the streets of the city around them were choking on an influx of refugees. The juxtaposition of the two realities crashed into each other in Tilly's mind, and he began to see just how big the cracks in the system were.

Hiro moved without hesitation to a sectioned-off area to the right of the basin floor, with Shuji following. Tilly made to follow but caught a subtle gesture from Shuji to not completely enter the area. Instead, Shuji motioned for him to stand behind it. Tilly took his position and looked up, scanning the different groups of senators, each separated by the fringe of their togas. There was a gold group, which was by far the largest, and the others were green, silver, red, and blue. The blue group was the smallest with only four members, three of which were older turtle-type people.

Tilly's observations were interrupted by the booming voice. "The trial has begun! The accused stands ready. What says the prosecution?"

Tilly traced the confusing echoes back to a smaller formal seat to the left of the large throne, in which sat a satyr in an all-black toga with white fringe.

Then a ridiculously coiffed satyr in a nearby floor section stood from his seat and shouted to the crowd in a high tenor voice, "Before us, my fellow countrymen, stands the last lord of a useless people hampering the returning glory of our empire. In his cowardice, he has taken what he could from our coffers and run from his duties as a citizen." He paused there, allowing the crowd to build a murmuring response.

Smiling to himself he continued. "Even in this they have failed. Hiro Matsumoto has been derelict in his duty to subjugate new lands for the empire and has grossly misused the resources given to him so generously by our divine emperor. For this most heinous crime among many others, we have called Hiro Matsumoto here on charges of treason!"

The echoes of his proclamation continued to reverberate into the upper levels of the amphitheater making them seem like they came from a legion of accusers instead of a single voice.

"How answers the defense?" the bass voice asked from the formal seat next to the throne. In response, Hiro slowly stood, seeming to be in no rush, and took a long moment to eye the gathered senators and the crowd above.

"Many have questioned my people for generations, viewing our entrance into this noble empire as insincere. It is especially clear to the rest of us that a very particular group in this senate will always call our allegiance into question. They have done so for centuries, questioning the usefulness of any non-satyr race. None of this is new.

"However, I do reject the accusation of failure in our order of subjugation . . . We have succeeded in subduing the Abomination that had threatened the empire's outpost. There is now nothing stopping our advancement further into the frontier. Neither do I accept the accusation of cowardice. I have bled many times for this nation, and even now, my people are bleeding and dying for the empire's continued existence. No, neither of these charges hold any substance, and I am happy to discuss either point further . . . But it will never be enough." He stopped there, glaring at the spectating crowd above the senators. Under his unforgiving gaze, the murmuring dulled.

"I am here because of my race, and my continued refusal to bow to the Purists, who wish to further enslave us." He then turned his flat stare to the large group of gold-fringed senators, leveling an accusation of his own. His words did not echo up and down the chamber like the prosecutor's had; instead they rang out once before settling down on the faces and shoulders of all those in attendance. Their weight produced either thoughtful frowns or sneers depending on the section of the audience.

The judge on the smaller throne kept his face impassive as he moved through what seemed to be a traditional order of trial before the senate.

"What evidence does the prosecution bring?"

The coiffed satyr stood back up, throwing a quick sneer at Tilly's group before turning to the judge. "We have a copy of the emperor's mandate, which compels this mongrel people to establish a satellite outpost for the empire in the frontier. A location that was very costly to obtain from the *Cartographers Guild*, I might add! The empire further graciously advanced a loan to establish a secure transport to the site for the agreed number of rodents . . . ahem, people, and their supplies. Yet all we received in return for this unprecedented generosity were delayed timelines and requests for additional aid! All of this points to an obvious misuse of resources, and even further, a malicious twisting of the emperor's goodwill!" the satyr finished, his voice rising to a fever pitch as his face reddened with passion.

This statement started some quiet discussion in a smaller group of senators wearing togas fringed in green. However, the largest group of senators, all wearing the gold fringe, were animated and even cheerful as they pointed and murmured at the prosecution's points. Tilly took a closer look at the green group, trying to place them with some of the political parties he had heard from the informant's report. Their group was mid-sized and was made up of four satyrs in exceedingly rich apparel along with two gnomes, one dwarf, and one dark elf. Tilly decided that these guys had to be the Economist party, the overstated richness of their dress speaking even more loudly than their concern over possible misuse of empire funds.

"What evidence does the defense bring to trial?" the judge continued impassively.

At his question, Shuji stood and managed an impressively graceful bow despite his considerable girth. "Noble ladies and gentlemen of this august and time-honored body, I am both grateful and humbled to stand before you as a ser—"

"Get on with it, you windbag!" someone shouted from the higher seats. Many laughed at the heckling, yet the judge's face showed his first expression of the day. A deep frown creased his otherwise smooth, apathetic face.

"It is a privilege to be here in this chamber while it is in session! That privilege can and will be revoked for any that choose to interrupt again," he said gravely without turning to look at the crowd. There must have been magic involved because even though his statement was uttered with quiet menace, it easily carried through the entirety of the stands. He then waved his hand at Shuji to continue.

"Ahem, yes well, as I was saying . . . I am the appointed logistics officer for this venture, and we have many detailed reports outlining each of our expenditures. We have not only kept track of the empire's resources but also of the considerable sum that was raised privately by our own people to make this venture possible. We have lost many more lives than we projected due to the unforeseen threat we faced in our expansion efforts. These figures are all outlined in the weekly reports we sent.

"Our figures were formed on the understanding that this was a relatively quiet zone of the frontier, newly discovered. It is because of this we undertook this project with only a token fighting force. If not for the ability granted by this senate to allow double classing for some of our citizens into militia we would have been swept away. Lord Hiro lost the last of his formal retainers and almost lost his son in the fighting.

"Again, all of this is detailed in our reports. For those of you who somehow did not see the reports, we endured attacks every night by infected and enslaved creatures from the surrounding mountains for weeks, turning our designated area of expansion into a warzone. Despite all of this we managed, with the help of this human, to end this threat with *no additional resources*. The land is prepared, the outpost is established, and now thanks to the constant fighting, the surrounding forests are almost clear of all wildlife. Contrary to the prosecution's case, we are happy to report a full success in our objective, despite the unforeseen obstacles." He finished his statement in clipped, formal tones, allowing a small amount of frustration to show through his otherwise respectful and magnanimous demeanor.

After his statements, many in the senate started to turn and quietly speak with one another. The gold-fringed group's expressions grew stormy, and Tilly saw an older satyr at its head turn around and look up to the stands with a thunderous expression. The red-fringed group of senators (made up of several scarred and burly members of mixed races, including three minotaurs) applauded Shuji's conclusion. The green group's discussion grew even more animated as they whispered back and forth amongst each other.

Nice job, Shuji! Tilly couldn't keep a satisfied smile of vindication from showing on his face.

Then the prosecutor's reedy voice broke up the chatter of the crowd.

"As is the prosecution's right in trials where there are no unbiased witnesses, we move to employ the *Truth Domain*." A murmur of excitement met that statement from the upper crowd. This action settled down the gold-fringed group while the other senators leaned in, letting their side conversations die off.

"This action is deemed appropriate by this judgment seat. You may call a single witness. This court will not be used as an excuse for political maneuvering," the judge replied gravely. Tilly had to hold back a snort at that. *A little late to pretend to be above politics, don't you think?*

Upon hearing this limit to one witness, the prosecutor furiously wrote on some sort of thick papyrus glowing with a silvery light.

"Who does the prosecution call at this time?" the judge asked, his tone shortening at the delay.

The prosecutor watched the page intensely, ignoring the judge for a moment.

"If the prosecution is unpr—"

The prosecutor's head snapped up and almost shouted, "The prosecution calls the human Jonathan Tillman to the *Domain* as a witness!"

Shuji jumped to his feet. "Your honor, this man is not under any accusation. He should not be made to stand trial."

"He is not being accused of anything besides poor taste in friends!" the prosecutor snapped back, before continuing. "He is being called as the most reliable witness this court can question, and hopefully from him, we can get something resembling the untainted truth," he finished, a vehement gleam shining in his eyes.

"The court will allow this, as long as the human understands he can not be incriminated by any statements he makes under the influence of the *Domain*. We are here to discover the guilt or innocence of Lord Hiro and the lapin venture, nothing else."

Shuji's face fell, and a look of defeat darkened his features. He turned to Tilly as if in apology and as soon as his expression couldn't be seen by the crowd he winked before leaning in. "Just be yourself. We are almost certain you will do much more harm to our opposition than to us."

"The witness is not to be prepared!" the prosecutor shouted.

The judge gestured to the empty space in the basin directly before the two thrones, where a glowing circle of arcane markings had appeared.

"Please step into the enchantment, human. You will not be harmed."

CHAPTER TWENTY-FIVE

The Truth? You Can't Handle the Truth!

Tilly suddenly found himself at the center of attention for the entire arena. He felt shabby in his patchy leathers and primitive axes, not to mention the grimy state of his body. He took a moment to be glad they couldn't smell him . . . well, he assumed they couldn't.

None of this, however, seemed to bother the assembly. The whole crowd leaned in excitedly while he slowly moved toward the enchantment. The collective weight of their attention made his movements feel awkward and self-conscious, and as he neared the circle, one of the perimeter guards came forward with a dagger. It was enchanted and glowed the same color as the arcane writing that formed the perimeter of the circle.

"Hand please," she asked in a bored voice.

Tilly put on his "nothing surprises me anymore" Senior Firefighter face and mirrored the impassivity of the guard trying to appear much more unaffected than he was. He stretched out his hand, which shook only slightly, and the guard took it and pricked the center of his palm with the dagger, which surprisingly didn't hurt. A single drop of blood welled up, and she flicked the dagger tip with the drop of blood toward the enchantment, which flashed in response to the introduction of his blood.

"You may now enter," she continued formally with a bow before stepping back to her place on the wall.

Tilly stepped in, trying not to hesitate as the unknown magic enveloped him. The golden light touched him but didn't feel like anything, and Tilly himself felt no different having stepped fully into the circle. He did see a status effect appear next to his health and mana at the top left of his vision.

Truth Bound

Tilly pulled up his notification log to see if it gave him any more information.

> *You have been affected by the enchantment **Domain of Truth**. You are now **Truth Bound**. For the duration of time, you are within the enchanted area you may not speak anything you know to be false and will be predisposed to share what you feel to be the most true response to any posed question.*

"Jonathan Tillman, both the prosecution and defense have the right to ask you three questions before you are released from the *Domain*. Then we will hear closing statements and vote. Are you ready?"

Tilly swallowed down the lump in his throat. Dive into a fire, no problem. Maneuver through the dangerous political currents without drowning . . .

"I feel absolutely unprepared for this, but I guess I don't have a choice." The answer gushed from his mouth without thought and was met by smiles and small laughs all through the crowd.

Even the judge allowed himself a smirk. "Well this institution is only interested in the truth, something that hopefully needs very little help in being shaped or understood. Prosecution, you may ask your first question," he said with a wave of his hand.

The satyr in the prosecutor's box nodded sharply and reviewed some notes he had written down on the silvery glowing page before speaking in a slow deliberate tone as if talking to a toddler.

"Mr. Tillman, in your time with the accused, have you seen any behavior or heard anything that showed less than full commitment to the empire and its people?" he asked, eyes intensively focused on Tilly's guileless, thoughtful expression.

Before Tilly had time to even think of how to answer the question, his mouth was opening. "It is my understanding that the lapin people are citizens of the empire . . . And everything I have seen from them speaks of a people just trying to survive threats both domestic and from abroad." His words had a clipped almost robotic cadence to them, and Tilly was surprised by the formal way that his thoughts emerged. Not that it was anything he didn't believe. It was just spoken clearly without any forethought.

At his words, the prosecutor's face screwed up into a sneer, and he furiously started writing on his glowing sheet again. The judge turned toward Shuji and Hiro. "Defense, what is your counter?"

This time Hiro stood up, and with that same unhurried coolness that had marked his presence during the whole affair he said, "Jonathan Tillman, what was your impression of our village when you first arrived just a few days ago?"

Tilly's mind noted the sharp interest provoked in several senators of the non-gold parties, and he guessed that it had something to do with Hiro establishing him as completely new to the lapins and probably the empire as a whole. His mouth, on the other hand, didn't care one lick about his observations and simply rattled off his uncolored opinion.

"Well, I arrived near death from my encounter with the **Corruption** in the mountains. I was hoping you guys would be able to provide some protection or an answer to the problem that was clearly consuming the surrounding wilds. But what I found when I recovered was a people who had almost lost hope. It looked to me like you were barely hanging on. This impression was further confirmed when you sent me back out into the forest to deal with the problem instead of doing it yourself." He winced internally at the slight bitterness that had entered his tone as he finished describing his impressions. He had understood Hiro's obligations to his people, but he couldn't help but think that they had on some level mishandled the growing threat early on. There was no way they should have ended up being dependent on him to save them.

The silvery page in front of the prosecution lit up, and the prosecutor nodded to something he found there before looking up with a smirk. Hiro, however, just took his response in stride and nodded before sitting down.

"The prosecution's next question," the judge said, gesturing to the prosecutor.

"The prosecution finds it interesting that you were sent off alone to face something that was clearly far beyond your ability to handle. Their race has something of a reputation amongst this governing body to be . . . unreliable. In that vein, have you seen or heard your lapin companions pursue any goals that run counter to the empire's wellbeing in their pursuit of 'survival' as you put it?"

At this Tilly tried to control his mouth before it opened, desperately trying to take inventory of all that he had witnessed. But it was hopeless. His response seemed to completely skip his front brain, filtered through some deeper place, and then immediately made available to the assembly.

"I don't know what the 'empire's wellbeing' means. From what I have seen it seems like you are currently losing a war. If these guys were given an important mission by the emperor, and you are calling them back on trumped-up charges, isn't that counter to the empire's wellbeing? In fact, the only treason I've heard about is by some guy named Marcellus."

Grumbling started to build in the crowd as Tilly recited his answer. From his tone, you might have thought he was talking about tomorrow's weather. Yet as his words sank in, the whole stadium erupted in shouting.

"Order! Order!" the Judge shouted from his seat, his voice barely drowning out the crowd.

Tilly's eyes locked on the same elderly satyr in rich gold-fringed robes sitting in front of the gold group of senators. His face had shifted from impassive to an achingly cold fury in a matter of moments, his eyes becoming beacons of icy hate.

"ORDER!" The judge's voice broke out once again, this time succeeding in damping the fervor of the crowd.

"I will have the guards remove any non-senate personnel that cannot control themselves immediately!" At that, the whole crowd quieted, even the senators stopped talking, and as if by some unsaid agreement, they all zeroed back in on Tilly, who couldn't keep the grimace off his face. What kind of shit had he just stepped into?

"I would remind this assembly, that what the witness speaks is only what he believes to be true, and is not grounds for any accusation without corroborating evidence." The judge spoke harshly.

Justice truly is blind, Tilly snarked internally.

"Defense, you have the witness for your counter question." The judge spat with a sharp gesture at the defense's cordon, all attempts at appearing unbiased having been forgotten. Today was not going how he expected.

Tilly turned to see Shuji covering up a smile with a cough. "Ughm . . . Yes, the defense wishes to ask the witness if he knows of any lapin plot to undermine or rebel against the empire. This will be our final question. No matter how he replies, the defense will rest until concluding statements."

Once again, a response disgorged itself from his gut, almost as if he was more of a spectator to this whole exchange than an active participant. As he began speaking he noted with some dark humor that the prosecution was furiously writing on his enchanted sheet, and it was flashing back in manic response.

"The lapins are planning for the possibility of this empire's collapse. I do not believe they want to bring it about. Although if they did, I don't think they would have to try very hard. Everything I have seen today tells me that this empire is in its final days."

Those words launched the crowd back into an uproar. The senators either started shouting and yelling at him, or turning to each other and discussing things furiously. The judge was shouting something to the guards, but his voice was caught up in a cacophony of the mob.

"Bastions! I pronounce this a closed session!" He tried again, shouting even louder, his voice barely audible over the din. But those same sharply dressed, scarred soldiers from the bottom of the stairs appeared all around the stadium and started moving through the stands, herding all the crowd above the senators out of the public entrances. Some fought and continued to yell; others seemed to take it in stride. A third and disturbingly large portion of the crowd seemed to think the whole thing was some sort of game, hooting and howling with the mob, trying to dodge the advance of the guard while waving drinks animatedly.

The guards did their jobs admirably despite the wildness of the upper audience, and soon the whole upper stadium was clear.

"This assembly will conclude its proceedings in order, or it will suspend any pending bills and motions until proper decorum can be achieved on the floor. This was always going to be the result when you include a human in your schemes. Now we will finish this trial and vote. The defense has rested. Prosecution . . . What is your final question?"

The coiffed satyr was thrown off by the sudden uproar, and his magical paper was no longer flashing any responses at him. He stood there for a moment looking lost.

"Prosecution! Do you have a question, or do you rest?" the judge demanded.

"Uh . . . Ahem, yes. The prosecution wishes to point out that this witness is unaware of our true state of affairs and the might of our empire . . ." he replied shrilly.

"This is your last chance. Do you have a question or not?" the judge snapped, leaning forward in his chair, disdain written all over his face.

"Yes! The prosecution wishes to ask the witness . . . Uh. . . . Ah! On what ignorant grounds could he possibly pronounce judgment over our state of affairs? He said himself that he had only just arrived on the plane a few days ago. Clearly, his ignorance is his undoing." He concluded in shallow triumph, his forehead shining with a layer of sweat, and his skin turning sallow.

In all of this, Tilly felt like currents he could not understand were shifting all around him. The feeling was as exhausting as it was frustrating. He had almost died yesterday, and here he was, being shifted like a pawn on the board by self-centered idiots who couldn't see the writing on the wall. But if they wanted the truth, then for better or worse, he was going to give it to them.

"The streets are choked with homeless and hopeless refugees, too hungry and weak to keep running from an army you apparently can't stop in the field. Those with the ability to do so, are packing up and fleeing to who knows where. Oh, and the fact that your upper class seems to have become completely divorced from reality. It was more important to them to show up to this trial for entertainment than it was to lead the people they have a responsibility to protect. By the way, where is the emperor? You are in crisis, and I don't see any leadership. I can only see a fast-approaching end and no obvious way to stop it.

"I may not know much, but it's pretty obvious that any of you not preparing for the empire's fall is a fool or delusional. Clearly, some of you know what is happening and are playing the situation to your advantage. I wonder where the 'Elder Marcellus' disappears to on his little outings beyond the wall?" Tilly finished, gasping for breath at the end of his tirade.

The senators and the judge sat stunned in silence, with the exception of the elder, hawklike senator at the front of the gold-fringed group. His face remained remarkably impassive, but his eyes burned with an extraordinary fury. For most of the senators, it was a thoughtful heavy silence. For the gold-fringed group it was the quiet of impending vengeance. As for the judge, his silence was rooted in a deep weariness that suddenly showed itself in the roadmap of lines creasing every part of his elderly, distinguished face.

Despite that, he was the first to answer. "Human, do not look at us in our darkest hour and think you know us. Once this place stood proudly for the rule of law, the truth of justice, and equal representation. Yes, we had an emperor, but ours was a republic, something much rarer than you yet realize in this world of monsters and legends. Do not be so quick to foretell our doom, for with us dies one of the last republics of Nephesh," he said solemnly, his words taking on an eerie weight of wisdom won through centuries of struggle and pain.

Then he closed his eyes for a long moment, and when he opened them, the impassive mask was back, the will to fulfill his duty as guardian of this storied institution hardened his resolve, and his voice once again rang out.

"Thus the questioning has been concluded. May we hear the truth and judge rightly by it!" he pronounced, his voice firmed by the millennia of tradition that preceded it.

"Human you may leave the *Domain*. Prosecution, defense, this assembly will hear your closing statements."

Tilly looked around in confusion, once again failing to embody any of the formality that surrounded him in the current circumstance. He awkwardly stepped back out of the circle and turned to take his place behind the cordoned-off section of the defense. On his way, he saw the coiffed satyr frantically writing on his pad with no response, and he caught a sad smile from Shuji before he schooled his expression back to one of professional interest.

Hiro stood as he passed by and addressed the assembly. "The defense stands ready . . ." At a wave from the judge, he continued. "You are correct, this human knows none of the histories of this empire or its greatness. But in some ways, it is that very knowledge that has made many of us blind to the possibility of its end. Make no mistake, this empire is in grave peril, and this body has far more important issues to deliberate than a false claim of a misuse of funds. A significant portion of this body will vote me guilty simply because of my race . . . and to them, I do not waste my breath on words. But to the rest of you . . . You know me, you know my people. We simply wish to survive what is coming, and we will not do so if this empire falls. We can not fall. We will not fall. That is all that matters." Then he sat back down, his manner just as cool and reserved as when they had begun. In fact through all of these proceedings the only member of the trial who had not seemed to be surprised by the proceedings was Hiro Matsumoto.

"The defense has been heard. Prosecution you will conclude your argument, or I will close and put this matter to a vote."

The satyr who had started the preceding with such vehemence seemed deflated, his magical communication thrown to the side. He looked up with a hard, bitter smile, something that spoke of a desire for mutual destruction.

"The prosecution stands ready . . ." he said, staring intensely at the judge, who again motioned for him to continue.

"This has always been an empire that holds the rule of law and the inherent rights of its citizens above all else. No one here denies the pressures we face along our borders. It is precisely because of these pressures that I stand before you at all, fighting for justice. By their own admission, these mongrels would have failed and squandered all that we had entrusted to them, if not for the miraculous intervention of a human. This is gross negligence of the highest order. On top of that, the prosecution knows it was unable to fully bring to light the history of malfeasance and quiet rebellion that this race has perpetrated throughout its history. They have undermined our greatness for generations, and it is they and others like them that have made us what we are today, a people on the brink. Do not give in to their petty mewlings. Remember your pride, and our great destiny. If we beat back this weakness here in this courtroom, we will beat it back on our borders, just as we always have and always will."

By the end of his monologue, his voice was once again ringing out with the passion of blind belief. This was a creature so committed to his ideals that he could not help but see every fact through the lens of his fervently held bias. The judge stood from his seat with a nod, and for the first time turned and addressed the assembled senate.

"The Cura has heard trial and will now put it to a vote. Ayes for guilty. Nays for not guilty. Noble senators, cast your vote."

CHAPTER TWENTY-SIX

Spite and Spittle

A glowing group of symbols appeared before the occupants in the lower arena seating. Some senators took a moment to deliberate before their group of symbols flashed and disappeared. Others didn't even look at the options before their voting enchantment display flashed in response to some unseen input and faded away.

Soon only the silver-fringed group of senators remained undecided, numbering eight in total. The Purist Party seemed to have enough members to make up just under half of the senate, and Tilly realized with some anxiety that it would be almost impossible for them to be voted innocent if this yet undecided party chose guilty, or abstained.

The front position of this smaller group was taken by a truly ancient satyr, his wizened face almost lost in the ridiculously long but thin white beard flowing down from his chin and upper lip. He sat there stoically considering each of the three symbols floating in front of him. He seemed to weigh the choice for an unhurried age with a look of focused deliberation on his face. Then in a break with all of his peers, he moved his hand in a deliberate motion and selected one of the options, making sure the whole arena could see his vote. The rest of his group hesitated briefly to look at each other before following suit with a series of quick flashes marking their decisions.

Tilly couldn't help but scan the crowd hoping for some hint of which way the different groups had voted. As he was taking in each group, he finally tried to put the names he had heard in the closet meeting to the groups before him. If his assumptions were right, then the silver-fringed group had to be the Loyalists . . . which from context clues, had something to do with the emperor. They held themselves rigid, ignoring the looks of the others in the arena, instead impassively looking to the judge, who seemed to be receiving the tally in real-time.

He sat there wearing a far-off look as lights danced before his eyes. Then suddenly, they were gone, and he was scowling down at the arena floor, ready to be done with this trial.

"The vote has been tallied at 36 nays, 30 ayes, and 0 abstained. Let the people of our glorious empire know that justice has prevailed . . . Hiro Mosimoto, before the eyes of those in this court, the emperor, and the heavens themselves, you are pronounced Not Guilty."

Upon his announcement, the entire silver-fringed group stood and filed out of the arena, leaving some in confusion, and others in outright animosity.

"You haven't voted for months!" One gold-fringed senator shouted at their backs.

"And now you choose to vote? For a filthy long ear!"

None of them replied as they filed through an exit, their absent response leaving its mark on the rest of the assembly, many turning and speaking to each other, trying to unravel the inscrutable choice of the Loyalists. Tilly couldn't quite see who was shouting, and as soon as he started scanning the gold group, he couldn't help but be drawn again into the frosty glare of the head of the Purists. He sat looking down at Tilly as one would look at a particularly skittery roach that was about to get stomped.

"Order, order," the judge called out in a tired voice.

"We have two more motions to move forward this morning before we break. All those not present automatically choose to abstain. Lord Matsumoto and delegation, you are dismissed."

At that Hiro and Shuji stood and moved toward the same arched opening they had entered through, with Tilly close behind.

"Hey . . . ugh, sorry about what I said up there about the village," Tilly whispered hurriedly as they exited the Cura.

Hiro kept moving down the stairs but waved off the apology like it was inconsequential. Shuji, however, turned and beamed at Tilly with his characteristically huge smile.

"Do not worry yourself, Mr. Tillman. You have been named *friend*! And you have once again proven your great worth to our people. If I may be so bold, it is probably we who owe you an apology. We had to come up with a plan very quickly, and we knew if we brought you along as an unknown, those nosy Purists wouldn't be able to help themselves. It worked out wonderfully! If our luck holds, we might even survive the coming calamity!"

Tilly almost missed a step as Shuji delivered the last words, seemingly without a care in the world. Then Hiro stopped suddenly on the steps, and turned back toward Tilly, his face drawn in a serious frown.

"This whole building is enchanted to prevent divination, but once we leave its protection, we will not be safe from being overheard until we lose ourselves in the city. This trial played out as well as it could for us. However, this means that they will try to end us with more overt methods, possibly as soon as dusk. We will leave this building and move fast, and I will tell you when we are relatively secure. Do not engage with anyone unless you see us do the same. They will find us, and we must do what we can to be ready." He delivered this in a steady but focused voice that broached no argument.

He was about to turn back down the stairs, but Tilly moved to stop him, lifting his hand to grab his shoulder, before thinking better of it and turning it into something of a hand raise.

"Look, Hiro, I'm with you and I understand that you have a lot more to worry about than me and my problems, but hear me out . . . I don't care if we are in the middle of a fight for our lives. Tonight, I need some answers," Tilly said, once again allowing some of the frustration of the last few days to color his tone.

Hiro didn't acknowledge the reach but did nod sharply at the statement, before turning to move. Shuji moved over and turned his bombastic smile on, once again giving Tilly a friendly pat on the shoulder before hurrying down after Hiro.

Guess that is a yes . . .

Tilly moved to follow distractedly, not for the first time worrying about how far beyond his ability circumstances had moved. He couldn't help but feel like a noob in a high-level zone. Nearly every possible combatant he had seen in the city was at least twice his level if not more.

Before he knew it, he was at the bottom of the stairs, and Hiro and Shuji were cutting through the crowd of squawking bureaucrats like a smoothbore nozzle cutting through fire in a fully involved room. There was something about the purpose with which Hiro moved that easily set him apart from his surroundings as they milled about amongst the tree-like pillars. Tilly followed in his wake, wondering if he would ever find his way in this world or be cursed to be caught up in this seemingly undeniable tide of events. Being treated like a hanger-on and told to follow was getting old. He shifted his jacket uncomfortably over his scar as he half-jogged to keep up with the odd loping gait that all of the lapin seemed to possess.

They made it through the crowds in the Cura and emerged at the front steps of the building to find the same satyr who had started all of this waiting for them with his formal servant. Tilly did note, however, that he lacked the guards that had accompanied him previously and hoped that this was a sign that he was no longer acting as an agent of the state.

His face was a storm cloud of anger, juxtaposed by the slack professional expression of his servant. He stood at the entrance of the Cura, clearly prepared for a public showdown, wanting to regain some face. Hiro didn't even bother to acknowledge him, simply moving around him like an inanimate object, Shuji following suit. This only darkened the satyr's already stormy expression, and his eyes flashed with fury.

Unfortunately, he was surprised by the move of avoidance and did not want to turn and look like he was following the moving lapins, so his eyes fixed on Tilly, who was a few steps behind the purposeful pair.

"You dirty, long-ear loving cur. How dare you besmirch my family's name in such a public setting," he declared in front of the growing crowd of onlookers. Apparently, they had known to anticipate this very meeting. The young aristocrat followed up his insult with one of the pettiest and most disgusting things Tilly could imagine. He spat in Tilly's face.

Now Tilly had been a firefighter for decades, and bodily fluids were a part of the job. He couldn't count the number of times he had been forced into contact with blood, urine, and even feces on duty. But in his many years . . . he had never been spit on. He had to admit, it did not agree with him at all.

Tilly saw red, and the sound of his throbbing heartbeat filled his ears. His whole body tensed like a fully compressed spring, and his side spasmed, releasing a sickly-sweet feeling of pleasure and relief. The sweet tingling spread up from his side and down his extremities, and he felt ready for anything. This world kept pushing him around, and it was time for him to start pushing back.

He didn't know what a level 38 Quaestor was, but all thought of consequences had flown from his mind, and his face cracked into a manic grin as goat spittle dribbled past his lips. A new flashing notification went unnoticed, as Tilly imagined rearranging the goat's chin.

The offender's sneer of hate momentarily ticked into a smirk at the sight of the reaction, and the steward's stance subtly shifted, the weight of his body moving from his heels to the balls of his feet.

Then Shuji, as if out of thin air, was between the three, interrupting the building tension with his unbelievably cheerful smile. He moved in front of Marcellus's heir with such a fawning expression that the satyr's satisfied smirk twisted into a rictus of confusion and disgust.

"My lord! I am deeply bereaved that this ignorant human has injured you and your family so unjustly!" he cried out, with literal tears forming in the corners of his eyes. Then he dropped to his knees before the satyr and started weeping at his feet, loudly. The transition was so shocking that it blew away Tilly's mindless fury like a brisk breeze clearing morning fog. The tingling remained in his veins but no longer demanded action.

Then Shuji raised the ridiculous performance to a new level, moving toward the satyr's legs and attempting to kiss them. As the possibility of being touched by such a base creature became a reality, fury reignited on Titus Marcellus's face, and Tilly saw his arm begin to writhe and glow with a dangerous purple aura. Shuji didn't even look up from his crying as the satyr raised his arm in a flash, preparing to bring it down in some sort of strike.

Tilly moved without thinking, some sort of eerie competence taking the place of his shock as he saw the danger Shuji was in. He activated [Resolute] as he dived over the prostrating lapin. A flash of purple shone from above as he lost view of all but Shuji, who was already moving as if having anticipated the strike from the beginning. Then a searing crushing pain exploded along his shoulders shattering his awareness momentarily before fading completely and leaving him gasping on the ground.

He quickly adjusted to the absence of the intense pain and pushed himself up from his position preparing to reach for his hatchets. He looked up to find looks of bewilderment on the faces of everyone present. The crowd that had formed to eagerly watch the events unfold broke out in exclamations of shock. Even the implacable steward was looking around with his hand in his jacket as if trying to identify the new unknown variables that had entered the field.

Shuji, the sneaky bastard, had somehow ended up ten feet down the steps in all the confusion, and he looked back up at Tilly with a chagrined expression on his face. The Quaestor, however, was the most put off by the change of events. His fury developed into a sort of near panic, clearly unused to being so out of control.

"You . . . Your human trickery . . . I demand satisfaction!" he finally stuttered out as his right arm started to twitch along with his face.

"That will not happen," stated a calm Hiro, appearing in the growing crowd with several of the scarred guards that Tilly had seen at the bottom of the inner steps. Hiro continued as if he was completely in control of the situation.

"You feel you have been insulted, and have in turn insulted and struck one of those in my retinue. It is now my responsibility to pursue satisfaction at my leisure, and be sure I will be doing so . . ." he said, nothing in his manner or voice changing, but still somehow impregnating his words with an incredible amount of menace.

The steward instantly moved between Hiro and his master, and the younger satyr choked on his furious reply.

"Shuji, Mr. Tillman, Come. It is time to take our leave," he said, once again turning to move down the stairs, the crowd parting before him like minnows scattering before a shark.

Shuji moved to follow immediately, and Tilly was only a second behind, following in Hiro's wake. As he moved, he couldn't help but turn back and shout over his shoulder, "That wasn't a human trick! You just hit like a little girl!" he called, wiping any remaining spit from his face. Was it childishness, sure. But sometimes you have to fight fire with fire.

A scream of fury followed them down the steps. "Mark my words, filth! You will be paste, smeared under my boot by the end of the day!" His words caused the already mumbling crowd to ripple with more animated discussion. Even that faded into the normal sounds of a bustling city as Hiro, Shuji, and Tilly moved out onto the promenade choked with every aspect of life.

CHAPTER TWENTY-SEVEN

Kowabunga

Now that it was no longer early morning, the city had come fully alive. They quickly moved off from the main promenade of the city to the smaller, less patrolled streets. Well, not so much less patrolled as absolutely packed. The city was almost choking on its own citizens, and several times they had to press through crowds of refugees so thick that Tilly felt as if he could hardly breathe from the bodies. The mood of the city, especially here, far away from the aristocracy, was a heady mixture of near panic and dark melancholy. The refugees they passed were either so forceful in their begging that it amounted to a near mugging, or so still that Tilly had trouble believing they were still alive.

It didn't matter to Tilly that the refugees were mainly satyrs, with occasional members of other races. What was getting to him all over again was the kids . . . They were everywhere, sometimes playing in small groups protected by wary adults. Other times they just sat against the edge of the street, showing a more deadened hardness that spoke of truly hellish experiences. The weight of the city's plight once again pressed down on him, and he felt a resurgence of the burning in his chest. The sensation clashed with the syrupy sweet tingling that was still throbbing up from his side, and he wondered how he hadn't thought much about the sensation until this moment.

Then he noticed the flashing notification icon in the corner of his eye. He was about to try to open it while following the lapins before remembering his hike through the forest and decided the thing could wait. Instead, he focused on keeping up through the press of bodies and tried to pay attention to his surroundings, Titus's threats looming in his mind.

Many of the houses and businesses they passed were abandoned by the more well-to-do owners of the city and had been boarded up. This opportunity had not been lost on the refugees who had taken to "repossessing" the buildings. This created a very post-apocalyptic feel as if these people were huddled in the ruins of a city, instead of taking refuge in the empire's capital.

Still, it was Tilly's first magical city, and despite the growing squalor he still spotted some awesome signs glowing with magic. Shops selling items and armor that he had only ever seen in video games. Not that he had much time to sight-see. Hiro led them through the ever-shrinking streets at an unforgiving pace, taking turns seemingly at random, and sometimes doubling back the way they came.

Then, just like the sun peeking out on a cloudy day, their surroundings changed. They moved out of the general population area and were now surrounded by ancient, well-kept structures that had a distinctly island feel. There was also a notable difference in the people. Almost everyone in this new section of the city was from the turtle race, and many of them walked around with an arcane implement of some kind.

Their pace broke down to a slow walk, and Hiro looked around as if waiting for someone. Shuji took a few deep breaths, trying to catch what he had lost in transit, and then looked over at Tilly with a smaller-than-normal smile. "We can't go to the lapin district. They would find us immediately, and even if we fought them off, some of our people would die in the process. So we are taking a small risk in delaying."

"I do not appreciate . . . the 'small risk' . . . you bring . . . to my people," an ancient voice wheezed as an extremely wrinkled turtle biped shuffled up to their group, leaning heavily on his gnarled staff covered in runes. Tilly thought he heard the sound of a seashore in the distance and looked around in confusion.

"Mr. Tillman, it is my pleasure to introduce Honored Elder Kihei Tide Caller," Hiro said, following his words with a deep bow to the much older creature. The turtle-man was flanked by many of his kind, although they stood a little ways off in deference. Hiro came up from his bow and continued. "Elder Kihei is the last elder of the honu people and the greatest mage the empire has left," he said introducing the honu elder and then turning to address him directly. "The charade is almost up, the city would soon implode, even without the Cult of the Serpent at the door. So we have come to make a deal." His expression was intense, yet still respectful as he looked directly into the eyes of the wizened elder, which sparkled with a vibrant intelligence untouched by time's advance. In the face of Hiro's offer, that sharp gaze narrowed in suspicion.

"We often . . . found ourselves allies . . . in the senate . . . Yet never once did you . . . ask us for aid . . . Yours is a proud people . . . and your scheme to survive is obvious . . . even to the point of being narrow-minded."

Hiro allowed himself a rare small smile at the words. "And I am sure your plan is well-rounded, conservative, and slow. This is happening faster than any of us thought, and I have already lost my son once because of pride. I will not lose my people by making the same mistake twice."

"Very well . . ." the elder stated, suddenly smiling, dropping his suspicion with deceptive ease.

"What do you need . . . from us . . . and what do you have . . . to offer?" Elder Kihei asked as if he had expected the offer for years. Those behind him, however, reacted in a comically slow display of shock. One honu literally took a full five seconds for his jaw to completely drop. Whatever was happening, it must have been unprecedented . . . Then, moving to the front of the growing crowd, a distinctive-looking honu arrived at the elder's side, holding a conch shell. He moved without the exaggerated slowness of the others and wore practical and travel-stained robes along with a vibrant blue scarf.

Hiro's small smile grew more exultant at the elder's response. "Is there any way we can be overheard?"

The elder did not answer but did tap his staff lightly on the ground. The sound of waves crashing against the shore grew noticeably.

"My gratitude, elder, we do not share this secret easily, for it has been guarded for generations by my people . . ." Then his smile faltered, and to Tilly's surprise, he saw Hiro take a deep shaky breath before nodding to himself and continuing. "When my people attacked this empire five hundred years ago, we did so because we too, were in decline, and our Moon Goddess thought it was our only chance to solidify our position in the eyes of the Land. As you know, this attack failed, and we became a conquered people, dishonored and relegated to vastly inferior classes as punishment by the emperor.

"This is all fairly well known. However, there are two facts known only to the royal line and a few close retainers. When our goddess saw we would fail, she chose to sacrifice herself instead of serving the empire's Rule of Law divine mandate. With her life, she bought two things for my people. First were the two *Mythic Bound* weapons that could only be used by the royal line," he said, gesturing to his sword.

"The second thing she bought with her life was a Sovereign Crystal. Our people have called it our *Promise* for generations, even though most don't know what it is." The crowd gasped at his words, and even the elder's eyes widened.

"When we first received it, it was in its nascent stage, and still required a gift of seventy-seven million *experience*. After five centuries, we are down to the last hundred thousand, and we had planned to use it to break off from the empire and establish a new kingdom on the frontier. This, of course, will not work under the current timeline. I have too many people left in this city and no way to move them. Neither can I come up with the rest of the *experience* in time to establish the new nation."

"Wait," Tilly blurted out, not even able to fathom how much it had cost the lapin people to donate that much *experience*. "Your people have just given up the chance to level for five hundred years to . . . uh, charge this thing?"

"That is correct, Mr. Tillman," Hiro said, briefly turning to the side to address the human before turning back to the honu and continuing to make his case.

"The majority of my people were forced to take servant or labor classes throughout our history here. They began certain stereotypes by leveling in those classes much slower than they should have to donate a portion of their *experience* to the *Promise*. This earned us the reputation of being lazy and unreliable, and we are widely regarded as a low-tier race, hampered by some sort of race-wide deficit." As he concluded, his eyes hardened, and Tilly could feel the passion and dedication that had fueled these people to make such a sacrifice.

"Always . . . So stubborn . . . I assume the emperor knew . . . some of this?"

"He knew that we would break from the empire rather than die here for ideals we did not share. He saw where this was headed and that he no longer had the power to stop it. He told me that as long as I didn't break any laws, or harm his people, he would not fault our desire to survive. Many now pursue the same end with much less honor."

"On this . . . we agree. I see what you need from us: . . . a way for all of your people . . . to retreat to your new home. . . . Now what . . . can you offer?"

At this, Hiro gestured to Shuji, who quickly stepped forward, his loud and fast manner somewhat at odds with the rest of the conversation.

"Elder Kihei, it is an honor as always, I have always been fascinated by your entries into the imperial—"

"Shuji!" Hiro growled.

"Ah . . . yes, so sorry. We had a formal covenant document prepared that would have rendered this in binding terms, but it was made as a contingency and does not include many of the pertinent variables that we currently face . . . But in essence, we offer you full access to the Sovereign Crystal to be housed on neutral grounds as well as a portion of the land we have subdued to be bound to your people until the new lapin kingdom falls or you choose to move elsewhere. We essentially offer you a place in our . . . confederacy," Shuji finished, rattling off most of the details in two breaths.

The elder considered the terms for a long minute, as those behind him spoke back and forth in slow mumbling tones. "Those terms sound acceptable . . . But I wish to add . . . one addendum . . . I too have . . . made a promise. . . . to our emperor . . . When your people flee . . . we request you take as many . . . refugees as you can . . . through the portal."

Hiro grimaced at the addendum, and slowly that grimace turned into an expression of smoldering anger. Emotion warred on his face as he searched for a counterproposal, and Tilly's chest tightened as he realized he was witnessing the other side of that same racial blindness he had experienced in the senate. He was growing to respect the lapin leader, and to see such a shallow shortsightedness in him hit Tilly like a gut punch.

He couldn't help but interject again.

"Listen, Hiro," Tilly growled, drawing all eyes in the conversation toward him.

"Your son named me a *friend* to the lapin people, and you offered me your sword. I have followed you without question for the better part of a day, getting myself in a world of shit along the way. Whatever equity I have with you, I'm to putting it on the table. You need to agree to this. We need to get as many people out as we can before this city is destroyed."

Hiro's smoldering anger evened out into something flat and controlled as he considered Tilly's words. Then with a slow deliberate cadence, he answered, "They will not destroy the city. They will conquer it. And yes, many here will become slaves to the Cult of the Serpent, but we can do nothing about that. The empire has failed all of us! Now we fight simply to protect whatever little we can." Hiro's voice did not rise as he moved through his response, but each successive word was laden with increasing amounts of bitterness. As each word landed, Tilly began to feel the weight of decades spent fighting for an institution that prospered off the servitude of his people.

"The *Ship. Is. Sinking.* We each must look to our own," he finished vehemently.

Tilly knew he was asking for too much from the man who was fighting to keep his people alive, but Tilly couldn't stop picturing the thousands of children littering the street, looking for some refuge from the war at their doorstep. Words poured out of his mouth before he could count their cost, or measure their implication.

"Fuck. That. If you want me with you for the rest of this little adventure, we are going to save as many of these people as we can. Or I am out." Tilly almost shouted, gesturing widely to the broader city behind him.

"I am afraid . . . That we feel the same . . . We can link the platforms . . . for your people to get through . . . but you must allow others . . . the same chance," the elder cut in.

"Human, as much as I appreciate your magnanimous gesture, how can we possibly house, let alone feed all these people," Shuji interjected desperately.

"We may have . . . some ideas on this front . . . We will contact you . . . mid-day tomorrow . . . and you will meet the others."

"Do not share the information I have revealed to you this day with these 'others.' I see that this conversation must continue, and I know we have imposed on your protection for long enough . . . I will come tomorrow," Hiro relented spitefully.

"Understood . . ." Elder Kihei sighed, gesturing to the honu next to him to come forward. The honu approached with uncharacteristically normal speed and handed a shell to Shuji. Even in the heat of the moment, Tilly couldn't help but notice the younger honu's scarf was drifting as if underwater.

"The divination is increasing in intensity, elder. Whoever they are sending is very powerful," he muttered, looking around as if something was going to pop out of the shadows at any second.

"Our guests know this . . . Franklin . . . Worry not . . . They are leaving now . . ."

Shuji pocketed the shell. "Yes, very sorry about that. We have a place to meet them set aside. We will be on our way," Shuji said, accompanying his words with another bow.

"I will meet your people, elder. We will see what we can do in the time left to us," Hiro said with a reluctant nod of his head. Then he turned to Tilly, his gaze turning cold.

"If it is not too much to ask, Mr. Tillman, we need to go now and get as ready as we can. They are coming, and after your performance today, they will have you in their sights as well. Whether you are with us or not," Hiro challenged.

Tilly returned his flat look, feeling slightly sheepish, but not at all apologetic. He quickly gave his own bow to the honu elder and then nodded in affirmation to the two lapins.

"Yeah . . . let's go. I hope you guys have one hell of a plan."

At that, Shuji barked out a laugh. "Ha! Yes, Jonathan Tillman! I believe you will love it!"

CHAPTER TWENTY-EIGHT

Sninjas

After a hurried walk through more crowded streets and twisted back-alley turns, they seemed to arrive at the edge of the city. The wall could clearly be seen in the distance, and the buildings became less residential and more industrial. Many of these seemed to have already been emptied, if not completely ransacked, and it was one such warehouse that Tilly found himself standing in front of as Shuji let out a cheerful huff of satisfaction.

"Good! Good. They left it exactly as I asked them," he said, shoving through a large, clearly broken wood gate. At one point it had probably been designed to allow wagons to move in and out of the ancient commercial-sized building. Now it sat wedged into the opening as if someone had jammed it back in place after illicitly gaining entry to the building.

"You asked them to leave it like this?" Tilly murmured moving through the doorway into a sea of smashed crates, clay pots, and canvas. Hiro was scanning the room in a businesslike manner while Shuji seemed to be fussing with something in a nearby crate and mumbling to himself.

". . . I know I sent them the correct scroll . . . Ah. Here we are!" he said, pulling a scroll from the rubble and throwing it open to reveal a surface covered in glowing script.

"Librarian arts, firefly swarm!" he stated in a strong ringing voice. The scroll hovered in the air for a few moments glowing brighter and brighter before the indecipherable words started to detach from the scroll and float all around the huge room. They danced in the air and lit the room, banishing the shadowy gloom of the unlit warehouse and giving it the feel of mystery and potential.

Tilly's notification icon began blinking again, and he opened it on reflex given that they had finally stopped moving.

> *You have entered a **Librarian's Domain**. All reading is 20% more effective, and you may benefit from any prepared seals the librarian has set over his Domain.*

Huh, Shuji wasn't kidding, they did have something prepared. Although Tilly wasn't sure how effective a library would be at keeping them alive . . . Then Tilly's blood ran cold at the sight of the notification just above the most recent one.

> *You have given into Corruption's influence and have gained 2% Strength and lost 3% Wisdom. **Corruption Seed** influence now: 7%*

"Shit." Tilly sighed, the heady sensation before his almost fight with the uppity satyr coming to his mind in sharp relief. Something had been affecting his mind, but he had been so caught up in the moment that he had barely noticed and then immediately forgotten the whole thing afterward.

Is it just going to keep running in the background, pushing every time I'm not paying attention? Tilly wondered, goosebumps running up his arms as he thought about something playing tricks with his perception. He was so caught up in the thought that he didn't even notice Shuji calling him.

". . . Tillman, excuse my interruption, Mr. Tillman! If you would be so kind, we need you to follow us to the center," Shuji said, looking back at Tilly with a mild but cheerful concern. He had already called Tilly several times, but he had missed it.

"Oh. Uh, Sorry about that, it's been a long couple of days," he said, doing his best to shake off the crawling sensation that covered his body.

Shuji took his slip in stride and quickly covered over the concern with a token cheerful grin. "Oh, of course! With the threat we face, it is no wonder you feel out of sorts. Well, not to worry, it will all be sorted out one way or another," he said with a well-meaning pat on Tilly's shoulder before moving deeper into the rubble, carefully following some path that only he and Hiro knew about.

Tilly quickly stepped after them, being careful to place his feet in the same places that Shuji did. As they navigated deeper into the large open building, Shuji started to explain, "This was once the hidden storehouse for all of our people's collective wealth and knowledge. When we got approval for our venture into the frontier, we slowly transferred all of it to the village before we were cut off from imperial support. Yet as a Librarian, I am only allowed one *Domain*, and we thought it best to keep mine here where we had long prepared for discovery. This was to be our last line of defense in the capital, and we thought it wouldn't be needed . . . Now it will have an opportunity to serve that purpose after all."

"So what, you have this place magically booby-trapped?" Tilly asked, looking around at the warehouse with new hope.

"What a fascinating turn of phrase . . . 'booby-trapped.' Due to the shared nature of our language on this plane, I can understand the basic meaning . . . Nonetheless, I digress. Over the years I have painstakingly set up many wards and seals to do my best to protect the treasures of my people. Alas, *Librarian* is not a militant class, and I am afraid my preparations are more creative than deadly."

Then Hiro broke into the conversation from the front. "They will be adequate, Shuji. We simply need to force their ace to show themselves before I enter the fight, or they will try to exhaust me with chaff. Normally, not even that would worry me, as it has been tried before, but I fear they have grown desperate at this late hour. I have no idea what the Marcellus family is willing to do now that the empire is on its knees. I will stay in reserve until I must intervene. You two must hold and distract them for as long as possible." As he finished laying out the plan, they arrived in a cleared center space about twenty yards in diameter.

"Shuji, how much time do we have left?" Hiro inquired, his deep, calm voice imparting a sense of control to his two companions, not that Tilly could see any sign of worry in Shuji's manner. The lapin had nerves of steel. This contrasted nicely with Tilly's noticeably shaking hands, which he stilled by gripping the handles of his hatchets. His thumbs ran along the hard, ridged texture of the Forest Spirit's antlers, and he remembered its stand against **Corruption**, and its warning not to wait until it was too late to do something.

Here he was, in way over his head, but doing his best to help the people in front of him. Just like he had done for years in the fire department before the grinding decades of the job had hardened him into what he had become in the end. He thought back to what it was like those first few years in the department when it all felt like it mattered, and he still had a family . . .

Tilly took a few deep breaths, finding the place in his mind that would turn on while he listened to radio traffic screaming down the road to a fire. Whatever happened, he had always done whatever he had to, so that everyone went home at the end of shift. If that wasn't possible, if someone had to lay it all on the line, it would be him. It wasn't something he hoped was true about himself—he knew it from experience. Over and over, this resolve had been tried and tested, and he had never left one of his team behind.

This was something that had always made sense to him in the fire service. The SOPs were clear, and the brotherhood was comfortable . . . At home? In the hospital? There was no playbook there, and he had often felt sure he was making mistake after mistake as he stumbled through life as a husband, and then a father.

But this? This made sense. He was just in another kind of building, knowing that he might not be the one to come out. He was with a small team, facing long odds against an unknown danger. He wasn't afraid of dying. In fact, with this thing inside him trying to turn him into one of those monsters, that might not be too bad of an outcome.

This was just another day.

And for better or worse, in his past life, he had come to live for these moments. His hands stopped shaking, and he relaxed his arms and shoulders, taking in as much information from his surroundings as possible.

Shuji had pulled out a large piece of papyrus and had begun folding it while muttering to himself at Hiro's question. Tilly realized with fascination that he was creating another magical origami shape. Fold after fold resolved itself into a large open eye that floated up from Shuji's hands and glowed with a malevolent dark red light.

"We are currently under divination, blood magic if I'm not mistaken," Shuji stated in a droning voice as his eyes looked off into the distance.

The eye started to glow brighter before it suddenly crumbled to ash. Shuji recoiled back as if struck, and his head whipped toward the entrance. The sun had almost set, and long shadows reached into the building from the street.

"The magic is much stronger than I expected . . . and with this level of blood rite, there can only be one explanation."

"Say something I can understand, Shuji! I don't know what any of that means," Tilly said, reacting to Shuji's sudden movement by pulling his hatchets from his belt loops and easing into a ready stance.

Hiro quietly drew his black-as-night sword and settled down on his knees with the blade resting upon his lap. "It is worse than we thought, someone has let Shadow Hunters past the city wards. We face the Cult of the Serpent tonight, and they have a special hatred for our kind."

"How close are we talking?" Tilly muttered, his voice growing quiet under the weight of anticipation for the coming fight.

"They know where we are, and they know that we have discovered their divination. They will move with all due haste under the cover of darkness," Shuji said, breaking from his reverie and pulling loose different scrolls he had cleverly strapped around his person under his voluminous clothing.

"Okay, well you guys think I took out that corruption singlehandedly, but I only have two moves. I can throw these hatchets and catch the things on fire," Tilly rattled off, suddenly afraid they were depending on some hidden martial talent from the human that had defeated the **Corrupted** tree.

Hiro simply snorted in response. "Yes, that will be perfect for sowing chaos. Do not worry. This plan depends on our preparation and my blade. You will simply be a distraction."

Tilly sighed in relief. "Perfect. I can be a distraction." Then almost unbidden, the heat in his chest built up and flowed down his arms, igniting the heads of his hatchets simultaneously. The sensation was new, and Tilly did his best not to flinch at the sudden conflagration.

"Yes! Good!" Shuji nodded in approval, looking over at the sudden appearance of flames.

"We have laced explosives throughout this perimeter and amongst the debris. Your fire will save me from having to ignite them," he said, cheerfully as he laid out the final scrolls before him.

Tilly watched his mana bar critically as the cost of igniting his weapons slowly recharged. Right now using the *Ability* twice had knocked his mana bar down 6 percent, and he would doubtlessly be recalling his weapons every time he threw them. How much did that cost again? He dropped his ignited hatchet and recalled it back to his hand immediately. It reappeared in his hand, still ignited. He saw his mana tick down another 2 percent.

Okay, so if the weapons did not hit anything then they would stay imbued, and to ignite and recall his weapon would cost him about 5 percent in total. That gave him approximately twenty throws before he was out, not factoring in his dismal *Wisdom* stat. Which was dropping further due to the freakin' **Seed of Corruption** trying to burrow into his soul . . .

"Well, twenty isn't bad, more than a typical quiver of arrows," he muttered to himself, watching the small but intense blue flame burn on the stone head of the hatchets. He had to admit, it was pretty awesome that he could create these blue flames now. His mind wandered back to the temple in the mountains and the blue flame that still burned on the altar.

A paper bird zipped in through the open doorway from the dark street and up to Shuji, fluttering erratically. Shuji waved it away, and it unfolded and slipped into his sleeve. His cheerful smile flattened into something more focused, and he whispered, "They are out there, surveying the building."

Hiro continued to kneel with his eyes closed, not reacting to the news while Shuji whispered something else under his breath, and a muted hush fell over the building, canceling out all the noises that had fallen into the background. The creak of the thick timbers of the old building stopped, and the breeze playing through the door also quieted.

"Shuji, what was that?" Tilly whispered and then gasped as even his voice had greatly reduced in volume.

"We can talk in a normal voice, Jonathan Tillman. This will keep most of what is happening inside a mystery to those remaining without," he said in a confident if significantly muted voice. Then his eye sharpened, and Tilly whipped his head back to the entrance, where the already long shadows started to thicken.

"Wait to attack until I have one of them immobilized." Shuji followed up, reaching for one of the scrolls before him slowly as if trying not to startle whatever figures were forming in the deepening shadows of the entrance.

The shapes resolved into four distinct figures. They were humanoid from the waist up with a long serpent's tail instead of legs. Two were male, with pairs of thin straight swords in their hands. The other two were female with long flat-bladed spears tipped with cruel-looking hooks. All four of their torsos were bare and absolutely covered with black tattoos that seemed to be bleeding ink, and each of their heads were wrapped in dark cloth that drank in the light.

They rose up higher on their snake bottoms and looked over the room again, seeming to confirm that there were no other occupants in the building. Then, as one, they focused in on the group in the center, nicely lit up by the paper fireflies. It was then as their eyes caught the light that Tilly saw they were pools of oozing blackness, just like the infected creatures of the forest.

Whatever the Cult of the Serpent was, they clearly had embraced another source of **Corruption** wholeheartedly. Tilly's side throbbed at the realization, and the fire in his chest roared in response. Looks like his new mantle was going to come in handy a lot sooner than he thought.

As one, the four figures rushed forward through the debris, showing a startling speed as they wove through the first rows of abandoned containers.

CHAPTER TWENTY-NINE

Silent Library

Tilly stood ready to make his move as Shuji reached for one of the scrolls and began to mutter. The snake warriors wove forward through the debris but were unable to jump over anything because of their serpentine anatomies. This keyed Tilly in to just how well thought out the inconspicuous barricades were. As they approached, Tilly's *Identify* kicked in:

> *Level 22, Shadow Hunter*
> *Level 23, Shadow Hunter*
> *Level 21, Shadow Hunter*
> *Level 28, Shadow Hunter*

Okay, not great, but not too bad. With his damage multiplier, he still stood a chance to actually make a difference in this fight. Then as they crossed the half-way point of the large room, Shuji's voice rang out. "Librarian Arts, *Flying Forms, Endless.*"

Several crates the warriors were passing exploded into glowing circles that shot out streams of paper at the nearby combatants. The forms unerringly flew toward their targets, and the warriors tried and failed to dodge, getting pelted with rivers of paper covered in meaningless script.

Assuming that was his cue, Tilly immediately let his two enflamed hatchets fly at the sword-wielding pair. He marveled at his increased accuracy as they both flew in easy arcs, the momentum arresting violently in the chest and back of the distracted creatures. They hissed in pain and reached for the painful new additions to their bodies. Tilly immediately recalled and let them fly again, deciding to keep the pressure on the same two targets. They, however, changed strategy. Instead of continuing to try to dodge the endless stream of paper projectiles the two wounded hunters sheathed their swords and faded into shadows, becoming intangible to the paper barrage.

The spear-wielding pair realized that paper was more distraction than dangerous and powered through the barrage. At about twenty yards they hissed something and thrust out their spears.

Tilly watched as the first two shadow figures shot forward through the air, the passage made visible by fist-sized glowing blue embers lodged in their incorporeal forms chewing hungrily on their shadowy substance. As Tilly's follow-up attack neared them, they ignored the spinning projectiles, which turned out to be a mistake. As soon as the flame-covered stone ax heads touched their shadow forms, they were knocked back into normal existence, with hatchets lodged deeply in their torsos. Having their *Ability* interrupted like that caused them to re-form around the hatchets. The morbid sight caused Tilly's grim mask of focus to crack, a small smile peeking through as he recalled both weapons back to his hands. Both warriors collapsed with blue fire consuming the black ichor that poured from their wounds.

"Librarian Arts, *Restricted Section!*" Shuji shouted next to him, bringing his focus back to the more present danger as the other two attackers extended their reach with two shadowy spearheads. The *Ability* elongated the Shadow Hunters' weapons, which slithered through the air toward the two defenders, effectively tripling their reach in a moment.

Enormous bookshelves exploded from the floor in front of them, sounding with a satisfying thunk as the attack was absorbed into the thick wood. Hiro's voice emerged from behind them, irritatingly calm.

"Do not allow yourself to be distracted. You are losing the initiative," he called from a relaxed kneeling position. Tilly realized that with the barriers in place, he could no longer see the approaching spear-wielders and jumped to move.

He randomly decided to break left, rounding the shelves to try to get ahead of his attacker, only to find one of the Shadow Hunters almost upon him. Tilly's *Dexterity* was high for his level, but the Shadow Hunter must have had a *Dexterity* build and reacted to his appearance much faster than Tilly planned.

"Librarian Arts, *Dictionary Inquiry, Endless,*" shouted Shuji from the other side of the shelves as Tilly dove to the ground under the spear wielder's thrust. Several *thunks* sounded from the other conflict followed by an outraged hiss, as Tilly felt the bite of his enemy's weapon rip into his thigh. The tip of her hooked spear elongated and twisted, slashing along Tilly's thigh mid-dive, and easily parted his protective leathers.

He attempted to roll upon landing, bringing up both his hatchets in a crossed block of the anticipated follow-up thrust. As expected, she was already upon him bearing down with her spear. Unfortunately, even though his instincts had been right, Tilly's block was woefully out of position, and her glazed black eyes flashed with elation as she stepped into her thrust.

Then a dictionary the size of Tilly's torso crashed into the shadow hunter's side, knocking her thrust off course. The dictionary was followed by another and then another, pounding the creature into the ground. Without hesitation, Tilly leaped toward the prone shadow hunter, some part of him reveling in the weakened position of his opponent. The burning sting of his wound drove up his adrenaline, and his breathing quickened.

His heartbeat pounded in his ears as he brought down both hatchets empowered with blue flame on his opponent's unprotected side. They landed like cleavers into the sides of soon-to-be butchered meat, and he gleefully ripped them back to hack again.

"More are coming, Jonathan Tillman," Hiro called in a flat voice. "That was only a test of our defenses. Ready yourself!"

Tilly looked down and saw that his opponent was already dead. He had been so caught up in . . . something, that he had been about to butcher a corpse. He stumbled back from the grisly scene with a creeping sense of horror. The throbbing in his ears reduced in volume, and he realized that the heat glowing in his chest was mingling painfully again with the pleasurable throb emanating from his side. He felt a tingling urge to abandon all constraint, like an itch at the back of his mind.

When had that started?

He looked toward the entrance and saw more forms emerging from the deep shadows pooling around the broken gate. His notification log was blinking, but he knew he didn't have time to read through it. Without pulling it up, he could sense that he had gained a level, so he just urged the free stat points toward *Wisdom*, hoping to stave off whatever was happening inside him. He hadn't done the math on keeping his [Resolute] Title, but he would worry about that later.

Ten more forms were disgorged from the shadow, slithering forth eagerly.

Shuji's voice broke into his stunned state. "As soon as they reach the outer perimeter, throw one or two flame strikes at the surrounding crates. Then take cover!" Tilly could tell he was yelling, but the words barely reached him. Nonetheless, he channeled more flame into his weapons and threw them hard at the perimeter. The charging warriors dodged easily, weaving around the crates that had caught fire. Tilly recalled and threw again, before ducking behind the large, newly erected barricades. He didn't know if his hatchets landed on target or not, but then he felt a huge woofing boom reverberate through the building. The silence effect muted most of the noise, but the force of the explosions rocked Tilly back, rattling the thick shelves.

The charging warriors, however, were thrown by the blast like rag dolls. Tilly looked over at Shuji aghast. He sure could have used something like that in the temple a few days ago! Shuji just looked back with a huge smile on his face.

"Those were our final gnomish explosives. Now we go out and finish off any still alive!" He punctuated his words with immediate action, rising from behind the barricade and swiftly jogging out among the flaming wreckage that was the front half of the room.

Tilly mirrored the move and saw that Hiro was already gone from his spot, choosing to take the opportunity to take down easy opponents as well. Then a voice cracked like a whip through the space. **"Enough."**

Tilly's eyes narrowed through the glow of smoldering debris and the haze of smoke. There at the shadowy entrance was a human-snake hybrid twice as large as the others with four arms coming off her distinctly female torso, each holding a scimitar with a barbed tip. Her eyes pooled with that same onyx-black substance, but none of her tattoos showed the running ink that the warriors before had displayed.

Level 58, Venom Assassin

Her eyes were focused in the middle distance of the debris field where Hiro stood over the dead body of another soldier. He turned toward her with a naked blade at the ready, darker even than her eyes.

"Always with your tricks and running. You should have died years ago on our glorious eastern march, yet here you stand caught hiding in another one of your warrens," she spat, revealing two wicked-looking fangs.

"I see your people have given in to the Abomination . . . Your Shadow Sunters are much weaker than they once were, Apepi," he replied cooly. The sound of a loud thud rang out from Tilly's right, and he shot a glance in that direction to see Shuji standing over another mangled snake warrior. He looked up sheepishly as he realized that his silence effect had been broken.

The snake lady however didn't even flinch as another subordinate was killed. "This is but another path to power," she said, lifting her arms to fully display her body covered with the dark, disturbing tattoos.

"With it, I have broken through the first bottleneck, and now it will be my pleasure to end you, *prey*," she said, her eyes glazing over with anticipation.

"You know nothing of power," the level 52 Samurai Lord declared, lazily bringing his sword back as if preparing to sweep it in front of him.

Her eyes flashed in response to his movement, and she sucked in air, inflating her abdomen to a disproportionately full state.

"Do not breathe in any of her filth!" Hiro shouted, before stepping forward and swinging his sword with unbelievable force. Tilly felt the blade pull the entirety of the room forward with its movement, before suddenly tearing free of the tension and ripping the air around it, creating a sweeping arc of jagged darkness.

"Waxing Shadow!" His shout reverberated through the space like the thrum of a particularly deep bass note.

Tilly watched stupefied as a jagged arc raced through the air toward the Venom Assassin, growing to the point where it could not be dodged. The assassin crossed all four of her blades in a blocking motion as the leading edge of the arc crashed into her. She seemed to catch the majority of the damage on the blades, but the attack did interrupt her inhalation, and she prematurely released an explosive breath.

Out of her mouth flowed a torrent of sickly-green smog populated with disturbing, wriggling black shapes. It rushed into the space filling the room and rolling toward Shuji and Tilly's position like an oncoming wave. Hiro exploded forward up out of the roiling smog with a downward swing aimed at the source of the breath attack, and Tilly flung his head around looking for nonexistent options to counter the atypical attack.

Shuji muttered something, and scattered papers rose up around him and started spinning around him, forming a vortex of disrupted air. The clangs of metal hitting metal started to fill the space, cutting off the breath attack. But the sound was far heavier than you would expect from a sword strike. These reminded Tilly of the time he had heard a steel I-beam accidentally detach from a crane and strike the steel frame of the building stories below.

Tilly took a deep breath in just before the wave reached him, ready to hold it for as long as possible, and was surprised to feel his armor changing once again to its yellow Sun Salamander form. With its protective covering over his mouth and nose, he hoped it would make some difference. His eyes began to water, and his exposed skin started to sting and then burn.

A shout of vindictive triumph sounded from the Venom Assassin, and Hiro grunted with pain before answering with a snarl of anger and a bellow laced with power. Blackness bled out from the epicenter of the conflict and overtook the poison area effect in moments.

Tilly felt like there was nothing more he could add to the fight besides hunkering down and trying to survive the increasingly deadly environment. He stumbled in the unnatural darkness toward the sound of a hacking cough in Shuji's direction. The snake woman's boastful voice filled the room. "You think I need to see you to kill you, little rabbit? How much longer do your companions have, do you think?" She cackled gleefully.

The only answer Hiro gave her was more crashing sword strikes, each one somehow sounding heavier than the last. He was obviously now holding his breath too, but Tilly was sure his *Endurance* was more than high enough to last a few minutes more. Unfortunately, *Endurance* was one of Shuji's lowest stats, and his coughing grew more ragged as Tilly approached. Tilly's chest had just begun to tighten with discomfort at the lack of oxygen, and he marveled at his body's new ability to take punishment. At the same time, something in this fog seemed to be trying to worm its way under his protective layers of armor, focusing on his side, where the throbbing sensation seemed to almost wriggle in anticipation.

Then, even amongst the clanging strikes, the sound of Shuji's shuddering exhale and the absent follow-up inhalation stood out in Tilly's dark world like a beacon. The soft, whirling sound of the paper vortex died, and Tilly groped forward for his companion.

Of all the things Tilly had experienced in his life, the sound of someone struggling to breathe still hit him the hardest. Particularly, he had fallen asleep far too many nights to the sound of a pair of small lungs fighting for air. It is a sound that comes back to you late at night when you are alone in your bed, too tired to sleep. A soundtrack that had played incessantly in the background of Tilly's life ever since he had lost his daughter to lung cancer. He hated hearing Shuji's last struggling breath.

He was the one who was supposed to die nobly in the line of duty. He had entered environments filled with carcinogens too many times to count and yet had never once popped positive on the yearly cancer screenings. Then, by some ironic twist of fate, his daughter had developed a persistent cough when she was six, and it had only gotten worse and worse over months.

Some deep part of himself, the wounded animal that had been backed into the corner too many times, snarled and lunged forward. He had always wished he could do something . . . anything to make a difference in his daughter's struggle, and now here he was in a magical land with his friend dying right in front of him!

It couldn't end here.

The warmth in his chest that accompanied his flame *Ability* compressed into a fiery pinprick before exploding into a nova of bright-blue heat. Suddenly the darkness in the area around him was banished, and blue flame rushed out from him in every direction, eagerly consuming all of the black shapes and patterns that had sustained and intensified the smog's effect. For just a moment, Tilly saw that the twisted black shapes around Shuji had formed some sort of eldritch creature, and it had been busy trying to shove itself into Shuji's mouth.

The flames pounced onto the creature, and it curled in on itself in the silent impression of a scream as it was consumed by righteous fire. The air left behind the fire's wake was hot, dry, and completely clean, and Tilly smiled as he heard Shuji take that long-awaited breath.

Suddenly he felt his brain being pierced by an ice pick, and his legs buckled beneath him. Darkness crept in on the edges of his vision as deep bone-wearying exhaustion overtook his body. The last thing he remembered seeing was **"Mana: -10%"** flashing at the top of his receding vision. Then a different kind of darkness overtook him. Not some magical domain, or the fretful darkness of nightmare-filled sleep.

Rather, it was the peaceful darkness of long-awaited rest. Only available to those who give all they have and hold nothing back. His body was forcing him to shut down after burning far past his reserves, and Tilly no longer had any will left to fight it.

CHAPTER THIRTY

Getting Better/Worse

Tilly groaned, rolling over on some padding that was doing a terrible job cushioning the hard stone floor.

"We need to leave soon if we are going to make the meeting." The deep bass of Hiro's voice cut through the fuzziness of Tilly's mind, and he looked up from his mat to find the Samurai Lord squatting down in front of him, with a focused scrutiny. He showed no obvious injuries, but his armor was damaged in a few places. The warehouse was now populated by about a dozen lapins, moving around, cleaning up, and packing whatever valuables were left in the wreckage.

"Where is Shuji? Did he make it?" Tilly blurted, his last moments before losing consciousness coming back to him in sharp relief.

At his question, the hard cast of Hiro's face softened, and a smirk might even have peeked out from the normally cloudy expression. "He will be fine, I think. He recovered shortly after I slew Apepi. He then proceeded to fuss over you much of the night. You activated an *Ability* without the mana to sustain it . . . a feat very few have managed and lived to speak of. Once it was clear you would recover, he went out to gather information and ready our people to flee in secret."

"How long was I out?" Tilly grumbled as he rubbed his temples trying to ease the phantom throbbing that cropped up at the memory of the excruciating pain he had experienced at the end of the battle.

A lapin moved up to them and offered both water flasks. Hiro nodded to him and took a deep drink, and Tilly matched him, suddenly terribly thirsty and hungry. He realized that he hadn't eaten the entire previous day, and wondered if that was due to his increased *Endurance*. Would he be able to forgo eating entirely at some point? Whatever the answer was, he was starving now.

"You have slept for fourteen hours. My people have arrived after hearing that the premises were secure, and they are now making it ready for our departure. There will be no trace of our battle by this evening."

At his words another lapin, this time a female lapin, approached with some boxes made out of bamboo. Hiro took his, and Tilly nodded in thanks before accepting his and lifting off the top. The inside was compartmentalized with a section for rice, more of the glazed carrot mixture, and some grilled fish. Tilly grabbed the accompanying chopsticks and started eating with fervor.

Hiro joined him at a much more sedate pace, occasionally pausing to eye the human who had become so entwined with the fate of his people. Tilly allowed himself the luxury of wondering out loud some of the many questions that had accumulated over the last week in between bites.

"So I get that we were attacked by the Cult of the Serpent last night. But it seemed like you knew them. Also, aren't they supposed to be in an army moving toward this city as we speak? How did these guys get in?"

"I have met Apepi and her hunters many times in battle. I once led the empire's mobile skirmishers. The satyr specialize in their square formations and are very difficult to beat in the open field. Something that my people found out long ago. But war is a mobile thing, and they have traditionally relied on a mix of irregulars and mercenaries to fill the mobility gap. Apepi fulfilled a similar role for the other side, specializing in assassination and marauding."

"How did you beat her? She was like six levels above you." Then, not being able to help himself Tilly reactivated **Identify** and was not surprised to note the change in Hiro's Identifier.

Level 53, Samurai Lord

"There is much you have yet to learn about power on Nephesh. We did not always have these numbers assigned to us, and while in some ways they can be helpful, in other ways they can be very deceptive. For example, you have two weapons, yet you wield them like an infant when you are not throwing them. I have a hard time imagining you defeating anyone with skill in close combat, no matter the level."

"I already tried to learn dual-wielding . . ." Tilly muttered, abashed.

"I mean no offense, Jonathan Tillman. Without basic instruction and the risk of real bodily harm, you can neither advance nor learn any significant martial skills. We will rectify this shortly. Your weapons and *Abilities* were otherwise very effective against our foes, especially considering their altered state . . ." At this he trailed off, once again looking at Tilly expectantly, as if waiting for some explanation. A part of Tilly twinged at the memory of the throbbing that had filled him mid-battle. He tried his best to cover over his feeling of unease with a follow-up question.

"Yeah, I would love some training with these," he said with a gesture at the hatchets looped into his belt.

"But what about how they got in, didn't you say that the Marcellus family would be sending people after . . . Uh, never mind, I figured it out on my own. The Marcellus family have some kind of alliance with the Cult of the Serpent and are working to undermine the empire any way they can."

If Hiro noticed Tilly's attempt at subtly changing the subject, he didn't show it. "Yes. We have suspected something of the sort for some time. They own the Purist Party completely and have used that influence for great personal gain over the past decades. In fact, as the emperor has declined, many have whispered in tavern corners that it is Augustus Marcellus that should next sit on the throne . . . They are fools, all of them if they think the serpent ever honors his agreements with anything more than a token effort."

"So where is the emperor? Is he dead? Sick? Can you even get sick here?" Tilly asked, excited to finally be scratching the itch of curiosity that had plagued him at every turn.

"He has not been seen in public in over a year. The Loyalists are completely silent on this subject, and no one has had success at divining their minds on the matter. I can tell you, however, that if he still lives, the emperor is ancient. He was old when I was born, and the stubborn goat had held on these last decades by sheer will. I know he was a just ruler once, and much of the filth we see infecting this empire is more a result of his decline without a successor than anything he has done." Hiro finished thoughtfully.

Then another lapin approached and whispered something indistinct to Hiro. He nodded in response and smoothly got to his feet. "Shuji sends word of the location of the meeting. We will leave in a few minutes. Prepare yourself, I will meet you at the entrance," he said before turning to leave. Then mid-turn he paused and looked back.

"Jonathan Tillman, we have declared you *friend* . . . We do not take such things lightly. I have entrusted you with many of the deep secrets of our people. If you need something, do not hesitate to ask," Hiro said, that same focused scrutiny coloring his gaze.

Tilly almost spoke up in response before catching a lump in his throat and settling for a nod of thanks. The emotions his burden was stirring up were just too raw . . . He would figure it out himself without bothering the already stretched leader. He had to.

Hiro nodded back and then moved over to some of his people working through the wreckage. Swallowing down his tide of emotion, Tilly pulled up his notification log and winced at the text sitting amongst battle notifications and level-up notifiers:

> *You have given in to Corruption's influence and have gained 7% Strength and lost 10% of your Wisdom.*
> ***Corruption Seed** influence now: 14%*

Sure, there were other things to read. He had finally been awarded dual-wielding for his hatchets. That had probably occurred during his dismal attempt at blocking and then opportunistic follow-up strike on his attacker. He had leveled up his **Ax Throwing** and what he had done at the end of the battle was a new *Ability* called **[Blue] Flame Expulsion**. Yet the elation that had typically followed these notifications in the past was muted.

> ***Corruption Seed** influence now: 14%*

What did this mean? How did he stop it? He figured that until he thought of something better he would dump every available point he could into *Wisdom* to try to offset this weird debuff while still keeping his [Resolute] Title. **Corruption** was his biggest long-term problem, but if he died in battle today it wouldn't matter much. Now that he had the insurance of negating one blow per day, he wanted to keep it. He was about to see if he could set the **Corruption** *influence* next to his mana and health on his always visible HUD when he felt suddenly drawn to take a bird's eye view of his character sheet and get a good feel for where he was going.

He laid a critical eye on his new character sheet.

> ### Jonathan Luke Tillman
>
> **Level:** *12 (26,000 exp to next level)*
>
> **Display Name:** *Tilly*
>
> **Race:** *Human*
>
> **Class:** *Son of Flame*
>
> **Titles:** *[Harbinger], [Resolute], **[Origin's** Champion], [Corruption's Host], [Trusted Gaijin].*
>
> **Health:** *100% (+1.2% per minute)*
>
> **Mana:** *100% (+0.8% per minute)*
>
> **Status Effects:** *Minor Corruption [Hidden]*

Stats:	Abilities:
Constitution: 12	-[Blue] Flame Strike: Channel the fire within you to strike at your opponents. Each strike leaves a smoldering ember at the point of impact and does damage over time. Ember damage is stackable. This Ability has been augmented by your mantle and does 200% more damage to Corruption.
Endurance: 71 (78.1)	
Dexterity: 28 (30.8)	
Strength: 10 (10.7)	
Wisdom: 13 (11.7)	
Intelligence: 8	-[Blue] Flame Expulsion: At the cost of 50% of your total mana, you channel the fire within you into a wave flowing from your center, impacting everything around you in a sphere. Ability scales with mana. This Ability has been augmented by your mantle and does 200% more damage to Corruption.

Equipment

Origin's primitive stone hatchets: +10% to Dexterity. **(Legendary, growth type)**

+Imbued Ability: Recall.

Origin's primitive leather armor: +10% to Endurance.
(Legendary, growth type)

+Imbued Form: Sun Salamander leather.

Skills:

-**Forestcraft** *level 12*

-**Identify** *level 17*

-**Cooking** *level 12*

-**Beginner Hatchet** *level 10*

-**Animal Processing** *level 9*

-**Stealth** *level 7*

-**Herb Lore** *level 3*

-**Ax Throwing** *level 9*

-**Dual-Wielding (Hatchets)** *level 1*

Titles:

[Harbinger]: *One touched by **Origin** to bring about change. "None may interfere." This and all other **Origin**-related Titles, Abilities, and items will be changed and seen as unremarkable by any deity or deity-aligned faction.*

[Resolute]: *Your Endurance stat is higher than all of your other stats combined. As long as this remains true, you may completely negate one fatal blow per day.*

[Origin's Champion]: *You have accepted the mantle of Champion from **Origin**. This will augment your skill and Abilities over time to reflect your new nature.*

[Corruption's Host]: *You hold within your body a Seed of Corruption. This entity's progress has been slowed by divine interference, but it will take every opportunity to grow until it has subsumed your will. Seed's influence: 14%*

[Trusted Gaijin]: *The highest honor that can be bestowed on a nonlapin by the ruling class. It marks you as "friend" to all lapinkind, and they will be immediately predisposed toward offering you any help they may have.*

Right now, his base stats added up to exactly equal to his *Endurance.* But he had not lost [Resolute].

I guess, I have to actually lose the lead to lose the Title.

He also saw how he had tapped out his mana reserve so easily at the end of the fight. **[Blue] Flame Expulsion** cost a whopping 50 percent . . . That was probably a great crowd-control opener, but not something to lean into deep in a battle. Unless he could get his hands on some mana potions or something! From what he had seen, these potions seemed more like luxury items than normal gear for the fighting classes.

He reviewed his build one more time . . . he had a magic physical range attack, he finally had a skill to improve his close-quarters combat, and he had just learned a crowd-control pushback. With his main stats, it looked like he was headed toward some sort of berserker-dodge-tank build with damage-over-time multipliers for the bigger enemies. Overall he felt like his class was starting to make some sense. Add in his growth-type armor and weapons, and he might stand a chance of making something of himself in this crazy world.

He set his empty box aside, took another long pull from the water flask, and got up, dusting himself off. He would soldier on, and do whatever he had to in order to save these people. That would start with finding a way to get as many people away from this insane naga army as possible.

He spotted Hiro standing in the shadow of the entryway talking to a couple of lapins in servants' clothing and jogged over. His mana and health were both at 100 percent, and for the first time in days, he felt pretty good . . . *really good.*

"If I keep this up, I might actually get strong enough to kick some bad guy ass," he quipped to himself as he moved easily through the remaining debris. He enjoyed the feeling of warmth that permeated his chest, as well as an energetic almost ticklish pleasure that was thrumming down his upper extremities from his side. Where the two sensations met in his lower ribcage, there was some slight discomfort, but that was to be expected after such a tough battle the night before.

CHAPTER THIRTY-ONE

The Cost of Compassion

Hiro handed Tilly a cloak at the entrance and threw a matching one over himself. "We do not know the capabilities of the enemy's network, but if there is even a chance the enemy thinks we are dead, it will be to our advantage." He then shrugged deeper into his hood and moved out into the deserted street.

They moved with their heads down, and Tilly tried to mimic Hiro's suddenly slumped shoulders as he lost some of the purposefulness of his steps and blended in with their surroundings. The streets became more crowded, and they found themselves in good company, moving through crowds of refugees, worn and weary from their hopeless flight.

Soon Tilly didn't have to try at all to effect a hopeless look to his gait as they moved through crowds of hundreds, then thousands of people doomed to whatever fate awaited them once the city fell. There were too many . . . Hiro's words from the day before seemed less cold and more pragmatic as Tilly tried to wrap his mind around the logistics of moving these people to some sort of extraction point. Or even if they succeeded, what would they do for shelter? What would they eat?

A ruddy shame began to burn on Tilly's face as his demands from the day before felt childish. He couldn't help but wince as he thought through just how much the Samurai Lord carried on his shoulders. The leader had been working toward his people's freedom for decades, and now Tilly, among others was putting even more responsibility on those bowed shoulders.

Hiro took him to the side of a building near a particularly busy intersection and grunted to him in a low voice, "Follow me at a distance. We will be entering a shop across the street, but we must not be seen together. I'll go in first, and you follow a few minutes after. We are to move to the back of the shop and request a view of some of the more exotic species."

"What kind of shop is it?" Tilly questioned back, trying to talk out of the side of his mouth as a patrol of guards moved through the crowd at the intersection.

"Ah . . . I should have warned you. We are meeting in the residence of the only other known human element in this conflict. She apparently has quite a few connections pertinent to our cause."

Before Tilly could ask another question, the guards shouted to a nearby group of hooded men standing in a huddle and demanded that they reveal themselves and state the nature of their business in the capital. Hiro's eyes hardened, and he nodded firmly at Tilly and then moved off around the edges of the crowd toward a line of shops.

Tilly's mind was reeling. The memory of the teary-eyed woman barging past him at the top of the Cura's steps came to the forefront of his mind. Much of the strangeness of his situation had just been shoved in a box at the back of his mind labeled "stuff I'll deal with when I am not about to die." But the prospect of meeting another human was suddenly extremely intriguing. Someone else who had been sent to this world from his own and would understand some of his questions on an experiential level!

Tilly growled softly to himself as he shoved the straining lid of the box back down and found a mental lock to fix the latch. He could have a party asking questions later when the possibility of genocide and slavery was no longer looming over the surrounding population.

He watched out of the corner of his eye as Hiro's figure approached a door particularly crowded with refugees to a shop with some sort of stylized plant emblazoned on a sign over the door. Tilly watched the storefront for a while longer and realized under prolonged observation, that the crowd of refugees around the shop were all adolescents or children, and some of them seemed to be much more alert than the other groups Tilly had seen populating side streets and alleyways throughout the city. Hiro entered without a problem, and Tilly remained on the corner, waiting.

After a few minutes, nothing had gone wrong, and Tilly decided to go for it. He crossed the street as unassumingly as possible. None of the children looked up at him or even acknowledged his presence, but Tilly could tell they were distinctly aware of him nonetheless. Another thing that became apparent as he moved through the small crowd toward the door was that they were sick. All of them.

He could hear it in the troubled wheezing breath of a little female satyr to his left. He saw it in a small gnomish boy who had a disturbing rash spreading over his neck and face. When the boy caught Tilly looking, he scowled up at him and then looked away, the sudden contraction of his skin causing a few of the sores to weep a dark gray substance. A hacking cough sounded behind him, and he suddenly couldn't just keep walking past them toward the door anymore.

His feet froze in place, and he found himself kneeling down in front of the wheezing satyr girl propped up against the storefront. Her eyes had a glassy sheen as they struggled to focus in on the large shadow that had just blocked out the afternoon sun. Tilly's medical training kicked in as he assessed rales in the lungs and an altered consciousness, which could be due to septic shock or a prolonged viral infection. He wished he had some antibiotics or fluids to give her, but he wasn't on the engine anymore, and he would have to work with what he had.

"Hey, sweetie . . . I can hear you having a little trouble breathing. Anything in this shop that can help you?" Tilly asked, the typical gruffness drained from his voice in the face of her plight. He realized he didn't care how impossible the odds were. Helping these people was something he had to try, or he wouldn't be able to live with himself. He couldn't stand by and let these people be conquered and sold into slavery.

The girl looked up at him confused, but the young gnomish boy with the rash chimed in next to her. "The lady inside has already tried all the normal things. None of them worked. She is keeping us around to try out some stranger reme- dies . . . But I don't think they will work either." Then his voice cracked in hope- lessness, covered over by anger.

"We came here to be safe from the Scale-bellies, but look where that got us. Sick and without family." Then the boy spit to the side, long-kept fury smolder- ing behind his eyes. When he saw Tilly looking over at him, he quickly looked away, wiping his shining eyes and refusing to say anything further.

Tilly choked up as he looked back around at the children huddled around the door to the shop. Some seemed watchful and were eyeing him with curiosity, while others like the little satyr girl were in a daze. The weight of their helplessness threat- ened to topple him over from his kneeling position and he reached for some- thing . . . anything he could do for them.

The ever-present fire that he now felt in his chest stoked itself. It didn't grow any hotter. Instead, it built up pressure until it overflowed up his throat and hov- ered, just behind his closed mouth. Following some deeper instinct, he took a deep inhale and then released his breath right into the face of the little girl. No flames appeared, but he did feel some drain on his mana and the feeling of heat bloomed in between their faces. Her short curly hair moved gently in response to his breath, and she closed her glassy eyes at the sensation.

The strangeness of his action hit him, and he looked around suddenly embar- rassed at the refugee children that were watching him. He got up, pretending that nothing had happened, and wished that he hadn't done something so strange to a little girl that had no idea who he was. She had already experienced enough. He quickly moved to the door, and the sound of the gnomish boy reacting to his odd behavior followed him in.

"Tinkerer's balls, that was weird. He just blew in Aurelia's face . . . looked like probably had stinky breath, if you ask me. Glad he didn't . . ."

Tilly hunched his shoulders at the comments as the door swung closed and found himself in an open room filled with plants. He had yet to get a chance to enter a magical shop, and he was not disappointed at finally getting to experience something truly magical. The large open room was chock-full of all kinds of plants, each housed in different sorts of magically maintained environments.

Different sections held different crystals above and below them, providing separate kinds of light and temperatures. One tuft of grass in a clay pot to his left was swaying in a breeze that did not exist; another blood-red flower seemed to tip its petals toward him as he walked past, delivering a distinct impression of hunger. Tilly suppressed a shiver at the thought of another plant trying to eat him and quickly moved through the maze of tables and shelves covered in plants to the back counter where a bored-looking female minotaur sat checking a scroll and grinding some seeds into a paste with a mortar and pestle. Tilly approached and drew back his hood.

"Hi, I was wondering where I could go to see some *more exotic species?*" he stated, making sure to get the phrasing just right.

"Gods, I do hate that Librarian of yours," she said, looking up from her work with a frustrated expression.

"I mean, we know there is another human in the city now, and there is only one lord of the lapin people . . . Do they think I'm an idiot, that I wouldn't know who to let through without a code phrase?"

"Well, I was ju—"

"No, no. Don't bother," she interrupted. "Just go through the door and up the stairs, mister spy man. The rest of the '*cabal*' is up there." She swung up part of the counter on a hinge and gave him access to the door to the back.

"Uh, thanks," Tilly said, a little of his frustration bleeding into his voice at the misunderstanding. He moved past the minotaur and through the doorway when he heard her voice call after him.

"Oh, and do not piss off my master. I don't care if you are both humans. She has enough on her plate, and we don't need another of your kind bashing in here and trying to mess everything up by *helping.*"

Tilly just scowled in response, not bothering to correct yet another set of assumptions about who he was and what he wanted based on his race alone. He moved up the narrow stairs on the left of the hallway that sat behind the doorway and noticed his notification icon blinking again. He toyed with the idea of bringing it up, but then he heard a harsh voice ring out from the other side of the door at the top of the steps.

"Why don't you stop being an ass and tell us, Cornelius! Is he alive or dead? How can we make any plan if the old monster is an unknown variable?" a voice demanded sternly from the other side of the door.

Notification log forgotten, Tilly opened the door to a simple large open room dominated by a center worktable that was surrounded by six contrasting figures.

They each turned to him as he entered, studying him with expressions ranging from curiosity to suspicion. Unfortunately, the latter expression was held by the speaker of the question Tilly had heard through the door.

She did not seem at all excited to see him, and her near hostility irritated him in a way that was difficult to pin down. Maybe it was the fact that she hadn't even noticed him yesterday, or the fact that he was the only other of her kind in the entire city, and yet she eyed him like he had just been caught eavesdropping or something. The feeling that accompanied being identified pinged in his mind, and he went ahead and identified them all back.

Directly to his right was Hiro, who stood erect with his arms crossed, nodding to Tilly in solidarity. Then there was Elder Kihei, who leaned on his staff wearing an expression of subtle amusement. Next to him was the other human, whose name he did not know. **Identify** labeled her as:

Level 32, Botanist Surveyor

She wore the same safari-style white blouse and pants with a long leather coat over it all that had a ridiculous amount of pockets. To her left was an impeccable armored satyr covered in scars. He only offered the human a cursory glance before turning back to the map covering the table.

Level 62, Bastion of the Empire

Next to him was a portly minotaur in relatively rich robes who was sitting comfortably in the only chair in the room, although it did not seem to be doing well holding him.

Level 49, Caravan Leader

The final member was an older satyr in formal-looking servants' garb, with a prominent badge trimmed in silver pinned to the front.

Level 41, Imperial Steward

"Why is he here again?" she stated in frustration, pulling the attention of the room back to her.

"He may mean something to you, Hiro, but he's only level 12. What could he possibly have to add to this discussion?" she said, leaning over the table and staring at Tilly like a full trash bin that no one wanted to take out. That was the last straw for Tilly. He was tired of all the unearned hostility thrown his way without him getting any chance to defend himself.

"Look, lady, I don't know what I did to piss you off, but I'm just here to help those kids out on the street, and if you—"

"Don't you dare speak to me about helping the children!" she shouted, suddenly furious. "I haven't slept in days, trying to find some way to beat this accursed malady that has infected them. You don't get to come in here—"

The door slammed into Tilly's back as it was suddenly flung open. He turned to see the female minotaur from behind the counter barging in carrying the little satyr girl in her arms. Following behind her legs was the same little gnomish boy from the front of the shop.

She laid down the little girl with exaggerated care on the table, and the whole room was filled with the crackling liquidy sound of her breathing.

"The children say *he* did something to her, and she started getting worse. She now has a fever which was not recorded in her documented symptoms," the minotaur said, looking over at Tilly with open hostility now roiling in her gaze.

"Yeah, hold your nose when he talks to you! I'm pretty sure it was his breath," the gnomish boy added unhelpfully.

CHAPTER THIRTY-TWO

Negotiations

S hit . . . " Tilly cursed under his breath.

"Just perfect!" the woman said, barging past the elder and Hiro to join her colleague over the child. She placed the back of her hand on the little girl's head and pulled it away immediately. She whirled around to face Tilly, her eyes flashing with rage.

"YOU! Tell me what *Ability* you tried to use, and its effects. Now," she demanded, thrusting the fingers of her right hand into his chest while reaching into one of her many pockets menacingly.

"I didn't use any *Abili*—" Tilly's agitated reply was cut off by the sudden sound of a deep racking cough from the girl. She was almost choking, and the minotauress lifted up her small convulsing form to attempt to give her a better angle to expel whatever she was dislodging.

The coughing was so violent that it completely derailed the conflict as all eyes moved toward the girl in concern, not even the hardest of their number able to witness the death of a small child with indifference.

With a final choking heave she spat out something dark and viscous on the table. It was terrible to imagine something like that in the girl's lungs. But upon expelling it, the girl displayed obvious relief, sighing and leaning back into the minotauress's arms and breathing easily for the first time.

Then to his horror, Tilly noticed the small black coagulations start to move on its own. Before he could even cry out, Hiro's midnight-black blade was flashing down on the table, destroying the substance and leaving a significant score on the work surface.

"What in the name of the gods is going on?!" the portly minotaur shouted, finally rising from his chair. The human woman looked back and forth between the stain and the little girl now breathing easily, clearly processing the new circumstances.

Tilly took advantage of the pause in the conflict to pull up his notification log and scan over the last few minutes.

Congratulations! *You have unlocked a new Ability:* **[Blue] Flame's Renewal.** *As a reward for unlocking an Ability not seen on Nephesh for several Epochs, you have been awarded the Title:* **[Hostile Environment].**

-**[Blue] Flame's Renewal:** *At the cost of 10% of your total mana, you impart the purifying nature of your indwelling flame, greatly increasing the recipient's ability to remove curses, poisons, and infections from their body. This Ability has been augmented by your mantle and does 200% more damage to Corruption.*

[Hostile Environment]: *Due to the unique nature of your physical body, foreign substances have a hard time persisting within your physical body. Poisons, Viruses, and Physical Curses will be 50% less effective against you. This Title scales with Endurance.*

Hiro took the time to look at each of the occupants in the room before sheathing his sword and calmly stating, "That is why he is in this room. He has shown remarkable ability against a new threat that we hardly understand, and if we are going to succeed in our endeavors, we will need him."

All the eyes in the room turned back toward Tilly as several things hit him at once. First, the sicknesses presenting in the children were being augmented by **Corruption**. Second, he was once again facing a problem way above his pay grade, and third, by some deus ex machina bullshit, he was the most effective means of combating this *thing's* influence on the world.

As each of these pieces fell into place, he had to fight down rage at the idea of their enemies using this tactic to bog down the healers and medicinal resources in the city. The Cult of the Serpent and their allies had clearly accepted **Corruption's** influence, and now even children were valid targets.

Amelia processed Hiro's words with a thoughtful groan, taking another look at the peacefully sleeping child.

"Why am I not surprised? I knew there was something magical influencing their debuff, but I could not dispel it, no matter what alchemical solutions I tried. The city's Temple of Light has been swamped for days with these cases, and they can barely dispel it, even with their focus on healing and purification," she wondered aloud, looking up from the girl to Tilly with understanding dawning in her eyes.

"I finally see why they think we bring calamity. It was bad before, but now with this infecting our weakest populations and you showing up just in time with some special *Ability* to beat it . . . I can't help but connect you with this turn of events."

At this, Hiro growled. "Think what you will, Mrs. Cooper, but the *Abomination* was assaulting our people a month before Jonathan Tillman arrived. In my weaker moments, I have begun to think there are still some gods left in this plane that care," he answered, matching the heat in her eyes with an authoritative coolness that did much to defuse the tension in the air.

"Look, I didn't ask for any of this. I'm just here trying to do my best. All I can tell you is that my system notifications call this stuff **Corruption**, and I have a strong feeling that it is breaking into this plane every place it can find purchase. I don't know how much the higher powers of this world know, but someone up there," he said, pointing up, "called **Origin** gave me a chance to come here and try to make a difference. I'm not proud of who I had become in my old life, and I'm trying to do better. So . . ." he said, thrusting out his hand, "My name is Jonathan Tillman. I was a firefighter back home, and now I'm something called a *Son of Flame* and because of events that transpired back near the lapin village, I am now supposedly a *Champion* of the deity **Origin** . . . I'm here to help."

He stood there awkwardly for a good three seconds as she blinked rapidly at the change of pace in the conversation before thrusting out her own hand and shaking his firmly, some of the icy regard in her gaze thawing.

"My name is Amelia Cooper, and a long time ago I was a landscape architect. Now I am a *Botanist Surveyor*. My *Abilities* can be used in combat, but are more geared toward harvesting, preserving, and capturing flora of the magical variety." She then let go of his hand. "I have been here for decades, and trust me when I say, you have a lot to learn if you want to survive, especially in your first year."

Tilly nodded. "Yeah, I got plenty of questions. What I can't seem to find is the time to get them answered," he responded wryly. Amelia quirked a smile and turned back toward the table.

"That is exactly why we are here today. We need to work together if any of us are going to survive the week, and it's time to start sharing notes. Heras, take the girl and boy back downstairs. Continue keeping watch for guards please," she said with finality, moving around her assistant and back to the worktable with the map.

Heras frowned in disappointment, but did as she was told, gently lifting the sleeping girl and shooing the complaining boy out the door. "Wait, does this mean I'm gonna have to smell his breath?" The retreating sound of his high voice traveled up the steps even as he went down.

"I think the Temple . . . will want to know . . . about this *Ability*," Elder Kihei chimed in.

"Exactly what I was thinking. As soon as we are done here, he can treat the children present and then move to the temple and after that the quarantine quarter," the Botanist responded without even looking over at Tilly.

"Uh, I'm all for helping, but that sounds like a lot of people. I'm pretty sure I can only do this *Ability* ten times before my mana runs out," Tilly cut in, more than a little perturbed that they were already trying to move him around like a pawn on a chessboard.

"He has been marked for death by the Marcellus family. He will stay with me, or someone of equivalent ability. They will find us again soon, and he is not ready to face what they will send next. Last night we fought Apepi and a full death squad . . . within the city walls."

At this, the scarred satyr soldier flinched as if struck, and the portly minotaur shook his head in disappointment.

"How many more do you think are within the walls?" the soldier asked gravely.

"Linus, it does not matter if they are within or without. We are a broken nation already. When their army arrives, they will find the way open to them. Marcellus, the Purists . . . others whom we do not know. They will all turn at the perfect moment, willing to be puppets for just a morsel of more power."

At this, the minotaur bristled and half rose out of his chair.

"Well, that is exactly why we are leaving tomorrow! The Great Caravan will leave, no matter what your Cura has to say about it. It is clear that there is no protection here for us, so we will move on. We are mobile people, and the Grey Steppe is more than enough to stop the snakes."

"We all know you are leaving, Cephalus. My question remains. How many will you take with you?" Amelia shot back in frustration.

"All of our people of course. But more than that I cannot say. Supplies are tight in the city, and we are no charity," Cephalus said, wringing his fat hands. Whether in fear or greed, Tilly could not say.

"We are authorized to open the imperial treasuries at this time to any and all efforts to defend the empire and her people. Can we convince any of the free companies to stay and fight?" the formally dressed satyr added in, speaking for the first time in Tilly's hearing.

"That is very . . . ah, generous of you. We will take as many as we can through the Steppe, but our people will not die in a pointless fight. Lord Hiro has said it. This city will fall. All we can do is save what we can while we still have a chance," Cephalus responded, sorrow coloring his tone for the first time.

"Who exactly . . . has authorized this . . . old friend?" Elder Kihei asked.

"You understand the fractured nature of the Cura . . . So we have been sworn to secrecy until this time. I am permitted to say this: His Majesty knows he has failed in his duties. He is not gone, as some have claimed. Rather he is husbanding all of his remaining strength to spend it when it is most needed. It is with his blessing that I am attending this meeting. We cannot save the city. But we will do what we can to save her people. Hiro, we know that duty alone has bound you to the throne, and your duty is almost up. But the throne calls upon your honor one last time. Take as many of the helpless that remain as you can. Consider a final order from your emperor."

Hiro took in the request, his resting frown deepening into something truly weighty, and Tilly saw the terrible conflict of duty and passion play out behind his eyes.

"I knew when he approved our venture there were strings. That old schemer has been planning for this for some time . . ." Hiro responded heavily, realizing that he had no choice but to risk the remainder of his people to save the others.

"He had many plans, and unfortunately they have come to naught. In the end, you have proved to be more loyal than many of the founding families of the empire, and for that he is sorry. But he does promise that a reckoning is coming," the old satyr followed up, attempting to placate the Samurai Lord on some level.

But at his words, Hiro's eyes only hardened. "I will obey, but here are my terms. One, my people will be first in line to leave. Two, I leave shelter and food as your problems to solve for however many make it through to our lands. In turn, your element will be treated as a third member state of the confederacy we will form. I offer you the same terms as the honu. Is that acceptable to all present?"

CHAPTER THIRTY-THREE

Heavy Breathing

Hiro took the time to make eye contact with each member of the meeting, waiting for their response.

Elder Kihei smiled slowly. "This is a terrible end . . . but also a hopeful beginning . . . for our peoples. The link . . . will be ready . . . by tomorrow evening." Hiro nodded in thanks to the ancient honu. He then turned to Amelia.

"At this point, my chief concern is the children. I am already liquidating my stores with Cephalus, and I will travel through the portal to support the refugees. I have been working on some ideas for the food shortage. The Cura was unwilling to partner with me, but perhaps this is better in the end."

Cephalus just waved away the look, knowing that he had very little to do with their alternative escape.

Linus, the scarred soldier, held Hiro's gaze for an intense moment and then replied, "My men, although spread thin, are moving through those that shelter in the city to find leaders among them. We are forming a militia of those willing to fight a moving battle through the streets. The Bastions will not flee. We will make our end here, and those who betrayed us will pay dearly before the day is done. Everyone not able or willing to fight will be ushered to the Grand Promenade. They do not know why they are being called to assemble, but I am afraid our plan will become painfully obvious as the day goes on. Hopefully, they will be close enough to the teleport hub that they can escape before we are broken. As of now, everything should be ready by tomorrow evening. We will miss all who choose to hide or ignore our warnings . . . but it is the best we can do," he said gravely, his hard eyes colored with bitterness and his shoulders squared against the terrible weight of the duty that lay before him.

Hiro then turned to Cornelius, the representative of the emperor, who had watched the reactions of the rest of those in the room carefully. He took a deep, tired breath and addressed the group.

"There are several treasures that will be gifted to this new confederation by the emperor. The staff of the palace will also stay with the city, as will the true loyalist families. We have our own end to make. But know that you have the emperor's gratitude, and we consider your obligation to the throne fulfilled upon the completion of this last request."

At that, some of the hardness in Hiro's eyes mellowed, and he slowly looked over to Tilly, speaking for the first time. "Despite what others may think, there are many ways to help. It is my opinion that healing the sick only for them to die tomorrow is not a wise course of action. However, you are no one's property. What do you choose to do with the remaining time?"

Tilly considered Hiro's words carefully and the threat of assassination that was sure to follow him leading up to the escape. He looked over at Amelia, who had schooled her face to an expression of indifference, and thought again of the children huddled around her door hoping for help. He wondered, for a moment, what drove her almost desperate need to save as many of them as she could.

In the end, even if it didn't make any sense, he seemed to be the only one who could do something about this new sickness. Sure, he could tag along with Hiro and probably do some good before the flight through the portal. It was the sensible and safest action in a very dangerous environment. But "sensible" and "safest" had never been the kind of words he used to make decisions.

He had spent his life running into burning buildings, not away from them.

"Lord Hiro, I appreciate your offer of protection, but for better or worse, I know exactly what I need to do to make a difference in this fight. If I can even free up one parent from having to carry a sick child, and they make it out because of it . . . Then it's worth it. It may not be much in the grand scheme of things, but it means a lot to me," Tilly said, matching the intensity of Hiro's gaze with fire of his own.

Hiro nodded slowly. "Then we will be parting ways. I will go to gather my people and get them as close to the square as possible. You will find us *before* the portal activates. Do not throw away your life saving those who are doomed. Save as many as you can, and then find us, my *friend*."

"I'll be there. Hopefully, with a thousand extra refugees in tow," Tilly replied, a shit-eating grin cracking his serious expression.

"In that case, I must be going," Hiro answered.

"My people and I are tasked with creating an entirely new nation, and we have a day to make ready," he said, before bowing to the room and making for the exit.

Following his lead, the others started to move toward the door, all going to make their rushed preparations before the operations tomorrow.

The minotaur handed Amelia a fat purse as he moved to leave. "My people will be by later today to recover your goods, and we will care for them as you have taught us. Take care of my third cousin, *sister*." Then he gave her a quick but powerful hug, which she endured with a huff, and then moved his considerable girth through the door.

Elder Kihei moved past them at a sedate pace, pausing to lay his ancient hand on Tilly's shoulder.

"Do not throw away . . . what is not yours . . . I see in you a hunger for worthiness . . . you might find it in death . . . but do not pay . . . such a price . . . lightly." He then nodded at Amelia with a grandfatherly smile and moved through the door.

The remaining two satyrs had huddled together in the corner for a few last-minute words, but seeing that everyone else had left, they looked up and moved past the humans to the door. The soldier just nodded at them both. The elder servant, however, paused at the door and looked back.

"Seldom has an empire of our small size held two humans at once. I have always thought that a boon, but you two are a credit to your race. Remember us as what we were, not as what we have become," he pronounced solemnly, the duties of the day taking a greater toll on him than they had on any of the others. He left the room with those words, his shoulders slumping for the first time as his pride bent before the terrible evidence of his people's failure.

"He is right, you know. When I first set up my business here twelve years ago, this was one of the most prosperous nations on the border of the Steppe. It was nothing compared to its glory days, but it still held to the ideals that made it great. No one saw such a rapid decline coming, and even with the losses of the last year, there was still this sense that the empire would continue, as it always had . . ." Some of the stiff determination she had exuded gave way to sorrow as she watched the empty doorway, before turning back to Tilly with a sigh, abruptly changing the topic.

"So, you can use that *Ability* ten times before your mana is exhausted?"

"That's what it says . . . Is there any way I can just shoot my screen over to you?"

She looked at him incredulously, as if the fact that he had been here for less than a week finally set in. "No. Some have *Abilities* to see part of another's character sheet, but it is extremely invasive. How long does it take you to regain your full mana pool?" she said, moving to another part of her work room, and starting to shuffle through some drawers.

Tilly gave his *Wisdom* regen a glance and did some quick math. "Probably a little over an hour and a half."

The *Botanist* dropped what she had been looking at and looked back over at him in shock. "Even at level 12 that is dismally low. You must be pouring almost all of your points somewhere else." She looked him up and down.

"It's not *Strength*, certainly not *Intelligence* . . ."

". . . *Endurance*," Tilly muttered in exasperation.

"I did what I had to to stay alive. I may have only been here for a small amount of time, but I've seen enough shit to fill a decade, and then some."

Her incredulous expression rose into mild surprise. "At least you will be tougher to kill than anyone expects at your level. Here," she said, pulling out a terrycloth sack from one of her pockets and handing it to him.

"I have a few tricks to help, but they are not overly powerful, so we best get started now." The sack felt like it had a mixture of dried herbs and seeds in it, and Tilly was about to sniff it when she slapped down his hand.

"Not yet, you oaf!" She sighed as he snatched his hand back, more out of reflex than from any pain.

"Do it when you are out of mana, or you will waste its effect."

Holding it away from his face, Tilly looked down at the sack and activated **Identify**.

---

*You have **identified** a Shaman's Casting Aid. When smelled this item will provide a temporary 200% increase to the user's Wisdom. This increase only lasts 100 breaths.*

She had already moved past him and was halfway down the steps when he looked up from reading. She turned back and gestured for him to get moving. "Come on, we have people to heal, assassins to avoid, and no time to waste."

He followed after the assertive Botanist as she descended the stairs brimming with renewed purpose. By the time he made it to the bottom, she was already giving her assistant orders. "Heras, please bring in the children and lock the front door."

The minotauress moved with a grunt of affirmation toward the door and opened it, giving indistinct instructions to the children outside.

"Can you help me with this? *Strength* is most definitely *my* lowest attribute," she said, already pushing against one of the center display tables holding several plants. Tilly moved next to her without a word and added his weight to the move, slowly shifting the table to the side, and opening up the center of the shop.

"Shame you have to give up this shop. It's one of the coolest and most magical places I have seen so far," Tilly said, straightening from the lift and looking around at the different magical enchantments and crystals.

"Yes, well Cephalus is giving me a family price on the goods, so it's not a total loss, but I will miss this little shop. Some of these plants have quite the story attached to them," she said, looking around wistfully as the children finished filing into the room. The process was difficult to watch as many of the more alert children had to help the weaker ones walk through the door.

"Alright children, I want you to bring the ten worst cases to the front. Cog, that includes you," she said as the gnomish boy immediately started shuffling to the back of the group.

"Young man, I have seen just how far that rash goes, and how you tear up every time something brushes against it," she admonished the boy as he hung his head and reversed course to the front, grumbling the whole way.

"Alright, but I'm not going first. I want to see a few others survive the smell before I try it myself . . ."

Some of the others looked around in fear at his words, and Amelia again spoke up, handling the crowd like a pro. "Now, now. I would hate to see a member of the proud gnomish race reduced to cowering in fear behind some of these gentler peers. Why, on your intellectual integrity alone, you should be first in line to test this for the others," she pronounced in an exaggerated tone.

Tilly watched, impressed, as conflict bloomed across the boy's face, before he screwed it up in resolution, causing some more of his lesions to ooze. "Fine. Hurry up, before I change my mind."

Suddenly the whole room was looking at Tilly again, and he was in the uncomfortable position of having to exhale in the face of a child in front of an audience. He had honestly never thought much about his breath. He kept a relatively clean mouth typically . . . But there hadn't been much of a chance to floss the last couple of days and—

"Come on!" Heras said, giving Tilly a healthy slap on the back. Tilly shot her a look before straightening up and taking a deep inhale, feeling the fire in his chest respond to his intentions and begin to kindle that same intensity he had felt earlier.

He felt the dip in his mana as simmering heat accompanied his exhalation and hit the boy right in the nose. The young gnome wiggled the facial feature without opening his eyes as if he felt a tickle. Then his expression relaxed into a look of surprise. "It actually didn't smell that bad, guys. Kind of reminded me of the furnace in my dad's worksho—"

He didn't get a chance to finish his sentence as his eyes rolled up into the back of his head and he collapsed on the floor, shaking. Several of the watching children cried out, and the rest just watched in horror as all the open sores on his rash began to sizzle and then smoke, releasing a horrible stench. Amelia quickly crouched down to the boy's side and lifted him in her arms, looking up at Tilly inquiringly, but all of Tilly's attention was on the small cloud of noxious fumes forming on the ceiling above the boy.

He could faintly see shapes wriggling in the twists and turns of the smoke, and without thinking, he imbued his right hand with a blue flame and leapt into the air, striking at the thickening cloud. It caught like a match to a hydrogen balloon, and instantly the smell was gone. Tilly looked around the room as they considered him in a new light, and he suddenly felt bashful again.

Once the children saw Cog breathing easily with small nearly healed scabs marking the place where he had previously sported the grayish, oozing rash, they were a lot more willing to be treated, and Amelia had to shout a few times to settle down the commotion.

"Alright, so once expelled, this substance has some form of malicious sapience . . . Heras, you handle anything physical, so Mr. Tillman can save his mana," Amelia directed.

"My pleasure, mistress," Heras growled, pulling a maul out from nowhere and standing at the ready. Tilly couldn't help but note that it was the first time he had seen her smile.

"Mr. Tillman, if you would be so kind as to self-administer the *Shaman's Aid*. That will keep us going along at a good pace, and please pay attention to your use of air once you take it. I believe it works off ambient mana inhalation, and you can stretch it as far as you are able to slow your breathing," she informed him as she lifted little Cog and moved him over to the side of the open space to lie comfortably and recover.

Tilly pulled the sack to his face and took a deep breath in, registering a scent that reminded him of a foggy early morning in a grassy field, still wet with dew. He felt his soul solidify slightly at the scent memory as his place in the world felt minutely more clear.

"Very good, Mr. Tillman, now slow your breathing as much as possible, and we will see just how many of the children we can move through before you run out."

They did just that, setting a pace of about one child per three minutes, with Tilly able to slow down his breathing to just three breaths a minute, probably due to his *Endurance*. With only a few deep breathing breaks, he made it through the rest of the group of twenty in under an hour. The whole exercise reminded him of bottle conservation drills back in the fire department. They would bleed the bottles down to their last 10 percent of air, and then see how long they could last on what should be three to five minutes of breathing time.

In the end, he had bottomed out his mana and recovered it several times, making sure not to overdo it like he had last night. He did, however, finish with a throbbing headache, and he gratefully took the tea Amelia handed him when offered. He looked around in quiet satisfaction at the children, all either resting or slowly coming to. They looked completely different than they had an hour ago, and Heras's maul was covered in a fading black stain. It looked like she enjoyed the smashing much more than a botanist's assistant had any right to if you asked Tilly. But who was he to judge?

He took his first sip of tea and immediately felt a cooling sensation begin to move up his head and into his frontal lobe, easing the migraine considerably.

"Wow, thanks. This stuff is incredible," he said, looking over at Amelia with gratitude.

"We have one day to cure as many people as possible, and it is going to take every alchemical and herbal trick I have to keep you going," she replied, with a slightly predatory smile.

Tilly missed her expression completely as a light bulb went off in his head.

"You have a plant shop, and you have the **Alchemy** skill . . . Do you by chance have an **Herb Lore Codex**?" he asked, a smirk curling at the corners of his mouth.

"I have become something of a plant enthusiast myself in my time here, and I have made a discovery that could change Nephesh as we know it." The smirk bloomed into a full-on idiot grin as he imagined her reaction to his achievement.

Amelia's eyes lit up at the possibility of a new genus or species discovered on this vast plane. Even after all these years, she had never grown tired of finding something novel or new and entering it into the magical tome. She'd had the honor of making nine discoveries herself in her time on Nephesh, and had to admit she was impressed that the new arrival had found something in only a week.

CHAPTER THIRTY-FOUR

Triage

The combination of healing so many children and then getting to talk about his favorite discovery on Nephesh left Tilly feeling giddy. Amelia's smile had ratcheted up to an uncomfortable level as Tilly described his fortuitous encounter in the forest and his discovered uses for the unknown magical tree. Her encouraging smile becoming something manic by the time she took out the tome to add his discovery to the **Codex**.

Tilly's eyes widened as he watched the book expand in size as she pulled it from her pocket. The cover was embossed with golden leaves and vines. Arcane symbols faintly shined on the surface of the material, which was a cross between leather and bark.

"And you are sure that your **Herb Lore** skill gave it no other uses?" Amelia asked at the end of the explanation, reluctantly jotting down his entry into the Plane-Spanning magical codex. It turns out her name would be marked next to the entry for every other owner of a **Codex** to see as long as the magic of the book accepted it as valid. At the last flourish of her reed pen, the page she was on flashed, and her words gained the golden sheen to match the others. Her eyes lost focus, and as she pulled up her status screen, her face lighting up in surprise, then chagrin.

"It seems that this entry was enough to finally get me to level 33 . . ." she muttered reluctantly.

"Awesome! Glad to help!" Tilly responded happily, looking down at the page in wonder as the Codex magically generated a simple sketch of the tree and its known uses. He completely missed the coloration in Amelia's cheeks as the final line generated for the whole community of Alchemists and Herbologists to see.

-Discovery inputted by Amelia Cooper, Botanist Surveyor.

Tilly looked up in almost childlike wonder as she closed the book quickly and shoved it back into a pocket. She didn't even look down as the book shrank to size and fit into the small opening. It was full-on, Hogwarts-level magic, and Tilly was tired of pretending that this kind of stuff was normal.

"I know we have a lot to do, but I have to ask. What is up with your jacket?"

Her eyes refocused from working on her private screens as she assigned her new stat points. "Well, this was a gift from some dear friends. When I came to Nephesh, I was deposited on the Grey Steppe, and they were having a lot of problems with an invasive species of plant from a certain irresponsible neighbor. A lot of my early work was in figuring out how to combat this incursion. Through that, I fell in with the caravans, and I was able to help them out of a very tight situation with an *Endless Locust Swarm* event that appears every thousand years or so. They were generous enough to give me this as a reward, and it has been invaluable in my work collecting and propagating plant life from many different biomes," she answered, her eyes taking a far-off look as she pulled on memories from a previous season of life. One filled with travel and adventure.

As she spoke, Tilly tried to gauge her age but was unable to get a clear read. She had an air of maturity about her but showed no wrinkles or gray hair. Without thinking he blurted out his next question while the minotauress assistant busily arranged the children and prepared the shop to be cleared out.

"You said you have been here for decades, but you look like you are in your late thirties . . . Do we stop aging when we get here?" he asked, excited to finally get some answers from someone who could understand just how crazy all of this was. In response to his question, she unconsciously moved some of her hair out of her face, and straightened out her jacket.

"Well, when I arrived I was in my mid-thirties, and I have been here for around twenty years. From what I understand leveling slows the aging process, and as long as you keep doing it, you don't age very much at all. At some point, I think you reach a kind of immortality, but it is well north of level 100. If you will excuse me, I need to grab a few more things from the back before we head to the temple," she said before abruptly turning and heading toward the back door.

Tilly nodded, oblivious to the emotion implied by her actions. He was far too busy thinking through the possibility of barely aging for a hundred years. He had already noticed that he no longer felt any of the aches and pains that had settled into his body after a lifetime of abuse. Plus, as he leveled he continued to get faster and stronger. He wondered how old he looked to the others . . . but it was hard to tell when it was your own face. He also had yet to see a mirror in his travels, and thinking of his appearance caused him to take a surreptitious sniff of his underarm. He hadn't had a chance to bathe in days.

A focused sniff made apparent what his nose blindness had kept hidden from him.

He was ripe.

Something flew at him from his periphery, and his new reflexes didn't save him from being hit in the face by another cloth sack of herbs that emitted a pleasant fragrance. He did manage to catch it on the way down from its initial impact and looked up to find the minotauress watching him from behind a display.

"Rub that one wherever you deem appropriate. It will help. I don't think anyone else will say anything, but my kind has a very good sense of smell, and . . . well, just do us all a favor," she said, looking back down at the goods she was packing. Thankfully most of the children were still out from their ordeal, but Tilly did hear a snickering laugh that sounded distinctly like a certain gnomish boy from behind him.

He refused to look at anyone as he reached under his leathers and rubbed the sewn sack on his underarms like deodorant mumbling to himself, "Sorry if I've been a little busy trying to keep everyone alive."

Then Amelia returned from the back with something that looked like a fanny pack, full to bursting.

"I see you don't have much in the way of equipment, I used to wear this before I got my jacket. It has minor weight reduction and expansion enchantments in it, as well as a durability charm. I have loaded it up with some of the basics. It should attach to your leather pants and still benefit from the overhang of your jacket," she said, looking up from stuffing the last items into the magical storage space. Tilly quickly pulled his arm out from under his jacket and hid it behind his back.

Amelia handed him the magical storage item and then looked over at her assistant.

"Heras, thank you for looking after the children. For those that don't have a group to return to, can you make sure they make it to the lapin rally point near the hub tomorrow?"

"On my honor, mistress, we will be there," she responded, patting her maul happily, an eager smile plastered on her bovine face. Tilly wasn't sure what about the next day's events made her smile, but he was glad someone was having a good time.

"Well, if I'm going to heal the whole city, we better get started, huh?" he said, trying to be friendly, but somehow coming across as awkward. His words caused Amelia to rub her eyes, and he remembered her statement about not sleeping for several days. He figured things like that would be more and more possible as his *stats* increased, but he couldn't imagine her being particularly high in *Endurance* as a Botanist Surveyor.

"Yes, we will do everything we can before tomorrow evening and pray that the enemy does not arrive before then. I hope you are ready, Mr. Tillman. I don't think you will gain any *experience* from this work, and you will be bottoming out your mana quite frequently over the next twenty-four hours. I will do all I can, but . . . it will not be pleasant. Some of my accelerants have some difficult side effects."

At her words Tilly's expression firmed, resolving into something much harder than he typically showed in social settings.

"Ma'am, at this point, we are talking about saving lives. I will do whatever it takes to help these people, and I won't stop until we are down to the wire." He followed up his words by strapping the small pack on the back of his belt line under his jacket, finding that it fit just like she said it would. Hopefully, it would last longer than his last piece of storage equipment.

Three cheers for a fantasy fanny pack!

Amelia took on a considering look as she processed his reply. "You know, Mr. Tillman, I have met three other humans in my time on this plane, and they have each proved to be repulsive or unbelievably selfish. Forgive me for my initial reaction. I just expected more of the same power-hungry mania I have found in our kind once we arrived here," she said, putting her hands on her hips and letting some appreciation bleed into her tone.

Tilly took a moment to bask in the acknowledgment of his choices so far, feeling a thrum in his veins that was becoming more familiar. Even with everything going on, he felt good. Better than he had in a long time. Subtle waves of pleasure throbbed up from his side, and he unconsciously adjusted his jacket to cover the scar that no one else could see. He was willing to admit that he had always been drawn to the idea of rescuing people and no small part of that was the attention he would occasionally get for his acts of service. Anyone who pretended otherwise wasn't being honest with themselves.

"Thanks for saying that, but I'm nobody perfect," he demurred, managing to school his smile. His response seemed to strike an unpleasant chord in Amelia, and as she heard it, she winced and looked away.

"None of us are, Mr. Tillman . . . Our kind doesn't get sent here for being perfect," she muttered darkly before straightening up, her face returning to the businesslike expression he was beginning to associate with her coping mechanism for stress.

"You are, of course, right. If we are going to make any difference, we might as well start sooner rather than later. How is your mana?"

"Almost refilled . . ." Tilly answered, struggling with whether or not to follow up on her last statement before deciding that it really wasn't his business, and it would be selfish to ask any more questions considering the time crunch.

"Good. Let us be on our way. Heras, I will see you tomorrow, fate willing," she called, moving toward the door and grabbing a cloak that hung on a peg there. Tilly followed suit, drawing up his hood around his features and closing the front of the cloak for as much privacy as he could get in the late afternoon sun.

"Bye, kids," Tilly said, turning and waving at the few children that were awake. The first little girl he had healed looked back up at him silently but after a moment gave him a wave and a brave smile. He could tell she felt better, even if she wasn't sure exactly what had happened to her over the last few hours. Her smile and the thought of what she had endured and would still endure before the week was over dampened some of Tilly's good humor. The rush of saving people felt a little more shallow in the context of the little girl and her struggles. He may have cured her ailment, but did she even have a family to go back to? He realized that her best-case outcome for the next few weeks was a life of hunger and makeshift shelter.

He followed Amelia out the door, and couldn't help but grow introspective. The siren song of the pleasurable feeling radiating in the background of his mind dulled.

What am I trying to prove and who am I trying to prove it to? Why did I really leave Hiro's protection?

Amelia lost herself in the crowd of people struggling through different stages of grief and hopelessness, and Tilly had an easy enough time keeping up with her brisk pace. He had a much more difficult time working through the complicated emotions the little girl's smile had brought to the surface. He tried to pin down the doubts he was feeling, but it was difficult. It felt like he kept getting lost in a fog of apathy. He knew something was nagging at him, but a louder internal voice urged him to keep moving and not worry about it.

Why wonder about all this? Just do what you do: Run in, save as many as you can, and get out. That's what heroes do.

Tilly was a simple guy, and spending time in self-reflection was not something he had given much time to. That little girl's smile had touched on deeper questions than he was prepared to answer. Was what he was doing even going to make a difference? Was Hiro right? Was this all for his own vanity?

He loved helping people. He always had. Seeing someone with an obvious problem and getting to solve it right then and there had always done it for him. It was the complicated problems he dreaded. The ones he felt powerless to solve that had always lodged in his brain like splinters.

House fire? Easy. Put the wet stuff on the red stuff. Simple as that.

A homeless schizophrenic man who had the police called on him because he kept rubbing his bloody hand on a gas station window? No clue how to help.

For some reason, those sorts of situations had hooked into his mind and never left. That man hadn't wanted to go to the hospital and refused to listen to the police when they asked him to stop his manic vandalism. He wouldn't even listen to Tilly and the other medics as they tried to put bandages on his injury. The man had screamed and smirked as he waved his bloody hand around. In the end, he had been arrested, not because it was what was best for him, but because there were no other options.

Those were the calls that had stuck with Tilly through the years. He had found himself more and more frustrated and jaded by the state of the world and the ones left in the margins, who wouldn't or couldn't get help. His daughter's fight with cancer had almost been icing on the cake after ten years in the department. Negative emotions and memories started to well up from deep in his chest as his thoughts started to spiral. The fog of cheerful apathy started to thin.

Just do what you can to help people. Make a difference. Don't worry about all of this other stuff.

His simple driving directive seemed more and more shallow as he thought about it. It had defined his past life, and apparently, he had barely broken even on the "cosmic scale." Just like before, he was shoving down everything too big to handle, pushing forward from one emergency to the next. Unprocessed emotions from his past failures and his current circumstances built in intensity beneath his chest, and suddenly, amid his downward spiral, he noticed the fire in his chest had roared to life in response to something . . .

He stopped walking, all of his attention taken by the conflict raging in his torso between the positive apathetic fog and his fiery emotional response to the unnatural suppression of his internal environment. The apathy promised relief from the pain, pushing with a subtle throbbing pleasure that had been emanating from his side almost nonstop since he had awoken. It urged him to keep going, keep moving. Don't stop. Don't think.

The girl's smile and the feelings it had touched had awakened his internal flame. The thing that had been building in him since his first hours on Nephesh that he had come to associate with the source of his burgeoning magical powers. This was the place that had been augmented by the Blue Flame on the altar. The magic that he pulled on to purify each of the children.

Now that he was paying more attention, he could feel it actively trying to consume the pleasurable influence of **Seed** in his side.

At some point, Amelia noticed that she had lost her companion, and looped back around to find him standing still with his eyes closed, an expression of intense concentration on his face.

"Johnathan. Are you ok?" she said, some concern entering her tone, even as she looked around to make sure they weren't garnering too much attention. Fortunately for them, the surrounding refugees were good camouflage when it came to losing attachment to time and place.

Tilly's eyes flew open as he returned to the present. He looked around abashedly and collected himself before whispering, "The last few days have been a lot . . . I'm good, I promise . . . I can explain later."

She watched him for a moment more, searching for any further signs of instability before nodding and taking him at his word. "Very well, the temple is a few blocks away. You can't miss it. The steps and street in front of it are crowded with the worst cases in the city."

Knowing that he was so close to the people who needed his help grounded Tilly, but this time he made sure not to lose track of the feeling of conflict that was raging in his torso. He wasn't going to let that go again. He opened his stat sheet and grabbed the Title he had almost forgotten about and mentally put a tracker up under his health and mana.

Corruption's influence: 14%

"I'm ready. Let's make the most of whatever time we have left," Tilly responded. Amelia nodded firmly, not noticing the grim turn Tilly's tone had taken. She turned back and began to move through the crowd again. Tilly followed her, hiding his tightly clenched fists in the sleeves of his robe. His newly realized emotions simmered under the surface of his granite will.

CHAPTER THIRTY-FIVE

The Sick and the Dead

B efore they turned the corner onto Temple Row, Tilly was hit by the smell. It was more than the funk of hundreds of unwashed bodies kept in one place for too long. The air was thick with a tang of rot that settled cozily around Tilly's nose and would not dissipate no matter how he tried to cover the orifice. He marched forward, dutifully following Amelia's vector as she angled for the corner of a building that sat on the intersection of Devotion and Temple Row.

Soon after the smell came the sounds of shouting,

"Please, she is dying!"

"Light's Mercy, is there no one left to perform the *Purification*?"

"Where is the Lady Light now that we need her?!"

Tilly stayed in stride with Amelia, and they slowed as the temple came into view. There were hundreds of petitioners in the street around the entrance to a squat stone structure with a tall tower emerging from its center, shining with a steady light. Everyone in the crowd was either escorting someone who was extremely sick or on death's door themselves. Most of the crowd was pitiful to look upon, but a few continued to cry out in rage and despair to haggard-looking clergy at the entrance of the temple and their grim guards.

"Have mercy, Mother!"

"We know you keep the best magics for yourselves. It's time to open up!"

An elderly clergyman was moving through the crowd handing out linens and water, and his head cocked up wearily at that last call. "How many times must we tell you! The Mother Superior is only able to cast so many times a day. We must let her rest between healings, or the only reliable way to be cured will be gone!" he shouted in the direction of the last voice of malcontent.

Tilly looked over at Amelia, wondering where she wanted to start, but her face betrayed her surprise at the sight. When she looked over at him, it was with an expression of chagrin and guilt.

"This is much worse than it was two days ago. If we move into this crowd and start healing, we will be mobbed. I had hoped to get to work without garnering too much attention. But it seems like this will be impossible to do and remain completely anonymous," she said softly, chewing on her lip, eyes shooting back to the crowd as she tried to think of a way forward that didn't end in chaos.

Tilly's face settled down into heavy grim lines as he read the situation. "The temple is locked up tight to give the healers time to rest, and if we start working on the people out here, we might get mobbed. Even if we don't get rushed once we start, there is zero chance of not being found out by those in the city who want me dead . . ."

Amelia's eyes widened as she suddenly stopped chewing her lip and looked back at the elderly man making his way through the crowd.

"If they are limiting entry, maybe we can use that to our advantage. I think I can get us in, and if we can convince the clergy to work with us, then we can pose you as another faceless priest and heal as many as possible, hopefully without being found out."

At this, Tilly shrugged. It was better than risking a mob. He had seen a few of those in his day, and they were no joke. Add magical bullshit into the mix, and he was absolutely sure it was something he did not want to mess with.

"Let's go for it. Hiro didn't seem too hot about me revealing myself to this Temple, but it's probably the best of our options," Tilly said, shrugging the hood of his cloak even deeper over his features.

Amelia gave him a halfhearted smile. "I should not have brought this option to the table so flippantly. I hadn't thought this through nearly enough. Move over to that wall across from the crowd, and I'll be back, hopefully with a way in."

Tilly nodded his assent, and Amelia moved down the street and through the crowd. Tilly had lost sight of the older clergyman and hunkered down against the thick stone wall of the building across the street while waiting for Amelia to return. He idly looked up and down the road, noting that there were not many temples in the temple district, and almost none of them were as well maintained as the towering temple of light at its center.

The temple's wall he leaned on supported a curvy structure made up of domes and arches that was topped by a statue of a richly dressed dwarf holding a hammer in one hand and a scale in the other. The compound looked ornate, but the walled gates to get in were firmly shut. Tilly guessed it was a deity for craftsmanship or commerce or something . . .

Just then Tilly heard the voice of the elderly clergyman ring out tiredly from the midst of the crowd.

"Alright, that's all the water and linens I have. The guards are going to come through and collect the ones from yesterday. Do not give them any trouble, and for the Lady's sake, please don't hold on to what we gave you yesterday. We will cleanse them and bring them back out as soon as we can. Dirty and diseased bandages will not help any of your cases." At his words, two of the guards moved to a couple of very large wheelbarrows at the bottom of the steps and lifted glowing face coverings to mask themselves against the crowd.

Tilly couldn't see where the elderly clergyman was, but he saw the two guards begin to move through the crowd and receive the discolored linens from the sick and their keepers. Anxious murmurs rolled through the people as they unwrapped and uncovered sick family members or infected limbs. Then the process was broken by wailing in the distance.

"Father! Father, answer me! Oh gods, he's dead. We have been here for two days with nothing but rags given for our trouble, and now he is dead!" The voice was growing more frantic by the minute, and the energy of the crowd was starting to shift. Other yells started to rise up indistinctly from the crowd, and Tilly was afraid he was about to see them break out into a riot. A very sickly riot.

Then the haggard-looking woman in white robes stepped forward from the entrance of the temple. She had not spoken yet in Tilly's hearing, but instead of trying to gain control of the crowd she simply raised her hands and staff before starting to chant. A golden light radiated from her, and the crowd closest to her quieted as it washed over them.

The priestess gritted her teeth as she chanted, and more light flowed out from her in bursts of concentric light. This had a more powerful effect than any sort of violent crowd control Tilly could have imagined, and everyone fell silent as the light washed over them all. Even Tilly felt a distant echo of the massive area effect.

Warmth trickled into his body where the light touched his skin, and it moved through him, relaxing knots in his shoulders and easing the last of his headache. If this was the edge of the working, what was it like in the center of the area of effect?

Suddenly the chanting cut off, as blood trickled down from the priestess's nose and her eyes rolled up into the back of her head. The crowd seemed mollified and then even concerned as she collapsed on the steps in front of the main entrance. The guards surrounded her in a protective formation even as the clergyman's voice rang out in anger.

"Light have mercy, Dinah! You were supposed to only be supervising," he shouted as he rushed through the crowd. Once he arrived, the formation broke, and his hand lit up with more minor magics. He rattled off some orders to a pair of guards who gently lifted the priestess and took her inside. He then turned and addressed the crowd.

"Look, I know you are suffering. This is not easy for any of us, but in case what you just saw didn't make it clear. We are doing *everything* we possibly can to fight this. Only our most senior members can completely cure you, and they are pushing far past their limits with the support of the rest of us. Please remain calm.

We will see as many of you as we can today," he said, some of the fire leaving his expression as he scanned the crowd before looking farther and farther out until he found Tilly across the street. Even at this distance, Tilly could feel the curiosity burgeoning on his brow.

Just as Tilly processed the look, Amelia appeared back at the edge of the crowd and made her way over to him. "Mateus is the steward of the temple, and he has been by the shop several times to restock when their normal shipments were delayed or short. He says he is willing to get you in without being seen, but he stressed that we had better be telling the truth. I assured him we could deliver on what we promised, and even with our relationship, I'm not sure he would have relented if I hadn't told him you were another human . . . That got his attention," she said, turning and eyeing the crowd warily.

"So is there a back entrance we need to get to or something?" Tilly asked, craning his neck from his position to try to spot some previously unnoticed alleyway.

"Uh . . . I'm afraid not. The plan is somewhat more involved than that. I hope you are as resistant to this infection as your magic seems to be," she said, digging her hands through her pockets. Tilly stared at her for a moment as she flashed an apologetic smile his way and gestured for them to move toward the outskirts of the crowd.

As they quietly arrived at the edge, Tilly saw the cart approach, piled high with soiled linens, and the bones of the plan clicked into place. He looked over sharply to Amelia, who was tying a thick square of cloth over her airway that had several more of the deodorant balls tucked into cleverly sewn pockets in the center.

After she finished, she handed him a similar cloth and a few more of the fragrant herb bundles. Her eyes were serious, and Tilly caught the slightest hint of a challenge in them as he moved to follow her lead.

The guard kept moving toward them, and Mateus's voice rang out from the steps. "I have just been informed that we will start seeing patients again in the next few minutes. Each of you has a number, and you will report to the guards when called. If you make trouble or try to harm another child of Light, we will confiscate your number. If you do not have a number, please report to the guards, and one will be issued to you shortly."

This was clearly a speech he had given many times, but still, the crowd broke into orderly action. Maybe it was part of the magic of the priestess, or maybe it was guilt over what had followed, but they moved into orderly queues, and in all the shuffling, a guard looked the other way as two humans hopped into the back of the cart and covered themselves in damp and discolored linens of various shapes and sizes.

CHAPTER THIRTY-SIX

The Good Guys

Ghhaaahhh." Tilly breathed in explosively, emerging from the putrid pile of unmentionables like a swamp monster being birthed from primordial soup. He tumbled out of his cart, almost bumping into Amelia as she emerged from her cart with much less drama.

"Acolyte, channel a basic cleanse for as long as you can. We won't get much out of them with this smell clouding the room." Tilly looked up to see the same elderly clergyman from outside. Upon closer inspection, Tilly saw that he was a satyr of the almost human variety. It seemed he had accompanied both the carts to conduct a quick interview of his odiferous guests.

Tilly found himself in an austere but neat waiting room with what looked like a few benches and cots for the sick. He thought this might be where they triaged people before they were seen by someone on a typical day. The temple steward stood with his arms crossed next to a nervous-looking young elf in priestess robes and a few guards. Behind them, lying on one of the benches and propped up by pillows, was a sleeping woman well past her prime. She was wearing more ornate robes than anyone in the room, and Tilly assumed she was one of the more powerful members of the temple. She appeared humanoid but had a green tinge to her skin and leaves instead of hair.

The young elf clasped together her hands and began to chant a hymn. The song washed over the room, and Tilly felt it press against and then saturate his armor, which seemed to almost drink in the magic. He heard hissing and popping from the piles behind him, and the almost overwhelming stench was slowly reduced. The young woman's voice began to grow hoarse as if the chant was somehow becoming more difficult the longer it went on until she finally cut off with a fit of coughing. Tilly moved forward unconsciously in concern, but the guards moved to block him immediately.

"Hmm, your concern is appreciated, human. I am Steward Mateus of the temple of the Lady Light. Amelia has dealt with me honestly for years, and we are taking her at her word. She says you can do something about this sickness afflicting our city . . ." He trailed off, not quite asking a question. Tilly waited a moment to see if he would continue, but then he just stood there, leaning into the awkward pause. So Tilly just picked up where he left off, trying to decide what was "need to know" and what was dangerous to share.

"Well . . . for starters, my name is Jonathan Tillman, and almost as soon as I arrived here on this plane, I was set against the force responsible for this 'sickness.' My system tells me it's something called **Corruption**. The lapin outpost was under siege for weeks by creatures infected and eventually enslaved by this same force. Now we have proof that the members of the Cult of the Serpent are under its effects too. Although, I believe they have partnered with it willingly.

"Something strange happened to me as I fought to cut it off at its source near the lapin village. I gained a patron deity, and my class was altered. Now I'm basically the antidote to this stuff," Tilly said, hoping that was enough to let him get started without involving him in any divine politics.

In response, the steward slowly nodded, taking in the human's story before shaking loose his hands from his robe. "Yes, well give me just a moment," he said, as arcane symbols lit up around his hands and one eye flashed with the same color as the symbols. Tilly felt the same tingling he normally felt as he was identified, but the feeling continued to intensify as if something was pressing in on his very soul. Then the fire within him kindled to a deeper heat in answer and pressed back against the metaphysical weight releasing a *wumph* of pressure, washing through the auras of all present.

The steward's eye flashed back to normal, and the symbols around his hands flickered out. He visibly flinched and shook out his hands as if stung. "Interesting, I have been blocked before, of course. But I have never quite felt so . . . rebuked," he said, trying to process what he had just seen.

Just how much was he supposed to share with this unknown element? They were obviously working hard against this incursion, and they didn't seem to be profiting from it in any way, but he thought back on his Title of [Harbinger]. Whatever **Origin** was, it didn't seem that well known by anyone he had interacted with so far, and he was hesitant to step into another divine radar. He already had the attention of one god, and that seemed to be more than enough.

I mean, he didn't even know where **Origin** stood in the grand scheme of things. He might be the big "G" God to all of these other little "g" gods, but who was supposed to tell them that? Or it might be the other way around. He just didn't know enough to safely pick a side, and he certainly didn't want to be some sort of evangelist for a god he knew nothing about.

If it wasn't for the fact that he was stuck fighting **Corruption,** something that **Origin's** power seemed uniquely suited to do, he was pretty sure he would already be looking for a way out of this Champion Mantle thing. It just screamed "strings attached." After another second of thought, he decided to partially level with the steward.

"Look, Mateus, I am the *Champion* of a deity that does not want to be discovered . . . I think. Honestly, I'm not sure, but I would rather not figure that out right now. What I do know is this; I have an *Ability* that can expel this stuff from anyone's body. I can help with a lot of the people you have out there. I'll just need somebody on hand to destroy what comes out and recharge me when I reach empty."

The steward's face slipped from disbelief into confusion, and Tilly thought that he probably lost him completely somewhere around needing to destroy a bodily expulsion.

"Look," Amelia interjected, rescuing the derailed conversation. "The little ones that you sent to me have all been cured. I know that none of their cases were too advanced, but I don't think it matters with his *Ability*, and he can cast it ten times before running out of mana. He has something this city needs and is willing to help. We just need to use you for a little anonymity."

As Amelia described how many casts he could do in one sitting, the young priestess looked up in hope, and even the sleeping matron cracked an eye, proving that she had not been sleeping at all.

"What did you see, Mateus?" the matron asked, with a dry voice that reminded Tilly of the crunching of leaves. He turned to her in concern as one of the guards rushed forward with a cup of glowing water.

"Nothing overly concerning, Mother. He is not Demonic-Aligned, and while I sensed no ill will, I was limited in my gaze to the knowledge that he is a hybrid caster with a relatively small well. The best direction that the Lady was able to give me was that he probably fell within the realm of *Chaotic Good*," he reported crisply, some of the concern he had shown for the priestess outside coloring his tone once again as he addressed his leader.

"Well, it's not like we have many options. None of our healings cure this 'Corruption.' We have been reduced to supporting me as I cast an **Advanced Banish**. Bring in the first one, and we will watch as he uses this *Ability*. If what he says is correct, then we will place the full support of the temple behind him and see just how many people he can cure before he is wrung out," she ordered, before taking a thirsty drink from the offered cup. Tilly saw that she sat up with some considerable effort. She was beautiful in a stately way, but her face was drawn with deep exhaustion, and he wondered just how long she had been pushing herself.

"Jerin, bring in the first," the steward ordered the guard nearest the door who nodded and left.

"Wait, Mateus, we need something to hide his identity," Amelia interjected. "He has already had to face off against Shadow Hunters within the city walls, and the Marcellus family has marked him for death. We came in here to hide him long enough to actually do some good . . . Do you have any robes of the *Forsaken* on hand?"

The church members in the room flinched at the mention of enemies already in the city, except for the Mother, who just sighed. "I wish we had more than just the spare uniforms on hand. Dark days are ahead for this city, and while the Cult wouldn't dare to touch us, we will only be able to shield a few from their wrath . . . Fetch him the uniform, and delay the first patient until he is ready."

Another guard rushed off, leaving the steward with only two guards and the junior and senior priestesses. Tilly was about to thank them or ask about the *Forsaken* when the elder priestess spoke again, issuing more orders as she considered the changing circumstances.

"Mateus, I want you to have another *Discerning Eye* ready. Focus on whatever is expunged from the patient. We may not be able to fight in the physical battle, but this is our supposed realm of authority, and I have hated having nothing but questions and apologies for our flock." To which the steward nodded seriously.

Just then the second guard returned with a simple white uniform draped over one arm. He held it out in reverence to Tilly, who took it reluctantly and tried to figure out how to put it on over his existing kit.

It included a face wrap with a shining lantern of some sort emblazoned where his forehead would be and a tabard with an oversized hood. As he handled it, his **Identify** pinged, and he pulled up the description.

> **Robes of the Forsaken.** *Worn by warriors of the Light who have forsaken all other ties and covenants to do battle with Demon kind. +10 to Wisdom. Demonic-sourced mana will be 50% less effective in mental and spiritual attacks.*

As he struggled with the unfamiliar cut of clothing, Amelia stepped up and helped him find the right way to hang it over his leather jacket. "I thought of this disguise because they are always swooping in to fight for the light-aligned factions and then fading away. Their abilities are as legendary as they are mysterious, and their identities are one of the things they forsake when they take up the class, so the news of healings at the temple can be pinned on the mysterious *Forsaken* Order instead of the new human freshly arrived in the city," she said pulling up his cowl to cover his now-covered face. She stepped back and nodded to herself.

"These are a loan, human. I hope the *Wisdom* will help you in your efforts, but neither you nor we are ready for the consequences of you donning that uniform officially," Mateus said seriously off to the side.

"But you must admit, it does suit him . . ." the Mother said thoughtfully behind him.

"Ma'am, I'm pretty sure I am taken. But I do hope my guy and yours are friends. By the way. After all this, do you mind giving me some pointers on how to contact a deity? If I'm gonna keep fighting this stuff, I want to know who I'm fighting for . . ."

Before she could answer, the first sick person came in. She was a smaller minotauress who would have towered over Tilly by a foot if she was standing up straight. Instead, she shuffled in front of the guard on a swollen leg that could be smelled as soon as the door opened. It was wrapped up with multiple layers of bandages, but those did nothing to hide the rot. She stiffened at the sight of Tilly in his uniform, but then hesitantly explained her situation.

"Good afternoon, your holiness. Thank you for seeing me. The caravan leaves tonight, and I didn't want to be a burden in this state. My company had taken a contract a month ago to escort some villages fleeing the Scale-belly advance, and in that action, I took a barbed arrow of theirs to the knee. This would normally be nothing to my kind, and I didn't think of it for days, even as it continued to worsen. Then it started to smell and swell up. Our healers couldn't do anything about it, even when they invoked the *Bright Ancestors*. So I was sent here."

"Come forward into the Lady's light, child," the steward said calmly as if he knew exactly what was about to happen. She hobbled into the center of the room before Tilly and Amelia, and she smiled at the minotauress in encouragement.

"You may proceed," Mateus said, and it took Tilly a moment to realize the steward had been speaking to him. He took a step closer to the minotauress and kindled the flame in his chest before breathing out deeply in front of her. She blinked rapidly in surprise before beads of sweat started to appear on her brow.

"Describe what you are experiencing, child," Mateus said in a kindly tone, even as his eye flashed again. She answered through clenched teeth.

"I know not what the Warrior has done, but I felt a burning enter my body through his breath. It has settled into my leg and centered on the wound. It is burning fiercely!" she said, gritting her large bovine teeth tightly against the pain. Then she grunted, and the sound of something popping issued out from under all of her bandages. They had not been clean when she came in, but in the seconds following the sound, they were soaked in an unsettlingly dark maroon color.

"Cut those off!" Mateus barked, glaring at the bandages with his shining eye. The guards quickly complied, and as soon as they pulled the bandages free, they began to animate, wiggling like a hundred little appendages.

"Great Ancestors!" the minotauress huffed in relief, even as Tilly stepped quickly forward with an enflamed fist to consume the bandages. He had once again found himself moving almost by reflex at the sight of the **Corruption**, calling his blue fire even as he moved to attack the creepy manifestation.

The rest of the room, however, looked at the man in the *Forsaken* uniform with various expressions of shock or surprise, except for Amelia who wore a look of smug satisfaction.

"Ancestors Light be upon you!" the newly healed minotauress said moving her now normal appendage. Nothing but a slight burn scar was left to mark the wound, and her eyes shone with admiration as she glanced back up at her savior.

"Thank you, sister, that will be all. Many more to see today," Amelia said, stepping in and pulling her around to face the door again. As soon as she was out, Mateus spun on Tilly.

"I understand your fidelity, believe me, I do. But we are not the only branch facing such a malady. Please, you must tell me as much as you can," he said, his eyes showing an almost feverish light. The elder priestess stepped in to blunt some of the steward's enthusiasm.

"We understand you are here in charity . . . Do not be pressured by our needs if you can not share." the older priestess stated from her perch on the bench. She had watched the minotauress leave with a new hope sprouting within her. She didn't need a name to recognize something good when she saw it, "Whether we hear the story now is of no consequence. We are obviously on the same side. *May the Light always prevail*," she said, her tone heavy with meaning at the last phrase.

Tilly looked back and forth between the people in the room and thought again about his interactions with the Administrator and then the blue flame in the temple. They had said nothing about hiding their existence, and while he wasn't sure what informing this faction about more of his experience would do, Tilly couldn't help but feel like these were the good guys. It wasn't the name or even the fact that they seemed to be a religion focused on healing and demonic opposition. It was the look on their faces when they discovered that he was actually able to destroy whatever was infecting the populace. It wasn't greed or fear. It was relief. They were just happy to finally find a way to help, and that dispelled any lingering suspicion he had with the group in the room.

He was already involved in some sort of cosmic power struggle . . . what were a few more deities in the mix?

"Alright, give me a few minutes before the next one, and I'll give you the CliffsNotes version," he relented, deciding to go big or go home on telling them everything he knew.

Mateus gestured at the guard near the door to wait. "Human, I do not know what cliffs have to do with this, but any information would be greatly appreciated."

Tilly just winced at the misunderstanding before deciding not to bother with it, and continued with a short version of his story. "Well, I woke up on Nephesh about four days ago . . ."

CHAPTER THIRTY-SEVEN

Exorcizing is No Joke

Tilly cut out many of the details but did share **Origin's** name as well as the exact words of his [Champion's Mantle] Title. He almost asked if they could get rid of the **Seed,** but decided against it after recalling the words of the Flame at the altar. If it took a Divine Boon to remove, then it would probably take more than a few clergy to solve the problem. Plus, with so much on their plate, it wouldn't be right to bother them with his problems too . . .

The steward left with the elder priestess to send a report. She had introduced herself as Rowan with a smile before leaving to update her superiors. They left behind a few guards and the younger priestess who had recovered from the effort of channeling *Cleanse* on such heavily corrupted materials. Amelia set up a miniature chemistry lab on the other side of the room and started brewing up different concoctions as the patients filed in, one after another.

They fell into a sort of rhythm where Tilly would purify as many patients as possible out of his mana well, then rest, recovering with the aid of either Amelia's latest herbal concoction or one of the young priestess's support *Abilities*. Unaided, he could recover his mana fully in about 50 minutes, depending on the mana recovery aid, that time could be cut down by 20 to 30 minutes.

He would spend the time between healing sprints focusing on his breathing while trying not to be overwhelmed by the side effects and debuffs that he was racking up and then removing as the *Botanist Surveyor* and *Priestess of Light* worked together to get as much casting out of him as possible without hitting a medicinal or magical dead end.

---

*You have received the **Potion Toxicity Debuff**. Any alchemical treatment you receive for the next 12 hours will be reduced by 50% in its effectiveness.*

"I have toxicity again," Tilly said, after rubbing some of the salve Amelia had given him on his chest and face. It would supposedly widen his "dantians" temporarily and allow his natural rate of recovery to increase in all areas for twenty minutes, giving him a 40 percent gain in mana regen. Make that 20 percent now that the debuff was back.

They had cured over one hundred and twenty people at this point, and Tilly wasn't the only one hurting from the constant work. Both guards leaned on their weapons, sweat staining their protective robes. They had to face a new temporary manifestation of **Corruption** after every patient was purified. None of the manifestations were especially dangerous on their own, but they could not be allowed to escape, and the varied nature of their appearance kept both of the guards on their toes, as Tilly tried to keep from intervening as much as possible to save mana.

The priestess, whose name was Triss, also wore a haggard expression as she choked down some sort of bitter-smelling tea that Amelia had handed to her to keep her own mana regen up.

"I can cast **Purifying Radiance** one more time, but after that, I think you will have to deal with the debuffs another way. Even though we have kept my well from bottoming out, I am closing in on mana exhaustion, and will be useless to you if you need me to boost your *Wisdom* again," she said between grimacing sips of the tea.

At that, Amelia looked up, eyes red from the repeated brewing and processing of raw magical herbs. "Yes, well save yourself until we run out of all options on my end. Speaking of which, Jonathan, I have one more thing to use that will be extremely beneficial to your power base and clear out any build-up of impurities in your system. With your *Endurance*, it should be safe to use, but it will not be pleasant."

Tilly's head pounded as he tried to focus on breathing and the source of his power. The internal flame showed no signs of flagging, unlike its surrounding vessel, which felt strained and sore from the constant emptying and filling. He had not yet had a chance to spend so much time actually focusing on his internal environment, and even in short bursts he had found the practice incredibly enlightening. At this point, if he added up all of his recovery sessions, he had probably spent several hours breathing deeply while focusing inward on the sensation of his flame, experiencing how his mana interacted with his physical body.

The flame seemed to flow out of him in specific patterns, each one manifesting a different *Ability*. His **Flame's Renewal** built right below his lungs, stoking as he breathed in deeply and activated it. Then it would surge up from his center, through his mouth, and out with his breath onto the target. It didn't burn exactly, but after over a hundred uses in less than twenty-four hours . . . every empowered exhalation was accompanied by a sharp, needlelike pain that ran up the route.

He tiredly looked over to Amelia and held out his hand. "Sure, why not . . . Give it to me, and let's get through the rest of these people. I can keep this up as long as you guys keep topping me off," he said in between slightly ragged breaths. He didn't know how much he had left, but he was sure of one thing. If they had to shut down the operation, it wasn't going to be because of him. Behind his back, Amelia shared a look with Triss, who just shrugged as she continued to choke down the bitter tea.

Amelia

Amelia was confounded. Tilly hadn't mentioned **Mana Exhaustion** once.

With her help, she had hoped he would be able to purify fifty patients before hitting one roadblock or another. At his level, his physical body just couldn't take much more abuse than that, or at least that is what she had thought.

A normal magic user of his class could run through his full mana reserve three or four times in a row before the infamous **Mana Exhaustion** debuff struck. Depending on the nature of the usage, you could lose consciousness or even lose the ability to move mana through your pathways for hours. Typically the onset of the debuff was preceded by crippling pain that made casting impossible. But, Amelia had never met a mana user who had such a crazy ratio of *Endurance* to *Wisdom*. For all she knew this could be typical of his build. Nonetheless, he seemed to deal with herbal toxicity just like everyone else, and it was time to use her last resort.

She reluctantly pulled out a bundle from one of her pocket spaces.

"I am going to hand you a leaf that I need you to hold under your tongue for ten breaths. You will want to spit it out, but you must hold it for that long. It will cause a chain reaction throughout your body that will force you to expel 70 to 80 percent of your short-term impurities over the next five minutes. We will leave the room, and I am sure the guards will be able to bring you something to use to handle the . . . impurities. Also, I suggest you remove your clothing for this, as it will be quite messy."

She gingerly took the plump purple-veined leaf from the bundle, handling it with a protective cloth, so as not to let the powerful reagent touch her skin, and placed it on the bench next to her human companion.

The whole **Origin** explanation had been as new to her as the others, but what he had mentioned about the Administrator had taken her back decades to her own Transference and the mess of a life she had left behind . . .

Jonathan's voice interrupted her reverie as he eyed the leaf, a curl of distaste tweaking his lips, "Naked, huh . . . you saved the best for last, didn't you?" he muttered before beginning to shed his patchwork primitive armor.

Amelia was once again taken aback. She had expected some pushback at the mention of such a strange method of detoxification, or at least a request for clarification. But he just tiredly complied without any hesitation, and it was almost as if he trusted her . . . Many shied away from taking anything but the tried and true recipes from licensed alchemists. However, her class let her discover new uses for flora much more readily than most who typically gathered for potion producers. This, in turn, allowed her to come up with new recipes much more frequently than others, using all kinds of unique and rare plants she came across in her travels.

"I have tried this on a few subjects, and some have even reported stat increases after using it, so there should be some benefits to outweigh the . . . cost," she stuttered quickly as she moved toward the door, not ready for how fast he had begun to disrobe. She didn't bother to mention that she had only tested it on herself and Heras and that his results would be a fascinating addition to her body of data. The priestess was right behind her through the door. The guards remained, one of whom was pushing forward a bucket with the toe of his boot.

Tilly just nodded tiredly at her to show his understanding before pulling his furred leathers over his head. She turned away as the door shut and sat in the hall for a few minutes as the sound of retching and bowel cleansing sounded out from the room. The priestess looked over at her, aghast, and Amelia gave a nervous chuckle in reply.

"I promise you, this method is by far the most effective way to use the leaf. It will allow me to re-use several of the recipes I have already employed to keep augmenting his mana regeneration . . . And I would never give a patient something that I had not tested on myself first. This particular method is just a bit unorthodox."

". . . Unorthodox?" Triss grunted through half-lidded eyes as another round of retching began.

"It sounds more like torture."

Jonathan Tillman, 12 minutes later

He shakily pulled on the loaned *Forsaken* hood and tabard.

"That should be it . . . much easier to cleanse than those awful bandages," the priestess said, false cheer ringing in her voice.

One of the guards, the taller humanoid that displayed much more hair than the other, helpfully added, "He must have produced his body weight in waste . . . I have never seen such a thing in all my years at the temple."

"Yes, well, that was to be expected considering the toxic load we had put on his system. Even your order's **Purifying Radiance** does little to remove actual toxicity. Rather, I think it is more focused on removing the negative magical side effects of a wide range of maladies," Amelia chimed in, leaning into an academic tone as if they were all in a lecture hall, and there wasn't a putrid bucket of waste sitting in the corner.

Meanwhile, Tilly took a deep drink of the provided church rations they had brought into the room at some point and a mechanical bite of some sort of spongy bread. The taste from the leaf still hadn't quite left his mouth, leaving behind a bitterness so acute that he felt like every tastebud on his tongue had puckered into a painful tension. Water and food were helping, but the process was slow.

He had wiped down as well as possible, and the priestess had taken away most of the smell with that handy cleanse of hers. But he couldn't shake the memory of slime oozing out of his pores as his whole body convulsed and squeezed out waste from every orifice. He felt like a tube of toothpaste, rolled to the very top of its cap.

"Well, I don't think I ever want to do that again, but you were right, Amelia," Tilly said as he mentally dismissed the new notification on his screen, and looked over at the Botanist, who had already begun the process of brewing another concoction.

"I gained a point in *Constitution* and *Dexterity*. According to the system, the changes I have undergone so far have racked up a lot of toxins. So despite how terrible that was, thank you," he added, actually pleased to get something out of that nightmarish experience. His mana was nearing 100 percent again, and while the ordeal had furthered his exhaustion, it had also left him with a strange clarity that lent him a mental sharpness that was out of place with his circumstances.

"Ulnas, can you send the next one in? I'm ready to keep going," he asked the guard, a steely determination underlying his tone. The hairier of the two guards left while the other reluctantly picked up the "cleansed" pot and removed it from the room.

Soon enough Ulnas returned with a satyr woman holding a baby that had an unhealthy grayish pallor and was breathing far too shallowly. Tilly straightened up from his slump against the bench and moved forward, gathering in a breath as his flame stirred and trying his best to ignore the feeling of hundreds of tiny knives that had begun to stab the pathway leading up his throat to his mouth.

CHAPTER THIRTY-EIGHT

Out of the Frying Pan

Every breath brought the sensation of jabbing needles back to his throat and lungs. The last twenty castings or so had been true agony, each empowered exhalation accompanied by an unconscious deep groan of pain. Through the agony and the gasping breaths of his short periods of recovery, Tilly numbly repeated his mantra. "One more . . . one more, and I'll stop."

The priestess had long since passed out, and they had found another exhausted member of the temple to replace her, but apparently, they could no longer do anything about his damaged mana channels. Instead, they stood by to support the guards and serve as a second line of defense against the manifestations.

Even Amelia had collapsed at some point—not sleeping for days and her constant magical brewing had caught up to her. At first, she had pulled a bench over to continue brewing while seated, and then a little while later, the sound of soft snoring emerged from her corner of the room as she sat slumped over her temporary worktable covered with beakers, cauldrons, and burners.

Tilly's world had narrowed to one gasping breath after another. After a blank few minutes, he realized it had been a while since the last person had come in. He had signaled for a break to regain some mana and had lost track of time. Through the fog of pain and fatigue, he looked up at his mana bar, which was blinking for some reason, but showed 12 percent. Enough for one more . . .

"Ulnas. Bring in the next," Tilly croaked, allowing his head to loll to the side and catch sight of the guard who was leaning heavily on his weapon. He just nodded tiredly in response and moved through the door, before coming right back through, bristling with a sudden energy as a surprised smile lit his face.

"You are one stubborn Aurochs, human!" he shouted, the exhaustion disappearing from his form like fog before a rising sun.

"That's all of them. The Mother Superior started casting in another room hours ago, and together, you have managed to get through every petitioner. That is it, you have done it!"

The gears in Tilly's mind slowly ground together, trying to process those words.

"*Done?*" he said, too tired to hold back the tears of relief pooling at the corners of his eyes.

Even through his fog, he felt the burden lift from his shoulders. He had given his *best* . . . There were no others who would die because of his lack of will. He let out a half chuckle, half sob as his shoulders slumped in relief and his body sagged much deeper into the bench against the wall. He saw several debuffs active on his status, and each came with a timer.

Minor Exhaustion: 6 hours remaining
Potion Toxicity: 10 hours remaining
Mana Exhaustion: 14 hours ({Partially Resisted}, {Localized}) remaining

None of them gave him a good notion of how long he had spent in the temple. He only knew that they had arrived sometime in the early evening. "How long till morning?" he croaked out again, as the other guard rushed over to bring him some water.

Tilly pulled some into his mouth and swished it around, trying to wash away the feeling of sandpaper scratching down his throat.

"It is several hours yet until dawn. We have orders to guard you as you sleep, and we will wake you in the morning," Ulnas stated solemnly, his pride in the work they had done evident on his face.

At that, Tilly let out a groan of relief and stretched out on the bench. Improved *Endurance* or not, he was utterly spent. In fact, he was past spent, having long since entered the fugue state he had sometimes found at the fire station on a double shift with no sleep. For decades he had operated at a functional level well past the limits of exhaustion, and it was good to see those years still meant something here.

He decided to look up at his notifications through slow, heavy blinks, wondering if there was anything he needed to know before he slipped away to unconsciousness. The screen came up, and he mentally filtered out all the healing, debuff, and cleansing notifications. The mental filters resolved into five distinct announcements from the system, and they danced before his bleary eyes, refusing to resolve into legible lines. He screwed his eyes shut to try to clear the bleariness and once closed, began to forget what his goal had been in closing them. The blanket of darkness was deeply soothing to his perception, and he gave up struggling, allowing his consciousness to slip away.

The newly filtered notification screen remained obediently visible before Tilly's closed eyes, happy to stay as long as it was needed.

Congratulations! You have unlocked a latent aspect of your class *Son of Flame.* Unlike other classes with stricter Ability pathways, your class originates from the First Epoch. The numerics assigned by the system are more flexible for you and can be bent and at times broken depending on your need and force of Will. Minimums and Maximums as estimated by the system cannot fully define your Abilities.

Congratulations! You have reforged the mana paths along which **Flame's Renewal** flows. It is now defined as **Flame Renewal+**. They have been broken and remade in the heat of a purifying flame, and once they fully recover from this trauma, they will be 100% more effective, allowing you to cast the same Ability for half the mana cost, or empower it to twice as effective at full cost.

Congratulations! You have emptied and filled your mana well over 24 times in 24 hours! By this action, you have forcibly expanded your well and your ability to fill it. Wisdom + 3 and Intelligence + 5.

Warning! Due to recent gains, you have lost the Title: **[Resolute]**

Congratulations! You have pushed far past your limits for the sake of others without a promised Quest Reward or Experience. You have done so motivated by deep pain and longing. This has been noted by the system and you have been awarded the **Title: [Scarred Heart]**

[Scarred Heart]: Any goal you pursue motivated by the depths of your soul will be met with an unparalleled opportunity by the system. Even a broken heart can produce unimaginable strength.

Jonathan Tillman, 6 hours later

Tilly was awoken by the sound of the door shutting harshly and urgent whispers coming from the front of the room. His head felt like it was stuffed with wool, and his mouth was unbelievably dry. He licked the roof of his mouth trying to produce a drop of saliva to no avail and cracked his bleary eyes open to try to find some water. The blue glow of a screen was shining in his face, and he tiredly dismissed it to get a better look around him.

The backup priestess was gone, and Amelia was still slumped over her temporary worktable, snoring. The guards were both by the door, sharing an intense conversation with the steward.

Tilly groped around until he found the water pouch before sitting up with a groan and pulling the canteen to his lips, taking deep, thirsty swallows as the lukewarm liquid slid in between his teeth and cooled the harsh gritty sensation covering the interior of his airway.

"Mr. Tillman, we had hoped to let you rest for a while longer, but the situation in the city is . . . ah . . . deteriorating rapidly," the steward said as he saw Tilly sit up. He was wringing his hands nervously.

"What's happening? How long have I been asleep?" Tilly mumbled, the fuzziness in his mind clarifying to a throbbing headache as he came fully to consciousness.

"The sun rose a few hours ago, and the Great Caravan left sometime in the night. It was thought that the Cult's forces would still be hours away, but it looks like our reports were wrong. They have been spotted from the walls. How our diviners missed this, I do not know, but the city has almost devolved into a riot . . ."

Tilly's headache throbbed deeply as if to emphasize how truly shitty today was going to be. As far as he knew, everything people would need to leave wouldn't be ready until this evening, and that was a hell of a lot of time to hang around with an army at your door.

"How many are there, and what is the state of our defense?" Amelia's tired voice groaned from the other side of the room. Tilly looked over, noticing her mussed hair and a drool stain on the collar of her shirt. Her eyes, however, contrasted completely with those signs of recent sleep. They shone brightly with an almost manic determination.

"The home Phalanx and two auxiliary Phalanxes are positioned to intercept. The walls are manned by a mixture of the city guard and the private guards of the noble houses. The **Emperor's Bastions** have been seen moving through the city, but no one knows how many there are or what they are doing. As for the enemy . . ." At this, Mateus's formal-sounding report devolved into a choking sob.

"There are reported to be ten thousand naga warriors of various levels, with accompanying elites . . . and they are driving a force of fifty thousand before them. Made up completely of irregulars—"

"What sort of irregulars have they been able to get in those numbers? Are they mercenaries?" Amelia asked, shocked.

"It is reported that they are employing some method of converting conquered citizens into war slaves. I can only imagine that these forces are a result of the sacking of our last remaining satellite city. They will be used as fodder to throw against the Home Guard and exhaust its resources."

"Let me guess," Tilly cut in, a hollow tone of despair filling his voice, "These 'war slaves' have black eyes and display berserker levels of aggression."

"Yes . . . The Cult employs blood magic that can be powerful and compulsive at times, but we have never seen anything like this. It's worse than the rituals of undeath some of our demonic enemies use. At least those conversions result in a loss of levels and must be accompanied by a controller of some kind. Is this related to the curse-empowered sicknesses we have been combating in the city?"

The color had long since drained from Tilly's face as he considered what the people of the city were about to face. "Yes, it's all connected. Those people have been **Corrupted**. Once it progresses that far, I don't think there is any sapience left in them. They will do everything possible to spread the infection. They will devour and kill, while any who remain relatively intact will be added to their number. At least that is how it happened with the forest creatures surrounding the lapin outpost."

At his words, Mateus's frown deepened, and Amelia shot up from her seat and started grasping her equipment and shoving it into various pockets. "I have got to find Heras and the children. If we are to fight, I would do so protecting them," she said as urgency sped her movements.

Tilly got up and began to remove the cowl of the *Forsaken*. "Hopefully they have already met up with the lapin contingent, and if so, that means I'm going with you. We will help anyone else we can along the way."

"Wait! Please. We can protect you here in the temple!" Mateus said desperately as the two made preparations to leave. Amelia totally ignored him while Tilly threw the balled-up uniform to one of the guards.

"Sorry, Mateus, I don't think that is an option for either of us," Tilly said shortly as he grabbed some of the bread and hurriedly shoved it in his mouth, chewing as fast as possible. He had learned long ago, that you always ate and drank what you could, when you could, before going out on an unknown engagement.

"The gift you have cannot end here in this fight! We have received word to recruit you if possible and send you through our network to the **Shining Isle**." Alarm bells went off in Tilly's mind at the desperation creeping into the steward's tone. His hands drifted to his hatchets, as he turned to give Mateus a hard look.

"Whatever your orders are, we are leaving. We have promises to keep." At his words, Amelia looked up, reaching into her pockets threateningly, prepared to back up Tilly, no matter what happened with the church. That was the second time Tilly had seen her reach into her pockets like that, and he couldn't help but wonder what exactly she would pull out of there if threatened.

Mateus raised his hand in a conciliatory manner. "No. Despite what you may think, no one here will force you. But many across the plane need your abilities, Mr. Tillman. This is not an isolated incident, and the Church is struggling with her allies to contain it. With our backing, you could truly skyrocket in power and help countless others while doing it," the steward pleaded, his eyes imploring Tilly to see reason.

Tilly allowed his words to sink in and thought through the possibility of his death in the coming fight. Was he being selfish? The church of the Lady Light seemed like the real deal good guys. Who was he to say no to helping all those people? These thoughts and more swirled through his head and seemed to reverberate through his body in time with the throbbing of his headache. Doubt crept in, and his normally decisive manner was once again struggling to find a way through the confusing morality of this conflict.

But in the end, he reluctantly shook his head. To say yes to Mateus's offer would mean having to change who he was on a fundamental level. He had made *promises*, and he couldn't break them and be the kind of man he wanted to be. Maybe that was wrong, but he thought again of the little girl lying in the shop, and her small courageous smile.

If doing the right thing meant abandoning her . . . His heart firmed, and a note of clarity resolved through the cacophony of contrasting desires.

As if in response to this revelation, he felt a deep echoing thud in his chest, and he started, before realizing it had been a single beat of his heart echoing through his whole body. It pushed back the throbbing of his head, suppressing the ever-present invasive sensation of the **Seed**, and even enveloped the burning heat in his chest. All of these dissonant forces combined to form something solid and sure under the power of its influence.

Something in the steward's eyes changed, and he relented before a voice sounded from the hallway past the open door. "Very well. If you must go, you will do so with our blessing." The Mother Superior came into view from the hall, looking as tired as Tilly felt. **Identify**, finally pinging as she entered.

Level 62, Elder Priestess of the Lady Light

"I have a blessing I can give both of you that might just help you survive the day. I can only cast it once a week, but this feels like the right time to use it, don't you think, Mateus?" she said, looking over at him with a small smirk playing at the corner of her mouth.

CHAPTER THIRTY-NINE

Into the Fire

Amelia had just finished tucking the last of her things into her coat, and at the priestess's offer, she looked over at Tilly and shrugged. "I think we should take all the help we can get."

"My thoughts exactly," Tilly said as she smoothed out some wrinkles in her coat and moved forward to stand next to Tilly before the elder priestess.

"Except for the cool-down, it is a very simple blessing. It lasts for six hours and will give you divine insight into your surroundings. Providence will guide your steps," she said, smiling.

"A week cool-down for that?" Tilly blurted before receiving a sharp elbow in the ribs from Amelia.

The Mother Superior smiled, and began to chant, pulling her hands from her voluminous sleeves and waving them in esoteric patterns. No light emitted from her blessing like Tilly had seen with other priestesses, but Tilly could feel something settling over his body, like a warm blanket.

The priestess's eyes flashed, and she finished with, "Light protect you and guide you," before collapsing. Mateus barely kept her from hitting the floor as she fell, and Tilly rushed forward in concern. But the steward waved him away with his free hand. "This is only because she, like you, has pushed herself far beyond her limits these last days. Now go. The blessing will make itself known to you as you move. May the Light shine upon you," he intoned as he and one of the guards moved to support the priestess and carried her over to one of the same cots they used for the sick.

"Thanks for everything, guys. I won't forget you, and if we make it out of this, I'll be in touch," Tilly said nodding to the steward and the guards.

"No, it is us who must thank you. Your arrival was nothing short of miraculous. The Light always finds a way," Ulnas said seriously, his fierce smile filled with gratitude.

"Mateus, a pleasure. I have always appreciated the work you do here, and I am glad to have been a part of it in the city's last days," Amelia said solemnly to the steward as he fussed over the elder priestess's prone form. He smiled in reply and shooed them away.

"Don't worry about us. Our order reserves the right to revoke this temple. It has a high cost, but if needed, we can all be called back to the Isle in a moment."

With that, they both turned and headed toward the exit of the building. When they emerged from the large front entryway they found a line of grim guards standing at attention on the steps facing out into a city bathed in morning light. What would have been a somewhat peaceful vista was marred by the sound of distant screaming and the general roar of upraised voices from the populace.

Tilly's eyes were immediately drawn to a pillar of black smoke rising in the distance over another part of the city, old instinct drawing him toward the fire even as he tried to remember which way the teleport hub was.

Amelia moved past the guards, who saluted before returning to their grim vigil, and then paused at the bottom of the steps as if in indecision.

"What are you thinking? Should we find where the lapin contingent is setting up and see what Lord Hiro is planning?" Tilly asked, coming up behind her.

"That is precisely what I was going to do, which would require us to move that way." She pointed toward the city center with a thoughtful expression. "But I feel something pulling me in a different direction. I believe it is the blessing of the Mother Superior . . . But how far do we trust something like this? Does it take into account our own goals, or does it prioritize our survival above all else?" She pondered, tapping her foot and looking in the direction she had pointed.

"Well . . . if this is a powerful *Ability*, then I'm sure it will turn out to be more than just a 'danger compass.' Let's move in the direction you know we need to go as fast as we can, and if either of us feels anything change, we will let the other know," Tilly said slowly, as he too felt a slight tug away from the direction they needed to go.

"If it is warning us of immediate danger, it's best to be prepared," Amelia said as she reached into her main right-hand pocket and pulled out a full staff, Mary Poppins style. It looked like a simple length of grayish wood whose only distinct feature was a sprig of budding growth at its top. With her other hand, she fished out a bundle of something. Tilly pulled out his hatchets, following Amelia as she moved down the street with a purposeful stride, staff at the ready.

Tilly's health and mana were both at 100 percent, but he still had two debuffs remaining from the night before:

Potion Toxicity: 4 hours remaining
Mana Exhaustion: 8 hours ({Partially Resisted}, {Localized}) remaining

He didn't really understand the second one, but he imagined it had something to do with the faint pins and needles sensations he felt in his lungs and throat every time he exhaled. He was happy to see the blessing also up on his HUD below the debuffs:

Light's Blessing of Insight: 6 hours remaining

Temple Way was more or less abandoned, with only a few other edifices showing a guard presence at the front entrance, the others being shut up or left abandoned. Only a few of these factions seemed to think they could weather the invasion, but Tilly didn't imagine the nagas would be very friendly to other deities.

Amelia took a turn down a side street that pointed more directly toward the center of the city, and she suddenly stopped in her tracks. Tilly felt a slightly more urgent tug back toward the Temple of Light as he walked up next to her.

The side street looked abandoned, but they both looked at each other as the pull of the blessing redoubled in strength, urging them not to head down the street.

"We continue. I would rather face this ready than be surprised by it later," Amelia muttered under her breath, dropping her cloth sack at their feet and then moving forward at a more cautious pace. Tilly jogged in front of Amelia, keeping his hatchets at the ready.

"Unless I miss my guess, you are more of a back-line combatant, so let me take the lead, alright?" he said through the side of his mouth as he continued. She nodded, scanning the suspiciously empty streets.

Tilly wished the priestess had given them more information before passing out, but then again, he doubted something like this functioned the same way every time it was cast. The tugging grew even more insistent until it felt like someone was pulling the back of his jacket. He was about to give in and suggest a longer route when the sound of clapping echoed up and down the street. Tilly's head snapped up to the source and found an ornately dressed satyr with two giant thugs in house guard uniforms emerging from a shadowed doorway a little further down the street.

Tilly's face grew hot, and he felt the phantom dribble of spit slide down the side of his face as he once again took in the sight of the smug Marcellus family scion.

"Ah, I should have known you two rats would find each other. I hear you have been getting involved in things far above your station, Mrs. Cooper," he sang, with a smile that oozed scorn. "And you," he said turning his gaze upon Tilly, "the resources my family has wasted on you are unconscionable, you little cockroach." He spat, his smug mask cracking to reveal the mania that hovered just under the surface.

During Titus's short monologue, Tilly felt the Blessing cease its pulling backward, and he glanced behind them to see a couple more thuggish guards stepping into the mouth of the side street. They were trapped.

His **Identify** populated their levels and classes.

Level 26–28, Marcellus House Guard Elite. X 4

Shit, way too much for him to handle, and no **Corruption** damage bonus either. He hoped that the Botanist Surveyor had some ass-kicking in her, because if not they were fucked.

"Run on my signal," Amelia hissed through clenched teeth, obviously seething with fury at her mistake in ignoring the blessing's guidance.

Tilly's hands were itching to throw one of his hatchets, and he didn't want to leave her to handle this fight, even if she could.

"What are the little rats chattering about?" the Quaestor sniggered, moving closer.

"I hope you aren't leaving our surprise party so soon! What about our guest of honor?" He gestured grandiosity at the other side of the street. There the Marcellus House Steward emerged from an abandoned shop's doorway, holding a small squirming gnomish boy in his hand.

"I'm sorry, Mrs. Amelia!" Cog cried pitifully.

"I left Miss Heras to try to find my family, and these smelly bastards caught me!" he snarled out through a sob, before receiving a sharp cuff across the head from the steward.

"You will speak with respect when referring to the master."

The boy cried out in response, and Tilly's fury grew cold and terrible as he noted the bruises already marking the boy's face and neck. Amelia's hissed next to him.

"You slimy pile of Aurochs dung! You would hide behind a child?"

At that Titus Marcellus snorted with laughter. "This creature is no child. It is little better than an animal. Besides, we brought him for fun, not because we needed him. Steward, you may dispat—"

"Wait!" Tilly shouted, whipping his head around to drill his gaze into the level 38 Quaestor. Panic and fury mingled in his chest as the situation rapidly devolved before his eyes.

"No one here has done as much damage to your name as me, and honestly I have loved every minute of it, you traitor," Tilly snarled, not having to fake any of the goading delight he felt at insulting the satyr.

"Aren't you the nagas' errand boy? How does it feel to be a toy to the Scalebellies?" Tilly continued, showing every one of his teeth in a fierce grin. A glimmer of a plan had formed in Tilly's mind that vaguely involved him starting a fight with the Quaestor and giving Amelia space to attempt a grab on Cog. But somewhere between giving a voice to his feigned fury and goading Titus, his blood began to boil. Something about his utter self-centeredness, even as the city pulled itself apart around him, drove Tilly up the wall.

He *hated* this piece of shit. The emerging plan sank back down into Tilly's subconscious as his world zeroed in on Titus Marcellus.

The half smile, half sneer fell from Titus's face and was replaced by raw, teeth-grinding fury. "You hairless ape. You have no idea what your betters are doing, but I look forward to showing you just how far out of your depth you truly are," he said, rolling up his sleeves.

"Stay back, I will take care of this buffoon myself," he called to his guards before turning to Amelia. "And don't even think of trying anything. If you so much as twitch, Evander will stick the ugly little midget." At his words the steward made a knife appear in his hand as if by magic, placing it almost gently upon the boy's cheek, and Amelia gasped in dismay loudly, before muttering rapidly under her breath to Tilly.

"If you can distract them for even a few seconds, I can get him free and take care of the goons behind us."

But he didn't respond. It seemed like he didn't hear the words at all. His attention was consumed by the tattoos revealed on the Quaestor's right arm. They seemed to bleed ink, just like the ones on the Shadow Hunters. They called to him and disturbed him at the same time.

The roaring throb began pounding in Tilly's ears, and his heart beat wildly as his mouth went dry. The **Seed** in his side began to writhe, its tendrils reaching hungrily for more. The veins in Titus's right arm wriggled in response, like recognizing like, and the blood drained from Tilly's face as his eyes met the satyr's grim smile.

This fucker knows.

"I had wondered what this sensation was . . . I kept thinking that you felt familiar, yet I had no reason to know you. Then when I let the Shadow Hunters over the wall, and I felt their **Corruption**, I finally discovered the source of our bond."

Amelia's wary eyes left the steward, and looked over at the Quaestor in confusion. "What is he talking about?" she called, taking in the cursed tattoos covering the writhing skin of Titus's arm. They had both seen similar eldritch movements hundreds of times by this point, and her expression fell as she put together what he was implying.

With dawning horror, she looked over at Tilly. "Jonathan, what is he talking about?" she asked again more urgently.

Tilly's mind was sluggish; the sweet feeling of hatred sung in his veins, drowning out reason and shame. He was going to tell Amelia, he was going to tell Hiro, but not like this. Not from this pompous ass. His avoidance and his shame came roaring to the surface before being drowned in fury. This was all *the stupid goat's fault* . . .

His surroundings, Amelia, and even little Cog fuzzed into the background as his breathing grew ragged and the color drained from his vision until everything was painted in shades of gray and black.

Titus Marcellus smiled warmly at Tilly. "You can hear its song, can't you? It's an offering of freedom if only you let yourself go . . . Show us your true self, APE!" he finished with a high-pitched squealing laugh.

"Jonathan!" Amelia shouted.

Tilly heard none of it. Not the antagonizing of the satyr, not Amelia's cry. He only heard the throbbing beats of his pounding heart and the roaring of his hatred.

He was going to chop this fucking goat into pieces.

CHAPTER FORTY

Just Deserts

Amelia Cooper - Level 33 Botanist Surveyor

should have trusted my instincts! she thought furiously to herself.

Her mind was whirling as she tried to take in the tumble of new information while simultaneously gaining some sort of control over the situation. She silently activated the mana in the *RageSpore* packet she had left at the mouth of the side street. She felt them greedily gobble up the stored energy and puff out an invisible mist of airborne fungi, that if inhaled, would produce confusion and extreme aggression in a target after thirty seconds. For better or worse, things would drastically change in half a minute.

She couldn't believe after all of his supposed efforts to stop this infection he was already under the **Corruption's** influence. She didn't know if he was a willing host or not, but the Marcellus scion's words had sent him into a frenzy. When she saw two black tear stains streaking from his dark watering eyes, all of her naive hope came crashing down around her.

"Jonathan!" she yelled, trying in vain to shock him out of **Corruption's** influence.

She fought back the familiar tang of regret and failure as she took in his complete lack of a reaction. Instead, a grisly smile ripped across his lips, and he stalked toward the vastly more powerful Quaestor like an absolute idiot. The satyr seemed to relish the challenge and was happily showing off his arm, which was infested with the same eldritch malady. She could tell that the tattoos were meant to somewhat contain the influence of the foreign substance, but that was a fool's errand. The magic of the seals was already clearly fraying, a fact underscored by the Quaestor's barely contained manic aggression. With both of them caught up in whatever this was . . . she just might have a chance.

Another small sob sounded out from behind her, and her grip on her Budded Staff tightened as she whipped her head back around toward the gnomish boy.

Twenty-five seconds.

She quickly checked her connection to the *Strangle Vine* cutting she had instructed each child to keep on their person. It weakly responded from Cog's pocket, and she was thankful that she had renewed a connection to each cutting as the children were healed yesterday. She could channel **Frenzied Growth** into any willing plant as long as she maintained her mana imprint. A seed could hold the pattern for longer, but it would take too long to sprout for any immediate defense. So she had mangled her last two living specimens, subdividing them until almost no life potential was left. Then she had imbued and distributed them to each child, with a stern order not to lose the little length of vine.

Even as a cutting, this plant was notorious for its rapid growth, and with her *Ability,* it should be enough to protect him when the time was right. She had to wait until the disturbingly impassive steward was distracted.

Twenty-two seconds.

The Marcellus scion reached into his robes and withdrew a sceptrum, a foolishly ornate weapon that had become fashionable amongst the young aristocrats in the last few years. This one, however, glowed with purple light as the smirking Quaester flourished it needlessly a few times before matching Jonathan's approach with a proud forward step.

"I'm not surprised, really. A brute like you would long for such comfort this substance offers," he admonished the approaching human, flourishing his tattooed arm again.

"There are methods to tame its influence while still reaping the rewards . . . But I am sure you received your imbuement through something vulgar like a bite or scratch!" he wandered idly, before whipping forward with a sudden and open swing.

The opening attack wasn't particularly powerful or fast, but he was twenty-six levels above Jonathan's *Son of Flame* class, and it showed. Jonathan immediately reacted to the obvious swing but was simply too slow, and was going to at least receive a bludgeoning blow to his shoulder. Amelia winced in sympathy while maintaining her internal count.

Then Jonathan seemed to be jerked to the side, and Titus's eyes widened in shock as the strange movement put him just out of reach of the swing.

Seventeen seconds.

Jonathan wasted no time, showing an astonishing battle sense even under the effects of **Corruption**. His ax heads flared with an angry blue flame, and he swung them at the Quaestor from opposite directions, taking advantage of his opponent's off-balanced stance after the surprising missed swing.

The Quaestor easily batted away the clumsy attack with his glowing metal rod. But his smirk was gone. He did not like being surprised by such a weak opponent.

"You are quite the cockroach, aren't you? I am growing weary of your antics. Bug!" he spat, accentuating his final sentence with wide-sweeping strikes that Jonathan barely blocked. Even with the obvious telegraphing from the overconfident Marcellus, each blow knocked him further on his back foot until he was up against the side of the jutting storefront from which the ambushing party had emerged.

Jonathan felt the wood behind him, snarled, and lunged back at Titus recklessly. His face was a mask of animalistic fury, as he rejected the reality of his circumstances completely. The lunge was received full-on by the satyr with open arms and a smirk. Jonathan's full weight didn't move his opponent at all, and the Quaestor brought down his sceptrum viciously on Jonathan's back, causing an explosive grunt to sound from his violently emptied lungs.

"A tackle?" The satyr sniggered, before lazily slamming another blow down on Jonathan's back. The second blow knocked him to the ground, and Amelia's whole body tightened, willing the spores' effect to hurry.

Five seconds.

"How positively juvenile," he yelled before aiming a kick at Jonathan's prone form, which once again slid just out of the way of the blow without any corresponding movement from Jonathan.

It's the Blessing! Amelia cheered internally.

Maybe it was burning out its influence to physically move him in his altered state, but Amelia was glad to see the *Ability* could operate with such nuance. While each of its influencing movements on Jonathan hadn't been particularly preternatural in speed, they had been so inexplicably well-timed that the result was just enough to extract Jonathan from more bodily harm. It wasn't foolproof, but it would have to be enough.

Any second now those two goons should start showing symptoms.

"How unbelievably frustrating!" the Quaestor yelled, his voice cracking manically.

"Very well, if the child won't stay still for his discipline, I will have to hold him down. **Chains of Judgment!**" he shouted in a high-pitched whine. Spectral chains shining with purple light appeared around Jonathan's wrists and yanked his arms upward and back until he was hanging from them with his back against the same wooden storefront.

Shouting could be heard from back down the street, and both of the thus-far inactive guards flanking the fight looked over with suspicious expressions. The Quaestor didn't react, totally absorbed in his "lesson," and to Amelia's horror, he followed up his *Ability* by thrusting his sceptrum through Jonathan's shoulder, pinning him to the wood of the wall behind him.

Cog cried out in horror behind her, and she whirled back around hoping to catch her chance at the distraction.

"There! That should help you keep still for the rest of our little game," Titus screeched.

The guards maneuvered around him to get a better view of what was happening further down the street, where the two others had inexplicably begun to brawl. They were shouting obscenities at each other with their weapons lying forgotten on the street.

Amelia watched the steward carefully. As soon as he craned his neck around the boy to peer coldly down the street, Amelia flooded the cutting with mana.

Jonathan Tillman - Level 12 Son of Flame

The boy's cry, along with the shock of being impaled, cut through the angry gray mist of hatred that had clouded Tilly's mind. He blinked rapidly as his vision cleared, and he saw Titus's delighted expression leering at him. In an instant, the situation crashed into Tilly's awareness along with a crushing shame that he had once again given in to **Corruption's** influence.

Tilly saw Cog held tight by the steward, with a knife drifting near his cheek, and Amelia posed on the edge of her feet as the guards nearest to him started to move back down the street.

"Crete! What in Justice's Upright Teets are you doing?" the guard on the right shouted back down the street toward the other two, who seemed to have begun brawling. This was lost on Titus, who was pulling back his fist in slow motion as he carefully took in Tilly's expression, almost shuddering in pleasure.

Over Titus's shoulder, Tilly saw Amelia lean forward on the balls of her feet as a faint green nimbus glow emitted from the staff. At the same time, something exploded out of Cog's pocket and Tilly smiled as Titus's fist connected with his face, shattering his perception and causing stars to flare in front of his eyes.

"What's so funny, you Neanderthal!" Titus shouted as the green thing latched onto the steward's arm and rapidly grew up around his extremity. He shouted in surprise, and Tilly was amazed to see Titus not even flinch as he leaned even closer to Tilly's face, screaming.

"Answer me!"

It's not too late, I can make this right, he thought as a fatalistic joy flooded Tilly's heart.

He may have fucked up, but there was still a chance to get Amelia and Cog out of this. He took in a deep breath, kindling the mana in his diaphragm and triggering excruciating pain throughout his over-drawn mana channels.

Titus leaned forward, expecting a plea for mercy or a cry of pain. Instead, Tilly exhaled, tearing open metaphysical wounds and releasing invisible flames all over the Quaestor's face. Titus looked at him in confusion for a second as he tried to register the heat blooming on his face. Then his eyes clouded over, and he released an animal-like scream.

The guards were at a loss, first turning in confusion toward the steward's surprised shout, then back to the sound of their master's screaming, not quite able to keep up with events. In the chaos, Tilly mercilessly headbutted Titus's reeling form, and Amelia's staff whipped around to bludgeon one of the guards on his head.

Titus Marcellus stumbled back, continuing to scream in agony as the writhing forms under his arm started to tear themselves free, attempting to escape the purifying flame. The steward had dropped Cog in an effort to shift his knife to his unbound hand, and Amelia followed up her blow to the first guard by whipping her hand out of another pocket and flinging dust in the second guard's face. His thick shortsword clattered on the cobbles as he started to hack and wretch in response to whatever hellish substance she had just introduced into his system.

"Take the boy and go, Amelia!" Tilly shouted hoarsely, while arduously pulling his ruined shoulder forward on the weird scepter thing that Titus had been beating him with.

Cog scrambled away on all fours as the steward began hacking at the still-growing vine reaching around his throat. The guard Amelia had initially whacked was backing away from her, sword at the ready, and Titus continued to scream as black tendrils ripped themselves free from his arm, leaving it a mangled mess.

With a final heave, Tilly pulled his shoulder free and found to his surprise that he was still clutching both of his hatchets in a death grip. Without thinking he immediately flung the one in his uninjured arm at the guard closest to Cog while igniting it in flames.

The guard grunted as it lodged in his back with a meaty thunk, and Amelia looked over at him, obviously torn on her next step. The tentacled horror had almost fully detached itself from the Marcellus scion, and the steward had carved bloody marks along his shoulder and neck, freeing himself from vinelike growth that had emerged from Cog's pocket.

She reached down and grabbed Cog, throwing his small, terrified form over her shoulder, and gave Tilly a flat look. "No one is sent here because they are good."

Then she frowned apologetically and skirted around the tentacled thing that had almost completely pulled free from Titus's body. As soon as she was out of range she turned and sprinted down the street away from the remaining combatants. The guard who had been hacking up a lung was recovering, and Tilly quickly recalled his second hatchet from the back of the other who had been reaching around pointlessly to remove it. These guys were pretty much all *Strength* and *Endurance*.

Only one of the two guards who had spontaneously started fighting remained standing. He came limping toward the main group with a conflicted expression on his face, leaving the other guard crumbling in a bloody pile at the intersection.

That left three wounded combatants, one writhing horror, and one aristocratic brat still screaming hoarsely in pain. All of whom were at least 14 levels above him . . .

Mana: 93%
Health: 45%

Tilly took a deep breath as they all took in the horror. By some unspoken arrangement, the guards zeroed in on him as the greatest threat and turned to advance. He clutched his newly recalled hatchet in his good arm and held on to the other one weakly as the gaping hole in his shoulder leaked blood.

Then a small paper bird flew into his view.

"Jonathan Tillman! My tracking sigil informed me that you are injured. Do not worry! Help is on the way!" the bird declared in Shuji's voice for all to hear. His opponents' eyes narrowed at the words and the steward's creepily calm voice issued out a command.

"Kill him and get the master away from the specimen."

CHAPTER FORTY-ONE

Low-Speed Chase

Everyone was injured in some form or another. Well, except for the tentacled manifestation of **Corruption** which had just finished separating itself with a sucking pop from Titus. That thing seemed completely fine.

The beaten guard and the guard with the hatchet wound in his back stalked toward Tilly, their thick shortswords in hand. The third guard shuffled warily toward Titus, who was still gasping on the ground in shock. All the while, the steward took in the scene coolly.

The manifestation's appendages quivered, and several of them homed in on the approaching guard as it stood over the body of its previous host possessively.

"Mr. Evander, I'm not sure this thing is going to let the master go," he said hesitantly, as more of the appendages tilted toward him at the sound of his voice.

"Shut up, Trivus, and do your job. You know it cannot survive long outside of a host. Do what you have to do, and end it. Retrieve the master," the steward droned as if giving a particularly boring lecture.

"Easy for you to say. I hate this stuff . . ." he muttered darkly, even as the other two arrived within attacking range of Tilly and split to either side to box him in. He held up his hatchets in what he hoped was an intimidating manner, but his left arm screamed at him in pain as he tried to raise the weapon above shoulder height. The guard on that side smiled, and Tilly stirred up his mana prepared to surprise both of them with **Flame Expulsion**.

They were both 14 levels higher than him and seemed to be free of **Corruption**, which would have been his only trump card against them. So the best he could come up with was a full frontal assault using the main chunk of his remaining mana.

"GARRAAGGHH!" The sound of a gurgling scream cut through the impending conflict like a knife, and all three combatants turned to the incredibly disturbing scene playing out behind them.

The manifestation had pounced on the approaching satyr in a burst of speed, and the guard was furiously stabbing at it with his sword. Unfortunately for him, the thing didn't care about the grievous wounds being inflicted on its center mass. It was busy putting all its effort into shoving as much of itself into the openings on the guard's face as possible.

The guard's two companions were slack-jawed at the horrifying sight, and while Tilly found it equally disturbing, he had unfortunately seen far too much of the **Corruption's** nature for something like this to throw him off. The steward was also taking advantage of the distraction. Skirting around the two, he made his way over to the now-unconscious Titus.

Tilly knew it was now or never and struck viciously with his good arm at the guard to his right. Even taken completely by surprise, the man's sword still came up for a block, but just too late to catch the head of the hatchet as it buried itself in his shoulder. The second guard spun back toward the fight even as Tilly followed up his strike by ramming his shoulder into the guard on the right for all he was worth.

Hitting him felt like trying to force open an industrial steel door. Nonetheless, he caused the guard to stumble back two steps. In the craziness of the conflict, the guard had not been expecting the ferocity of the attack or the immediacy of the follow-up. He responded with a weak thrust from his back foot, and his partner tried to grab Tilly from behind, but he was already shooting the gap created by the move. Before they could fully react, he was behind the guard on the right, breaking out into a full run, dropping the hatchet in his weak arm in favor of building speed.

"Get him, you idiots!" the steward shouted as he dragged Titus's body away from the now collapsed guard and the quickly disappearing appendages of the manifestation.

Tilly was several steps ahead, almost at a full sprint when he heard both guards curse and give chase. He thought that with his emphasis on *Dexterity,* he would have an advantage in speed, but that idea was quickly put to the sword by the sound of heavy breathing drawing up behind him.

Tilly's shoulder injury shot jagged pain through his body every other step as he pumped his arm as best he could. The guards were faster than him but not by much, and he was going to make them work for every gained foot. He blindly sprinted down the street in the direction Amelia had gone and desperately hoped he was moving toward backup, not away from it.

The side street opened up to a main thoroughfare about ninety feet ahead. He could see people moving panickedly in a single direction, but he wasn't going to make it. The hooved feet of his pursuers were now hitting the cobblestones just behind him in loping rhythms and he could almost feel a strike that was about to land.

He churned up the flame in his chest desperately and reached for the compressing sensation that had accompanied **Flame Expulsion** the first time he had used this *Ability* against the **Corrupted** poison fog. The flame inside his chest roiled and then shrunk to a nova pinprick in his chest, just as he heard a grunt of effort behind him.

The compression reached its bursting point and exploded out of him in a sphere of blue flames. He held his breath just in time as they washed over him in a pleasant heat. The guards behind him were not as prepared. If they had seen the attack coming, they probably could have sheltered behind their extremities and gotten away with superficial burns. Especially with their obvious *Endurance*. But midchase? They suddenly found themselves running into a wall of fire, eyes open to the flame, gasping in lungs full of superheated air.

The huge mana expenditure left him feeling even more tired and hollow than he already was, but he pushed on for another ten steps before recalling his hatchet and turning back toward his foes.

Both guards were hunched over covering injured eyes and heaving dry, painful-sounding coughs. Tilly didn't give them any more time to recover, launching an enflamed hatchet at one with his good arm, and then shifting the second hatchet to his right hand and throwing that as well. They were stationary targets at about twenty-five feet, and Tilly easily scored significant hits on both of them at the base of their necks in the gaps of their armor.

Not waiting to see how they reacted, he spun and continued his flight, emerging out into the crowded street a few moments later. The street was choked with citizens all heading deeper into the city, and the sound of fighting could be heard in the opposite direction of their fleeing. Tilly could vaguely see the walls in the distance back the way they came, and the road curved slightly up ahead, blocking their destination. Not that many of them probably knew where they were headed. They just wanted to get as far away from the fighting as possible. The emergence of a wounded human from the side street seemed to go unnoticed as they continued to push and shove further down the street. He entered the flow of refugees, buying himself some time.

He had barely and miraculously escaped a situation that should have been his end. With this realization came the galling pain of having lost control again . . .

This time for much more than a moment of unbridled rage. Something about Titus and the way he reveled in revealing Tilly's infection to Amelia had sent him into a spiral. He had blanked out, only coming back to himself at the sound of Cog's scream. Sure, he'd done everything he could to help Amelia and the boy get free, but that did little to cool the burning shame at the thought of almost being responsible for their deaths.

It had clearly put them in danger to not know he was as much a liability as an ally, and all the excuses he had spun up to delay telling people now seemed shallow and self-centered. Everything he hated in Titus . . . Part of him wanted to pretend that **Corruption's** influence had been some unstoppable internal influence, but that just wasn't true. It pushed him, urging him to lose himself in his darker nature, but it wasn't forcing him along a path he didn't already want to walk.

Asking for help had slowly grown into a no-fly zone over the decades, and he especially hated being seen as the one who held back the team. This drive had propelled him into training time after time, as he pushed to make sure he was never the one lagging behind. He was deeply uncomfortable with needing any-thing from anyone else, and the **Seed** had played that part of his mind perfectly.

Now here he was knee-deep in his bullshit plan to fix himself. At least no one else had gotten hurt . . . this time.

He kept moving, looking back over his shoulder. There was no way his hasty strikes had finished the sturdy pursuers. Builds like that were born to take hits and keep going. Without the 200 percent bonus, he simply didn't have the attack power to win out against such powerful opponents. Not to mention they could have a healing potion or something.

He thought for a moment about following the crowd toward the center of the city but discarded the idea. That was probably exactly where they would look for him to head. Plus, the crush of the crowd was only getting worse further in.

So, reluctantly, he turned perpendicular to the flow of the crowd and started moving at a slow jog in the direction of the opposite street. Those fleeing treated him as just another obstacle and flowed around him as he moved at a decent pace, looking to find another side street. Then he spotted a break in the buildings ahead. He hopped and dodged around through the stream of people, hoping that the gap had an outlet on another street.

Then Tilly's blood ran cold as he heard shouting intermingled with coughs from behind him.

"Where is he?!"

"Who here has seen a human? Guard business!"

Tilly ducked into the cool darkness of the opening to the alley, hoping he had not been spotted. The relief Tilly felt shriveled up and died at the sight of the dead-end thirty feet into the opening.

There were two doors in the alley, and Tilly desperately threw himself against one, finding it firmly barred from the inside. The other was the same, and he backed away from the barred doorway, looking around for any other options. The walls were made of crumbling stone and went up three stories on both sides. He had to have picked the two tallest buildings on this street to hide between.

"This way!"

The shouting sounded closer. Apparently, the sight of an injured human didn't go as unnoticed as he thought. His eyes flicked up to his HUD as he gingerly swung his arms back and forth a few times, willing his shoulder to heal faster.

Health: 62%
Mana: 45%

There was no way he could turn and fight cornered. While he still couldn't lift his right arm above his shoulder, the strength in his grip had returned. It would have to do. He moved to a particularly crumbly streak in the stone wall and reached up to grab hold of a jutting stone just above his head with his right hand. He pulled up and stepped into a crack next to his left knee, thankful, for the first time that he was wearing moccasins instead of stiff, clunky boots, which would have made climbing impossible. He awkwardly reached to his left for another crack and bit back a moan as he grabbed it, securing his weight on his injured left arm, freeing up his right to reach higher up the wall.

He pulled up and wedged his right foot a few feet higher than his left and repeated the agonizing formula again and again. Like climbing the tree to gain a vantage in the forest near the lapin village, Tilly knew what he was doing would have been way past impossible with his old body. His balance and physical control were far beyond what they had been back on Earth. Not that he could particularly relish in his new abilities. Every time he secured himself against the wall with his left arm, the gaping hole left by that lunatic shot a bolt of pain through his whole body.

But climb he did, one agonizing foot at a time. He had probably made it two-thirds of the way up when he heard the sound he had been dreading.

"Shit, those farmers said he ducked in here. Check the doors." Tilly froze at the sound of voices at the entrance to the alley. He did all he could to turn his billowing effort-filled breaths into the silent gas exchanges they were meant to be.

The sound of two booming crashes thundered up from the ground. "They are barred fast. Do you think he made it inside?"

"No, you idiot, any door with a working lock has been shut up for days. He has to be here somewhere," the second guard growled before the alley filled with a long, silent pause. The toes on Tilly's right foot burned, wedged into their current crack, and he had of course had to freeze right as he was leaning into his left arm again. His whole body trembled with the effort, and he slowly, silently tried to shift his weight to another handhold. Then the mortar under his left hand cracked and a stone fell to the ground, landing with an incriminating crack.

Tilly winced, and then cursed as the sound of an evil chuckle echoed up from the ground.

"Of course, what else would a monkey do? He scampered up a tree, Attus! Stay here and make sure he doesn't come down. I'll find another way onto the roof to meet our new friend."

The discourse was followed by another thunderous crack against the barred door. Tilly redoubled his effort to reach the roof. He could not afford to get there after the guard. His fingers and toes were far past cramping in effort, but still, he kept shoving them in cracks between stonework like a fat kid reaching for candy. Two more blows and Tilly heard the door give way.

"I'll see you at the top, Monkey Man. You are going to pay for every little trick you pulled back there!" the brutish Elite Guard shouted up mockingly. Tilly's only answer was to continue gasping for breath as he hoisted himself up one hold at a time.

The sound of subsequent doors being destroyed reverberated out into the alley, and Tilly silently thanked God for doors as his mangled right hand finally reached the lip of the building and he heaved himself over the side. He collapsed, gasping for air, while scanning the roof for its access point.

There! A warped wooden trap door lay closed at the other end of the flat-topped roof. Tilly hauled himself up to his feet and recalled his hatchets, hoping he could get a jump on the brute.

Then the door exploded upward, and the guard quickly pulled himself up through the opening. Tilly threw a hatchet at his climbing form, but in an impressive display of *Dexterity,* the guard whipped up his shortsword and batted it aside.

"Uh-uh . . . I know your tricks now. There will be no more of that. It's time to have a little chat," he growled menacingly, holding up his blade in a guard position, ready to ward off another throw as he smoothly pulled the rest of his body through the opening. Tilly's mind raced, as he attempted to think of a way out, and the guard started to stroll forward, sword at the ready.

"Attus, I've got 'em. Come on up and join the fun!" the guard shouted triumphantly down to his partner before continuing.

"You are gonna pay for what happened to Trivus." His continued, false cheerfulness drained away as he addressed his quarry.

"Seems to me that had more to do with your boss than me," Tilly responded, shifting his eyes to the nearest roof, trying to gauge the possibility of a jump. Unfortunately, the look wasn't missed by the guard.

"None of that now. Can't have you breaking your neck and ending our talk early. Attus! Get your dumb ass up here," he shouted again and frowned as no response came.

Then Tilly felt hope bloom in his chest, and he lifted his weapon while recalling the other, taking a ready stance of his own.

He did his best to mask his emotion with a scowl of pain at the wound in his shoulder and fixed his eyes firmly on the approaching guard, making absolutely certain not to give away the long-eared figure silently flowing up and out of the opening in the roof.

CHAPTER FORTY-TWO

Buying Time

Even in his peripherals, Tilly recognized her as Mochizuki, the female lapin servant they had met a couple of days ago upon entry to the city. But this time she was not dressed as a simple servant. Layers of black cloth were cinched tight around her waist and the beginning and end of her extremities. The gear was reminiscent of a classic ninja outfit, but something about the looser clothing around her torso and extremities made it hard to tell exactly where her body was within the shifting fabric of the flared-out cloth. She padded up behind the guard, completely silent, focused on her opponent.

"I don't think your friend is going to answer," Tilly shouted, stalling for a few more seconds. Oddly he felt the Blessing tug at his arm, and he took it to mean it was encouraging him to attack. It hadn't given him anything useful since the fight, and he thought it might have burned through all of its available energy keeping him alive back in the side street.

"Shut your Gob! Att—"

Tilly cut off the response by throwing his hatchet with his good hand, which the guard easily batted aside, and then smiled. They both knew Tilly didn't have time to recall and block with the weapon at his current skill level, and the guard squatted slightly, the muscles on his hairy goat legs bunching for a lunge.

Just before he sprung forward, his eyes widened slightly and his head jerked around, suddenly sensing something.

It was too little too late.

Kunai had appeared as if from thin air in Mochizuki's hands, and the guard moved too slowly to avoid the double critical strike, as one plunged into his neck and the other was thrust up into his armpit, above the protection of his cuirass.

The guard let out a choking gasp, and his legs gave out, as Mochizuki led him to the ground almost gently, before ripping out her knives and wiping them on his armor padding. She gracefully rose to her feet, and flicked the blades out, making them disappear into the folds of her robes.

His **Identify** insistently confirmed her previous class tag over her head.

Level 13, Household Servant

At this point, it seemed more like a joke than helpful information. Clearly, his level 17 skill was far from infallible.

"Gaijin," she said in greeting, meeting his eyes with a serious expression only allowing a hint of satisfaction to dance in her eyes.

"I sure as hell am glad you are on my side. That was intense." Tilly breathed in relief, before recalling his other hatchet and looping both of them on his belt.

"Yes, well things are going very poorly for the city, and by extension Lord Hiro's plans. They are here too early, and our escape will be contested every step of the way," she said, gesturing toward the wall. As if her motion somehow turned up the volume on the battle in the distance, the roar of the fighting and dying washed over Tilly's senses. In the rush of his personal danger, he hadn't yet taken in the view that this vantage provided.

Tilly could not see the battle happening on the other side of the wall, but he saw the battlements flanking either side of the gates crowded with soldier-like figures. Flashes of some sort of large-scale magics were occasionally bursting forth like beacons from over the wall, but there were no signs of enemies in the city yet.

"Look closely at those atop the wall . . ." Mochizuki instructed as she moved up to his side and took in the view. He squinted, just barely able to make out that most directly over the gate wore the matching uniforms of the city guard, while the rest of the force on the walls was formed from different units wearing all sorts of armor. This was true for the whole rest of the wall actually, but the forces were especially crowded near the front gate.

"What will happen to the forces outside the wall?" Tilly asked quietly, fairly sure he already understood the answer.

"They are the last two Phalanxes of the august, 'Thousand Phalanx Empire.' One of which had to be bolstered by any veterans in the city guard. They will all assuredly die. They went knowingly to buy us time . . . Unfortunately, not as much time as they had hoped," she said with a deep frown.

"What makes you say—"

Then before his eyes, he watched as the unified guard standing watch on the wall suddenly collapsed in on itself in infighting, satyr against satyr. The private forces on both sides suddenly attacked the last few hundred guards manning battlements above the gate.

"Those sons of bitches! Wait, you knew this was going to happen? Why aren't you doing anything?!" He whipped his head around in mounting fury at the betrayal of the people those guards were supposed to be protecting.

She returned his freshly stoked anger with cold, hard eyes, and some of the heat drained from his expression.

"I paid a heavy price to obtain this intelligence. I passed it off to my superiors, who shared it with their counterparts last night. What follows is their best attempt to salvage an unsalvageable situation." Then she looked him up and down before reaching into the folds of her flowing robe and pulling out a familiar red potion.

"We have precious few of these left for the coming battle, but you will need it," she said, calmly handing it over to him.

He took it and knocked it back quickly, scowling at the feeling of sinew and muscle knitting back together at a hyper-accelerated rate. He eyed the battlements again and saw that the guards were holding remarkably well for a group that had been "surprised." They had almost instantly formed disciplined ranks against the bilateral attack.

"Didn't you say all the veterans had joined the Phalanxes?" Tilly asked in confusion.

"I did. That was the official line, anyway. It seems there might have been a mix-up. The private forces of the houses will use their position to force open the gates, ending the siege before it begins, but not so easily as they had planned," she said, a sad smile tugging at the edge of her mouth.

He looked back toward the road where refugees were still rushing toward the center of the city.

"How long until the honu can get a stable portal up?"

"That entirely depends on if they are able to proceed uninterrupted. Without interference, they will be done in the next hour. But you can be sure the bones of our plan have also been discovered, and the enemy would be foolish to allow us a back door. There are contingencies we hold in reserve that have been kept from me for operational security. But I have a part to play, as do you if you choose to take it. In essence, we must do all we can to delay the enemy and safeguard our escape."

Tilly took in his HUD as he swung his arms back and forth, not quite trusting the numbers.

Health: 100%

Mana: 34%

Corruption's Influence: 22%

"Yeah, I'm willing to do whatever I can to help, although I don't see how much of a difference I can make . . ." Tilly said, trying not to let his low mana and growing **Corruption** drown any remaining hope he had for the situation in the city.

She nodded as if expecting the answer, before pulling out a small metal sphere covered in arcane writings. "This arrived from the palace along with a few other treasures from the imperial vault. It looks like the Ancient Sovereign is planning some sort of last stand, and he wants to bleed the enemy as much as possible before that occurs."

Tilly took the item and looked down at it in curiosity. Under his gaze, he felt some of the fire in his chest kindle, and the symbols marking the sphere started to take on a blue glow.

Artificial Endless Path Microcosm - ???

As his **Identify** pinged, the warmth from his center reached down through his outstretched arm to touch the item, and he felt it begin to . . . resonate.

"Not yet!" she said, snatching the sphere out of his hand, she then juggled it back and forth between her hands like a hot potato.

"If you channel any mana-based *Ability* while holding this sphere, it will cause a multiplicative feedback loop . . . that is what Shuji said, anyway," she answered before handing it back to him gingerly, the arcane glow having diminished as soon as it left his hand.

"So with this, I empower one of my *Abilities*?" Tilly said as he tucked it carefully into his fantasy fanny pack.

"Not exactly. I am told it had no upper limit of input and is extremely dangerous to use. Lord Hiro seemed to think you were suited for such an item. Something about having unusually resistant pathways. It will continue to recirculate the mana back through your channels, increasing every cycle until you lose control of the circuit. Then it will release the *Ability* at whatever multiple you are able to achieve."

"So, like a magical bomb or something?"

"Yes. The Emperor's Bastions will reveal themselves when the gates are breached in a counterstrike and you are to join up with them and deploy your *Ability* at the optimum moment to disrupt the enemy's momentum. It seems that they are content to sit back and throw their fodder at us, so we will not risk escalating the fight any earlier than we have to. We will meet each threat with our bare minimum of force so we can delay the deployment of their Aces for as long as possible. Once the real fight begins, very few of us will make it out unscathed."

"So, magical bomb, but not until we absolutely have to. Got it. What will you do?" Tilly asked, a self-deprecating grin on his face.

"They have been infiltrating the city for hours with advanced units to destabilize our escape plan. I am to search and destroy any of these elements I can find before they reach our base of operations or our people," she said, moving casually back a few steps from the ledge.

Then she looked at him, and he felt a previously unnoticed pressure release on his mind. His **Identify** pinged, and the words over her head shifted to an entirely new level and class.

Level 32, Ninja Infiltrator

She winked at him, and before he could say anything at the awesome reveal, she sprang forward and leaped the twenty-foot gap between buildings, before blurring away across the rooftop, her form startlingly difficult to track, even in broad daylight.

That was one hell of an exit. If I live through the day, I have got to get one of those.

He looked around lamely, finding the trap door and heading down to the street the old-fashioned way. He didn't bother with the body of the guard. He doubted the man had anything Tilly could use besides the healing potion he had probably used to cure his wounds early in the chase.

Tilly followed the trail of destruction back down through the building and emerged to find the second guard dead on his knees with a shocked expression forever frozen on his features . . .

"Yeah, really glad she is on my side," he muttered to himself before heading toward the exit of the alley at a jog. The street was entirely clear at this point. Everyone had gotten the word that some sort of last-ditch escape effort was being made at the center of the city. He hesitated for a moment at the entrance to the street and pulled up his notification log to see what he had to work with.

He scrolled backward, confirming that he had not gained an actual level from the fights he had participated in, although he had picked up a couple of skill levels.

> *Congratulations!* Your skill **Beginner Hatchet** has leveled up. Now level 11.
>
> *Congratulations!* Your skill **Dual-Wielding (Hatchets)** has leveled up. Now level 3.
>
> *Congratulations!* Your skill **Ax Throwing** has leveled up. Now level 10.

He continued to scroll up and . . . *Shit, how did I miss this?*

He had lost [Resolute] due to the stat gains in the Temple, and he had gained another Title called [Scarred Heart], but it didn't seem like it would be much help in the next hour. The same was true for the sweet improvement he had gotten to his **Flame's Renewal** *Ability*, although that did explain how it was able to ruin Titus's day so thoroughly. No, the only real choice for Operation Magical Bomb was his **Flame Expulsion**.

He had begun chewing on a truly stupid idea. One that, if it worked, would be a legendary cheat on the game mechanics of this world. But he absolutely needed that [Title] back. Which meant he had to gain at least one level before activating the Microcosm. All while somehow getting up to the required 50 percent mana he needed to activate his *Ability*. He double-checked his character sheet to make sure he wasn't missing anything.

Jonathan Luke Tillman

Level: 12 (2000 exp to next level)

Display Name: Tilly

Race: Human

Class: Son of Flame

Status Effects:

Minor Corruption [Hidden] -15% Wisdom +10% Strength, Potion Toxicity: 3 hours remaining All alchemical items are 50% less effective, Mana Exhaustion: 7 hours ({Partially Resisted}, {Localized}) remaining

*Titles: [Harbinger], [**Origin's** Champion], [Corruption's Host], [Trusted Gaijin], [Hostile Environment], [Scarred Heart]*

Stats:

Constitution: 13

Endurance: 71 (78.1)

Dexterity: 29 (31.9)

Strength: 11 (12.1)

Wisdom: 16 (13.6)

Intelligence: 13

Equipment

Origin's *primitive stone hatchets: +10% to Dexterity.* **(Legendary, growth type)**

+Imbued Ability: Recall.

Origin's *primitive leather armor: +10% to Endurance.*
(Legendary, growth type)

+Imbued Form: Sun Salamander leather.

Skills:	*Abilities:*
-**Forestcraft** *level 12*	-**[Blue] Flame Strike,**
-**Identify** *level 17*	**[Blue] Flame Expulsion, [Blue]**
-**Cooking** *level 12*	**Flame's Renewal+.**
-**Beginner Hatchet** *level 11*	
-**Animal Processing** *level 9*	
-**Stealth** *level 7*	
-**Herb Lore** *level 3*	
-**Ax Throwing** *level 10*	
-**Dual-Wielding (Hatchets)** *level 3*	

Tilly cursed inwardly as he recounted his total non-*Endurance* stats. They were sitting at 82 to his *Endurance's* 71! That meant he actually had to gain two freaking levels before he could gain the Title back. This was going to suck . . .

A dark thought caused him to chuckle to himself as he started to jog toward the main gates of the city. He felt like a ticking time bomb with this **Seed** inside of him, and now they were sending him to be a literal bomb against the enemy.

Alanis Morissette would be so proud.

CHAPTER FORTY-THREE

Band of Goat-Brothers

Jonathan Tillman

On his way to the front gates, he saw a couple of faces furtively peeking out of windows, and one brave drunk who seemed to have chosen to meet the invasion head-on with a stuttering song. Aside from them, it seemed like everyone had gotten the news and was getting as far away from the attack as possible.

Twenty minutes of jogging through the city toward the point he had seen from the roof resulted in him finally emerging from a side street onto the extremely long promenade that started at the front gate and cut a straight line to the teleportation hub at the center. The crossroad he had found let out just a few blocks from the gates. Looking up, he saw that the battle for the gatehouse was almost over, the traitorous private house guards having slowly worn down the city guard veterans.

He glanced back toward the center of the city and could just barely make out the crowds in the distance, which would be massed like sitting ducks around the hub until the spell was complete. Far beyond them at the other end of the promenade was the imperial palace, which stood aloof, somehow still feeling removed even at the imminent destruction of its seat of power.

"Human! Get out of the street," came a whispered shout from the shadowed doorway of a building across the street.

Tilly squinted at the origin of the voice. It was one of the extremely muscular and scarred guards Tilly had seen at the steps of the Cura. He was standing half hidden in the door of his building with a great vantage of the fight on the top of the wall. Tilly's **Identify** pinged.

Level 44, Empire's Bastion

"I'm here to help, Lord Hiro sent me!" Tilly called back, suddenly aware of possible watchers from the top of the wall. He ducked back around the corner, keeping his line of sight with the soldier, but removing himself from the sight of any on top of the wall.

The soldier gave a hard nod of acknowledgment and glanced up at the wall, watching for a few breaths, before gesturing sharply for Tilly to make the crossing. Tilly sprinted from his cover, crossing the wide street and ducking into the large doorway.

The soldier moved to the side to let him pass, keeping watch on the wall, and he entered into a large stone atrium with booths at the other end. The space looked like a processing area for customs and taxes for those entering the city. But Tilly barely registered the space, his eyes immediately drawn to the group that had claimed this as their base of operations. The entire room was filled with soldiers in different states of readiness. Some sharpening their already sharp swords, others playing dice, and a few actually napping. Each had a torso-sized shield close to hand and a spear within reach. A few glanced his way curiously as he entered, but none seemed concerned, trusting the man at the door to not let anyone in that was a threat.

There was an air of confident menace that permeated this group. Looking over the room, Tilly got the impression that he might be amongst the last and greatest fighters the empire had to offer. He hadn't thought to ask but was sure they didn't hand out the class Empire's Bastion to just anyone. Off to the right of the door, Tilly spotted Linus speaking to a few other older especially grizzled-looking satyrs. Tilly headed over to report for duty, and the small group around Linus parted at his approach, all hard men, giving him cool, measuring looks.

"Jonathan Tillman, this is about to become a very dangerous place. If you have a message, give it quickly," Linus snapped, obviously short on time and patience. Tilly was suddenly so nervous he almost replied, *Dangerous? Danger is my middle name.*

Instead, he coughed and looked around again. He had been in plenty of rooms filled with hardened firefighters when a rookie walked in on his first day. Hell, he remembered his first day as a rookie. There was nothing like the divide between those who had been in the shit and those who hadn't. Even with everything he had seen and endured the last week, he immediately knew he had not been in the shit like these guys. This wasn't another military unit. It was a family forged in blood and iron. As casual as it may seem, he could feel his otherness within their deeply ingrained prebattle rituals.

"I . . . um. I'm here to help," he said to the small group around the commander. They stood there at ease, broken-in armor oiled and polished to a shine. Their simple weapons practically vibrated with a potential for violence. Before these practitioners of violence, the hatchets on his belt felt like little toys, and he wished he hadn't already stuttered in his answer.

"Ha! We would love to have you with us, little man!" boomed a voice just beyond the leadership huddle. Tilly couldn't keep his jaw from dropping as a huge muscled physique detached himself from the wall. Tilly was sure he was a satyr like the others, but he didn't share the goat-legged feature of many of his fellow soldiers. A large almost entirely goat head sat atop a perfectly humanoid body. Well, it would be humanoid if humans grew to be ten feet tall. This guy could give the minotaurs a run for their money.

"Maybe when the press gets thick, we can throw you over the line as a snack to the enemy!" He guffawed, his goat mouth somehow forming human words in an oddly fascinating display of dexterity.

Tilly's mouth got ahead of his brain, and he spoke without thinking. "Actually, Gigantor, you hit the nail right on the head," he snarked back.

Linus's frown deepened at Tilly's pithy reply. "Explain yourself, human. Time is short, and this is no place for humor."

"Look, I know this is a one-way mission for you guys, and I am sure you are more than capable of completing it. But I have been given something from the imperial treasury. It can greatly magnify one of my *Abilities*. When paired with my unique effectiveness against the kind of enemy that will be coming through that gate, I have the potential to eliminate a significant amount of combatants in one go." Tilly rushed through the situation, almost without taking a breath.

Linus paused, considering Tilly's words and weighing them against the risk of changing the battle plan at such a late hour. After a moment, he made sure Tilly understood the mission. "As soon as the final guards fall, the gate will be opened. The enemy is holding back and hoping to flood the streets with these **Corrupted** without losing any other resources. Our directive is simple. Form up in the center of the gate and hold for as long as possible. If you believe you can aid us in our task, then welcome aboard. What do you need to activate this item of yours?"

The disturbingly beady eyes of the giant-goat-man drilled into him from over the commander's shoulder. Tilly had a hard time telling if he was smiling or snarling as he respectfully waited for the commander to finish the interrogation.

"Well, it should be straightforward once I have enough mana, but I need to gain two levels before I can activate it to its full potential. As for your plan, I can work from behind the front line and use my ranged attack, which is my best anyway. Once I am ready, I'll charge the *Ability* as much as I can, but I need some way to get as far behind the enemy's lines as possible before releasing it. It is an area of effect that marks me as its center."

The commander's hard, calculating eyes shone for a moment at that final piece of information, "Alright, Gorock. You're on babysitting duty. Keep him alive and behind our lines. When he is ready, throw him. Everyone clear on the plan?"

"But, sir!" The giant recoiled as if struck.

"Shut your big mouth, Gorock!" one of the well-worn sergeants snarled. The goat-man ignored the officer and looked like he was still going to object.

"You will do as I command, and on top of that, if he does manage to live after this half-baked plan, you are to retrieve him at all costs. If he can do what he says, they will need him at the center of the city."

That declaration hit the huge soldier like a hammer blow.

"Sir, please! I must die with you . . . the men . . . I will not run like a coward," he pleaded, choking back what might have been a sob.

"There is plenty of dying to be had today. I'm sure you will have your pick of opportunity to die, but you will do so after you complete the mission," he said firmly, looking away from the warrior and scanning the large room. As he tallied up their resources one final time, granite resolve settled over his features. He became again what his men needed, something immovable.

"I have seen what he can do against this new enemy. If we can keep this resource available to our remaining citizens, then we will," he finished.

"Sir!" called the soldier watching the gates. "They are breaking into the mechanism room now! You want me to activate it?"

"Hold on that," he called back, brushing past Gorock and Tilly, the matter settled in his mind.

"Wait until the gate is a quarter open, then break it. We want them drawn to our choke point."

Then he turned to the room, and bellowed out, "All right boys, this is it! Form up on me!" As if by magic, every soldier in the room was rising to their feet, shield in hand, weapon at the ready. It was as if they hadn't been relaxing at all.

Commander Linus turned through the doorway and jogged out, followed by the seventy or so soldiers that made up the Empire's Bastion unit. Their movements were smooth and disciplined, showing no hesitance or confusion at the orders.

"Come on, little man." Gorock sighed, as he hefted his door-sized shield, and brought up the rear of the formation. Tilly looked down at some abandoned dice on the floor, took a deep steadying breath, and drew his hatchets. He found himself nauseous and thirsty all at once, but it was time to go. He was still so new . . . but he could feel the significance of this mission. This was the best place for him, and he wasn't going to back down from what could possibly save hundreds if not thousands of lives.

He shut down his mind and moved, catching up with the giant goat-man as he ducked through the doorway. Fighting fire had been one of the few things in life that he excelled at. He was decisive under pressure and could read a change in the environment even as fire raged all around him. But none of that set him apart from the crowd. The thing that made him different, was his ability to lean completely into his training without hesitating or second-guessing. Once he entered a burning building, everything else faded away until only muscle memory and instinct were left. The past was gone, and the future narrowed to a razor edge of clarity. *Take another step forward and do what you were trained to do.*

Of course, he didn't have any training when it came to fighting with ancient weaponry against a charging horde of monsters . . .

The controlled shout of the commander broke through the din of fighting on and beyond the wall, "First rank, shields up! Second rank, spears at ready! Third rank, filter in as needed. If you see a brother go down, pull him back and fill the gap!" He never stopped advancing to the gate, which was just beginning to crack open. The sound of men screaming and the inhuman gurgling roars of the **Corrupted** pierced through the sliver of an opening like a knife through sutures, reminding Tilly that thousands of soldiers had already fought and died today.

The gate continued to open outwardly, and the soldiers in front of him flowed unhurriedly into formation, three lines deep. They might as well have been on the parade ground for all the concern they showed.

"Now, Threstus!" Linus called to the soldier who had kept out of formation. The satyr held a large conch shell at the ready above his head. At the command, he broke it against the wall, and the sound of crashing waves rose and drowned out the tumult of battle. Blue symbols raced up the wall from the point of the break, and the private guards began to call and point out the Bastion's activity to their superiors.

When the arcane symbols hit the top of the wall, the whole section above the gate lit up in glowing blue markings, and the sound of crashing waves turned into a roar that reminded Tilly of a waterfall. The traitorous guards above shouted in alarm, backing away from the edge of the wall and the brilliant azure glow emanating from the stone.

Then the deafening sound suddenly cut off for a long second of silence before water exploded like a geyser from the top of the wall, knocking all of those standing on the battlements off at an outward angle. Tilly realized this must be some sort of failsafe embedded in the magic of the walls to repel an attack if the gatehouse was lost. No one had told the noble houses that this existed, even though they were the ones who had been assigned to hold the wall.

Screams of confusion and terror emerged from the battlefield beyond the wall as the private guards of the noble houses found themselves amongst thousands of mindless **Corrupted** consuming the dregs of the formations that had recently been the last of the empire's Phalanxes. As hundreds of new soldiers fell in among their number, they gleefully turned and fell upon the new presence in their midst.

Through the twenty-foot opening of the stalled gate, Tilly saw many of the guards take the three-story fall unscathed, only to be set upon by **Corrupted**. These guards may have been assholes, but they weren't weak. Many grouped up in twos and threes to take out ten or twenty of the creatures before going down themselves. Tilly was starting to see just how well-designed this plan had been. Let the enemy proceed with their plan as much as possible while delaying them every step of the way. None of these counterattacks were designed to be decisive victories. Rather, they had been strung together to rob the enemy of momentum every step of the way.

"The Cult believes we are finished!" Linus bellowed, drawing attention to the now open gate. **Corrupted** turned from the recent distraction, and fixed their dead all-black orbs on the new prey.

"They think they have faced a true Phalanx and defeated it!" Linus shouted at them again, his voice rising in volume. He eyed the tens of thousands of **Corrupted** creatures that had once been citizens of the empire he had sworn to protect. Tilly saw rage there, blazing up from deep sorrow at all they had lost. But none of it softened the stony resolve that was carved in resolute lines across the commander's features.

"Bastions, shields up! HOLD THE LINE!" His voice rang out in several octaves at once, and Tilly realized that the commander had just used an *Ability*. In one motion, the front rank locked their shields with a thunderous clang, and a golden light showed in an almost opaque barrier of radiance about a foot in front of the first rank.

The **Corrupted** seemed to understand that some sort of challenge had been issued, and howled in fury, charging toward the open gate, and the prey that filled the gap.

The commander's voice again rose, exploding in several octaves at once, "DON'T GIVE THEM AN INCH!" The golden radiance intensified and filtered back, washing over all the ranks. It even shone on Tilly who had positioned himself about five feet behind the last rank next to Gorock who wore a melancholic expression. Or at least that's what Tilly thought it was. It was hard to tell on a goat's face.

"Our glorious last stand, and I'm stuck next to a Baby-Man . . ." he muttered to himself, just loud enough to hear over the din of the coming charge of **Corrupted**.

Tilly was barely paying attention, instead watching as three buffs appeared on his HUD. He quickly pulled up his notification log to make sure he knew exactly what he was working with before he got caught up in the heat of battle.

CHAPTER FORTY-FOUR

Thermopile Monopoly

> *You have been accepted into the formation of the **Empire's Bastion**.
> While in formation, you are affected by **Shields Up**, **Don't Give an Inch**,
> and **Hold the Line**.*

> ***Shields Up:*** *Any offensive attack against the shield wall is reduced by 25%
> in effectiveness while formation is held.*

> ***Don't Give an Inch:*** *All enemy knockback Abilities are negated
> as long as the formation is held.*

> ***Hold the Line:*** *All passive regeneration rates are doubled while in formation.*

That last one was a game-changer! That would boost his mana regen up to almost 3 percent per minute. That was still pitifully low, but it felt huge. He set his mental floor at 40 percent mana so that he would never be more than three minutes from activating **Flame Expulsion**. He flicked closed the log and checked his mana and health.

Mana: 55%
Health: 100%

He inflamed his hatchets just in time for the front of the enemy's charge to hit the line. Gorock looked over and snorted at Tilly's forearm-sized weapons, while Tilly watched engrossed as the tide of **Corrupted** crashed against a golden wall projecting from the shields. As soon as they hit, they slowed significantly and hit the seemingly unmovable secondary wall of shields, having lost almost all of their momentum.

Then, as if they were a single entity with many appendages the second rank of soldiers thrust their spears over the shoulders of the shield bearers, impaling the first and second ranks of enemy combatants. As the spears were withdrawn with whiplike quickness, the first rank followed up the thrusts with businesslike sword strikes, mowing through any **Corrupted** that remained standing. The soldiers showed incredible discipline in their positioning through all of these maneuvers. The first rank never broke the wall, and the second rank continued to pull back and strike with terrible thrusts over the shoulders of their brothers. Tilly even saw one second-ranker strike through the neck of a **Corrupted** minotaur mid-attack as it bent down to try to gore the satyr in front of him holding the shield wall.

Very quickly the initial wave of attackers that had stormed over to the opening in the gate had been churned into a gory paste by the economical yet brutal strikes of the shoulder-to-shoulder fighters of the Emperor's Bastions.

Tilly nervously rotated the hafts of his hatchets as he watched the rest of the horde of **Corrupted** shift from the battlefield, drawn toward the noise of the new conflict. Tens of thousands of black orbs had fixed on the gap in the gates. Eyeing a **Corrupted** shifting into a shambling run about thirty feet in front of the formation, Tilly hefted one of his hatchets and threw it, feeling like a kid tossing rocks at the ocean. It hit, decimating the reanimated body as blue flames licked hungrily through the center mass of the target.

Then he threw another and another . . . Soon Tilly didn't even have to aim. He just kept throwing, enflaming every attack he could until his mana dropped below 36 percent. He was rewarded with a *level up* notification a few seconds later, as the blue flame from his strikes finished eating through its latest target. He mentally dropped all the points into *Endurance* and realized he must have been pretty close to leveling after his part in the fight with the guards.

By this time, the new massed charge was almost upon the formation, and Tilly dropped his arms and breathed deeply, trying to recover as much mana as possible. The second, much larger wave thundered forward, and this time, as it crashed against the shield wall, the crushing weight of thousands of bodies caused the formation to flex. Commander Linus stepped forward, waiting until it seemed like the formation was flexed to its breaking point, the men shouting in rage, as they dug their hooves in and pushed back against the weight of an army. Then his bellowing command broke through the tumult.

"BASTIONS, PUSH THEM BACK!" he shouted in that same multi-octave voice that seemed to be linked to the unit's magic. The aura around the unit intensified, and the second and third rank ducked low and rammed their shoulders into the body of the satyr in front of them. It almost looked like a scrum from rugby, and the unit collectively yelled as it pushed forward.

At first, it was just one step, then it was two, the radiance building with each step until it flashed and an explosive *WUMPH* sounded from the front ranks as the collective force of both sides rebounded back toward the enemy, sending bodies flying twenty feet into the air. Tilly watched in awe as the unit took advantage of the breathing room to reset, with the first rank rotating back to the third, and the other two moving forward one position. All of the first rankers were injured in some way, but they took up their new positions stoically, trusting in the improved regen to get them right before their next rotation up front. Gorock looked on like a boy on punishment, forced to watch as his siblings ate all the dessert at the table.

"It feels like you guys will be able to hold forever," Tilly marveled, wondering if his plan was even necessary.

Gorock bared his square goat teeth in what could have been a grin or a sneer but didn't say anything. Surprisingly, he heard Linus speak up from ten yards away, supervising the carnage as if he were a butcher, trying to decide how he wanted to divide up a side of beef. "Yes, at our levels, in group warfare, we are unmatched. But this is not group warfare. This is slaughter. And while we can endure for longer than any traditional foot soldier, not even we can hold out for more than ten or fifteen minutes at this pace."

As if responding to his words, the horde gathered itself back together and surged forward again. Tilly had only regained about 5 percent of his mana, but he enflamed his axes and launched them at the biggest approaching targets anyway.

"How much longer?" Linus asked. His voice was flinty but calm. Tilly's throws hit, and he recalled the hatchets eyeing his glacial mana regen.

"I don't know exactly, but I only have one level left to achieve, and it looks like these guys range from five to ten levels above me. No matter what I *will* activate the *Ability* before you are overwhelmed," Tilly affirmed forcefully, not willing to allow the possibility of the formation breaking just so that he could regain a Title, and improve his chances at survival. Linus nodded at that, then squinted up toward the top of the wall.

"Threstus, what is the enemy's disposition? Any elites moving forward?" he called up. Tilly whipped his head up and saw that at some point the same satyr who had broken the shell against the wall had scaled its face and was now positioned near the gatehouse looking out over the enemy.

"No sir!" he shouted down. "But the creatures in the center of the press have begun to cannibalize each other. Some seem to be growing in size as they consume more of their peers."

Linus nodded at the news as if the lookout had just informed him of the weather. Then he turned back to Tilly.

"Mr. Tillman, you and Gorock are going to join Threstus on the wall. Disrupt as many of these things from forming and reaching the line as possible. This will probably be better for your level gain and the elevation will be advantageous for your throwing plan as well," he stated dryly, obviously not putting too much stock in the plan succeeding.

"Yes sir!" Gorock growled, apparently excited to get closer to the action any way he could. Before Tilly could respond, he felt the giant grab him by the back of his jacket and his waist band.

"Hey, wha-AAAHH!" Tilly screamed as he was launched thirty feet in the air, his arms pinwheeling as he thudded into the side of the crenellations and urgently clung to them as Threstus reached over and hauled him over the side.

"What the fu—" Tilly started, but as he caught Threstus's grin, he clamped his mouth shut. He was the one who had come up with the projectile plan and he realized Gorock had wanted to see how he handled a smaller throw.

Tilly cleared his throat and straightened his jacket, before moving to the opposite edge of the wall to get a better picture of what Threstus had seen. On his way over, he saw numerous piles of javelins and a large ballista set and loaded every ten feet along the wall. He was again struck by a pang of fury at the thought of the hundreds of soldiers up here that could have been manning the defenses if not for the selfishness of a few.

Threstus called down behind him, "He flies just fine, Gorock. Get your big naked legs up here and give us a hand!"

Tilly crossed to the other side of the wall and got eyes on what was happening in the center of the horde. The **Corrupted** there were being pressed in from behind, but were unable to move forward and had begun to fight amongst themselves. This would have normally been awesome, but unfortunately, eldritch tentacles had started to reach between the raging creatures and draw them together, fusing them into amalgamations of black ooze and twisted flesh.

Level 32, Corrupted Amalgam

Tilly shivered and felt Threstus step up next to him. "Gods, that's disgusting . . . bet I kill more than you, Mr. Magic-Fire-Man," he snarked before pulling one of the nearby bundles of javelins over to his hooves and picking one up.

Mana: 38%

Tilly shrugged and enflamed his hatchets. Threstus heaved a shockingly powerful throw. and Tilly followed him, throwing his weapons one after another at the largest **Amalgam** he could see forming. It had begun to wade through its twisted brethren like an adult at the shallow end of the pool, but then Tilly's axes thunked deep into its torso of melded bodies.

Something about the composition of the new creature called his flame attacks to be super effective. The flames ate hungrily at the surrounding flesh, and the creature urgently tried to brush off the tiny-looking weapons but only managed to press them deeper and spread the flames to its arms, which threw it into a frenzy.

Threstus's throw blew another's head clean off, although it just kept walking like nothing had happened. Threstus clucked in annoyance as he saw Tilly's target start to flail in pain, spreading the fire on its arms to the **Corrupted** it was wading through.

Threstus quickly kicked up two more javelins into his hands and launched them at his target, hitting the points where its legs connected to the rest of its body. Both strikes were extremely effective, erasing the joints as if they had never existed. The creature collapsed to the ground, crushing some other creatures.

Threstus looked over, smiling, only to see Tilly recalling his hatchets from a charred circle of bodies, the blue flame having done its work. He frowned and muttered something about "cheating magic users" under his breath.

"That may have worked great against these things, but I can't do that again for another couple of minutes, and it looks like we won't have that kind of time," Tilly said in a hollow voice, as the rush of his triumph bled away. The rest of the **Amalgams** had started to move forward, and with at least fifteen targets still to go, Tilly started rethinking his 40 percent rule. The sound of shouting and occasional commands rang out from below, and the men down there continued to grind against the endless numbers trying to press their way into the city.

"Don't worry," Threstus said, launching another couple of terrifyingly powerful throws. If this guy could do this with javelins, what could a high-level bow user do?

"Commander has one or two more tricks to play before we are done," he continued, crippling another **Amalgam**, before hoisting another couple of javelins to throw. Tilly just lamely watched his mana tick back up, twisting in knots over how slowly he was progressing.

"What did I miss?!" Gorock huffed, pulling himself over the side of the wall.

"Not much, Forward Knees," Threstus quipped as he launched the weapons in his hands.

"Aim for the big guys. Whoever has the most knockdowns wins!" he said cheerfully as he watched another **Amalgam** fall. The rest were halfway to the wall by now. Gorock just grunted in acknowledgment and moved over to the nearby ballista.

"I thought it was 'kills.' I don't remember you saying anything about knockdowns," Tilly called, as he saw his mana finally tick up another five points. He was able to launch another pair of enflamed hatchets at the next closest **Amalgam**.

The exact same scenario played out, netting Tilly more than twenty kills for the price of one.

"Humans . . ." Gorock said disapprovingly as he hefted one of the tree trunk ballista bolts above his shoulders.

"Always able to find something to complain about," he finished with a grunt as he lobbed the bolt in a perfect spiral that arced through the air until piercing through an **Amalgam** and biting deep into the hard ground beyond. The creature tried to pull free but was stuck at a forty-five-degree angle with no leverage to move forward or back along the body of the bolt.

"Yes, yes. You very strong. Congratulations," Threstus muttered dryly, before throwing again, hitting his target perfectly.

These guys are machines! Tilly thought, but as Tilly looked over the seemingly endless enemies, fear churned in his gut at the hopelessness of their position. Less than a hundred against tens of thousands.

Tilly flicked up his character sheet, checking to see just how much exp was left before he regained [Resolute]. Deadly or not, he would activate the Microcosm before he regained the Title if it came down to it. He couldn't just watch them die.

Level: 13 (45,000 exp to next level)

He quickly followed up that query by pulling up his battle log, filtering through the updates to find how much he was getting per **Amalgam** and **Corrupted** kill. It looked like 7,000 exp for a big guy and 500 for the normal **Corrupted** on average.

Still, a ways to go, and they were almost out of time. Both Gorock and Threstus took out another **Amalgam**, while Tilly tried to decide if he should just try to activate **Flame Expulsion** without waiting for the mana or Title. He had done it before, and if he was probably going to die anyway, might as well risk **Mana Exhaustion**.

"Guys, I'm holding back, trying to conserve mana for the big move . . . but things aren't looking good. Should I go for it?" Tilly called, reaching into his fantasy fanny pack for the magical orb. The **Amalgams** were almost at the gate now, and Tilly ground his teeth in indecision.

CHAPTER FORTY-FIVE

Soldiers of the Line

Tilly felt a restraining touch against his forearm as he reached for the Microcosm. "Just wait. Commander's not done in yet," Threstus said, watching the approach of the **Amalgams** with hard eyes, a javelin ready in his other hand.

Just as the **Amalgams** reached the shield wall, Tilly heard the commander's voice explode from down below, "BASTIONS, PUSH THEM BACK!" A concerted yell of effort followed, and then the same concussive resulted, which looked even more spectacular from above. Once again bodies of **Corrupted** went flying back as if hit by a freight train.

"Third Rank, ON ME!" followed the shout of Commander Linus, before the bodies had even finished landing in the distance. The **Amalgams** had all been knocked down or at least put off balance. Tilly quickly counted nine lying supine or on all fours before the formation, barely out of reach of the first rank.

The first rank stood ready while the third rank leaped out from behind the first two, in an extraordinary feat of coordinated athleticism. Tilly saw that they were each suffused with the same unit magic that had empowered the other commands, their speed and grace having practically doubled.

The radiant warriors fell upon the twisted creatures still trying to get off the ground. The **Amalgams'** builds heavily favored *Strength*, and their ponderous movements to get their unnaturally formed bodies back off the ground were far too slow to avoid the countercharge.

The satyrs flowed over the hulking downed forms, hacking at limbs until they were severed from the main body, and then quickly moving on to the next. The repelled group of regular **Corrupted** was already back on its feet and moving back into the fight, but not before the third rank had completely dismembered seven of the **Amalgams**.

"FALL BACK!" Linus shouted from the midst of the glowing squad. They all turned and ran, the tide of **Corrupted** close behind. Tilly saw the magic wink out one by one, as the soldiers fled back toward their lines and the shield wall.

Tilly had pulled his hands away from the orb and was itching to throw his hatchets to support their retreat. Threstus and Gorock did their best to provide cover fire for the retreating unit as the first rank split neatly. Every second shield turned on its axis to allow room for the incoming members of the unit to dive through the openings.

Even with all of this, Tilly saw one, then two soldiers taken down by the manic tide of **Corrupted** following at their hooves. Gorock pinned one of the last two **Amalgams** to the ground with another ballista bolt, and Threstus furiously rained down projectiles while the third rank made it back through the line and the shields crashed shut behind them.

At this point, Tilly was trying to crush the bone handles of his weapons in his grip, anger and frustration warring for supremacy in his mind. The desperate backward chops of the two who had been caught by the **Corrupted's** countercharge, felt like they had hit Tilly in the guts. Should he have done something? Was he right to be saving his mana like this?

Just then a Bastion on the first rank was yanked forward by a particularly large **Corrupted** and was torn apart before his brothers could free him from the mob grabbing at the momentary weak point in the line.

"PUSH THEM BACK!" the command rang in response, and another explosion of supernatural force gave the line yards of breathing room to rotate ranks, putting the most rested second-rankers in front to take the next crashing charge. Tilly watched his mana tick above 40 percent again, and he enflamed and threw his hatchets at the last **Amalgam**, which was trying to regain its feet after receiving another blow of concussive force.

It and everything around it died in a blaze of hungry blue flame. Recalling the weapons brought him back down to 35 percent, and he once again chafed at his pitiful *Wisdom* stat. Not that he could do anything about it now. Too much depended on him being able to overcharge **Flame's Expulsion** with [Resolute]. If he died before he could ramp up the power high enough, it would all be for nothing.

"Eyes up boys," Threstus called, gesturing with a javelin back toward the middle of the horde. Another bubbling soup of conflict and grotesque creation was brewing.

"How many times can you guys push and countercharge like that?" Tilly asked through gritted teeth, each minute progressing tortuously as more soldiers fought and died below him at the gates.

"We probably have two or three push rotations left," Threstus answered off to the side as he hunted for another pile of javelins.

"We will save them for high-value opportunities. Otherwise we will keep the rotation piecemeal based on injuries or casualties. We will hold them for as long as possible. Every minute here is one more minute for our charges to escape," he continued, unable to mask the grim note that had slipped into his light tone.

Eventually, Tilly's mana ticked back up past 40 percent, and he enflamed and sent his hatchets hurtling through the air again, hurling them to near the limit of his range, to disrupt some of the disturbing fusion happening at the center of the horde. He allowed himself a grim smile as the two **Amalgams** trying to fuse both caught fire and collapsed onto the crowd of creatures below.

"How close are you, little man?" Gorock's gravelly baritone interjected from nearest the ballista as he threw the last of the bolts over the wall horizontally to log roll and crush at least ten of the **Corrupted**.

"I need about two more of the big guys and then about three minutes to regen what I need for the *Ability*," Tilly snapped urgently as he watched his mana tick back up slowly. His eyes flicked to the center of the Horde, where he saw the giant horror snatch a few more of the recently created **Amalgams** and pop them into its recently formed maw. The thing's mouth was the size of a full wagon, crammed with a mix of jagged bones and floppy flesh.

Level 55, Corrupted Colossus

"Yeah, I don't think we have that long . . ." Threstus snarled, and then his eyes snapped away from the **Colossus** and focused in on Tilly with an almost feverish brightness. "Is the main problem mana conservation?"

"Affirmative. I can take them out but not fast enough if I save mana for the bomb. Or if I burn through to get the last level I need, I won't be able to overload and explode afterward," Tilly answered quickly. Threstus blinked a couple of times at the wording before a death's head grin broke out across his face.

"Melee it is! Gorock, make a hole, buddy. If we are going to die, it's not going to be up here on a wall. We are soldiers of the Line after all!"

Tilly barely had time to compute that insane string of sentences when Gorock bellowed, "Finally, some action!" before crouching down and leaping over the wall crenellations in a standing jump. Tilly watched his flight down slacked-jawed. Midflight the warrior pulled his XL-sized spear from behind his back and unsheathed his shortsword. He landed with a boom about ten yards in front of the gate entrance, and bellowed again, this time making a sound somewhat resembling a bleat . . . if it was about five octaves lower than a normal goat.

He crushed several **Corrupted** to paste with his landing, and his bellow did something to those around him, causing them to stagger. He followed up the effect with huge sweeping strikes with his spear that clearly was much heavier than it appeared in his hands. It mowed through the enemy like a scythe through grain.

Threstus jabbed him in the side with an elbow, having drawn two of the Roman-style shortswords at some point. "You better hurry human. We have some power-leveling to do and not much time to do it in." Then he too leaped over the side of the wall, having the gall to actually add a swan dive into his fall, before landing on a few of the enemy, crushing or stabbing several before rolling to his feet. Then the pair were back-to-back, sowing death and dismemberment in equal measures and somehow managing to not get swamped in the tide of battle.

Holy shit . . .

It was one thing to recognize that his old human limits were meaningless. It was another to realize that pretty much the whole battle plan now hinged on him jumping down three stories from the top of the wall into a whole crowd of **Corrupted**.

Then a sound so deep it actually shook the wall blasted forth from almost formed **Colossus**, and Tilly's mind blanked. That familiar switch flicked inside of him, and he just decided to believe what he needed to keep moving. He had trusted his equipment a thousand times in roaring fires, even when every human instinct screamed at him that the few inches of treated fabric wouldn't be nearly enough to protect him.

He had decided his gear could take as much punishment as it needed to for him to get the job done. Now, in the same way, something in him snapped, and he knew his body could take something like this fall and keep fighting. He had monstrous *Endurance* for his level, and while he understood he was probably going to die today, it wasn't going to be from falling.

He blanked, removing his conscious mind's control of his actions, and suddenly, the wind was rushing past him and his stomach was up in his throat. He didn't remember jumping, but that was kind of the point. The best way to do something your rational mind refused to do was to turn it off. In the second he was in the air, he managed to be glad that he had at least kept his body feet first. An absurd image of him belly-flopping in the lake when he was fifteen almost caused him to smile, and then the insane moment of mid-air suspension ended, and he plummeted to the ground.

It came up punishingly fast and struck the soles of his feet like the world's biggest sledgehammer. Thankfully, he didn't lock his legs, resisting as they collapsed, trying to capture as much of his momentum as possible, before slamming down into his shoulder and rolling several feet like a rag doll.

"Get up, little man! Not the time for a nap," Gorock shouted, somehow already standing over him warding back the enemy with wide-sweeping strikes. Tilly groaned but was already pushing up from the ground, finding nothing broken. In fact, the only pain he really had was a throbbing in the bottoms of both feet and his left shoulder.

Health: 89%

Before he could celebrate his first "almost superhero landing" a **Corrupted** satyr in guards' armor was on him, trying to bite down on his neck. Before Tilly could even yell in shock, its weight was suddenly gone, and Threstus was above him pulling him up.

"Come on man, we are here to get you *experience*. You need to get in the fight!" he shouted as if Tilly was confused about their purpose here in this endless sea of enemies.

"PUSH THEM BACK!" came the shout from somewhere behind them, accompanied a second later by another huge boom and the flying of bodies. Tilly found his hatchets in his hand, not really sure how they got there, and he started hacking wildly at anything that came close. Gorock was everywhere, keeping most of the enemies on his side at bay with his spear and finishing any that came close with that huge meat cleaver of a sword that only looked normal in his hand due to his huge proportions.

Threstus was equally impressive, whirling around with incredible grace, somehow holding down most of his side without ever staying in one place. Not that they could cover all 360-degrees of the surrounding enemies. Tilly was almost immediately breathing extremely heavily as he did everything in his power to keep enemies from piling in on him. They didn't so much fight as throw their body weight at him, trying to bog him down. He was shoving back the ones who got through as much as he was hitting them with any sort of ax strike.

"BASTIONS, ON ME!" came the multi-octave shout from behind him. Then, the battered unit of satyrs were flowing all around him glowing with golden intensity as they mowed through the surrounding enemies like grass.

"Threstus, you better have a good reason for breaking formation." Commander Linus's voice cracked out like a whip as he pulled up next to the trio.

"That's almost the last of our *Unit Magic*," he finished in a lower voice looking around at the men fighting all around him sadly. Then he called out in an authoritative, but unenhanced voice, "Bastion, Form Up. True square, Eight by Eight!"

The glow sputtered out all around them as the men suddenly broke off their charge and quickly formed a square with the commander at the center. Threstus saluted and reported in a much more businesslike voice than he had used atop the wall. "Sir, the human stated that he could not make the current time frame while using mana-burning *Abilities*. So I made the call to go full melee and see if we could help him make time—"

His words were cut off by a deafening roar from the **Colossus** and the crash of a new tide of **Corrupted** against the new formation. The worn soldiers were still holding back the onslaught, though it was a close thing. Tilly noted, between gasping breaths, that the only men left in reserve in the third rank were his trio and the commander. The rest were needed for a thin second rank and a full first. There would be no more rotating out.

Linus just nodded, rolling with the shift in a battle that he could do nothing to change. "You two, take the leading right edge. I'll take the left," he commanded, moving to take his self-given position. Then he stopped and turned back around, finding Tilly's eyes with an intense look. "Tillman, get it done." Then he turned and was in the midst of the soldiers on the left front.

Threstus's eyes were flint as he turned away from the commander to Tilly. "Time to learn what the Line is all about."

Gorock simply bellowed before rushing to his assigned position, with Threstus behind. The flame at Tilly's center blazed in approval at the courage and honor the soldiers around him showed. None hesitated in following commands that would assuredly lead to their deaths. He found his fear quashed beneath the weight of expectation he had seen in Linus's eyes. If he was going to die, he was going to make it count, shoulder to shoulder with brothers bent toward the same purpose.

He rushed into the second rank of soldiers and added his weight to the line trying to counter the unstoppable press of the **Corrupted** horde.

Not a single member of the unit expected to live out the next few minutes. But the formation would hold, and the enemy was going to pay a bloody price for every step.

CHAPTER FORTY-SIX

Bombs Away

Jonathan Tillman - Level 13 Son of Flame

What do I do?" Tilly shouted from his newly received position in the Bastion formation.

"Stand behind the guy with a shield and hit as many enemies as you can. You don't have to kill them, just participate. You'll see!" Threstus shouted over the melee, already thrusting over a combatant's shoulder to impale two separate **corrupted** like a macabre shish kebab.

Gorock had already unslung the huge shield from his back and jumped the line, swinging his sword in punishing arcs as he cleared the area directly in front of the right corner of the formation. He acted as a tide breaker against the enemy, trusting the men behind him to take out anything coming for his flank.

Tilly added his desperate thumping attacks to the rhythm of butchery being played out in front of him. Any time an enemy flung itself onto the shield wall or reached through to attempt a grab or swipe, Tilly was there. His weapons bit through corrupted flesh and bone alike. It was chaos.

It was horrifying.

It was glorious.

Then the ground trembled with a deep crashing reverberation. Tilly threw his head back and looked up, craning his neck to a painful degree. There, towering seventy feet in the air was the **Colossus**. It had finally gained its feet and victoriously released a booming roar that sounded like a foghorn the size of a city bus. It had been formed from thousands of bodies, and while it didn't have eyes, Tilly felt it when the protrusion that seemed to be its head turned toward their dwindling formation that still managed to block most of the gate.

This was it.

They were out of time. Bile rose in Tilly's throat as he realized he had failed. Even if he activated now, he doubted he would be able to make a dent in that thing without being able to overcharge the *Ability* far past his limits. He roared in frustration, furiously redoubling his hacking, taking swipes and bites from the enemy as his pace became more reckless.

He had given these men hope . . .

He had *lied* to them.

Tears started free-flowing down his face as he viciously hacked at every enemy in reach. Each chop of his weapon did nothing to reduce his growing certainty that he had failed. He railed against the unfairness of it all, flailing almost wildly over the shoulders of the shield bearers in front of him.

Then he felt the mental ping that indicated a *level-up* notification. His icon was blinking, but that couldn't be right. He had only done a fraction of the work that should have been involved to get the last chunk of *experience*. He gave the command to place all of his free points into *Endurance* and pulled up his log.

Congratulations! You have regained a lost Title, [Resolute].

Threstus noticed him stepping back from the line in confusion and yelled over. "It's the Line. We all share in the experience as we fight! Did you get it?"

In wonder, Tilly looked over at him, and nodded dumbly, before reaching into his fantasy fanny pack for the Microcosm. Threstus's gore-covered face, flashed white with a smile and he yelled over to Commander Linus, "Commander! It's a go!"

Another earth shattering footstep sounded out through the battlefield, as the **Colossus** lumbered forward.

"Collapse the Square! Four by Four!" the blood-covered commander shouted. Exhausted Bastions threw off the weight of the tide one last time, and stepped back smartly, covering each other with thrusts and stabs as they collapsed the square to half its former size. This exposed open portions of the gate to the enemy, and some began to slip in past the much smaller formation.

Tilly saw none of this as he watched his mana tick up to 50 percent.

It was time.

He held the orb in front of him and activated **Flame Expulsion**. With his newly developed internal awareness, he saw his mana pathways light up with a blue fiery glow, as they sent energy to his core, and his core itself began to condense the building pressure to forcefully expel flame at the apex of the *Ability*. Time slowed as the magic of the orb activated.

It began to burn in his hand and the markings across its surface began to shine and whirl. He felt its magic entering his body, and race along his pathways, creating a shadow network of the ones already activated by his skill. Just as he reached the point of full compaction at his core, something happened, and all of the energy drained into the shadow pathways much more rapidly than it had compacted.

"Wait, wha—" he began to exclaim in disbelief before his mana suddenly pounded back into his activated pathways, twice as dense as it had been before. It reentered his pathways with an almost physical blow to his body, and he flinched as he attempted to channel it back toward his center. It was uncomfortable, but not impossible and his awareness of the outer world dimmed as his inward focus grew sharper.

"Gorock, I think it's your moment, Big Guy!" Threstus shouted as another step from the **Colossus** shook the ground.

Tilly gritted his teeth and pushed the newly condensed mana back through his pathways to the center where the *Ability* took over and began to condense it. As it reached its climax, the mana drained away again into the shadow pathways of the *Artificial Endless Path*, leaving Tilly feeling like a wrung-out dishrag.

The feeling lasted another hollow moment before mana crashed into his pathways again. At four times the normal load, the metaphysical blow doubled him over like a punch to the gut. As the impact disgorged its payload, it felt like molten lead flooded his veins. He screamed as he forced it back down along his pathways to his core. The **Flame Expulsion** took over and condensed it again. At this point, the *Microcosm* orb was shining like a miniature star, burning the skin off of Tilly's clenched hand. His consciousness receded, and he dimly realized that if he wanted to stop the feedback, he would have to let go of the orb. His body was on fire, and ethereal flames licked up and down his torso, as he bore the weight of twice his normal mana capacity.

The **Colossus** took another step toward the formation, its movement deceptively slow as it lifted its tower-sized leg and slammed it down just twenty yards away.

Tilly's whole body locked up as he screamed, torturously fighting with everything he had to compress his supercharged mana fully. As soon as the *Ability* reached its threshold, the immense pressure momentarily lifted from his aching internal network as the *Artificial Endless Path* drained it all away. In the clarity of that aching emptiness, Tilly activated [Resolute], the ragged scream dying on his lips.

Gorock had, at some point, arrived beside him as the Bastions fought on, their formation slowly eroding before the endless tide of the enemy army. He stood by, watching the approach of the Colossus with unbridled glee.

[Resolute] slid into place, encasing Tilly's body and mind in an impenetrable moment. In a single shining flash of clarity, Tilly understood many things at once. He was about to get hit with mana eight times denser than his pathways were designed to handle, and while he was sure [Resolute] would protect him from the effects of such an overload, he was not confident in his capacity to control such power. Even as he had this thought, the burning orb in his hand began to turn to slag, the enchanted metal melting in between his fingers.

"Throw me, NOW!" he shouted, his eyes flying open. What had felt like a burning liquid in his pathways previously now hit his network like a living river of plasma. His pathways would have disintegrated except for the intervention of the many-hued energy that had reinforced his network like scaffolding, holding them up under the load for a single cycle. The rainbow coalescence coated the insides and outside of his pathways, guiding the destructive force all the way to his core where it began to compact a final time.

Gorock lifted him with ease and reared back before launching him into the air with terrifying speed. A scream once again tore itself from Tilly's lips. He was mid-arc, flying directly toward the chest of the **Colossus** when time stopped.

Tilly's awareness was once again elongated and deepened as he became locked in the crosswinds of space and time. He could still think, but it was not a linear experience. Instead different aspects of his situation bloomed in his consciousness at once, and he processed them simultaneously.

First, something had gone wrong with the feedback loop of the Microcosm. He assumed that almost any foreseen use of the item had not factored in the presence of a Title such as [Resolute] and thus it had failed when pushed past a third feedback loop. The mana had returned to him at the appropriate density, but the item had melted to his hand, leaving him unable to drop it and break the connection.

But something else was happening. As it had melted, the enchanted hyper-imbued metal had made contact with his sleeve, and a notification had appeared on his log. One that he was able to comprehend instantaneously once he understood its existence.

Congratulations! *You have been subjected to an extreme environment while wearing* **Origin's** *primitive leather armor, activating a hidden growth prerequisite. You are currently caught in an infinite mana feedback loop and have provided your armor with an enchanted material to pattern a new form. When in Mana Overdrive, your armor will take on characteristics of the Nullspider hide. The enchantment found on the item sacrificed to your armor will be overlaid on the Nullspider hide in this form, allowing a full experience to mana conversion at 100 exp - 1% mana regen. Conversion will continue until mana usage or experience flow ceases.*

His leather armor had turned matte black all over with silvery metal inlays that looked suspiciously like a mix between the surface of a computer chip and the nervelike pathways of his mana channels. These newly carved paths had taken the place of the Microcosm in the feedback loop and were still pushing extremely dense mana through his battered, but thankfully protected mana channels.

Finally, his was not the only hidden surge of mana on the field of battle. Tilly was able to sense a steady but dense flow of red-aspected mana flowing from the front lines of the battle back toward the ranks of the Cult's true army. There, they had set up some sort of large ritual, and it was feeding off the deaths of this conflict.

These realities settled into his consciousness and then time hiccupped forward, like a CD skipping. The **Colossus's** foot was lifted to its apex, ready to slam down and crush the entire Bastion formation, while Tilly flew past in an arc that would have him hitting the creature center mass. All of this as his **Flame Expulsion** finally reached its pressure limit, and his world exploded in blue flames.

Some distant part of him noted the feeling of impact upon a solid perpendicular surface, but most of him was consumed with the raw terror of being a conduit for impossible amounts of energy. As the initial wave of his *Ability* released at eight times its normal magnitude, the lines on the new form of his armor lit up and began to receive an influx of . . . *experience*. It was taking this source of energy and converting it to raw mana that continued to power a channeled version of **Flame Expulsion**. Until the *Ability* ran out of enemies to consume, he was trapped, frozen in a vortex of influx and output.

To make matters worse, [Resolute] had stopped protecting his pathways after the initial wave, and they were being put under extreme pressure from continuously casting his strongest *Ability*. He tried to scream, but there was no oxygen— his flames had consumed it all. He persisted there in this confluence of power and agony until suddenly the influx stopped, and he began to fall, his unconscious form limp as it crashed to the ground.

Threstus Marcellus - Level 44 Empire's Bastion Subcommander
Two minutes earlier

Threstus wasn't sure what was going to happen when Gorock tossed the human at the disgusting monstrosity. He knew that the man had been gathering mana for something he referred to as a bomb, but he didn't know how effective it would be against this creature. No, this was where the Bastions would make their end.

Gods, how has it come to this?

At least he could die here with his brothers and do his duty one last time, making some small atonement for the incredible debt his family now owed the empire and all of its citizens. To think they would stoop so low for the favor of such a power was horrendous. Thinking about his past as the previous heir to that death trap of a family was one of the few things that could darken his otherwise cheerful demeanor.

He was about to continue to fight on the line, to hold for a few minutes more when the unthinkable happened. The human's attack exploded into the form of a blue shooting star, hitting the **Colossus** in its center and then releasing an expanding mass of blue flames. The creature let out a much higher pitch call of distress before stumbling back. All the while the flames continued to grow into a miniature sun.

"Commander!" Threstus shouted looking over.

"I see it. Bastions, PROTECT!" The last of the collective Unit Reserve Mana washed over the formation, and they all withdrew even tighter into the square with supernatural grace. The second rank unslung shields and held them above their heads while the first rank continued to guard against outward pressures. A golden aegis much more potent than the slowing effect of the shield wall was projected in all directions, and the entire unit hunkered down under extremely dense layers of protection.

This formation had been developed hundreds of years ago to protect against large-scale destructive attacks that could sometimes be unleashed by an enemy. They had pulled it up just in time, as flame began to rain down all around them. None of them felt the intense heat behind their collective magical shield, but outside their formation, they could hear thousands of the creatures release a collective screech of panic and pain.

CHAPTER FORTY-SEVEN

Fighting Retreat

Linus - Level 62 Bastion of the Empire, Commander

B *linded Justice, that was one Pit of an Ability!* the commander mentally cursed, all the while watching for the outside environment to clear.

The human had come through. At first, he humored the plan because it required little to no change to their assignment. They were to create an irresistible opening for the horde so that they wouldn't swamp the wall and the city. Then hold them there as long as possible. They were to be a shield that delayed and drew out the enemy.

These orders had come from the emperor himself, and Linus still held out hope that the notoriously slippery patriarch had one or two tricks up his sleeve. He had not hesitated to lead his men to this duty, and they had followed, one and all. Even the Marcellus boy hadn't balked at the one-way mission. They had all known what it meant when they took the vows. Access to the empire's most coveted class, but bound to a sacred and strict code. Every soldier here had long since left any other life behind.

When the human had come, claiming he could make a significant dent in the enemy's numbers, it had taken Linus all of two seconds to decide to risk committing a small amount of resources for a possibly huge payout in extended time for their operation. Fewer enemies meant less pressure on the line, which in turn would buy them a few more minutes. He had repurposed Gorock, who wasn't much for line fighting anyway, and then thrown the Marcellus in on the scheme because if that brat wasn't given something to play with, he always became trouble. Subcommander or not.

They had of course forced him to remaneuver from the most favorable ground, but at that point, it had not mattered; all of their careful planning about to be demolished by the newly formed **Colossus**.

So he had chosen to advance the formation and protect the human, as he finished whatever endgame casting scheme he had been gifted by the emperor. After a minute of vicious fighting on the line, he was ready, and Gorock had thrown him right into the pathway of the approaching **Colossus**. Linus watched with a critical eye, judging if he would have to leave the men and fight this creature himself using a final trump card. Yet his eyes widened in surprise as the *Ability* unfolded into an absolutely devastating attack.

It.

Was.

Glorious.

Not only had the human's flames proven to be extremely effective against this type of combatant, but they had somehow been multiplied to the third tier of power. They seemed to emerge endlessly from an angry sapphire sun. The Marcellus yelled over to him, just as he realized that the flames risked expanding over the whole battlefield.

"Commander!"

"I see it. Bastions, PROTECT!" he **Commanded**, pulling on the dregs of the unit reserves to activate one of the most famous of the Phalanxes formations. One augmented by layers of magical and physical protections.

With his **Battle Sight**, Linus saw the endless horde of creatures turned into a smoldering field of charred remains in a matter of moments. Then the epicenter of the flaming attack flickered out, and he noted the human falling from his position in the sky above the battlefield. He had not been able to hold on to consciousness through the experience and hit the ground like a rag doll. Linus examined him more carefully with **Battle Sight** and confirmed that the human was still alive. Linus wasn't about to lose a possible strategic resource like that!

"Formation BREAK! Gorock, Threstus, retrieve our human! I don't care if he is in pieces. I want every one of them back in the middle of this formation NOW," he **Commanded**. The formation lost its supernatural composure, and exhausted men stumbled and fell where they stood, far past the point of exhaustion. The line was never meant to hold in such conditions, and he had been forced to burn through every bit of their reserves to survive this long.

"On it, sir!" replied Threstus as he and Gorock sprinted from the line through the field of still-smoldering corpses.

As they made their way through, Linus's **Battle Sight** drew his attention toward some sort of haze flowing back to the enemy's lines. He watched as even the smoke from the flame was drawn by an invisible stream of energy toward the Cult's forces.

He frowned as he realized another ace had been revealed. The Scale-bellies were using this battle and its deaths for a large ritual of some kind. His eyes narrowed in consideration.

Gods he hated blood magic. He would take an honest **Fireball** any day of the week over that vile form of power. It asked a steep price, and its practitioners were always looking for new customers to pay.

Now that he was looking for it, he could see trails of black-and-red blood weaving through the sea of corpses back toward the naga front lines.

He was no wizard, but he would bet his pension that whatever they were doing with the blood of tens of thousands of creatures would not be good for the city or its citizens . . .

"Rom. Get over here," he called to the youngest surviving member of the unit.

"Sir!" he replied after stumbling over to Linus's position, covered in viscera and gore. The young, but impressive, soldier looked like he had nothing left to give, and swayed on his hooves before his commanding officer. He looked exactly like Linus felt, not that he would ever show it to the men. Bastions were always ready to serve, and they did their best work when all others gave up and quit.

"You look a little tired, soldier. Should I give this assignment to someone else?" Linus barked, loud enough for the others to hear.

"No sir!" he said straightening. There was a fire of defiance in his eyes as several of the older members snickered nearby.

"Good man! I need a runner. Find Lord Hiro at the hub and let him know that the naga are probably summoning their god. There is a *Cataclysm* ranked ritual underway, and without a significant counter, our delay tactics will be for naught."

"It would be my pleasure, sir! I'll get it done and head back to continue the fight immediately!" he shouted, now ramrod straight.

"Dismissed! Oh, and Rom, more than a thousand made it through, but do not engage with the **Corrupted**! I need this message there ASAP. Am I clear? Aside from the subcommander, you have the highest *Dexterity* in the unit, and I expect you to use it!"

"Sir, yes sir!" he replied, saluting and then jogging through the men, back toward the gates.

"What's the new plan, sir?" one of the men called, slouched over his shield. Linus noted with some satisfaction, that even now, the man held a good grip on his gladius.

"Well, men, we are going to double-time back to the refugee front. We will destroy any of the creatures we come across en route and reconvene with the rest of our forces facilitating the evacuation of the city. Our delay tactic here was a success." He paused, making sure to make eye contact with the forty-six soldiers left alive after the brutal fighting.

"Good job, men. When people whisper the name *Bastion* in hushed honor, you will be the one they think of. I have never been more proud to call myself one of your own," he finished gravely, a glint of fierce pride showing in his eyes.

The men each stood to attention, each finding a way through injury or exhaustion to offer him a solemn salute. They were knitting back together slowly and would be back in the fight when he needed them.

"Commander!" shouted the Marcellus brat as he jogged back toward their lines, followed closely by Gorock, cradling the human in his arms as if it was his infant.

"Would you believe this idiot is still alive? A few broken bones and unconscious, but that's it!" Threstus crooned happily.

Good, they still had the human, an essential asset. The Bastions weren't done yet, not by a long shot.

"Copy that. Bastions move out!" he called, turning to lead the column. He prayed to whoever would listen that the emperor had one more trick up his sleeve. The Cult was summoning their god, and the empire had run out of those a long time ago.

Jonathan Tillman - Level 14 Son of Flame

Something was seriously wrong.

Tilly's perspective was doubled as his psyche warred against the feeling of being in two places at once.

Part of him was being carried somewhere. His mana pathways had been cut to ribbons by the endless flow of power, and the **Corruption** within him wriggled hungrily now that it was not boxed in by the network of blue flame-aspected mana flowing within him. Tilly knew he wasn't going to die, but he worried he would never be able to cast again if left in this state.

If this had been his only perspective, he would have stayed blissfully unconscious, but simultaneously as he was lying unconscious in that broken state, he was also floating above the battlefield in the same location where he had unleashed his eight-fold **Flame Expulsion**. He could see the transparent outline of his ghost-like form and watched as streams of ruby energy were pulled in the direction of the Cult's army and funneled into a giant ritual circle there.

Two threads of multi-hued energy tugged at the core of his incorporeal form. One, he knew, went all the way to his physical body, where it continuously relayed the agony of his broken state back to him. The other was also pulling on him, but not in any direction that he could tell. He focused on it, trying to understand just where it led but to no avail. He knew it was there, pulling on him . . . but maddeningly, it was impossible to locate. It was like having a constant itch that he couldn't reach. He cursed in frustration, his ghostly form making no sound as he decided to turn and fly back to his body, ignoring the other thread for now.

Suddenly, his form was buffeted by waves of malevolent energy that started to build from within the ritual circle, and he felt himself start to tear apart under spiritual pressure. Whatever he had done to achieve this form, it clearly wasn't stable, and he panicked as the faint lines of his form started to blur and fade.

What would it mean for his normal self if this form of his was destroyed? He tried to shoot back toward the city, but let out a soundless scream as he realized he could only move at a sedate float. His awareness began to slip as he saw motes of himself separate from his body and be carried away on the waves of spiritual pressure emanating from the ritual.

The second thread, the one he couldn't follow, tugged on him again, even more insistently. In a panic, Tilly grabbed at the thread with his will like a drowning man snatching a lifeline. Instead of trying to follow it, he mentally pulled on it as hard as he could, hoping he could pull himself away fast enough to survive the onslaught of energy.

His diminishing self suddenly felt like it was trying to squeeze through the eye of a needle, but Tilly kept pulling, desperate to get away from the creeping annihilation promised by the proximity of the ritual.

POP.

He was through and in the exact same place as where he had been a moment ago . . .

But now everything around him was frozen in time. Even the waves of energy had stopped in their tracks, and before him floating in the sky were two ethereal trees, whose canopies touched each other forming a natural arc. Between the two trunks was a spinning vortex of many-hued light, and his now visible second thread was leading right into the portal.

Tilly tried to find his first thread and discovered that while he could still feel its tug, it no longer seemed to lead anywhere.

Well . . . that wasn't right. It did lead somewhere, but right now he was somewhen . . .

Trying to figure it out completely hurt his already pounding head. He had always loved time travel movies, but no matter which theory you chose, it never ended in a simple logical bow.

Anyway. He could either enter the mysterious portal or pop back through the needle-sized hole in time-space and be destroyed by the raging sea of energy.

He shrugged. Beggars can't be choosers . . .

He followed the thread until he was engulfed by the whirling many-hued energy. As he entered the portal, he was struck by the thought that this energy looked exactly like the energy that had held his pathways together after he activated [Resolute].

CHAPTER FORTY-EIGHT

A Glimpse Past the Veil

Tilly felt like he should have stumbled as he was hurled through the other side of the portal. Instead, his momentum was immediately arrested as he cleared the plane. He found himself floating in the middle of a shady grove of trees with a moss-strewn stone path leading forward. He was still in his ghostly form, so he couldn't feel the calm cool air of the forest, or smell the slightly damp grass in the dappled morning sun, but he took them in anyway.

He looked down at the thread of rainbow-like energy pulling him deeper into the woods with gentle insistence. He hoped that whatever this was, it would help him get out of the mess he had found himself in on the other side of the space-time aperture.

He looked up to check his log and realized it was gone! In fact, his whole HUD was gone, and he realized they must not work outside of time. He had also lost access to them the last time he had frozen in time before the Flame. He tried to pull up his character sheet with mental commands to be sure, but none responded . . .

Now that he had time to think about it, he really didn't like losing access to his system interface. Most of the time it seemed like he was losing a game he didn't know the rules to, and the *Notification Log* had been the one constant equalizer in his desert of information.

Well I'm flying blind, what else is new? Tilly thought as he let out a long, silent sigh and floated forward. Wherever he was going, he would understand even less than usual.

He moved forward at a sedate pace, finding the forest to be oddly soothing, even frozen in time as it was. Sunlight danced through gaps in the foliage above, and he smiled as he continued to float forward like a segway cop in the park. The trees became more sparse and patches of grass and wildflowers became more frequent.

Then he heard it, something just on the edge of his comprehension. At first, it sounded like the tinkling of bells, and he wondered if he was imagining it. But the farther in he went down the trail the louder it got, until he was sure it was an actual sound. When juxtaposed with the almost nonstop, fight-for-your-life environments he had been moving through his whole time in Nephesh so far, the peace of this place stood out like a strange beacon. The cynical voice in his mind insisted that there might be some sort of enchantment or glamour at work, but the feelings he was beginning to feel did not avoid his mental scrutiny. He felt totally in control of his thoughts, even as some of the ever-present, low-grade panic that lived under the surface of his mind started to drain away.

Soft, light harmonies began to accompany the bells, followed by gentle rhythmic beats. He had never been the biggest music guy, but what he was hearing now moved him deeply. This wasn't just any music. Its ebb and flow spoke to something much deeper than a simple melody ever could. He realized that if he was in his actual body, he might have been unable to move farther forward without being overwhelmed.

At this point, the forest had almost completely opened up and the path led up a gentle hill set at the beginning of a small valley. Now that there were no trees blocking the horizon, he could see he was at the heart of an impassable circle of mountains.

How hard would this place be to find in my physical form? That is, if it even exists in the real world. He laughed to himself at that last thought. What did "real world" even mean anymore?

He continued his leisurely float, not noticing as the lines that made up his incorporeal form became more defined and present. There was something in this environment that was enriching his soul. It didn't just feel good. It felt right, like some part of himself that he didn't know was missing was slowly being restored to him.

He crested the hill and let out a silent gasp. The mountains, the valley, and even the ground beneath his floating feet faded away in contrast to what was the source of this extraordinary environment. The camera lens of Tilly's awareness rotated, throwing everything else out of focus as his whole being feasted on the epicenter of this song.

There at the center of the small valley, swaying gently in an absent breeze was a **Blue Flower**. Those words, "blue" and "flower," were pale, empty things compared to the reality unfolding before Tilly. Describing what he saw as a "blue flower" felt like trying to describe the ocean to a person who had lived in the desert their whole life. There was a gap there that nothing but experience could fill.

The Flower swayed in time to the music, and the longer Tilly watched, the more he was able to understand. Dancing faintly all around the Flower, were ribbons of color, slowly being woven into the very fabric of reality and fading away.

No, that wasn't right; the ribbons were not fading. Tilly could almost make out the pattern they continued to form as they augmented everything aro—

"That's enough, little brother." The voice struck Tilly like a slap, and he tore his eyes from the entrancing scene before him.

The voice had been firm, but kind in its interruption of Tilly's gaze as if the speaker understood the joy Tilly had discovered, and the price he was asking Tilly to pay by pulling his attention away.

Tilly was shocked to see an orc the size of a small building smiling down at him. Next to him was a hammer that literally hurt to look at. He even felt some of his form bending and twisting toward the weapon as he gave it any attention and he quickly glanced away. The impossibly muscular warrior looked sheepish once he noticed Tilly's discomfort and nudged the hammer behind his huge form with his foot.

"Welcome to Memory's Womb, little brother," he said, smiling, his large yellowish tusks doing nothing to take away from his genuine warmth. Without thinking Tilly asked the first question that came to mind, mouthing the words, but producing no sound. *"Please, can you tell me what* it *is?"*

Even as he asked, he struggled not to turn back to the Flower and its song, starving for the answer that would ease the ache of longing that had emerged in his soul. The fact that he couldn't audibly produce words didn't seem to faze the giant orc at all. He smiled and nodded as if he had been waiting for Tilly to ask.

"That is the anchor point for all **Beauty**. From it, hope, joy, and courage flow, working themselves into the great **Weave** of the hearts of men. I believe you would be most comfortable calling it **Origin's Bloom**." He smiled guilelessly, seeming happy to have someone to talk to.

Origin again . . .

The music around him grew fainter, and the jarring pain radiating from his second thread, the one that drew him back to *time,* back to reality, made itself known. Another mystery, another demand on Tilly even though he was already giving all he had. Even here he could feel the **Seed of Corruption** straining against him, trying to dig deeper into his body. If they had brought him here because they wanted something more from him, they were going to be sorely disappointed. He didn't have anything left to give.

Tilly felt tired. Tired of always giving. Tired of never being enough.

The orc's beaming smile slowly sank into a frown, somehow watching the internal war play out within the ghostly form of Tilly's soul. "You carry too much weight, little brother . . . Some things must be laid down if we are to realize our purpose," he grumbled.

Yeah, well it's been a hard week. I'm doing whatever I can to prevent a genocide, and even if we somehow get out, I will probably turn into a monster. Whatever else **Origin** *wants, you can tell him, I'm not interested.*

The words and the deep bitterness they represented erupted out of him, flowing from his center like puss from a wound. He was trapped, and there was no way out. Whatever **Origin** was, he seemed to be indifferent at best, and cruel at worst. Tilly was done being forced to do someone else's dirty work. He had given all he had, with little to no support from the deity.

The writhing pain present in his physical body radiated through the thread and up into his psyche, like nails on a chalkboard. Notes soared around him, a ripple of melody and wind winding its way through the valley, unhindered by time and space. The song met the silence of his agony and blanketed it in peace. Tilly remembered the little girl and her sad smile of hope. One that spoke of a small, courageous choice, even when faced with the possibility of terrible pain. The choice to believe that things would be okay.

Something only a child could do.

"Look again, little brother, but not too long. You are here in spirit now, but the weight of this sight would sever your connection to your mortal form at its current level," the orc insisted, looking back wistfully at the center of the valley. Tilly found himself following the orc's gaze before he had even consciously made the choice to do so.

There the Flower stood. It did not glow, nor did the music it produced overwhelm Tilly. In fact, it did not demand attention at all.

Nonetheless, it was absolutely captivating. The pain waiting for him at the other end of the thread to his body continued to clamor, making its dreadful promise of future suffering and unavoidable failure. But here, now, Tilly felt a small portion of the deep pain he carried like armor around his heart . . . melt. Maybe, just maybe, there *was* a purpose in all of it. Some greater drive to move forward than the fear of failure that had kept him running from one pain to another his whole life. Through that small opening, he felt a minuscule portion of the song enter his being and radiate back through his thread, somehow touching his physical body.

Tilly couldn't tell what was happening, but something was being restored, both here in his ethereal form and there in his physical body.

"Now you begin to see, little brother," the orc said, calling Tilly's attention back to the present.

Tilly turned back to the orc reluctantly and winced at the bright hopefulness of his smile.

"Who are you, and why do you call me little brother?"

"You are a guardian of one of the **Great Secrets**, and so am I. I was called Thunder's Descent once . . . You have found the **Flame** in life, and I have guarded the **Bloom** in death," he said, still smiling. The last word hit Tilly like a ton of bricks. Tilly's attention was immediately drawn to the faint insubstantial nature of the orc's outline. It was barely perceptible, but Tilly realized that the orc,

Thunder's Descent, didn't have a physical body either. Although his form was almost completely substantial despite his disembodied state.

"Why me?" Tilly mouthed, his eyes once again drawn to the second thread, the one that still pulled him to the **Bloom**.

"Yes, good question! My vigil here is almost done, but we will see each other again before its end, I think. It was good to meet you, little brother. Come find us when you are ready to lay down this **darkness** you think you must carry." At his words, Tilly felt the tug from his time-bound thread grow more substantial, pulling him back toward the tree line. He stubbornly resisted, attempting to anchor his form with his will.

"Lay it down? When I chose to cleanse the corruption from the Temple, I gave up that chance. Now it's only a matter of time," Tilly mouthed frowning in confusion as he fought to stay in the place.

"No one can decide that but you. You cling to control, and because of this, you are losing the very thing you fight so hard to keep. We are all slaves to something. Our only freedom is to choose what we will serve," he urged, his eyes imploring Tilly to understand even as his tusk-filled smile remained easygoing.

The force of the pull redoubled, and Tilly began to move against his will,

*"Wait! I'm tired of being left in the dark! What is **Origin**? What is **Corruption**, and how am I supposed to do anything about it?"* He silently screamed in frustration, furious that he was once again being yanked around without any answers.

"We may not know all the steps, little brother, but that shouldn't stop us from joining the dance!" Thunder's Descent called after Tilly as he built up speed. Annoyingly, the orc even included a small dance with his parting words.

The peaceful forest path flew by in a blur, and Tilly felt like a fish on the line by the time he was pulled through the portal. Before he could get a handle on what was happening, he was at the time-space needle hole, being yanked through. He felt like the last bit of toothpaste getting squeezed from the tube. The aperture had grown smaller, and he realized that it had been slowly closing the whole time he was in the valley. It felt like his entire form was being smushed through an opening the size of a molecule, moving at a ridiculous speed to make it in time.

Then, just before he escaped the shrinking hole, he felt something vibrating down the thread that had led him to the Flower.

*One last thing, little brother. You might find yourself a little changed after your visit to our valley. The **Great Secrets** do not need anything from you. Rather, they seek to give to all. Good Providence **Guardian of the Flame**. May your path be straight, and your eyes full of light.*

Pop.

He was back through the other side of *Time*, and he was immediately assaulted by buffeting waves of malevolent energy emerging from the ritual. Tilly immediately curled into a ball, trying to protect as much of his essence as possible from the onslaught of foreign energy.

But . . . the onslaught never came. Well, that wasn't true. The waves continued to crash against him, but he no longer felt that ghastly ripping at the edges of his form.

He looked down at his ghostly hand in wonder, noting that it was far more defined and detailed. While he still felt the energy flowing all around him, it could no longer destabilize him on a spiritual level. *"Hell yeah! +1 to the magical flower of destiny!"* he exclaimed dryly. He felt around for that second thread and noted that it was gone, cut off as the aperture closed. A surprising amount of sadness accompanied the realization, and he shoved down the strong emotional response.

The orc had said that he had to find the valley again in order to get rid of the **Seed of Corruption**. At least that is what Tilly thought he had said . . . The simple-seeming orc had been deceptively evasive. Well, that was a problem for future Tilly. A man who managed to survive whatever shitstorm was building up at the other end of the battlefield. He needed to get back and warn the others. He shot through the air at double his previous speed, which while nice, still put him at a fast walk . . .

This was going to be frustrating. But while he couldn't do anything to move faster, he could at least review his notification log and try to figure out what had just happened to him.

CHAPTER FORTY-NINE

Back in the Fight

While floating through the air, trying to catch up to his body, Tilly pulled up his notification log and tried to get a grip on what he had just experienced. He scanned over the events, starting with his impact against the **Colossus** and moving through how the notifications described what had just happened to him. Nothing seemed completely out of place, but events continued to unfold in such a way that he was always at the epicenter of the conflict between **Corruption** and those who chose to resist it. The more he thought about it, the more he realized that while he had chosen his direction at every fork in the road, the events that transpired after each of his decisions displayed subtle evidence of divine interference.

The mutation and adoption of the Microcosm by his Legendary set of leather armor seemed like it should never have happened, and yet here he was. Now the owner of two different armor forms that had manifested just in time for him to face an extraordinarily dangerous environment. Tilly scowled at the thought of being subtly manipulated even if the interventions had resulted in something positive so far. His eyes ran through the list of log entries, trying to pull out the essentials before he made it back to the Bastions.

---

*Through your actions, you have created a mana-experience loop. This has not been seen on Nephesh since the third Epoch. This experience has indelibly marked your soul and imparted you with the Ability **Mana Overdrive**. You may perform Abilities without paying the mana cost in exchange for unused experience stored in the subspace of your soul at a rate of 100 experience : 1% mana recharge while wearing the **Nullspider Set**. Your character sheet has been modified to reflect such.*

---

*You have defeated a **Corrupted Colossus!** You have been awarded*
539,000 exp. Level up!

Congratulations! *You are now level 15.*

You have earned 5 stat points to distribute plus 2 points in Endurance and 1 in
*Dexterity from the class **Son of Flame**.*

Congratulations! *You are now level 16 . . .*

Congratulations! *You are now level 17. 20,000 exp until the next level.*

You have earned 5 stat points to distribute plus 2 points in Endurance
*and 1 in Dexterity from the class **Son of Flame**.*

---

*You have activated **Mana Overdrive**. All experience you earn through the use*
of continuous mana-based Abilities will convert to mana at a 100:1 ratio
until the flow of experience stops.

*Experience consumed by **Mana Overdrive**: 3,234,907.*

Congratulations! *By attacking and defeating an opponent more than 4x your*
level with a suicidal frontal assault, you have earned the Title: [A Divine Wind].
When you attack an opponent more than double your level while holding their
full attention, you gain a 25% bonus to your attack power.

Warning! *Your soul has been reforged in the flow of immense amounts of mana,*
and the trauma of this event has temporarily torn your spirit from your body.

Congratulations! *You have learned a new skill, **Spirit Walk**.*
Spirit Walk Level 1

Your Spirit Form has entered into an incredibly rich soul environment and
has been strengthened by the primordial energies found in its presence.

Spirit Walk Level 2

Spirit Walk Level 3 . . .

Spirit Walk Level 7

He immediately tried to assign the stat points from his levels but found that he was unable to. Freaking ghost form . . .

Well, now he had a pretty good idea of his strategy going forward. He didn't want to lose [Resolute] again. If he was being set up as a counter to the biggest bad guy around, he needed to hold on to the one thing that let him survive a hit way above his weight class. That meant that at least half of all points gained would have to go to *Endurance*. It was painful to even think about, but he just didn't have the luxury of creating some sort of solo adventurer, jack-of-all-trades kind of build. For now, he would dump the majority of the rest of these points into *Constitution*. He needed to get back in the fight as soon as possible.

Mana Overdrive was insane. The *experience* price was steep, but the fact that he had the option to keep in the fight even after he hit zero mana was a godsend. He loved having another option besides relying on his pitiful mana regen in the middle of a fight. Gaining levels was essential, but not as essential as staying alive. With this, he always had an emergency fund of mana if he was desperate and there were enough low-level enemies around.

This *Ability*, in combination with the Titles [Resolute] and [Divine Wind], was going to be the ace of his build. He didn't love it, but it looked like his days as a DPS-Tank were only just beginning. He just had to hope that his reckless min-maxing in *Endurance* would pay off and keep him alive in his next laughably unfair matchup. **Spirit Walk** was also super interesting, and the DM in him had some ideas of how the skill could be applied laterally to overcome obstacles and gain intel. But it probably wouldn't be useful in the near future.

So, a couple of levels, a new synergy in his Titles and *Abilities,* and one non-combat skill that should be useful in the future. Overall, he had advanced pretty well over the last day . . . but his progress did nothing to shake the feeling that he was falling behind. It felt like he had been entered into a race that he had no chance of winning, and every step forward just solidified his hopeless prospects of succeeding.

So much for a tutorial or a nice friendly starting area . . . Well, there had been horned rabbits, so he shouldn't complain too much.

He minimized the log and found that he was already moving over the promenade. He allowed himself a smile of dark satisfaction at the trail of destruction left by the moving engine of blades and shields that was the remaining core of the **Emperor's Bastions**.

Even at his slow pace, he was gaining on them as they dispatched the milling groups of **Corrupted** who seemed to be pulled in a thousand different directions by the maze of intersecting roads and hiding prey. However, the majority of the remaining **Corrupted** were drawn into the conflict playing out at the leading edge of the Bastion formation as they continued their relentless march through the middle of the city.

Even with most of the **Corrupted** accounted for, a horrible symphony of screams and terror began to rise from the rampaging wave of invaders emanating from the front gate. The enemy combatants that had made it through, and avoided engagement with the Bastions were free to sow chaos throughout the city. Tilly was thankful that the true organizers of the city's defense had already concentrated the majority of people at its center.

He scanned ahead of the moving formation to the immense crowd of citizens at the city center. There, standing in a thin defiant line was a group of armed refugees holding back the most forward element of the **Corrupted**. They stood fast against the thin but constant stream of enemies as the quickest of the shambling creatures made it to the concentration of life at the city center. Luckily, the line looked like it would have no problem holding until the Bastions reached it. Then Tilly looked back at the enemy lines and saw the energy radiating from the ritual slowly coalesce into a serpentine physical shape.

The sight renewed his sense of urgency, and with a silent growl of frustration, he pushed forward with his will, while simultaneously pulling on the thread that led to his body. He felt his pace pick up slightly. It wasn't enough . . .

Tilly narrowed all of his mental focus until his whole world was the task of reaching the moving formation faster.

The gap between him and the soldiers closed, and he got a better look at how bad of shape the Bastions were in. The forward line was made up of the least injured of the unit, which meant that they had all their limbs and were not bleeding out. At the center of the kind of Bastions still in the fight was the commander, covered in gore and limping forward with a clipped efficient gait. Not that those with obvious injuries seemed to be at any sort of handicap. The line of soldiers leading the formation continued to cut down the enemy and ram them out of the way as the whole group moved inexorably forward. The sides were held by spear-wielders, using the reach of their weapons like poles on a river raft, thrusting into occasional enemies and pushing them off to the side.

Finally, the rear was almost entirely being held by Threstus, who tirelessly dispatched **Corrupted** who attempted to flank around the sides or catch up with the formation from the rear. The soldiers at the center of the unit displayed an impressive litany of ghastly injuries and seemed to be keeping up pace by spite alone. In the middle of it all was Gorock with Tilly's body thrown over his shoulder like a sack of flour going to market.

The sight of his body as a burden added even more urgency to his flight, and he used it as fuel to eke out another slight increase in speed. Finally, he was floating above the shambling soldiers. None of them looked up or noticed his presence, confirming his hunch that he was undetectable to most senses in this form. As soon as he reached Gorock at the center of the formation he extended his hand to touch the back of his physical body.

The contact removed any sort of priority between spirit and body, and his perceptions doubled. He was suddenly looking through two sets of eyes, one perspective looking down at his slumped form, the other flaring open to take in the sight of Gorock's ridiculously shapely hamstrings. Then both perspectives blurred and merged in a nauseating multidirectional fusion.

"Uuuhhhggg." He gasped, choking back some bile as he returned to his physical form. The muted sensations of his injuries hit him full force as he returned fully to his body, and he immediately put 6 points in *Endurance*, 5 in *Constitution*, and 2 each in *Wisdom* and *Strength*. Bringing his *non-Endurance* stat total to 96 and his *Endurance* to 97. His ribs were still cracked, and there were hairline fractures in several other sets of bones, but all of them were well into the process of healing. The almost 50 percent increase in his *Constitution* would be a huge help in speeding that process up.

"Is Baby-Man awake?" Gorock rumbled, his basso voice vibrating through Tilly's body from its position on the warrior's shoulder, causing his ribs to grind together painfully.

"Guh . . . Yeah, I am. Mind if I walk, big guy?" Tilly gasped out between painful breaths, trying and failing to take some pressure off his mending ribs. Gorock hefted him up and then set him on his feet with surprising gentleness. The formation didn't notice or slow at his waking, but Tilly found he was able to turn and adopt the same stumbling, exhausted gait that was being used by most of the members of the unit. A few of the nearby soldiers looked over at him and nodded.

No cheering or thanks. Just a silent nod of acceptance. Tilly knew from experience that the respect of such men was much more precious than praise, and he nodded back, attempting to match the hard, weathered expression of impassivity that so many of the veterans wore.

"You did good, Baby-Man. I especially liked it when you exploded. You should do this again very soon!" Gorock exclaimed enthusiastically.

"Don't think I have any more of those in me for a while . . ." Tilly ground out, splitting his attention between keeping up the march and trying to get a handle on what had happened to him internally. He could tell he was on track to recover physically, but metaphysically, he was a mess.

He focused internally as he mindlessly stumbled forward and could feel the shattered state of his mana pathways. This caused the normal flow of mana through his body to slosh out and pool in different sections of his network. He could still move his magic, but the act had become wildly inefficient and resulted in a painful pressure around shattered areas of his nervelike mana pathway network. Hesitantly, Tilly tried to recall his hatchets from wherever they had gotten to. But the wave of anticipated pain never came. Instead, as the magic moved along the pattern it used to recall his hatchets, he felt the presence of a previously undetected blanket of cool energy, underpinning and repairing the broken parts of his network. After a slower-than-normal period of time, his weapons appeared in his hands, and he looped them.

His concentration wavered as he tried to get the hang of observing his internal structures while on the move, but eventually, he was able to fall into a shuffling rhythm and turn his attention fully inward to watch the flow of mana within his body and observe this new, beneficial energy. While he couldn't *see* color in this state, the energy had a feeling of deep blueness, like glacial ice, or the relief of an ice pack on an inflamed injury. He watched as this strange energy was slowly being absorbed to reknit his pathways. Then it clicked: this energy was the same color as his ghostly form when he **Spirit Walked**. According to his log, he had absorbed a small portion of the Primordial energy around the **Bloom**, causing a huge increase in the strength of his Spirit. It must be these gains that his physical body was processing, and the excess energy was being used to restore the metaphysical network that made up his mana pathways.

The spiritual energy was slowly breaking down and rejoining with his integrated self, fueling the highly accelerated spiritual regeneration he was observing. He wondered just how long this process would have taken without the "chance" encounter in the hidden valley.

"Formation halt!" shouted Commander Linus from the front.

The sound of battle had become almost white noise to Tilly as he had found his meditative rhythm. But the sudden call to halt jolted him from his inward-facing state, and he found the Bastions finishing the last of the **Corrupted** between their formation and the ragged but determined line of refugee militia.

They had made it to the hub.

CHAPTER FIFTY

Trouble Magnet

The line of volunteer militia was about three deep in most places and had held back the **Corrupted** so far. Many of the refugee fighters were tradespeople or farmers holding makeshift weapons, but they spanned the promenade in a protective line about fifty feet in front of the mass of refugees. Behind them, there must have been over 100,000 people pressed in as close as possible to the teleport hub.

"Who commands here?" Linus called.

"That would be me," stated a decrepit old satyr woman with a bloodied gladius in her hand.

Level 38, Guard Captain (retired)

"They said they needed someone with experience, and I had plenty of that. Plus it's been a few decades since *Lick* here has tasted any blood," she stated with a ghastly smile showing missing teeth.

"Yes. Well, you have done admirably considering the circumstances," complimented the commander, not at all fazed by her almost ghoulish smile.

"I need to find Lord Hiro, and my men need a few minutes to rest and recover," Linus said curtly, wiping his sword off on a rag he produced from somewhere before sheathing it.

"Alright, slugs! You heard the youngster. Part in the middle, then re-form! No lingering! We will maintain line discipline, or I will personally give you a *lickin* you will never forget," she snarled in an impressively loud voice.

Not surprisingly, many of the volunteers moved almost immediately, nervously looking over at the ancient guard captain with actual fear. Tilly wasn't sure if they were more afraid of her or the hundreds of **Corrupted** they had just faced and defeated.

The line of refugee militia parted, many of them showing relief at the appearance of some actual soldiers. The faces of those who had taken up arms displayed a mixture of grim determination and barely controlled panic. But they were maintaining discipline well enough under the command of the guard captain. Of course, there was no guarantee that they would hold in the face of what was coming.

That would change with the support of the Bastions. No matter how beaten and exhausted they were, each soldier maintained a look of stoic indifference as they moved through the gap in the line. The severely injured in the center of the formation with Tilly seemed to be playing a game centered around who could ignore the greatest injury. A satyr a few paces ahead of Tilly was missing most of his right arm, but walked on his own through the gap, still carrying his shield and spear on his back and his sword in the remaining hand. He wore a stoic expression as some of the militia muttered and pointed at him. Tilly was sure that even without an arm, he was still worth fifty of the volunteers.

As they all filtered through, Linus started barking orders. "Alright, I want you to set up against that building over there. Rations and water! Severely injured are to take a **Soldier's Rest**. Subcommander, I'm leaving you to it."

The gap closed just as quickly as it had opened, just as the loose mob of **Corrupted** trailing the formation sped up at the sign of new prey. The volunteers were uncoordinated and disorganized, but they moved quickly enough to fill in the line.

"Weapons up, you fat pieces of Auroch shit. They bite! So don't let their heads in close!" the Guard Captain shouted, turning her watchful eyes over the loose defensive formation they had set up. They took the loose charge of the scattered **Corrupted** with only one or two losses.

Tilly turned from the fighting and hurried over to the commander who was re-wrapping a blood-soaked bandage around his almost-healed quad.

"Commander, I saw something while I was in the air," Tilly reported simply, deciding he didn't need to go into the full story.

"Mr. Tillman, it's good to see you up. Come with me. We need to find Hiro," he said, moving away from the men, and gesturing for Tilly to follow. Like almost everything else they did, as Tilly turned from the Bastions' position, they uniformly collapsed into sitting or lying positions. Tilly grinned briefly. If these men were anything like the boys back in the department, they would be able to sleep standing up if they needed to. He hurried to move up beside the injured commander who was making his way toward the crowd with a quick limp.

"Sir, I think I know why the main bulk of the Cult's army has hung back instead of capitalizing on our depleted numbers. They are using the deaths of the battle somehow, collecting the energy for something big, although I don't know what," Tilly huffed out in between quick strides. The reality of the odds against them settled down on his shoulders, causing him to feel even more out of breath.

"It's been noted, and I sent a runner. The way I see it, we only face two true possibilities. One, the emperor, *may justice preserve him*, has some sort of last counter prepared for something like this; or two, whatever they are bringing to the battlefield crushes us. Either way, it's above our pay grade. In times like these, you learn to do what you can, and not worry about the rest," he remarked stoically as they moved. Tilly followed a step behind, trying to school his breathing through the pain of his ribs knitting back together.

He couldn't help but be impressed by the commander's even-keeled demeanor. He must have been absolutely dead on his feet at this point, but he let none of it show. He simply carried on, back erect and eyes level. Tilly could almost feel his purpose reverberating through every step, undampened by the near loss of all he had sworn to protect.

Tilly had led small teams in dangerous situations. He knew that on some level it was always an act—one that you maintained for the rank and file, giving them something to depend on even when their world was falling apart. When it came to good leadership, this all registered as par for the course in Tilly's mind. But something about Linus's courage and fidelity to his cause touched Tilly in a way he could not quantify. He found his shoulders relaxing slightly as he followed the satyr toward what would undoubtedly be more conflict. The weight he was carrying became fractionally lighter as he began to understand that as dark as things would get, he wouldn't be facing them alone.

For some reason, that made all the difference.

The crowd ahead was mostly facing forward, clamoring for a spot closer to the hub and hopefully salvation. The closest of the crowd, however, were more focused on observing the thin line of militia holding back the **Corrupted** than adding to the press that was clearly not making progress forward.

This created a growing murmur of awareness as Commander Linus approached with a strange fur-and-leather-covered human in tow. They parted respectfully as the pair neared, but only as a little way into the crowd. Once they got to the true press, everyone was facing away toward the hub still hundreds of feet forward. Tilly was above average height in the crowd of shorter-statured satyrs and could see that each road leading to the hub was similarly packed, with a barrier of magic holding them back. Past the barrier and the honu maintaining it, were only a few other figures in the large opening.

Tilly could just see the imperial palace in the distance and noted a silvery haze rising from the building, like heat off asphalt on a summer day.

"I think I can see Hiro ahead in the hub past the barriers. We just have to find a way through."

"Make way in the name of the emperor!" bellowed Linus in his commander's voice. Many almost automatically pushed to the right and left to part the crowd just enough, but not all were so accommodating.

"The emperor? Why would you invoke such a weak name at a time like this?" hissed someone to their right. Tilly turned to look in confusion, thinking that the voice sounded a little off when Linus flashed by him, blade already out.

Before Tilly had even registered what was happening, Linus was exchanging lightning strike blows with a naga wielding two scimitars.

Level 45, Shadow Hunter

The surrounding crowd screamed and scattered as four other figures shed their draping cloaks, and enchantments fuzzed out around them, revealing four other Shadow Hunters ranging from levels 25 to 29.

Tilly's stomach clenched in tension as two more surged toward Linus, whose blade had already found his attacker's guts. The other two were already facing him and struck like the coiled serpents they were.

Tilly's pathways screamed as he forced his mana to respond in desperation and recall his hatchets from their loops, to his hands, bringing them up in a cross-block just in time to check the spear thrust of one of the serpents. Unfortunately, he was no master of close combat, and the best he could do to mitigate the horizontal strike of the second attacker was to step into the blow and lower his shoulder, hoping to not lose his arm in the process. He felt his healing mana pathways shudder, protest, and strain at the usage in their injured state.

The blade of the second spear sheared through his armor and parted his flesh until meeting the top of his humerus, jarring his right arm with its impact. All three warriors looked at the point of impact in surprise. Despite the full swing, it had stopped an inch deep.

Looks like a 97 in *Endurance* wasn't just for blowing smoke up his ass.

Tilly capitalized on their shock and hooked the first attacker's spear shaft with the bearded head of one of his hatchets. Simultaneously, he yanked for all he was worth and dropped his second weapon to bend his pinned arm at just the right angle to grab the length of the second attacker's spear.

Both attackers attempted to pull their weapons free, and Tilly resisted for only a moment, screaming in defiance at the trauma of once again having a weapon piercing his body. As soon as they shifted their weight and leaned back, Tilly felt himself losing purchase at their superior strength. Instead of continuing to pull, he suddenly kicked off the ground, adding his weight to their leverage and launching himself at their bodies.

He crashed into them in a tangle of limbs, all technique forgotten as he degraded the fight into a desperate brawl. He chopped with his remaining weapon at one and hooked an arm around the neck of the other. In turn, the one he was choking immediately locked down his legs with its long snake tail and began to squeeze in retaliation. The other dropped her spear as the hatchet impacted her shoulder with a cleaving thunk. She produced a knife with her free hand and thrust it right at his abdomen with a wild glee shining in her abyssal eyes.

The thrust pierced into his stomach but caught on his abdominal muscles, digging in painfully, if shallowly. In the press of bodies, Tilly did the only thing he could think of and rallied his barely functional pathways to gasp out one more **Flame's Renewal** into the faces of both of his opponents. They, like the others Tilly had encountered, were covered in black tattoos bleeding dark ink all over their bodies, and at Tilly's *Ability*, their skin immediately began to bubble.

Both screamed in fury and agony, and the one wrapping Tilly squeezed even harder around his legs, causing his recently healed bones to creak. The second ripped out the tip of her knife to thrust it again, mad with rage.

"That is enough of that." Linus snarled in disgust as his gladius whirled overhead and then smoothly cut through both of the nagas' heads at once. The double decapitation was truly epic, or so Tilly would have thought if he hadn't been suddenly showered in blood darkened by **Corruption**.

He pushed himself free from the slack appendages and sputtered as he tried to wipe the clotting mess from his eyes.

"Apologies," came the sound of Linus's voice as Tilly felt a cloth press into his hand, which he desperately began using to wipe the viscous liquid from his eyes, spitting all the while.

"I thought the situation called for speed over cleanliness," he continued dryly.

"No, you made the right—BLLAAARRRGGGG!" Tilly vomited, his body forcefully ejecting any of the foreign bodily fluid from his system. Along with the pain of his recently won wounds, he felt a stinging prickly sensation building around the bleeding opening. Amidst all of the horrible new sensations he was experiencing, he was glad to feel the flame at the center of his chest kindle and begin to warm his whole body.

"I think . . . their blades . . . are poisoned," he gasped out between a few lingering dry heaves.

"What is your status? Can you continue?" Linus demanded, looking back toward the hub.

"Yeah, I'm good. Fucking up stuff that tries to get inside me is becoming my micropower," he said shakily as he straightened up.

Health: 56%*
Mana: 82%*

He was sure that the system had all sorts of details and caveats on those numbers, but he didn't care. His [Hostile Environment] Title would have to step up and take care of the poison, and his mana pathways would just have to suck it up along with him. This wasn't a fun day for anybody, and his complaining pathways were just going to have to get with the program.

He used the cloth to try to mop off the blood beginning to mat in his short beard and hair. The stuff all over his body was going to dry and smell, he just knew it.

CHAPTER FIFTY-ONE

Above My Pay Grade

Tilly handed the now filthy rag back to Linus with a smirk, and the satyr took it with a frown. He pinched it carefully between two fingers and gave it a flick, and Tilly watched in dismay as it began to glow before releasing a starburst of energy and returning to its original state as a freshly laundered square of cloth. Now that Tilly thought about it, he had seen the commander bust out the same square a couple of times in the last hour. And it was always fresh.

"Standard issue for officers," he said matter-of-factly, not at all succeeding in hiding a slightly smug demeanor behind his mask of professionalism. Tilly sighed, coming to his feet and wiping off the front of his primitive but already clean jacket. When juxtaposed with the disgusting layer of grime that was slathered over almost every inch of exposed skin . . .

"Okay, Mr. Magic Cloth, I'm ready to keep moving," Tilly said dryly as the scattered crowd started to return from their panicked press at the edge of the streets. Linus nodded and continued forward as if the attempted assassination was just another thing on the to-do list. Tilly looked back for a moment at the bodies that they were leaving in their wake and realized that they didn't bother him. Not the near-death thing. That sucked. It was the savagery of Nephesh that he was weirdly okay with.

So many people moved through life never breaking a bone. They worked on a computer and played Call of Duty in their off time. They had never seen someone burned alive, never felt the force of arterial blood as it escaped the vessel it was meant to animate. Gruesome shit still happened all the time, but most people lived protected lives that kept them insulated from just how brutal life could get.

Tilly hadn't.

And in some messed up way, he was thankful. There were a lot of firsts for him in this new life. But leaving dead bodies on the street wasn't one of them.

"Make way in the name of the emperor!" Linus shouted again, drawing the attention of all the nearby eyes toward him. As he followed the yelling officer, Tilly realized that the bastard could have just pushed his way through the crowd. He had been intentionally drawing attention to himself as an agent of the emperor, hoping to instigate any more attacks or hidden traps the enemy may have planted in the crowd.

It was a good plan . . . it just would have been nice to get a warning.

Just then, a blaze of blue magic showed from their destination, and the people around them started to cheer and scream in desperation all at once.

"That would be the portal going up. We need to be there, now!" Linus shouted back, doubling his pace to a slightly hobbled jog as he pushed through an increasingly panicked crowd that was already as tightly packed as possible.

Linus had no qualms about forcing his way forward, increasing in ferocity as he shouldered people aside. "Emperor's business! Let us through!" he barked out as the surrounding crowd worked its way into a frenzy that only the hope of salvation could have birthed.

Tilly stayed in the commander's shadow, even grabbing on to his armor at one point. The press had become so thick that as soon as Linus moved through a space, it would begin to collapse back on Tilly with the weight of thousands of bodies. The experience was claustrophobic, to say the least.

Thirty feet ahead stood a barrier of empowered rushing water that held back the panicking refugees. Beyond that, sitting like a beacon of hope, was the re-enchanted teleport platform, which supported a newly created stable portal. At each corner of the platform was an ornately outfitted honu moving through motions, continuing to empower the ongoing spell.

"How do you feel about getting thrown again!" the commander called over to him, the noise and press of bodies becoming too thick even for him to navigate without actually hurting people.

"Three in a day? I'm in," Tilly shouted back.

Without any preamble, Linus turned and grabbed Tilly's waistband and jacket, crouched down, and lobbed the full-grown man over the crowd to crash into the protective barrier guarding the hub.

Tilly was proud to say he didn't scream as he flew through the air toward an opaque magical barrier. The oddest moment of calm reflection hit him as the barrier loomed before him.

I guess the human mind can adjust to any kind of trauma if it happens frequently enough . . .

Just before he was going to hit, there was a flash, and the barrier opened in front of him, allowing him to crash behind the line of honu casters. Tilly barely felt any pain from the crash landing. It was mildly uncomfortable, but he could tell he wouldn't be developing any road rash or bruising. He had the throwing part down. Now if only he could figure out how to land.

His sliding roll came to a stop right at the feet of a honu with a particularly glorious light blue scarf. "How are you, friend?" he asked in a light tone.

"Oh, hey, Franklin! What are the chances, huh?" Tilly chuckled, staggering to his feet.

Linus landed with a few staccato clacks as he skipped forward a few steps to arrest his forward momentum. Franklin just looked at the both of them before gesturing behind him as if this had all been a part of the plan.

"We have the portal online and connected to the other end. Unfortunately, we can't just open the barriers. I am afraid the resulting stampede will crush us. The elder and Lord Hiro are working on something near the platform. You better go see what they need," he finished, eyeing the crowd with tight concern.

"Thank you, young Tide Caller," Linus said respectfully before heading off. Tilly shot off a saucy wink to Franklin before following after the commander. They soon approached the platform adjoining the portal, where both respective leaders were orchestrating the operation.

". . . a good point. . . . Fortunately . . . I have a . . . solution." Tilly caught the tail end of their conversation.

Kihei turned away from Hiro and offered a kind smile to the approaching pair before lifting his staff and slamming it to the ground. The sound of crashing waves suffused the hub, and Tilly saw the magic of the barrier blocking all entrances to the hub ripple and change. Azure energies moved from Kihei's staff and connected to each of the barriers present. Then each wall of infused water responded to his magic by growing a path leading straight to the platform, wide enough for three to pass at a time.

Yet all were still barred from walking these newly created paths designed to stop a panicked stampede. Except for the barrier before a wider road leading perpendicular to the main promenade. It alone opened, funneling those waiting onto Kihei's impromptu magical path. Tilly noted with a mixture of dismay and satisfaction that all of the figures that rushed the gap were lapins. In fact, that particular street was entirely filled with lapins, and they moved quickly to the platform, not hesitating to jog through, obviously having been prepared for just this occurrence.

The rest of the crowd saw this and howled in frustration. Some even began attacking the barriers, which showed no signs of weakening under the control of Elder Kihei.

"Mr. Tillman. It is very good to see you alive, here with Linus no less! You do not disappoint," Hiro said, looking over with a warm smile.

"Hiro, I see your negotiations paid off . . . what about all the others?" Tilly said, not at all trying to hide his disquiet at the sight of clear favoritism.

"This world is a cruel place, and all you can do is protect what is yours. I think you will come to understand this in time. Until then, know that my people will all be through in minutes, and all the other barriers will open, allowing all those who can make it, a chance," Hiro rumbled, showing the human patience that he normally reserved for children.

"Did my runner make it here?" Linus interjected, not caring for moral debate.

"He arrived well before you and we sent him off to the palace. Shuji would have sent a bird, but the *Ability* is already active with Mochizuki. He lost track of her somewhere beyond where my people are stationed, and went to investigate."

"I'll head to the palace as well. Gods willing, he has something planned for the coming *cataclysm*. He had a plan for everything else."

"Many of those plans have failed . . . You will forgive me if I don't share your trust," Hiro replied shortly, turning to watch the remnant of his people rush down the magical corridor to the portal and move through.

A booming crack reverberated across the sky, and a reddish haze along with a network of fractures filled the area above the Cult's army. All of them at the center of the hub looked up as the crowd's shouting became screams of panic.

An unnatural-looking bulge formed in the heavens at the epicenter of the fracturing as something pushed through from a higher reality. Then with a terrible ripping sound, the sky burst, and blood rained down from above. Even this far from the epicenter of the ritual, a spray of blood misted over the city, inciting an even greater reaction of terror from the refugees.

It was one hell of an entrance.

A serpentine head the size of a warehouse pushed through the opening in the sky, followed by a long uncoiling body the size of the Empire State Building. Tilly, along with everyone else, looked up in frozen astonishment as the god of the enemy forces took the field.

Level ??? Deified Serpent of the Sixth Circle

Everyone stopped moving as the divine being looked around, surveying the battlefield and the city that was all but abandoned with its vulnerable neck exposed.

"Well done, Broodlingssss, you may now feasssst." A harsh hissing voice grated on Tilly's psyche, coming from everywhere and nowhere at once. Even at this distance, Tilly could hear the roaring cheer that rose up from the enemy's lines at the approval of their god. They would be charging the city at any moment. Tilly looked around at the others to see what they were going to do. Everyone else was grimly watching the emergence of the snake god. He saw that the lapin people were almost all through, and following on their tails was Amelia with her contingent of children.

That's right, they had planned to stage with the lapins . . . smart.

More interestingly, Tilly spotted Shuji hurrying in their wake, supporting a barely conscious Mochizuki.

He turned to inform Hiro and was surprised to see Linus looking in the complete opposite direction of the snake god. What the heck was he—

"**AHAHAHA!**" rang out harsh mocking laughter. It too boomed out with the immense weight of unbelievable power.

"**It's good of you to finally show your forked tongue, Nehebkau.**" Tilly struggled to track the source of the voice, looking all around before remembering Linus's hope-filled face. He followed his line of sight as the others on the platform turned to do the same.

"Now I see why he so closely guarded his plan," Hiro intoned as they all watched the silvery haze that had been coming off the structure start to thicken into tendrils of energy. The tendrils were emerging from every part of the palace, all leading to a nexus of energy at the top of the highest dome of the roof. There stood a figure that Tilly could make out in perfect clarity despite the distance. It was as if the immense weight of his power on the plane caused the nearby air to magnify his presence somehow.

Standing there was a proud ancient satyr, wearing ornate armor. The centerpiece of the armor was a golden cuirass with a blindfolded female satyr holding a set of scales on the front. He looked sickly, and the shadows coloring his face gave a severe cast to his features.

Level 98*, Emperor of the Thousand Phalanx Empire

His eyes showed the black tears of a longstanding **Corruption** infection, but some part of Tilly recognized another who was fighting back the influence with all he had. He didn't know what the asterisk meant after the level, but he assumed it had something to do with the streams of silvery energy entering his body from thousands of separate points.

CHAPTER FIFTY-TWO

Battle Medic

"Ah, the old goat livessss . . . No matter . . . I look forward to ssssnapping your bonesss one at a time as I sssqueeze the life from your little ssscity," the serpent exclaimed in a voice that permeated the capital and all its inhabitants.

"Enough of your incessant hissing. Are you going to attack, or will you let all my people slip away?" The emperor provoked the snake, waving magnanimously in the direction of the hub. His motions were a poetry of empowered potential, and Tilly could almost feel the pressure of his movements from where he stood. Although he did wish that those movements weren't drawing attention to over one hundred thousand fleeing refugees.

"The *Imperial War Array*!" Linus grunted, showing an uncharacteristic amount of awe. Tilly looked around and saw new hope blooming all over the platform.

The snake god began to coil in the air around itself, rearing back its head.

"Will this 'array' thing be enough to fight a snake god?" Tilly asked.

"It is not a 'thing.' It is an Epic Legacy skill that allows the emperor to empower himself at the cost of the lives of his willing subjects. It is rarely seen in our history and many thought it was lost," he said, almost breathless at the sight of his emperor returned in glory.

"What are you, compared to a god? Your time is finished. Lie down and die, PREY!" the snake hissed before opening its mouth wide and releasing a jet of green-tinted liquid at the palace.

The emperor raised his scepter and bellowed out in defiance. The walls of the city burst with silvery radiance and shot out a dome of silver energy that covered the whole city just in time to catch the serpent's venom attack. The toxic stream dispersed violently on the barrier, spreading the intensity of the attack over the whole skyline.

"It will take more than a little spit to reach me, Nehebkau. If you want this city, you will have to come and take it," the man said through gritted teeth. Tilly could tell he was bluffing but wondered if the snake god would let the insult stand. He also wondered why the snake god continued to attack from a distance with what was clearly only part of his strength. Both seemed to be planning on more than just a frontal assault, the snake god seeming content to stay back and drain the emperor's strength, while the emperor seemed to want to goad him into a charge.

"Ah, my friends! It is very good to see you!" a familiar voice shouted from the rear of the still-fleeing lapin contingent. Tilly had almost forgotten about Shuji in the craziness. Almost all of the lapins had made it through the linked portal, and Tilly saw several familiar figures bring up the rear of the first wave of retreating citizens. First was a hurrying group of children made up of many races that were being herded toward the portal by Amelia and her assistant, Heras. Behind them was Shuji, supporting the weight of a nearly unconscious Mochizuki.

"Shuji, report!" Hiro commanded, showing obvious concern over the semiconscious body of Mochizuki that the Librarian was practically dragging along.

"Yes, lord," he said, huffing as he approached. Tilly jumped down and moved through the stream of fleeing lapins, to arrive at Shuji's side and help him carry his burden the rest of the way to the platform.

"I found her making her way here with all possible speed. She is combating several high-level poisons at the moment, but I hope she will be fine with some rest," Shuji said, gesturing toward the heavily injured ninja. She was covered in lacerations, and several of them were oozing unpleasant dark liquids. Tilly kindled his power painfully and breathed out **Purifying Flame**, watching as she shivered unconsciously in response.

"She discovered a Marcellus unit of private guards moving to the east entrance to meet a group of the Cult's highest elites. The other three Cult generals are coming this way now under the distraction of the summoning, and they plan to flank us here. She retreated as soon as she saw them, but still, they managed to injure her before she broke away. I found her moving down this street only moments ago."

"Tsht." Hiro snarled in frustration, looking up at the two beings still testing each other above the city, and then back down the street from which Shuji had come.

"Thus is the way of battle . . . Kihei, our agreement has been upheld. Passage and haven will be offered to all who make it through the portal. I go to meet this new threat," Lord Hiro decided, leaping from the platform.

"I'm with you," Linus said, tearing away his gaze from the image of his emperor shining like a silver beacon as he held back the attack of a god.

"Heras, make sure the children get settled on the other side. I'm afraid I will be staying for a little longer as well," Amelia said, catching the situation as she ushered her charges up the steps. The assistant took one look at her master's face and nodded, seeing the grave expression she wore at the sight of all those who had yet to escape.

"Hope is not yet lost . . . Franklin . . . Go with them . . . We only need . . . a little more time." Kihei spoke quietly, still effortlessly empowering and augmenting the barriers but watching the conflict unfolding in the heavens with a critical eye. The layers of this battle were unfolding, and Tilly could see just enough to know that as crazy powerful as some of these beings were, they still needed to carefully avoid wasting their strength without knowing what their opponent had in reserve. He couldn't imagine how complicated battle strategy could get when you lived in a place with magical bullshit around every corner.

"I'm not in that great of shape, but I'm coming too. Whatever this poison is, I think you guys will need my help." Tilly sighed, laying a shivering Mochizuki down on the platform nearest to the portal, and then nodding to Shuji in appreciation.

"Of that, human, I have no doubt," Hiro said, turning to address the ones who would stay.

"Shuji, assist the rest of the evacuation as best you can, but make sure you and Mochizuki are gone before I get back."

"As you will, lord," he said with a deep bow.

Hiro turned and started jogging, the rest of the group following after. Franklin seemed to be uncomfortable with the speed, but kept up, while Linus caught up with Hiro and led the way. As they ran, Tilly shot a glance over at Amelia who was easily keeping pace wearing a serious but distant expression on her face.

"Do you know anything about who these elites are?" Tilly called over, trying for a professional icebreaker, while he warred with himself internally about whether or not to bring up his liability to the team.

"No, Mr. Tillman, I do not. I saw Shuji pass by only a little while before you did. I imagine they had planned to bring the rest of our hidden defenses to the fore with the emergence of their god. Then while we are all occupied, they would send in a flanking strike with their best fighters, snuffing out our escape," she answered, her explanation coming fast and clipped. She kept her eyes forward, and Tilly saw her pulling things out of her pockets in preparation.

"They are sending in their other three generals, each on par with what you and Hiro faced two nights ago. They wish to cut us off, while the main force takes a frontal attack," Linus added. "Hiro eliminated Apepi, so that leaves Ladon, Kaliya, and Jormun. They are extremely dangerous, and there is a serious possibility that some of us will not—"

He jerked to the side, attempting to dodge something that was moving too fast for Tilly to see. As Tilly attempted to register what had just happened, Linus stumbled to the side, an arrow having sprouted from his shoulder.

"COVER!" shouted Hiro as his sword lashed out of its sheath, intercepting another of the arrows. His eyes flashed in anger at having missed the initial attack. Linus stumbled to the side of the street and crashed through a barred door, Tilly following immediately after to administer whatever aid he could.

The inside was dark with all the windows still boarded, but Tilly quickly found Linus slumped against a wall breathing fast shallow breaths. His eyes were already unfocused, and Tilly called to him to try to get his attention. "Linus, how you doing, buddy?"

No response, just the continued black stare, and rapid breathing. Tilly moved forward and unclasped the cuirass from Linus's shoulder before carefully ripping away the clothes underneath to get a better look at the wound. The place where the arrow had punctured was red and puffy with a black veiny spiderweb of **Corruption** spreading out from the wound at an alarming rate.

"Oh no you fucking don't," Tilly growled, stoking the fire in his center again, and breathing out with a small cry of pain at the broken glass sensation of using his recently pieced-together mana pathways. For a moment of panic, he thought his *Ability* wouldn't be able to push through the damaged pathways . . . but it did. He was reminded of the time he worked on the scene of an apartment fire for twelve hours, his muscles obeying his commands despite having been broken down into numb facsimiles of their former structures.

Nonetheless, his *Ability* had an immediate effect on the wounded commander. His breaths came even faster, and the tendrils of darkness spreading from what was probably high-level **Corrupted** poison started to creep back slowly. Having addressed the first problem, Tilly tipped the altered conscious satyr forward in his sitting position and found the wickedly barbed arrow tip on the other side. He grimaced thinking about what would have happened if Linus had tried to pull this out on his own.

"Hopefully, you are too out of it to feel this one," he said grimacing as he wrapped his hand around the tip of the arrow and thrust it away from him, pulling the arrow out of Linus's back, through his shoulder.

"GGGAAAHH" the satyr screamed, feeling the pain, even in his muddled state. This poison was way too potent . . . It must have been another of the Cult's trump cards. If the poison could do this to Linus and Mochizuki, who undoubtedly each had a powerful defense against such things, then Tilly could only imagine what it would do to anyone else.

Seeing the wound now free-flowing with blood and dark, wriggling black forms, Tilly riffled around in Linus's tunic and found the magical cloth he had been showing off earlier. Tilly unceremoniously stuffed it into the exit wound and then leaned him back against the wall, allowing the satyr's own body to apply pressure to the dressing.

The spidering network of infection had stopped spreading and had even reduced a small amount, but still hadn't been expelled.

This poison has to be insane. Linus is still altered and nonresponsive . . . and we can't lose him for the rest of this fight . . .

Monstrous clanging began to ring out from the street as metal impacted metal in furious combat.

"Come here, you annoying plant bitch!" came another shout from outside the door.

Tilly mentally reviewed his *Ability*, trying to figure out why it wasn't as effective as it had been in the past. **Purifying Flame** greatly augmented the target's resistances, but that didn't automatically mean whatever they were trying to beat back was expelled. That had been the case for the much weaker grade infection in the city and with Mochizuki's shallow wounds. She probably had received a much smaller dose. But with the malignancy of this substance and its root in the satyr's brachial artery, Tilly realized he was going to have to be more invasive if he wanted to clear it altogether.

What else could he do? He doubted his purifying *Ability* stacked. He looked again at the entry wound, which had already started to dribble blood and black-tinged puss.

The sound of a hissing scream of pain broke Tilly's thought process for a moment, and he looked outside to see the area surrounding the door they had crashed through was choked with writhing thorny vines.

"You can't hide forever behind these little vines!" the disturbing voice howled outside the door, accompanied by the thwacking sound of a blade chopping through plant matter.

Thanks, Amelia.

Tilly looked back down at his patient, noting that his recovery was still stalled.

"I've got one more idea, man, but you are not going to like it," Tilly muttered looking down at his right hand for a second before holding out one finger. He focused in on it intensely and channeled his blue flame strike in a much more narrow manner. His mana pathways screamed in protest, but Tilly pushed through the shattered areas and inflamed his index finger successfully. An intense blue flame blazed to life, dancing up and down his index finger.

"You are running out of room little hum—AAHHHHH" the voice screamed from right outside the door, cut off violently by a meaty thunk.

"You know, it is very hard to find a poison that works against that disturbingly polluted body of yours. But I think you will enjoy this," Amelia called from farther beyond the door, having sprung some trap.

Before he could think about it any further, Tilly shoved his burning finger into the bleeding hole left by the **Corrupted** arrow.

CHAPTER FIFTY-THREE

Tipping the Scales

Tilly plunged his finger into the bloody hole, producing a soft squelching hiss as the writhing infection started to burn. Tilly winced as the smell of charred **Corrupted** flesh hit his nostrils again.

I'm beginning to hate that smell.

"GRRRAAAAAHHHH!" Linus shouted, grabbing Tilly's shoulder in such an intense grip that he felt his scapula flexing under the strain.

"AHHHH! Hey, I'm trying to help! Hold on!" Tilly yelled.

Like bacon on a hot pan, the tendrils of darkness wriggled one last time before sizzling into nonexistence, leaving behind a spidery network of molted burnt flesh. Tilly pulled his hand free with a wet pop and saw the wound begin to close before his eyes. He whipped his head up to check Linus's eyes and found a grim but aware visage staring back at him as the commander panted with the effort of fighting off the foreign substance.

Linus looked over at the blocked doorway and grunted. Without preamble, he stood to his feet and rolled his injured shoulder gingerly, before drawing his gladius to the sound of a thunderous clash from the Titans above the city.

"Come now, Dust Eater! Is that all you got? Give this old satyr the pleasure of hosting you in his city. It would be rude to come all this way and stay outside . . . Unless of course, you are frightened?" the emperor called out through what sounded like a clenched jaw.

"SSSSS, You are nothing before my wrath, Old Goat." The snake god hissed, breaking off the crackling sound of the impact of its breath attack against the magic barrier. Then there was a pregnant pause in which Linus and Tilly shared a look before a booming blast rattled the whole building and probably the city with it.

"FINAL VERDICT!" shouted the emperor, engaging some sort of *Ability*. A cacophony of giant metallic objects hitting each other whirled around something.

Then a snarling **"HSSSS!"** of fury resounded as whatever trap the emperor had planned came to fruition.

"Human, step back," Linus stated calmly, turning back to the vine-choked doorway. He did a pretty good job taking this all in stride, but this was Tilly's first time experiencing power on this scale, and he just nodded dumbly and moved to the other side of the room. The satyr commander who had been comatose moments ago, rolled his shoulders one more time and then rebuckled his cuirass, wincing as his fingers brushed the clotted mess of a magic cloth Tilly had shoved in the exit wound. With a slight squint, he ripped the cloth free from the healing wound, before flicking the cloth once to activate its enchantment, and then tossed it over. Tilly caught it, looking at the cloth and then back at the commander in confusion.

"Keep that," he said, his voice heavy with purpose. "Tell the men that an empire is more than a city, more than an emperor. It is a people and the ideals that unite them. At some point, we forgot that, but it is no less true today than it was at the founding of our nation."

"Linus . . . why do you need *me* to tell them?" Tilly said, goosebumps tingling up and down his arms as he began to grasp Linus's intention. Screams of fury sounded almost right outside the door before suddenly shifting to manic laughter.

Facing the door with an expression hard as flint, Linus breathed out two words: "*Terminal Bastion.*"

He spoke them so softly, with such heavy finality that they came out as barely more than a whisper. The whole room seemed to lean in as if wanting to hear more before an immense pressure was unleashed, rolling off Linus in golden waves of force. So much energy was coming off him that his hair was literally standing on end and small static discharges spontaneously started popping up near his body.

He gave Tilly a final small nod and then faced the doorway barricaded with dark, thick vines and disappeared. Tilly was deafened by the thunderclap, and he completely lost track of Linus as he exploded forward in an incomprehensible burst of speed, obliterating the vines in his way with pressure and momentum alone.

Tilly stumbled back against the wall, recovered, and rushed to the door to the sound of the blood-curdling laughter abruptly being cut off. He emerged into the street and froze for a moment as the enormity of the conflict outside sunk in.

In the sky above the city, the serpent god had been caught fully extended in a thrusting strike of its arrow-shaped head. Chains with links the size of houses had surged up from the edges of the city and bound the god, holding it fast in place just a few feet short of its goal. The emperor stood right in front of the snake god's unhinged jaw, his arms outstretched with a look of profound effort on his face. Black-tinged blood was dripping from his nose and eyes as he bent his whole will toward holding the divine being in place. The snake god wriggled forward, pushing against the mana-forged chains with all its might.

The sound of a wet, meaty *thrump* drew his eyes down from the sky and over to the right, where Linus stood over another headless naga corpse. This one was covered with red welts and black tattoos. The body had collapsed right next to the crumpled form of Amelia, who was curled up on the ground guarding a gushing wound in her abdomen.

Tilly immediately moved into a sprint toward them as Linus's head whipped up and his shortsword blurred to bat away another incoming arrow. Tilly shot a glance toward the eardrum-shattering clanging that had not let up since the beginning of the fight and saw Hiro engaged in a duel of blades with a giant four-armed naga wielding four scimitars in an almost continuous blur of strikes. Hiro's smooth, unruffled motions were unmistakable in their mastery of his chosen weapon, and while he bore numerous shallow cuts, his enemy showed far larger wounds.

Franklin, meanwhile, was doing his utmost to contain a group of twenty-ish satyr private guards along with Titus Marcellus himself. The honu was evoking a complex pattern of jetlike bursts of water in a constantly changing frequency to keep the group from advancing, but they had formed a wedge and were slowly moving through the maelstrom. He had kept them to one side of the street, and out of the other fights, but his gambit wouldn't last much longer.

Beyond all of this, a burst of light announced the arrival of Linus at his target. The two distant figures clashed and then separated, covering crazy distances with each maneuver. Tilly hoped Linus would be able to lock down the archer long enough for the battle to turn their way.

Then he was at the body of the dead naga, sliding to a stop next to the headless corpse. It had collapsed over its weapon, which was a spear shaped like a serpent. Tilly drew both hatchets as the thing suddenly tried to wiggle free of its master. It had a serrated blade held in place by what looked to be the jaws of a living snake gripping the tang of the spearhead. The serpent-body shaft wriggled and writhed, trying to pull free of the weight of its master's dead torso, but Tilly's hatchet was already swinging down on its neck as the creepy weapon registered his presence. His primitive stone blades collided with the shaft's scales and rebounded, causing the snake-head portion of the spear to whip around in a limited attempt to lash out at its assailant. Tilly slammed his moccasin down on the head, trapping the flat of the blade with the weight of his body.

Then with a grunt of pain, he enflamed his hatchet head, and slowly lowered the bladed edge onto the neck of the spear, watching for the coloration in the scales to change before pushing the blade into the skin and beginning to saw off the head. After a few passes, he reached the spine. The whole thing went rigid, and he lifted his unoccupied foot and stomped down on the back of his hatchet, completely severing its head from the body.

Turning away from the elite naga with the sapient weapon, he knelt next to Amelia who was curled into a fetal position in the middle of a sea of wrecked vine growth. Her knees were drawn up to her chest, and her face was buried in the plant growth in a heart-wrenching infantile defense reflex. Blood had pooled under her, and he didn't have a clear view of what sort of wound she was guarding, but he didn't want to move her if she was already gone. He laid his hand on her back, waiting as the shouts and clamor of the battlefield fell away and zeroed in on his patient's chest.

There it is.

An almost imperceptible rise of the ribs, indicating a single shallow breath. He felt for a pulse with one hand, while gently rolling her onto her back with the other arm. Her eyes were closed, and her arms were wrapped around a horrendous wound in her abdomen. The jagged edge of the spearhead had left a bloody mess of cloth and flesh that was still gurgling blood. Tilly gently lifted away the pieces of her shirt and found another network of black veiny infection reaching outward in all directions from the wound. Most concerning was the thick nest of tendrils actively reaching for her heart.

Shit.

This was much worse than Linus's wound, and he probably had double the *Endurance* Amelia had. He stoked the mana in his chest as intensely as the *Ability* would let him and breathed out over the wound, watching in frustration as it began to bubble in response. The wound continued to dribble out blood and clotted knots of **Corruption**. The only sign that his *Ability* was doing anything to the poison was that it had stopped spreading, leaving a root system that spanned all of her lower torso.

It isn't going to be enough. She'll either be turned into one of those things or die.

Tilly looked up in desperation, at a loss for what to do to help. He spotted Linus still chasing the archer and Hiro almost having dismantled his naga opponent but at the cost of numerous wounds crisscrossing his body. Worst of all, the contingent of private guards had almost reached Franklin. He probably had a minute left, max. Tilly looked back down at Amelia in distress, cursing his limited abilities. It's not like he had anything to actually help heal her; all he could do was burn as much of the **Corruption** as he could and hope that the additional trauma didn't push her over the edge.

He clenched his fist in frustration, letting out a shout of impotent rage. No matter what he did, he always found himself helpless when it really mattered. One more person he could do nothing to save.

Could I have done something different?

Would she have gotten this injury if I hadn't dived after Linus?

Would Linus have even been hit if I hadn't been running my mouth like an idiot?

For some reason, there, with little hope, and a city collapsing around him, Tilly thought again of the little girl outside the shop. The one that was now safe on the other side of the portal.

He couldn't answer any of his questions, and he would anguish over them later. For now, he had a fucking job to do.

Heat bloomed in his chest, as he shoved the weight of his guilt and uncertainty into that flame at his center, stoking it to an inferno. He unclenched his fist and opened his hand, sending the new heat at his center and down his arm to materialize as an intense blue and white flame dancing above his palm. Then with a deep breath and something that might even have been a prayer, he laid it gently against the deep, bubbling wound on her abdomen. The flame sizzled as it touched her waxy, corrupted flesh, and even unconscious, she shivered in pain, releasing a deep groan.

The flame sank into her navel, crackling as it consumed flesh and corruption alike. Tilly watched as Amelia's already shallow breathing quickened and her eyes fluttered. The glow from the flame continued to emanate from her even as her wound was cauterized and sealed, trapping the flame within.

"Amelia, I need you to hold on! We are getting out of here and those kids need you," Tilly growled down to her, tears falling on the new source of pain he had just added to her fragile wounded body.

It will work.

It has to work.

He stood up, heat smoldering in his eyes as he looked to the group of satyrs about to push through the area effect of Franklin's spell and reach the Tide Caller.

CHAPTER FIFTY-FOUR

Encroaching Darkness

Amelia Cooper - Level 35 Botanist Surveyor

Amelia was held suspended in a sea of darkness, drowning in its depths. A place that had haunted her dreams for as long as she could remember.

A place where nothing grew and no light ever showed.

Amelia! You will not speak to your betters that way!

Whispers surrounded her, buzzing like flies around a corpse.

We are sorry, Mrs. Cooper. You are just not what we are looking for in a candidate.

Here, she was completely alone, abandoned. Her only company, a continuous loop of accusations, replaying her past failures. They never stopped, never quieted.

We have exhausted every option, ma'am. You are just unable to have children.

This heaviness had pressed down on her chest many nights, waking her with its crushing presence until she could hardly breathe. But this time was different. This time she wasn't alone with her despair and its buzzing cloud of witnesses.

Something had weaponized her darkness, giving it terrible form. Now in its newfound sentience, she felt a terrible gnawing hunger.

Thousands of appendages reached toward her suspended frozen form. She had nowhere to run. There was no hiding in her own private hell. Just endless grief and fear. This new darkness thrived in the sea of her regret, pulling in her endless despair and multiplying. What started as an intruder grew into a multitude, surrounding her on all sides, radiating a cold hatred.

It would take her, twist her, and use her to destroy all she loved.

She curled in on herself and screamed for an eternity as its grasping hooks reached her floating form and began to tear and rip, gobbling up the edges of her soul.

She felt it invading her body, screaming in her mind, offering freedom. The complete and total release of utter destruction. An end to the pain. Its hatred of her made complete sense. She hated herself . . . didn't she?

She looked down again at the half-empty bottle of liquor and popped open the cap on her medication.

God, it hurt so badly, and even as the tendrils dug into her flesh, tearing and gnawing at the exposed parts of her being, an even greater pain started to build at her center.

A bright burning seared her navel, galvanizing it . . . purifying it.

From that place, flowed fury. A wrath like she had never known.

She had been here before. She had fought this battle and lost, and in the losing, she had given up hope completely. These voices had led her down dark roads, promising the cold salvation of oblivion. Then when she reached the end of the road and saw her destination, she tried to run.

Tried to fight.

But it had not been enough, and she drowned in that darkness. It had taken everything from her and now it was back. Demanding more. Eating away at who she was all over again.

Not again.

She dived into the burning pain at her center, stoking it, feeding it her outrage, her rejection, her denial of this *thing* trying to claim her.

The pain was incredible, but it was honest. It demanded nothing from her, besides that she burn, and to that burning, she gave her whole self. She fed it more. She fed the flame her pain, her mistakes, her fears, and her desires. She channeled all that she was into the growing inferno allowing it to consume her soul.

The tendrils increased their writhings, tearing into her at a faster rate, but it was pointless. Their hold on her was fading, burning away, leaving only a glowing corona of blue flame.

It blazed there, daring the tendrils to come closer and resume their feast. The tendrils curled back on themselves, fearing the destruction that always came with the flame. But the fire did not follow. Instead, it formed a protective sphere around the tiny mote of light at its center, glowing with an otherworldly iridescence that made the surrounding darkness seem but a shadow.

*Congratulations! Under immense metaphysical pressure from an invader, you have successfully formed an **Origin Seed**.*

Jonathan Tillman

The heat of Tilly's rage poured off him in cascades as he turned toward the group of Marcellus guards almost on top of Franklin. These bastards had abused and attacked his allies at every turn. Now, because of them, Amelia was lying in a pool of her own corrupted blood, fighting for her life and probably her sanity.

Strangely, the pain from his overused pathways had grown distant. Even the throbbing in his side, pushing him to revel in his hatred had been dampened. There was so much he couldn't do. So much that he couldn't change. Yet this reality didn't weigh on him like it had minutes ago. In this moment he finally understood his purpose.

The incessant buzzing of anxiety and the heavy chains of past regrets all fell away as his whole being focused down to the razor's edge of the present. The battles playing out before him sharpened in intensity until he entered into a moment of perfectly hanging clarity.

The crash and screech of clanging blades continued to sound up the street as Hiro finished his duel with the huge naga. At some point, Hiro had removed one of his opponent's arms, but in response, the naga had entered into a berserker state, and his tempo of attack had doubled. Black smoke poured out of his mouth as he released a continuous screech of animalistic hatred. Hiro met the onslaught stoically, an island of calm in the raging sea of strikes, only allowing the most shallow swipes through his defense. Yet, even they were taking their toll as Hiro became covered in a rusty red network of bleeding cuts.

The flashes of light that had accompanied Linus's strikes had ceased, and there was no sign of him or the enemy archer.

All three generals were either eliminated or removed as threats. That left Titus Marcellus with his cadre of twenty guards. The mosquito that Just. Kept. Biting. The embodiment of all that had eaten this empire from the inside out.

They advanced arduously against Franklin's onslaught of woven water jets. If they won out, then every remaining battle here would tip toward the enemy's hand, and pressure would come to bear on the hub and its escaping refugees.

Tilly didn't have to process this information. He took it all in along with a deep inhalation of fiery air. Indecision and doubt were gone; all that was left was purpose.

He would burn away the rot that stood before him.

His heart blazed in righteous fury, building up pressure inside him until it manifested in the form of blue fire wreathing his body. Wrath burned in his eyes as they glowed bright azure blue.

He felt light.

He felt certain.

He couldn't protect the whole city. He might not even be able to protect his few allies. But whatever power he did have, he would use to his utmost to push back against those who wanted to destroy all that he had promised to protect.

Reality snapped back into movement, and Tilly sprang into action.

Right before the lead guards reached Franklin, Tilly launched his hatchets, whirling with his throws to lend them even more velocity as he released. They shot off, small explosions of flame propelling them even faster as they impacted squarely in the flanks of the formation pushing toward the Tide Caller.

The fire was instantly quenched by Franklin's water *Ability*, even as the ax heads bit deeply into the neck and side of their respective targets. As the flame and water met, an explosion of steam was produced, bypassing all armor and shields as it left blistering welts on the guards all around the two that had been hit by his initial salvo.

Tilly kept up his forward momentum, sprinting toward the unit, calling back his axes and spinning again as he whipped them in furious arcs back toward the unit scattering in confusion at the unexpected vector of attack. The woven jets of water emerging from Franklin didn't let up, and steam again burst in their midst as two more guards were incapacitated.

The guards whom **Identify** pinged at levels 21 to 28, finally oriented on the new attacker bounding toward them. He was wrath incarnate, and fire flowed off him freely as he crashed into their slow-to-form ranks. Franklin coordinated his attack pattern, splitting off jets to avoid hitting his newly arrived ally.

"It's just one man! Kill him! Ignore the shellback!" a voice screamed from the back of the formation.

The nasally grate of his screeching command caused Tilly to smile.

Soon.

This new *Ability* flowed through Tilly as if he had been born to it, allowing him to constantly radiate blue flame from every part of his body in a continuous attack. The flaming aura simultaneously pushed his enemies back and enflamed each strike of his weapons. His close-up technique with his hatchets was almost nonexistent, but *Dexterity* was his second-highest stat, and even his rough motions held a certain deadly grace, allowing him to move from one enflamed strike to another without ceasing.

Not that his fighting style would have been called graceful. He looked nothing like Threstus moving his twin swords like a master painter attacking a canvas. When that man had fought, every moment had been purposeful and connected to the whole, creating a bloody work of beautiful devastation.

In contrast, Tilly was rage incarnate, and what he lacked in training, he more than made up in savagery. A shoulder tackle flowed into a strike against unguarded goat legs, before jumping up to smash his head against the chin of a guard trying to strike down on him.

His patternless rage combined with his constant aura of blue flame quickly caused the remainder of the guards to give him space. They all backed away in a loose circle as Franklin continued to punish those on the edges with jets of water.

He stood there for a moment gasping for breath, covered in bruises and cuts, none of which had managed to do critical damage.

His mana had completely run out at some point, and his armor had morphed into its **Nullspider Set**. He could keep up the full body flame as long as he kept taking down enemies . . . and them giving him space was exactly what he didn't want.

"What are you waiting for, you imbeciles! We have provided you with healing potions, now earn your keep!" the same voice screeched from outside the circle.

Tilly smiled and feinted away from the voice, before pivoting and sprinting right toward his favorite Quaestor and the guards who had the misfortune to be in his way.

"Stop him!" squealed the young aristocrat as Tilly charged the two guards and leaped into an insane attack, completely ignoring their defensive strikes. He tangled himself up with their weapons as he rode them to the ground, taking more shallow strikes in the process.

The guards screamed in outrage and then horror as blue fire cascaded over their exposed flesh. One tried to stab Tilly in the gut, but his outrageous *Endurance* demanded much greater strength than the guard could leverage from his compromised position. All the strike did was add to the network of cuts crisscrossing Tilly's body. The rest of the guards charged in behind him, just a few steps away, all probably rearing back to strike.

Tilly rolled with the tackle and pulled the guard who had stabbed him over his body as the rest of the unit attempted to rain down chops and stabs on Tilly's sheltered form. The now-charred meat shield took most of the initial strikes before Tilly kicked him up and rolled to the side. Then with a primal roar, he burst out a reduced-cost **Flame Expulsion**, giving him enough space to leap to his feet.

A huge blast of water hit the rest of the guards from behind as they stumbled back from Tilly's area of effect. This knocked most of them to the ground, and Tilly smiled a bloody smile at Titus as fire consumed the caked-on blood and viscera that had coated him for over half a day.

CHAPTER FIFTY-FIVE

The Final Gambit

Titus screwed up his face in a sneer, holding his scepter-spear at the ready. "Come at me scu—"

Tilly didn't even let him finish the taunt as he launched an inflamed hatchet in Titus's direction, sprinting after the throw. Several days ago, Tilly would have never been about to pull together the coordination or burst of speed necessary to follow such a motion with an immediate sprint. But now his *Dexterity* was three times higher than anyone back on Earth, and things that had only been possible in his imagination were finally becoming reality. Even with Tilly's comparative speed, Titus responded to his throw and follow-up attack with cold precision, showing years of experience and training. He neatly knocked aside the thrown weapon as Tilly approached his position, bringing around his other hatchet in a downward chop. He telegraphed the overhand strike heavily while simultaneously bringing around his empty left hand for an underhanded strike at the satyr's unguarded right side, calling his weapon back to his hand at the very last moment.

His opponent stepped into the attack just as Tilly committed, parrying the high strike and shoulder-checking the lunging human with his characteristic sneer. The aristocrat had read Tilly easily and positioned his body so that the second strike would be the completely off angle. The maneuver was completely unexpected, and more or less neutralized Tilly's surprise undercut as Titus entered into Tilly's guard with impunity.

But the smile never left Tilly's face as Titus chose to close the gap and grapple instead of gaining distance and time. That move probably kicked ass in the dueling ring, but Tilly was literally on fire, and that had very real consequences for this fight. Not that he could last much longer. Tilly could feel his **Mana Overdrive** coughing as it ran out of *experience* to convert, and he knew he had seconds before all of his *Abilities* ran dry. He needed this to be fast and dirty. So he snarled as he took the shoulder check in the chest and snaked his arms around the satyr instead of trying for another strike. He knew he was outclassed in this match-up, and he was already tired of the "dive in and catch everything on fire" fighting style he had developed, but those were the tools he had. And he would be damned if he didn't use them. The fire-aura Tilly was still going, and even with his far superior stats, Titus gasped in pain as flame started to impinge on his armor and exposed flesh.

The Quaestor knew his way around his weapon, and even with Tilly's unconventional fighting, he had seamlessly brought around his short spear from its parry to a thrust at Tilly's side. Tilly desperately tried to lock down the thrusting arm, but only managed to deflect it a little so that it cut a deep furrow along his back.

"Get off me, you cretin!" he hissed in pain, trying to gain enough space and leverage to push the human away from his body. But Tilly clung to him like a roach on the side of a swaying garbage bag, not wanting to give up on his main tactic.

With a yell and a monumental heave, the satyr succeeded in shoving Tilly away, causing the joint in his right shoulder to pop out at the sudden nonstandard tension put on it. To make matters worse, his new *Ability* finally sputtered out, no longer empowered by the *experience* gained from defeating surrounding enemies. He stood there gasping for breath with his left arm hanging loosely at his side, the head of his humerus painfully hanging by its tendon, out of socket.

That was it, his best effort, and this fucker was still standing. Superficial burns covered Titus's exposed skin, and much of his clothing was charred and blackened. But the disdain he radiated was palpable and undiminished.

"Is that it, you vile hairless ape? You are nothing before me. The main army is reaching the hub as we speak. All of this was just to pull out your elites while the rest of the traitors are slaughtered." He spat, his eyes bright with manic fury.

"Traitors? I knew your worldview was insane, but that is on another level . . . And I don't think things are as peachy for your side as you think. People are still escaping, right now, as we speak. All of the lapins made it out, which I'm sure you hate. And . . . all the guys you brought are dead," Tilly said, gesturing past the satyr's shoulder toward the now silent street. There, slowly limping toward them was Hiro, half helping, half carrying Linus, who had several arrows protruding out of him. The commander seemed to have aged decades during the fight, and his body looked like a shriveled husk.

Titus stepped smartly to the side of the street, taking the wall as cover on his left before looking back behind him. The huge naga swordsman was piled in a bloody heap farther down the road, and the sharpshooter was nowhere to be seen. Impressively, his face screwed up even tighter in defiance as he took in the two victorious combatants. Then he turned and spit on the ground in Tilly's direction. Tilly heard steps behind him and jumped to the side himself, looking back and finding a disheveled but unharmed Franklin walking through a maze of drowned bodies to join him in facing Titus.

"Seems you are all alone, friend . . ." Franklin said, his easygoing manner contrasting oddly with the group of dead bodies he stepped between.

"No matter, I will end all of you!" Titus screamed, his voice going shrill as he looked back and forth at the two pairs of exhausted combatants. Then a great metallic snap echoed through the city, followed by another, and then another. All five survivors on the street looked up to see the Divine Serpent writhing furiously, straining against its bonds and breaking them one by one. The emperor still stood before him, his arms outstretched in arcane effort, but the silvery light shining from him had dimmed noticeably. Black-tinged blood was streaming from his eyes, mouth, and nose as he fought to keep the serpent detained. Every new snap of the chains caused his whole body to convulse. Tilly could only imagine the backlash a spell of that size would unleash on the body of the caster.

The dying emperor looked down then as if he could feel their eyes on him. But he was not looking at the group on the street. Instead, he looked straight at the hub.

"This is all I have for you, old friend . . . A minute more, no longer," he said, all the bluster gone from his face, replaced by a deep sadness tinged with regret.

"You see!" Titus screamed with glee. "It's over! Your pathetic attempts to delay the inevitable have failed. Nehebkau was always going to triumph, and my father will rule this city, just as he was meant to," Titus screamed, turning his head back and forth, to keep both groups in his sight, his back firmly placed against the wall.

"Now, I will show you just how great the power of the coming age will be!" he cried, his voice almost breaking in its shrillness as he pulled his hands free from a pouch at his belt and brought something black and wriggling to his mouth.

Time slowed as Tilly broke forward in a run, trying to stop whatever was happening. To his left, he heard Franklin shout something as two high-pressured jets of water looped around Tilly to smash Titus off balance right before Tilly got there to tackle the insane satyr, reaching to grab the hand and whatever it held. Even as Tilly brought him to the ground, the sound of insane laughter and then choking echoed out into the street.

It was too late. The Quaestor had brought his fist to his mouth before Tilly had knocked it away and crunched down on whatever nightmare item he had been holding in reserve. The moment he did, Tilly felt his own **Corruption** begin to wriggle excitedly in his side.

Titus continued to choke, a rictus grin stretching the muscles on his face into a grotesque caricature of a smile. Black tendrils of **Corruption** reached out of his mouth and nose as the skin covering his face started to dance and contort wildly. Whatever he had ingested was spreading faster than any **Corruption** Tilly had ever seen. This wasn't going to be handled with a few chops of the trusty hatchet . . .

Tilly jumped to his feet, backing away just as Hiro arrived with Linus. "Mr. Tillman, can you do anything about this?" Hiro grunted as he shifted Linus's weight. Hiro was barely standing in his own right, and many of his own cuts showed signs of infection as well.

Titus's body began to convulse on the ground, and large appendages of his new occupant began to burst out of his skin as it took control of its new body.

Tilly glanced at his mana bar, and then at his fatally wounded friends. "I think this one is a big *nope* for me. Let's get out of here before this thing finishes doing whatever it is doing," he yelled over the sound of consecutive snapping chains raining from the sky above them.

"Understood," Hiro snapped grimly. Franklin rushed over to his side and took Linus's other arm, and they started moving as Tilly backed away, covering them with a hatchet at the ready. Tilly backed away another five or six feet until he was hopefully out of reach of the continuously growing writhing knot of tentacles and flesh that used to be Titus Marcellus.

Then he turned and ran, catching up to the three moving at a slow jog before him, before sliding to a stop and kneeling down next to an unconscious Amelia. She was breathing more normally now, but her abdomen was still a maze of burns and **Corrupted** veins, pierced through the center with a bright glowing light barely covered by burned skin.

Tilly winced as he pulled her up to a sitting position and then leaned his dislocated shoulder into her chest as he draped her leading arm over the opposite shoulder and stood up with some effort. He was stronger than he had ever been, but with his injury, it still wasn't easy. Luckily this was far from Tilly's first fireman-carry, and soon he was moving fast enough to catch back up with the trio moving ahead of him down the street toward the hub.

"EEEEEEYYYYYYY!" screeched the thing behind them, Tilly didn't even bother to look back. He had seen more than enough monstrosities for today and was happy to remain in ignorance as long as possible.

The injured group moved as quickly as possible, maintaining a stumbling jog as they fled the thing forming behind them. The divine snake shook free of the last few chains above them, and the hub came into full view. The crowds had been reduced by half, and Elder Kihei's barrier pathways were working overtime to keep the escape orderly and efficient as each portion of the crowd pressed forward to make it to the portal before the Cult's army broke through the thin line of refugee militia and remaining Bastions holding them off. The honu casters that had been maintaining the barriers before Elder Kihei had taken over were now lending magical support, bombarding the deeper ranks of the Cult's regulars with water jets and well-placed empowered barriers.

Finally the group stumbled into the square to the sound of crashing behind them and a victorious hiss of fury from above them. Tilly never stopped moving as he swung around his shoulders, hearing the left one pop back into place as he looked behind to locate their pursuer.

Rolling down the street like some sort of giant ball of eldritch fun was the creature Titus had become.

Level 54, Bursting Defiler

Then the sound of a gunshot-like snap of jaws exploded through the sky, followed by a weak gasp.

"Now . . . " the broken voice of the emperor whispered at a volume that could now barely permeate the hub. Tilly rocked back his shoulders and attempted to look up at a run. Between awkward, encumbered steps he was able to spot the emperor, his lower half completely gone. His body now ended in a gory line at his waist, with the divine snake's head rearing back for another strike.

Tilly and his companions picked up the pace even as screams of despair echoed all around them as many saw their last chance of escape cut off. Tilly's ribs billowed with effort as he approached a set of steps leading up the portal platform. The three other approaches were all choked with a flowing mass of panicked bodies as thousands of people tried to push even faster toward the portal. The portal itself remained stable even as the four ornately garbed casters at its corners withered away, using the last of their lives to maintain the magic.

Then all the barriers around the hub collapsed, and the rest of the crowds flooded the area, all control lost as the sound of crashing waves rose above the cacophony. Elder Kihei pulled his magic back in around him and started to glow a deep azure blue, floating up above the now unchecked crowds. Arcane symbols started to dance all around him, as he activated all the other platforms in the hub at once and began calling something through.

CHAPTER FIFTY-SIX

A Promise Kept

Each of the activated platforms started to emanate a feeling of crushing pressure, causing Tilly to stumble, jostling Amelia on his shoulders in his final steps to the portal. The crowds were now pouring in on each side of the platform, entering the tear in space from every direction.

As Tilly lowered Amelia from his shoulders, he was immediately pressed by the panicking crowds, almost getting pushed into the portal several times himself. A burdened Hiro arrived with Linus and Franklin a moment later and unleashed his killing intent, pushing the crowd back in all directions and forcing them to go around the group. Shuji rushed toward them, making full use of his girth to push through the crowd.

"Just in time, my friends! I take it you were . . . successful?!" he said, eyeing the giant ball of horror slowly rolling this way from the street they had just vacated.

"We have done what we can. Now we must take control of the situation on the other side. These people will only be escaping to more chaos if we don't establish order as they arrive," Hiro said tiredly.

Tilly said nothing in reply, gently placing Amelia in Shuji's arms and turning toward Hiro and Linus, expelling the little mana he had just regained in a **Flame's Renewal**. They both shuddered as their growing resistance to the foreign substance trying to invade their bodies was supercharged.

Hiro was right. The situation on the other end had to be pure chaos as thousands of panicked refugees arrived every minute in the village square. It would be an administrative nightmare to get it all sorted . . . Tilly shivered at the thought and looked around for an excuse to avoid it for as long as possible.

"Hiro, you and Shuji are definitely needed to handle all of this back at the village. But me? Whatever help I have left to give is probably best spent here," he said, looking back toward the **Bursting Defiler** rolling inexorably down the street.

Another explosive snap sounded above them, and they all looked up as the divine snake tipped back its head and swallowed its old enemy whole.

And . . . there goes the emperor.

Then Kihei's voice echoed through the crashing waves, somehow able to be heard even above the screaming and the battle happening at the entrance to the square. **"All who are not through that portal in the next two minutes will not survive,"** he grunted, his voice heavy-laden as if he was lifting a huge weight.

Hiro fought to suppress the shuddering that was running through his body as beads of sweat ran down his face. Linus had been rendered completely unconscious by the new power wracking his body, and Shuji stood there holding Amelia, looking torn. Franklin, however, nodded agreeably and moved away through the crowd to join up with the line of casters supporting the defenders of the square. The line was holding against the professional army . . . but barely, as it slowly backed toward the portal platform.

Finally, the Samurai Lord grunted in acknowledgment, and moved through the portal without any further fanfare, carrying Linus through. Shuji gave Tilly a hopeful smile and a wink before following afterward, with an unconscious, but stable Amelia in his arms. Tilly turned and jogged off, pushing through the crowd back in the direction of the monstrosity rolling its way toward the still numerous fleeing refugees.

He didn't know what he could possibly do with zero mana. He was all out of tricks . . . Maybe he could try a distraction, luring it away with an enflamed hatchet throw? He would regain enough mana for that in a minute or two . . . But that would be cutting it pretty close to Elder Kihei's timeline.

The glow from the other platforms grew more intense as Kihei's magic suffused the whole of the hub. The Divine Serpent, far above, slowly turned its head to the ants milling about in the city below.

"Bow before your God, sssslavesssss," it hissed out.

"You will gain nothing from this place," Kihei shouted, his voice hitting several octaves as it blended with the sound of the crashing waves now filling the city. Whatever prepared magic he had laid on the hub had linked each platform and had begun to weave a huge runic circle above the group of platforms.

"What is thisss? A little water magic will do nothing to harm me!" the serpent spat, its huge eyes narrowing at the enchantment forming below it. It began to build its own technique, gathering red and green energy in its slowly opening jaw.

Kihei's runic circle started to spin, whirling faster and faster as water exploded forth from the activated platforms. Each river-sized torrent crashed into the rotating spell above and was pulled into the working.

Empowered by the water it was taking in, the runic circle started to expand and stretch out into a rotating dome that covered almost all of the hub in an azure barrier of magic-imbued water. Before Tilly really understood what was happening, the barrier had lowered down in front of him, cutting off half of the remaining refugees from the portal. He could faintly make out the shock on their faces just feet away as their fates were sealed and they were left to the mercy of the Defiler.

Tilly looked around in desperation, wanting to find something, anything he could do to help those now trapped outside the protective barrier. The dome had dropped right in between the first and the second rank of the pressing Cult army, leaving only the front rank to keep fighting against the depleted force of refugee militia and Bastions.

The swirling sapphire dome seemed impenetrable, an absolute protection for those who had made it within and a damning blockade to those too slow to make it to the square.

The Defiler rolled in amongst the hundreds of poor souls and began to snatch refugees with abandon, its tentacles snaking out in all directions. Tilly pressed against the barrier helplessly, not sure what he could have done to stop the atrocity, but feeling a gut-wrenching guilt all the same. The hopeless looks of those just feet away from salvation raked his soul, as they collapsed to their knees, the light of hope snuffed out in an instant.

"Your petty defiancesss endssss here," the god snapped above them, the gathered corrosive energy flashing into a spell that took the shape of a green snake biting its tail, with a blood-red sun at its center.

Tilly glanced back down from the conflict playing out in the sky, unable to leave those just on the other side. Their eyes glazed, as the desperation animating their movements was cut off like a puppet's strings. He had seen that look so many times. They always looked at him the same way, confusion mingling with denial as they fought to hold back the yawning finality of sorrow. It was the look of acceptance, the small soul death that preceded a heart's last labored beats.

And, just as he had done so many times in the past, he turned away from those faces, the ones he couldn't do anything to help, and kept moving.

Kihei floated at the center of his huge spell as the magic continued to flow from the platforms to the circle at the top of the dome. His expression was now one of fierce concentration, glowing so brightly that Tilly could hardly make it out.

"When my ancestors first took sanctuary in this city and built these platforms, we were asked to promise one thing: that we would destroy it before we let it fall into enemy hands. Today that promise is fulfilled, and I break any ties of debt my people owe this place," he roared, departing from his normal slow pace of speaking as he grit his teeth in effort, and lifted his arms to direct the power city-shattering spell.

"You will not take what is MINE!" the snake declared as it unleashed a poison *Ability* that dwarfed the initial salvo he had used to test the emperor. If that had been its opening shot, this was the finisher.

"Fathoms of the Deep!" Kihei shouted. The flow of water leaving each platform multiplied by a factor of ten, now flowing at a rate that Tilly couldn't even begin to calculate. He had seen a video of engineers releasing pressure off the Hoover Dam once. The volume and rate of flow of that stream had nothing on what Tilly was seeing pour out of each of the fourteen platforms linked in the spell.

The fourteen engorged torrents of water hit the spinning runic circle at the top of the dome and burst through it in a twisting braid made up of millions of gallons of empowered water. The thought struck Tilly as he raced back toward the center of the hub, that he was looking at a far larger, empowered version of Franklin's combat technique.

A braid of water the size of the Colorado River and moving at probably two or three hundred PSI hit the stream of poison the Divine Serpent had launched and burst through its middle. It was simple physics. No matter how powerful, caustic, or heavy the serpent's ability was, it wasn't going to match the force being exerted by that much water moving with unbelievable speed. It blew through the beam of poison the size of a tree trunk and hit the giant serpent in the body like a freight train, forcing it thousands of feet higher into the air.

"The city will flood and this barrier will pull back until it surrounds only me, all who remain must flee. NOW!" Kihei shouted through the crashing waves of his spell to the last thousand or so refugees and their final protectors.

Tilly took one last look at the people getting slaughtered outside the barrier. On one hand, he hated what Kihei had done . . . but he had to admit there hadn't been any more time or other options. His mind raced through how close the defenders had cut every delaying tactic they had, all to give the people the most possible time to flee.

Refugees, honu casters, and the remaining Bastions all moved toward the platform now. Thousands had been left outside the barrier at the mercy of the Defiler and the seemingly endless ranks of Cult soldiers, but those inside did not stay to watch their fate. None were ignoring Kihei's urgent warning.

The new front rank of the Cult soldiers locked outside of the barrier parted. This allowed some of their casters to come forward and begin a counterspell aimed at the barrier. The Defiler seemed to realize it was being denied even more food and started thrusting its appendages into the barrier. Tilly doubted either would be fast enough.

Kihei continued to glow brighter and brighter as he floated there near the top of the dome, his hands outstretched, guiding the braid of super-pressurized water in a continuous attack. Tilly realized that the attack served two purposes as literal tons of water began to rain back down on the city, creating a deluge of rain like Tilly had never seen. The outside of the barrier was getting inches of rain a second, and the water level outside was quickly rising.

"You Will Not Take THISSSS FROM ME!" came the voice echoing from the distance.

Fighting through the hundreds of millions of pounds of force, the snake god came, wriggling and dodging shockingly fast. Tilly could feel the force of its fury as it fought back toward the center of the city, and its palpable wrath bore down with incredible weight on the hub. Many of the refugees around Tilly stumbled, crying out under the newly intensified aura of divine bloodlust.

Tilly's frown turned into a snarl of effort as he looped his weapons and knelt down next to an elderly satyr couple who had fallen to their knees in front of him. Even unable to walk, they were attempting to crawl to the platform and their salvation. He grabbed each of them around their waists, finding them grossly underweight, and threw both of them over his shoulders with a grunt as he stood back up.

The pressure of a god's aura fought against the motion, trying to shove him back into the ground, but he took one teetering step and then another as he pressed forward with all his will. There was nothing he could do to change this battle. He didn't have the power to fight these things or even affect events on a conflict of this scale. The syrupy sweet voice of the **Seed** redoubled its efforts to tempt him, giving voice to the dark cowardly place that hid behind boarded-up doors of bitterness in his beaten, scarred heart.

These two strangers are weighing you down!

All you can do is save yourself!

What is two more deaths in the face of thousands? These people are not your responsibility.

The voice whined and pleaded, venting out the injustice and outrage he felt at the impossibility of his circumstance . . . It may be right, and he might be throwing his life away by taking on one last burden, but he knew what was really at stake. His soul had taken a critical wound at the sight of so many deaths. He wouldn't . . . *he couldn't* leave anyone else behind.

CHAPTER FIFTY-SEVEN

The Great Escape

The barrier around the hub was shrinking at the pace of a fast walk. The enemies surrounding the dome redoubled their efforts to get in, taking the movement as a sign of the magic weakening. None seemed to notice that they were now up to their chests in water, lost in an orgy of their own bloodlust.

Tilly continued to struggle forward under the weight of a god's fury, which the barrier could do nothing to stop. Each step felt like lifting a mountain, and the shockingly light elderly couple that he had thrown on his shoulders initially continued to grow heavier the closer he got to the platform. It was almost as if the serpent's metaphysical desire was actively opposing the escape of its prey.

The increasing weight drove home just how exhausted Tilly was. With lingering injuries, deeply fatigued muscles, and a soul that felt stretched to its limit at the breadth of things it had witnessed in the last twenty-four hours . . . it was all too much.

With a scowl of effort, Tilly straightened his slumped shoulders and looked around to see how everyone else was coping. His lips quirked up into a snarling smile as he saw Threstus and Gorock leading the group of thirty or so Bastions just behind the exhausted honu casters and refugee militia. Their path moved perpendicular to Tilly's, and as they grew closer he saw that many of them were picking up stragglers of their own.

As Tilly watched, Gorock ducked down for a few moments and emerged towering over the group with five gnomes clinging to him as his huge legs continued to pump indomitably toward the portal. That whole group of tough bastards was going to make it, and so would he, as long as he didn't quit.

The thought of quitting caused his trembling legs to wobble, and he almost missed his next step. His foot dragged along the ground, getting under him just in time to stop from falling, as the weight kept shoving him down into the stone pavers mercilessly. The whole time, Tilly kept his eyes on the stoic Bastions.

If they could keep going, so could he.

He shifted the weight of the two, now unconscious, elderly satyrs and continued to march forward as the last of the refugees in front of him made it through the portal.

"**Enough!**" came the reverberating hiss, thrumming through Tilly's chest. The sound of water crashing against the snake's body suddenly ceased.

Tilly struggled to look up with both bodies on his shoulders sandwiching his head, but finally, by awkwardly bending backward, he was able to glimpse the shocking sight of the Divine Serpent free of the water braid. In a movement that was too fast for Tilly to track, the Divine Serpent somehow turned momentarily insubstantial to the water's attack and shot the gap between it and the top of the dome barrier, striking at it viciously as its form returned to its full physical state, including its twenty-foot-long fangs.

They dug into the flashing runic circle spewing red and green poison into the magic just above where Tilly stood. The snake followed up this attack by flexing its jaw closed while Kihei tried and failed to redirect the huge jet of water at point-blank range. Then with a final groan of effort, Kihei's voice whispered out through the sound of crashing waves.

"Time . . . Is . . . Up."

The dome began to flex under the pressure of the serpent's closing jaws, and Tilly grasped desperately at his empty reserves. He had reached the steps, but they might as well have been twenty feet tall for all the effort it took him to raise his knee high enough to plant his foot on the first rise. He kept his eyes fixed on the sight of the others stumbling and diving through the flickering portal. The Bastions followed up the last of the refugees, all of them helping or carrying one or two as they grimly continued to fight forward, not giving an inch to the divine opposition.

At this point, almost all of them were through, and those bringing up the rear were pushing forward for all they were worth. Tilly gritted his teeth in effort until he thought they might shatter, pushing his body above the first step with his trembling right leg. He leaned forward and immediately lifted and swung his opposite leg to take another rise, capitalizing on his momentum as much as possible.

Watching the others push on with no regard for the impossibility of their task pulled on something deep within Tilly. He wasn't the only one being asked to pay a price far beyond what should be possible. Yet without complaint, or even a flicker of doubt in their minds, each remaining Bastion moved through the portal, carrying far more than their fair share of the burden.

The fire in his chest which had dwindled down to a candle's smoldering wick, roared back to life. The change had nothing to do with his mana well or his abused pathways and everything to do with the broken, scarred soul that radiated a deep desire for significance. He wanted to be better this time . . . *He had to be.*

That wounded place in his psyche that insisted he was entitled to a better life wailed in fear as something *savage* rose up from an unknown depth. Suddenly the animal skins that covered his body felt comfortable, like they described some part of his nature he was only beginning to discover. The brutal stone-headed hatchets that hung on his hips were suddenly right in a way he couldn't explain. At that moment, fighting to climb the steps with the weight of the world pushing him back down, something snapped into place.

He had whined, cried, and complained in his past life. None of it had made a difference. With every step that wailing coward's voice was ground into greater insignificance, as Tilly stomped him into the ground with the force of an angry god's wrath.

His *will* hardened to flint, and his shaking legs pushed him up another step.

This world had thrown brutality and horror at him, day after day. The soft man he had been was dying, and something new stood in his place.

He was going to fucking make it.

There were no other options.

Finally, he reached the top of the stairs and looked up from his legs, gaining a clear view of what Kihei had become. His whole body was lost in a glare of deep, blue, pulsating mana, thrumming to the cadence of the crashing waves. Each of the streams of water feeding into the spell at the top of the dome began to shudder and lose their shape, before constricting in on themselves as all the space within the dome of the spell shuddered and then—

Popped.

Tilly stumbled onward, hoping to collide with the flickering portal in one last push. But the entire surrounding environment changed at the sound rejecting physics as he knew it. The crashing sound of waves ceased along with the pulsating light, and gravity had shifted, all the weight of the god's aura fading.

As he pushed forward to the portal a few feet ahead of him the effort sent him upward instead of forward, floating into the air as if he had fallen into the deep end of a pool and was kicking up to the surface.

The constricted flows of water feeding into the spell from the other platforms continued to compress, until they formed a sort of rootlike network, feeding directly into the light where Kihei had once been.

Above them, the giant serpent had stopped trying to rupture the dome. It had sensed something at the sound of the pop, the whole spell changing into something new and far more dangerous, and was now trying to disengage its fangs, shaking its head back and forth in an attempt to yank its body free. Tilly looked around in confusion, finding himself floating alone in the hub with the portal just out of reach. He was shocked to see the enemy army gone, as only the tops of the tallest buildings now showed through the torrent of still-rising water.

Tilly tried to kick forward toward the portal, but despite the water-like feel of the air, it did not offer enough resistance to allow him to swim.

He was so close!

In a flash decision, he lifted the weightless bodies from his shoulders, careful not to let them float off, and gently pushed them toward the opening. They floated the last foot of space between Tilly and the wildly flickering portal and disappeared in a final coughing flicker of power from the teleport spell that had held on this long by a thread. Then Tilly watched in numb acceptance as the portal disappeared, leaving behind a discolored haze in the air where it had blazed for over an hour.

The world around him seemed to be moving incredibly slowly as he floated. He looked up and saw the place where the serpent had inserted itself into the spell spark and flash in distress as the flow of runes started to collapse. This did not stop the spinning of the circle, or the slow shrinkage of the dome. Rather, it caused the movement of the mana to become erratic.

With its army gone, some part of the summoning must have begun to fail as well, and the serpent's form was growing insubstantial. It continued to struggle weakly to free itself, but Tilly could now see the disrupted energies of the spell entering into the serpent and pulling forth its red and green energy to power whatever the spell's climax was designed to be.

He twisted around and looked back to find that even the **Defiler**, which had successfully burrowed partially through the barrier had been caught up in the flow of the unfettered spell. It screeched in defiance, bleeding inky darkness into the deep blue flow of seemingly endless mana.

There wasn't even a hint of Kihei left. The center of the circle was nothing more than a blazing blue vortex of power as water continued to blast forth from the apex of the dome, drowning even the memory of the city in its azure torrent.

He floated there alone next to the faint haze that was once a portal as the barrier closed in around him, now only twenty feet away. There had to be a way out. He had come too far to believe it was all over. Not when he was so close.

His mind raced through everything he knew about magic in this world, and how he could interact with it. He doubted he could blast his way through the hazy scar left by the portal. Those two kinds of magic seemed to have nothing to do with each other . . . Then it hit him. He had just developed a new *Ability* that seemed much closer to the time and space nature of the magic he needed.

Tilly flung his will into the new space that hosted the **Spirit Walk** skill and activated it. This sort of magic had nothing to do with his mana pathways, and he felt it pulling on an entirely different source of energy. One that both moved through time with him and connected to the vastness found outside the bounds of the fourth dimension. His "spirit" pulled away from his physical form with little effort, like the shedding of a winter coat once you got inside.

Hostile magics assaulted his ethereal form the moment he pulled free. The interior of the dome was a riot of conflicting energies, each one screaming at him, *through him,* as he struggled to maintain the integrity of his form, reinforcing the boundaries of himself by sheer force of will. He pulled deeply on knowledge the skill imparted to fortify his being against the powerful flows of mana around him. He emerged a few feet in front of his body and was able to reach out and touch the place where the portal had been minutes before. The now-calcified statues of the four elder casters who had poured their entire being into the spell stood at the four corners of the platform, silent monuments to the heroic defiance of the city's defenders.

He could feel that the *space* there had been forcefully knit together with another location using brute magical force as much as anything else. This caused the composition of reality to be more elastic than it should be. The pattern of space-time was slowly rebounding to its immutable form of rigid structure, but the flux of mana within the dome was slowing the process considerably.

Having found his target, he focused his entire *will* on his ethereal hand reaching to touch the scar in *space.* Then, moving more by instinct than any sort of logic, he reached back and thrust his other hand into the chest of his physical form.

The hazy space he was touching felt like it was right in front of him . . . and yet, there was also the faintest sense that he was reaching through a hole toward something that he couldn't see. He focused harder on his outstretched hand, and slowly felt it double as if it was both out in front of him and incomprehensibly distant. Reality pushed against this unnatural doubling, and he shoved right back.

He focused . . . becoming dead certain that there was *still* a hole in space *right in front of him*, and it hadn't *completely* closed.

A harsh ripping sound tore the air as the recently repaired fabric of reality was forced open again and the sensation of doubling in Tilly's hand suddenly resolved. He turned his frayed will back to his body and attempted to drag it forward somehow, just as the barrier touched the outside shoulder of his physical form.

He desperately activated the portion of his skill that rejoined his spirit to his body while clinging to the space beyond the tear. The azure energy of the spell screamed into his system as his spirit became a conduit for the tear in space. The energies clashed in his body, and a thunderclap sounded from the center of his being.

The out-of-control energies of the wild spell flooded into the memory of the teleport spell form still lightly etched into reality by the sacrifice of the four honu casters. Then just for a fraction of a second, the entire spell flickered back to life, launching Tilly's body and spirit through space-time in a confluence of probabilities that should have never been possible.

In that moment, beyond space and outside of time, Tilly touched on something greater than either, and it pulled him into itself.

CHAPTER FIFTY-EIGHT

Reckoning

J onathan Tillman, you have a . . . talent for thinking outside the box."

Tilly came to on a rough-sawn wooden floor. He sat up, immediately reaching his hands to his head, ready for the onslaught of pain that he was sure would be coming.

"No pain can reach you here. You broke yourself down on the quantum level, temporarily removing yourself completely from time and space. Your imagination has bridged a gap of probability so great that you have just performed one of the most unlikely escapes I have ever seen . . . I hope you know that means quite a lot coming from me."

Tilly looked up in confusion and found himself in an achingly familiar cabin. *Grandad's place.*

He had only gotten to come here as a kid a few times before Grandad had died, but those summer trips "roughing it" had been some of his best childhood memories. The strangeness of his situation imparted a stolid pace to his thoughts as he struggled to come to terms with what he was experiencing. He turned slowly, breathing in the familiar smell of wood smoke, inspecting the shelf stuffed with tattered books in astonishment, and finally, stood facing the two chairs in front of the fireplace. It all felt so normal . . . That is, until he saw the burst of light come into being in his grandad's chair.

An extremely complex network of woven light settled itself in the overstuffed armchair, its shape somehow giving off the impression that it was sitting. The pattern of flowing luminescence was so bright and intricate that as Tilly squinted against its brilliance, he had trouble finding where the cabin ended and its form began.

As his eyes adjusted, he realized that there *was* no end to the network. Rather, it was seamlessly integrated into its surroundings. The strands of light grew less opalescent the farther from the central network they went, and they faded until they were completely transparent. But as Tilly looked closely he found that they were still very much present, weaving everything in the room back toward the center. Tilly uncomfortably followed the few strands that he could spot reaching toward him until they ended in his chest. He looked back up, his mouth dry and face slack as comprehension slowly dawned.

Despite how otherworldly the pattern of light before him looked, he addressed the vaguely humanoid shape in its midst.

"You are him aren't you?" Tilly said, addressing the Living Network with something approaching awe.

"It is not incorrect to call me 'Him,' although it is a little derivative."

Tilly could practically hear the teasing smile behind the words. In the face of that levity, his fury and sorrow from the last few hours came crashing back, displacing wonder. His mind flooded with questions and accusations. They rose up from the well of pain at his center, jostling for position on his tongue. Before he could make an active election, a few popped out, forming partial thoughts and then dying as he attempted to find some calm in the tumult of his emotions.

"Where were . . . How could you . . . All those people . . ." The questions rose and were choked off. Each one was like a boat capsizing under the onslaught of a stormy sea, not able to fully express the aching pain and furious resentment that suddenly swamped Tilly's heart.

In response **Origin's** light dimmed until a fatherly, caramel-skinned man sat before him in something resembling a mechanic's outfit. His eyes crinkled in compassion.

"Why don't you sit down? We have time, but I want to spend it well."

Confusion warred with anger on Tilly's face, before they settled into an uneasy truce of suspicion. He slowly approached, watching the now unassuming man sit leaning forward with his hands clasped in front of him. Those hands were dirty, but in the way that a gardener's hands would be after a long day working in the soil.

Tilly took his seat, struggling with what to say. **Origin** just sat there with a look of concern painted across his face in broad, clear strokes. Something about this kindly demeanor set Tilly even further out of sorts. He seemed to invite Tilly's questions, and for some reason this caused Tilly to hesitate, looking for the right place to begin.

Through it all, **Origin** sat patiently, maintaining eye contact in a way that invited . . . *something*. Demands for answers lived and died on the surface of Tilly's mind as he tried to reconcile his expectations with the calm reality that sat before him. Finally, he settled for the one that had haunted him for days as he fought against **Corruption** on multiple fronts.

"How could you let this happen? Can't you do something?"

"Yes . . . that is always a tough one," **Origin** said leaning back into his chair, with a sigh.

"If I wanted, I could wipe away all of Corruption. I could dispose of evil in a moment and claim the throne of the souls of men with power and glory . . . But I actively choose not to. And this is very painful. Both for me and for you . . ." Then he just stopped, looking at Tilly as if he was waiting for something. The silence lingered and then grew as Tilly realized that he didn't plan on continuing.

"And?" Tilly said shocked, expecting at least some sort of defense or explanation.

"And what?" Origin asked, a small smile again quirking the edges of his lips. He was infuriatingly cool in the face of the horrors Tilly had witnessed, both in this life and the last, and all of Tilly's hesitancy disappeared in a puff of smoke.

"WHY?!" Tilly shouted, snarling in rage as he gripped the armrests of the chair so hard that they creaked in protest.

Origin didn't even flinch at the sudden outburst. He just leaned forward into Tilly's anger and began to shine.

The mesmerizing network of complex woven light returned, illuminating a thick pattern flowing outward from his center in two opposite directions. Both continued to be revealed and illuminated until they reached out to an incomprehensible length.

Unable to help himself, Tilly tried to follow the pattern in one direction to its end. His vision doubled, and his mind flexed uncomfortably as he saw one end of the pattern both within the one-room cabin and in the infinite distance. Origin's voice echoed eerily over the boundless vista.

"I am, as we speak, standing at the beginning of Time, setting this work into motion. It is a very ambitious work . . . For I am creating something that has full freedom of choice, and I have committed to guarding that freedom until the end," he said, looking in the same direction Tilly had. Tilly could see the beginning of the immeasurable strands of existence, each being pulled into a Weave that started simply, yet beautifully. Origin's voice spoke again, drawing Tilly to look in the opposite direction.

"I am also, right now, standing at creation's final moment in Time, watching as what I hold most dear, becomes something far greater."

Tilly turned slowly, fighting to stay conscious as something akin to mental nausea took his perception through loops. The simple motion of turning his head juxtaposed sickeningly with the terrifying amount of distance his perception covered. As his perception traveled toward the other end of the pattern, he noticed that the Weave never stopped changing, increasing in complexity and beauty as it moved through time.

When Tilly finally found the end with his eyes, he could more than just see it: he could smell, hear, and taste just how supremely glorious it had become. All of his senses were evoked at once, and he was drawn into the very definition of

Goodness. It was the smell of freshly baked bread, the taste of summer's first strawberry, and the crescendo of a symphony all at once. The sensations wrapped around him, drawing him into an embrace that seemed to permeate every part of his being.

His awe returned, striking his soul with a thunderous truth he could not understand. As he struggled to comprehend just what he was seeing, a memory emerged. It rose out of the midst of the tension between his ability to understand and his longing to know.

He was back in his daughter's room, having just arrived home after a long shift. She had stayed up way too late fighting sleep so she wouldn't miss him.

And as tired as he was, he had charged into the room roaring like a lion and collapsed on his three-year-old in an impromptu tickle attack. The sound of her squeals of delight and laughter echoed through the room as the light of the pattern slowly faded.

His chest constricted, and he tried to remember how to breathe, struck dumb by the beauty and the sorrow that welled up in the wake of the memory. He turned back to **Origin**, who was once again in his human form, and was shocked to find him crying as he too turned away from the scene.

"Jonathan, I am so sorry about your daughter," he said as tears continued to stream freely down his face. Then, as if nourished by the steady flow of his tears, a small joyful smile bloomed.

"I am, however, happy to tell you that her story is not over. It continues in a different form, and you will see her *there*, at the end."

The words and the manner in which they were given cut straight to the heart of Tilly's bitterness. For, if Tilly was to believe them, then he would have to let go of all the blame and hatred he had hoarded in his heart for so many years. These were the knives he used to punish himself when he stumbled, the broken glass he scattered around his heart to keep anyone from getting close.

Another memory rose to the surface of his mind. His mother stood over him on his tricycle, an expression of shock and then hot anger twisting her face as she looked down at the shattered porcelain lamp. Slowly she lifted her eyes, her expression too dangerous for his young mind to comprehend. *"God dammit, Jonny! Why do you always break everything?"* she hissed at him, almost spitting out the last words. The memory sat like a weight in his stomach, assuring him that no matter what happened in life, everything he touched would end up in ruins.

The laughter of his daughter echoed again through his mind, joined now, by the courageous smile of the little satyr girl, whose name he could not even remember.

His eyes cleared, and hope beckoned to him, inviting him to something new . . . something strange and wonderful. He found **Origin** still there, waiting . . . *vulnerable*.

Tilly's choice mattered to him. And in that moment, under those eyes, Tilly was frightened to realize that he mattered.

That significance, something that he had chased his whole career in the fire department, gave him the strength he needed to lift the awful weight of guilt off his soul. The burden of decades of self-hatred fell to the floor as Tilly looked into those eyes and found a lightness he couldn't understand.

He would see his daughter again. He believed it.

"I am very glad you have chosen to try, Jonathan," Origin said, his smile less grating than it had been just minutes before. "Now it is time for you to return . . . there is much yet left for you to do."

Then Origin clapped his hands together and stood. Tilly flinched in surprise at the movement and stuttered. "Wh— Wait! I thought you said we had time?" Tilly stammered, scrambling up out of his chair.

"Jonathan, you have been here for five days. I do not think you would want to miss what is coming for your friends and the new nation you have helped start," Origin answered, his expression becoming somber.

"Aren't you going to help me with the Seed? Or at least tell me what to do to help Amelia. The purification Ability isn't enough. I don't know what to do," Tilly said, the urgency of his situation beginning to go off like a siren in his mind.

"You already have the answers to your questions . . . I will not take your freedom to choose from you," Origin declared, his face growing hard for the first time in their encounter.

"Now go!" The light and then the room itself started to fade around Tilly. He tried not to feel panic as the impending crash back to reality loomed in his mind.

"Can't you tell me anything else? I have no clue what I am doing out there!"

At this point, the figure and the cabin it had held together in the void were almost completely gone, but Origin's voice returned one last time.

"You are free. Nothing can change that. Use this great gift well . . ." Then the voice faded into the nothingness, leaving Tilly alone.

The blackness around him was absolute. His sense of place and even time was distorted by the infinite emptiness that was both endless and intimate.

Then a pinprick of light burst in front of him. He reached out toward it, as it grew into a marble and then a fist-sized hole of brightness. Tilly watched in fascination as he realized it was hurtling toward him, or he toward it . . . He couldn't tell, and before he had time to puzzle it out, he was colliding with the now truck-sized opening of light.

The harsh light of day assaulted his eyes, and a roaring filled his ears. He blinked rapidly as he covered his head in anguish, fending off the onslaught of reality. Slowly, shapes began to resolve out of the glare in front of him, and the roar reduced itself to incomprehensible noise and then finally the sound of voices.

One figure pulled itself away from the milling patchwork of shapes and colors, its form sharpening as it approached.

A face covered in a thin layer of gray fur leaned in close to Tilly, its milky white eyes looking deeply into his own as if they were looking through him, back in time, to what he had just experienced.

"Welcome home, Gaijin. You are among friends, and we are glad you have returned . . . from wherever you went."

CHAPTER FIFTY-NINE

A Good Night's Sleep

The scene behind Ichiro resolved into clarity before Tilly's eyes, and he found a much changed lapin village, if you could even call it that anymore. The wooden palisade was gone, and lines of buildings had been deconstructed to widen the road going toward the docks on the river and the valley outside the gate.

That valley had experienced an even greater transformation with the influx of new residents. All of the sparse forest leading to the base of the mountain far in the distance had been clear-cut. In its place was a huge milling camp of refugees, which was sprawled out around a square of timber longhouses as big again as the village itself.

"How long was I gone?" Tilly whispered with a hoarse voice, watching as the guards and other lapins attending to business in the village square began to point and exclaim excitedly, with several running off as soon as they realized who had arrived. It seemed like the only one who had actually been expecting him was Ichiro.

"A little less than a week I would say, hard to keep track with all that we have going on. From all reports, your trip to the capital was quite eventful," he said, a playful smile emerging under milky white eyes that still managed to dance with mirth.

"Eventful . . . sure let's call it that. Did everyone make it through alright?" Tilly asked tiredly, trying and failing to resist the leaden feeling that had returned to his limbs and now his eyelids as the events of the past two weeks caught up to him. His notification icon was going crazy, and at a mental inquiry he found that he had gained another level sometime after the fighting. Sluggishly, he thought about pulling up the screen . . .

Ichiro said something else, but Tilly missed it completely, feeling pulled in too many directions for his addled mind to follow. "I'm sorry, can you say that again?"

Ichiro responded by pulling him up from the ground where he had collapsed without noticing, "Come, friend, I made sure your place was kept ready for you. You must rest and eat," Ichiro said, leading Tilly by the arm as he stumbled forward. The shock of adrenaline at having arrived back within the bounds of space-time had left him feeling drained and shaky. It was like emerging from a sensory deprivation chamber and then being given heavy medication. Everything was too loud and bright, yet at the same time draped in the cotton fuzziness of pure exhaustion.

The walk to his little one-room house was a blur. Now that the weight of hundreds of thousands of lives did not hang on his shoulders he felt utterly spent. Even the strange conversation with **Origin** had left him feeling as wrung as a dirty dish rag.

His eyes kept scanning those around him in the late afternoon light, dreading the appearance of a weapon, yet too tired to do something if attacked. Something about Ichiro's steady gait and firm guiding hand on his arm did more than help him through the crowd of onlookers. It slowly pulled him out of his fight-or-flight state, and he began to trust that he had found some respite from the near-constant danger that had marked his new life. Before he knew it, he was lying on the pallet bed he remembered so fondly. Ichiro said something else, but Tilly was already asleep and didn't hear the door close softly on the quiet room.

He slept deeply, his soul lighter than it had been in a long time as he dreamed of a hidden valley with a flower at its center and a song so sweet that it plucked away the few worries and cares that tried to burrow their way into his respite.

What felt like weeks later, Tilly turned his head and nestled back into his blankets, but was started awake by an uncomfortably wet feeling against his cheek. He growled and lifted his head, squinting down at the offending patch of linen, and found it completely soaked in drool.

"Ugh . . ." He mumbled to himself, pushing up from the pallet and looking around. Nearby someone had set a huge container of water, and a tray of food, covered in different dishes. Tilly's dry, cottony-feeling mouth watered, and he stumbled over to the treasure trove of small ceramic bowls organized around a larger one heaped with rice. His stomach cramped as Maslow's hierarchy of needs demanded his attention one by one.

Tilly plopped down on the mat before the tray and mostly ignored the chopsticks in favor of pouring the contents of the assorted bowls down his throat and washing them down with huge swallows of water. All thoughts fled as Tilly entered into the almost meditative bliss of stuffing himself as fast as he could. Before he knew it, the tray was a mess of tipped-over dishes and spilled rice. He looked down at the mess he had just made, slightly ashamed, and thought briefly of trying to stack the bowls. But once again, his body made its demands known as his bladder pressed down angrily on his pelvis, and a sudden urgent need registered in his system. Ignoring these needs for days on end apparently did have some sort of consequence.

In fact, the feeling struck so powerfully that, for a moment, Tilly had to struggle to keep everything contained. He lurched to his feet, suddenly overwhelmed by a driving desire to find the little communal outhouse he had remembered from his last stay here.

He slid the front door open urgently and moved through, barely remembering to slide it closed behind him. Even at this hour, Tilly saw people moving with purpose up and down the street, each pursuing some task they thought was vital to the young city. He picked the direction that felt right and started moving down the small street. The village's transformation was unfolding all around him. Timber was laid in stacks everywhere, and the sound of sawing and hammering was already ringing out through the morning. Though, it was difficult to find a rhyme or reason for how things were being designed. Some buildings seemed to be actually under construction, while others seemed to just be outlined with piles of resources left in the middle.

Each time he passed a lapin, they bowed and smiled, as if they personally knew Tilly. Tilly tried to give each one a nod back, which painfully slowed his progress. It must have been the Title at work because he had yet to see anyone he knew. None of the satyrs he passed or the few other races gave him anything but the typical "Was that a human?" double-take Tilly had grown used to. Finally, he found the outhouse, marked by a rock-covered ditch flowing under the slightly elevated closet-sized building.

There were a few lapins in line when he got there, but they all stepped away as he arrived, bowing as they did so.

"No, guys, I can wait, I promise," Tilly said, waving them back in line and dancing in place. None of them even looked up at his attempts, let alone responded. The door to the small shack opened, and another lapin emerged, hopping out of the way as he saw Tilly, and joining in the bowing. They all just stood there avoiding his eyes as they waited for him to take his turn.

"Alright, alright. I'll be quick!" he blurted in a higher-than-necessary voice, extremely uncomfortable in the current situation. He nodded to each lapin on his way up to the door, feeling every bit like a fish out of water. As soon as he closed the door, however, he dropped all pretenses of control along with his pants. He had to bite back a groan of relief as he sat on the wooden seat, releasing the pressure sitting on his pelvis bidirectionally.

Once he was fully evacuated, he sighed in contentment. The last dregs of stress collected over the hellish week finally started to drain away as he took a moment to sit there and experience the sweet, contented comfort of a full stomach and empty bowels.

Then, remembering the line of people waiting outside, he looked around the small room . . . and his anxiety immediately ratcheted back up to eleven. The only thing he could find in the dim shack was a cup of plain sticks of various sizes, he almost picked one up to investigate when the smell hit him, and he gagged.

Never before had he felt so heavy a burden to deliver a people from such onerous bondage. He shuddered at the thought of how these sticks were used and experienced a pang of longing for his pile of Charmin leaves lying forgotten somewhere in this valley. Someone outside let out a cough, and Tilly looked around again in desperation, hoping against hope that something would just magically appear to rescue him in his moment of need.

Nope, just him and the shit sticks.

He churned his mind, squeezing every drop of inspiration he could from it.

Magic! Of course! He rifled through his fantasy fanny pack and found nothing that would work. Then he took another look at his sleeve.

His Legendary, self-cleaning sleeve.

With a grimace, he reached back to do the dirty, dirty deed and felt the armor tighten unnaturally around his arm and shoulder, constricting his movements.

"Hey! I don't like this any more than you do! One of us has to take the hit, and I can't self-clean!" he said, straining against the suddenly skin-tight jacket. It refused to budge, and Tilly growled in frustration.

Then it hit him. *Can't self-clean.* His mind flashed through a montage of moments when he had discovered new aspects of his powers:

His first enflamed strike.

Enflaming his fist to strike at a manifestation of **Corruption**.

Enflaming his finger to save Linus.

Wreathing his whole body in cascading blue flames that burned away everything but his skin, hair, and armor.

Burned away *everything*.

Tilly was shaken by the revelation and urgently focused on his sphincter, but this time in a way that agitated his mana into producing a portion of his power. He didn't need the entire *Ability* he had discovered in his final battle with Titus, just a small portion of it. The hot, but not unpleasant feeling of his own magically produced flame followed soon after, emerging in an extremely localized position on his body. After a few moments, a very particular smell filled the small room. Having been around fire most of his adult life, he had of course experienced the aroma of burning feces . . . But that didn't make it any less unpleasant.

Tilly held the flame there for five more seconds, even as the normally moist orifice became painfully dry. Then he released it, having eliminated everything he could and hopefully having cleansed the area. He sighed deeply in relief, then immediately regretted it, letting out a hacking cough. He quickly pulled up his pants and banged the door open, hoping that nothing odd had been noticed by those waiting.

The line had grown twice as long as when he had entered, each lapin present looking elsewhere, studiously avoiding the small smoky shack. Tilly cleared his throat in deep discomfort and all but ran past the line back toward his refuge. He didn't know what he would do when he got there, but anywhere was better than the scene of his probable cultural crime. Besides, he needed a place to sit and think for a few minutes. Once he was far enough down the road, he slowed his almost jog down to a normal pace. He almost jumped when a booming voice hit him from a distance, interrupting his squinting scan for the door to his room.

"Jonathan Tillman! It is good to see you awake!" Shuji's greeting resounded down the street. Tilly turned further down the street and found Shuji emerging from the exact door he was looking for.

"Man, it is good to see you!" Tilly grunted, happy to be leaving behind his most recent ordeal. As he approached, Shuji rushed forward and encompassed Tilly in a warm embrace.

"I'm afraid I never got the chance to say thank you for your help that first night. I shudder to think what would have become of me if you had not intervened," he burbled, suddenly emotional.

"Shuji, you saved my life like three times in the capital . . . I should be thanking you!" Tilly answered in exasperation, as he clapped the large Librarian on the back.

The lapin released the hug and gestured for Tilly to go inside. Tilly complied, eager to finally get some answers. Shuji followed closely behind, sliding the door closed and settling to his knees easily on the mat floor. Tilly attempted to match Shuji's relaxed seated position but ended up sitting like a kindergartener. The Librarian's tears were gone, and he once again wore his cheerful smile, a mischievous look twinkling in his eyes. Tilly was starting to enjoy Shuji's constant positive outlook. Whatever crazy shit was going down, one guy in the room would always see the glass as half full.

But, after a few seconds, Tilly began to recognize the unmistakable signs of someone who had gone days, or even weeks with little to no sleep.

CHAPTER SIXTY

AMA with Shuji

Shuji leaned in, excited, clearly unbothered by his tired state, "It is a very exciting time for us, even if many unexpected changes were required for us to move forward. Over the last week, we found ourselves with numbers far greater than what we had anticipated, and that has come with many logistical challenges that had to be addressed before we established ourselves as a faction. We find ourselves with several impossible gaps in our logistical capability that we hope to find a solution to later today . . ." he explained, allowing his smile to slip a fraction before forcing it back up to its full state.

"The hardest part for me has been, of course, giving up my quaint shop in the village. I had become quite fond of it, but others with more appropriate classes are taking over. Now it is nothing but administration work until we get a library established . . . Which I am afraid will not happen for some time. But look at me rambling on. I am here to make sure you are settled back in and advise you before the meeting this morning," Shuji said, a hungry gleam shining in his eyes at the prospect of learning something new.

"Well, all things considered, I think our escape went much better than expected," Tilly said, trying to catch up with events before being struck by a thought. "Wait! Linus, Mochizuki . . . Amelia! Have they recovered?" Tilly almost shouted as memories of their injuries hit him like a brick to the face.

Shuji's smile twitched downward for a minute before responding with his usual optimism. "You will see Linus at the council meeting this morning. He is not what he once was, but still serves the people. Don't tell him I said this, but it is probably better that he has taken the position he has with the former empire. Mochizuki made a full recovery, although I doubt you will see her much in the near future. Amelia has woken and seems to be at no risk of becoming one of those . . . **Corrupted**. Despite that, nothing we do seems to be able to clear away her current level of infection. She is out on the fields and pastureland now, working on a system that will hopefully be able to feed all of these new people. I am afraid in the short term that food will be one of our biggest challenges." Then before Tilly could ask about any others, Shuji slapped his hands on the mat in front of him decisively.

"Enough about others, human! I have been sent here to advise you before the meeting, and Hiro will not be gentle with me if you continue as you have been."

"What?" Tilly said, looking down at himself, before it dawned on him . . . It was finally time to get some answers! No attack, no running for his life. He could actually learn something about this world and the system that governed it.

"Oh, hell yes, Shuji! My bad, let's get down to it, can I ask you anything?"

At that, Shuji hesitated for a second, before answering, "I think it is best if we start with your character sheet. Lord Hiro is somewhat concerned that you have been . . . ah . . . haphazard in your choices so far, and he wishes you to have the best advice I can offer regarding your build going forward. I am by no means an expert, but this is within my area of interest, and we believe you could use the help," he said suddenly looking anywhere but Tilly's eyes.

Tilly's face, however, brightened considerably at the offer. "Shuji, I don't know if you think that's offensive. But no one knows more than me that I have been scrambling from day one. I would love your thoughts . . . But there is something I have to tell you first. It's time I was honest with you and Lord Hiro."

The last sentence just slipped out of Tilly's mouth, not at all premeditated. But now that it was out there, he found himself torn.

"Please, *Gaijin*, you are among friends, no less than any of our people in my eyes," Shuji said, concern coloring the edges of his reassurance.

Not suspicion.

Not disappointment.

Concern.

Tilly's voice caught in his throat for a moment, again feeling hesitant to burden the already tired lapin with his problems . . . As he thought about how best to put it, he felt the subtle throbbing emanating from his side, harder to notice than ever. Or did it feel weaker?

Maybe it is getting better . . .

Maybe I can manage it.

He looked back up into Shuji's earnest expression. He was genuinely offering help and cared about Tilly's wellbeing. That look pierced through Tilly's confusion, and suddenly, just for an instant, he was sitting back in that cabin looking into another set of eyes.

"Shuji!" Tilly blurted out, abandoning any careful shaping of his statement.

"When I went up to fight the **Corrupted** tree, it infected me with some-thing . . . Something that I think might be far stronger than anything we have encountered so far. No matter what I do, it is growing worse. I am afraid I might be becoming something even worse than what I burned down in the temple." The words tumbled out of him in a rush, seeming to rip free from the depths of his psyche. Then it was all out of him, and he felt . . . light. For better or worse, oth-ers knew.

Shuji leaned back on his heels and thoughtfully nodded to himself. His face grew serious as he considered Tilly's words, but his eyes . . . They still danced as if he was enjoying a joke no one else had heard, and he certainly didn't seem surprised.

"Shuji . . . did you already know?" Tilly asked hesitantly, trying to read through the expression on the Librarian's face.

"Yes, of course. Even if Ichiro had not told us, it would have been plain from several points of observation. But we are glad you are willing to share. This means you are willing to accept help, which does us great honor. What that help will be, however, must still be considered. It is part of the reason I am here, to find out how we must proceed."

Tilly let out a deep sigh, his shoulders straightening from a slump he did not even know was there.

He wasn't alone.

"Alright, Let's get to it. I haven't had a chance to look recently . . ."

Tilly pulled up his character sheet and started to read it out to Shuji, deciding not to hold anything back. This was his chance to finally get some questions answered and maybe even some decent advice on how to proceed.

Jonathan Luke Tillman

Level: 18 (2000/500,000 exp until next level)

Display Name: Tilly

Race: Human

Class: Son of Flame

Health: 100% (1.8% per min.)

Mana: 100% (1.5% per min.)

Corruption's Influence: 24%

Status Effects:

Minor Corruption [Hidden] -16% Wisdom +11% Strength

Titles: *[Harbinger], [Resolute], [**Origin's** Champion], [Corruption's Host], [Trusted Gaijin], [Hostile Environment], [Scarred Heart], [Divine Wind]*

Stats:

Constitution: 18

Endurance: 99 (108.9)

Dexterity: 35 (38.5)

Strength: 13 (14.4)

Wisdom: 18 (15.2)

Intelligence: 13

Equipment:

Origin's *primitive stone hatchets: +10% to Dexterity.* **(Legendary, growth type)**

+Imbued Ability: Recall.

Origin's *primitive leather armor: +10% to Endurance.*
(Legendary, growth type)

+Imbued Form: Sun Salamander leather

+Imbued Form: Nullspider, Mana Engine Enchantment

Skills:

-**Forestcraft** *level 12*

-**Identify** *level 17*

-**Cooking** *level 12*

-**Beginner Hatchet** *level 12*

-**Animal Processing** *level 9*

-**Stealth** *level 7*

-**Herb Lore** *level 3*

-**Ax Throwing** *level 15*

-**Dual-Wielding (Hatchets)** *level 8*

-**Spirit Walk** *level 14*

Abilities:

-*[Blue]* **Flame Strike:** *Channel the fire within you to strike at your opponents. Each strike leaves a smoldering ember at the point of impact and does damage over time. Ember damage is stackable. This Ability has been augmented by your mantle and does 200% more damage to Corruption.*

-*[Blue]* **Flame Expulsion+:** *At the cost of 25–50% of your total mana, you channel the fire within you into a wave flowing from your center, impacting everything around you in a sphere. Ability scales with mana. This Ability has been augmented by your mantle and does 200% more damage to Corruption.*

-[Blue] Flame's Renewal+: At the cost of 5–10% of your total mana, you impart the purifying nature of your indwelling flame, greatly increasing the recipient's ability to remove curses, poisons, and infections from their body. This Ability has been augmented by your mantle and does 200% more damage to Corruption.

-Mana Overdrive: You may perform abilities without paying the mana cost in exchange for unused experience stored in the subspace of your soul at a rate of 100:1.

-Wrath's Shroud: At the cost of 1% mana per second, you may enflame your entire body without physical consequence. You will continually produce flame from your core while this ability is active, and any attack you perform will automatically be empowered with your flame.

Titles:

[Harbinger]: One touched by **Origin** to bring about change. "None may interfere." This and all other **Origin**-related Titles, Abilities, and items will be changed and seen as unremarkable by any deity or deity-aligned faction.

[Resolute]: Your Endurance stat is higher than all of your other stats combined. As long as this remains true, you may completely negate one fatal blow per day.

[Origin's Champion]: You have accepted the mantle of champion from **Origin**. This will augment your skills and abilities over time to reflect your new nature.

[Corruption's Host]: You hold within your body a Seed of Corruption. This entity's progress has been slowed by divine interference, but it will take every opportunity to grow until it has subsumed your will. Seed's influence: 24%

[Trusted Gaijin]: The highest honor that can be bestowed on a nonlapin by the ruling class. It marks you as a "friend" to all lapinkind and they will be immediately predisposed toward offering you any help they may have.

[Hostile Environment]: Due to the unique nature of your physical body, foreign substances have a hard time persisting within your physical body. Poisons, Viruses, and Physical Curses will be 50% less effective against you. This Title scales with Endurance.

[Scarred Heart]: Any goal you pursue motivated by a deep heart desire will be met with an unparalleled opportunity by the system. "Guard your Heart, for out of it will flow Unimaginable Strength."

[A Divine Wind]: When you attack an opponent more than double your level while holding their full attention, you gain a 25% bonus to your attack power.

Shuji rubbed his mustache and muttered to himself as Tilly read, harumphing at certain points and nodding to himself at others. As Tilly finished his last Title, he turned toward Shuji, who didn't seem to notice he had stopped reading. Tilly himself couldn't help but catch that despite everything he had been through, **Corruption's** influence had still gone up two percentage points at some point in the battle.

That more or less overshadowed the joy he would have had at seeing the increases in his hatchet-related skills and the surprisingly useful **Spirit Walk** skill. The only other real change besides his level up was the new ability, **Wrath's Shroud** which seemed like a continuous lower-intensity version of **Flame Expulsion**. Whatever else it was, it would certainly be a useful addition, especially now that he had an alternative source of mana. Even if that source robbed him of leveling progress.

All of this and more tumbled around in Tilly's mind as he eagerly looked forward to receiving some sort of context for all the numbers and terms he had been interacting with since day one.

"Well, what do you think?" Tilly finally asked, interrupting the lapin's fugue.

"Ah," he said, breaking away from his musings. "You already had an interesting class when we first met, but now it has grown into a build unlike anything I have ever read about in the libraries. Am I right in my understanding that you do not receive new *Abilities* as you level?"

"Yeah. Instead, they come to me at moments when I experience intense emotion. But the process doesn't seem to be predictable. It just kind of happens."

Shuji continued to stroke his mustache thoughtfully as he began to get lost again in his thoughts muttering to himself. "Perhaps from a previous Epoch, his system compatibility seems both abnormally low and high for a Progenitor class . . ."

"What is a Progenitor class?" Tilly broke in again, beginning to feel like he was interrupting a private conversation.

"Oh! Goodness me! Mooning over new data like a fresh librarian's assistant! Very sorry, I am here to advise you after all," he sputtered, coming to himself again.

"Some of what I will share with you is theory, but much of our understanding of the plane and your place in it as humans continues to change. It is hotly debated whether we are a derivative of your world or the other way around. Most tend to see what happens on Nephesh as the leading edge of the entire cycle of existence. Our scholarship is very likely biased in this regard. Yet it is well known that in this place ideals, Concepts, and even certain embodiments of culture struggle for supremacy. To be a god on this plane is to embody an ideal or concept so completely that it determines your course of action as much as you affect its meaning. What we saw over the capital was the temporary manifestation of humanity's concept of the serpent, for example."

"Whatever it was, it's gone now. That guy got destroyed before I entered the portal," Tilly cut in, thinking Shuji would want to know.

"No, you saw its manifestation disrupted. The serpent will live on in some form as long as it has believers. The Cult itself exists to propagate terror of its power across the plane. It was weakened for certain, but not destroyed."

"Excuse me for saying this, but didn't your goddess die? That's what Hiro said."

"Not exactly. She gave up much of her sapience to empower the two swords that are our people's heritage, and create a sovereign crystal that has been our people's *Promise* through the generations," Shuji explained solemnly, enjoying the gravity of the legends of his people.

"Uggh! So many questions! Every time you answer one, another comes up! I want to know what this *Promise* is, but first, I want to talk about my character sheet and what is up with my class. I have gathered that other people gain *Abilities* along with their levels, but for some reason, I don't. What does that mean?"

"Ah, yes! Progenitor classes! It is well documented by interviews with your kind that time does not flow parallel here to your world, rather our two times, and perhaps others, weave in and around each other—"

At that, Tilly looked up sharply, the memory of what he saw in his grandfather's cabin burning brightly in his mind's eye. Shuji seemed not to notice.

"But both of our worlds progress together, and both have experienced Epochs of change. Not much is known about them besides that they mark a major shift in the way power and influence are defined by the system governing our world. They are generally referred to as—"

"Shuji," Tilly interrupted. "My class. What can you tell me about it, and what do you think about my stat distribution? I'm sure the rest of this is important. But that is what I need to know now."

"Ah, yes. My apologies. In these times, I get so little chance to share my passions . . . Well, it is my theory that your class is perhaps derived from the very first Epoch of power on Nephesh. The Epoch of **The Hunter and The Prey**. Any Concepts that have survived from that time are extremely powerful, and I believe your class is the current system's attempt to quantify the embodiment of an ancient power. We call classes not native to this Epoch, Progenitor classes. The system will continue to attempt to quantify your effect on the world, but the actual mechanics of your advancement will defy and at times, break the typical rules governing classes and powers on this plane." At this he paused, taking a moment to take in Tilly again, some hint of awe shading his eyes.

"Humans are almost always agents of change, renewing conflict in our world, and making sure established power structures are always in question. But I think you represent something much greater than that. I heard from the soldiers what you did outside of the city, and all of us saw the flames. Something like that should only be possible at much higher levels . . . but it seems you have arrived on the eve of great conflict on our plane, and in you, we find a way, perhaps, to counter the new dark power that is rising."

CHAPTER SIXTY-ONE

A New Hope

The weight of Shuji's prediction hung in the room like a stark light, casting everything they had spoken of in shadows of meaning. Tilly struggled for a moment under the idea that perhaps he was the only solution **Origin** had in place for what could be an entire apocalypse . . .

No. That couldn't be right.

What he had seen in that one-room cabin had changed him. He wanted it to be real . . . *He needed it to be real.*

But even if it was, part of him understood that a good ending did not automatically mean that all the lives he just helped save would continue unmolested. Whatever **Corruption** was, the priests at the Temple of Light had said it was emerging everywhere. Tilly didn't know what that meant for the people here, but the thought of what else they would face before this was all over sent shivers down his spine. That little girl was out there in that camp somewhere, and he was going to do everything in his power to make sure she had a chance to grow up. He jerked his attention away from his dark musing and back to the present.

"Okay well, all the world-ending stuff aside . . . I may have one of these Progenitor classes. But that doesn't change the fact that I have stats to allocate. Is what I have done so far idiotic? I know they are skewed, but I only did what I had to in order to survive, and then I got [Resolute], and I pretty much needed it to keep not dying. What you saw outside of the city is probably possible again, as long as I keep that Title."

Shuji nodded at Tilly's explanation, not at all looking like he wanted to accuse Tilly of making some grave mistake. In fact, he was uncharacteristically slow to speak as he mulled over what would be best for the build in front of him. When he did speak, it was in a thoughtful and hesitant manner.

"Yes, each of us must choose our path of growth, and I must say that yours is quite unique. I have read about a few cases where *Intelligence* has been maxed in a similar layout. Certain classes and races will even do the same with *Strength* or *Dexterity*. Each of these cases results in racially unique Titles for the build. But, I have never heard of a primary *Endurance* with a secondary in *Dexterity*. Perhaps the closest I can think of are Barbarian and Dwarvish builds which prioritize or at least balance *Endurance* with *Strength*. Yet, it can not be denied that your Titles and build are beginning to show some true synergy, which is very rare at such a low level. Then again, you have had a very eventful two weeks . . ." he finished, chewing on each word as if the problem before him was a tough piece of meat.

"So you think I should stay unbalanced? The reward outweighs the risk?" Tilly asked, not quite able to keep the satisfaction from his voice.

"To be honest, Mr. Tillman, I would never advise building such a path of ascension. But you are already here, and the usefulness of [Resolute], especially when paired with some of these other Titles and *Abilities*, makes it difficult to advise against. That being said if you face any other dangers besides the **Corrupted**, of which there are many, your damage output is far too low. As it stands now it is heavily dependent on your mana, not your *Dexterity* or *Strength*. So for now, as you split your stat points amongst *Endurance* and the rest, you must prioritize *Wisdom* and *Intelligence*. This will not balance you, but will allow you to continue to grow without stunting your ability to contribute to fights," he finished, pulling his hand through his Fu Manchu mustache with a flourish.

Nodding in agreement, Tilly pulled back up his stats trying to route a path forward. He was glad to have a good reason to prioritize some of his secondary stats over others. He knew every stat was important, but something about how the **Corruption Seed** gave him a backhanded bonus in *Strength* made him lean more and more away from the stat. Not that he could ignore it completely. His growth everywhere besides *Endurance* and *Dexterity* would be anemic, but he would make sure to invest 50 percent more points into the mana-centric stats than he did *Strength*.

Looking at his sheet again, he was struck by a question that had been nagging him for a while, "Oh! That reminds me! I have a decent handle on all the others, but what exactly does *Intelligence* do? I want to say it gives me a bigger mana pool or something, but all of my system readings are in percentages, so how does that affect my *Abilities* and their usage of mana?" Even as Tilly asked, he saw Shuji's smile tighten across his face as if he was holding back something . . .

"Ahemmm." Coughing, Shuji choked, before quickly stuttering out an answer. "Y-yes. No need to be ashamed, Mr. Tillman. *Intelligence* is difficult for many to grasp. I think your pool metaphor will work nicely in describing it. The costs of your *Ability* can remain the same, while the amount of mana invested in the same *Ability* will increase with every point in *Intelligence*. At some point, 1 percent of your mana will represent significantly more than it does now. For example, two mages can receive the fireball *Ability*, but if one of them has double the *Intelligence* of the other, it will result in a vastly different outcome from the same input."

Tilly's mind was once again taken back to the **Corrupted** hyena things that had stupidly circled the tree while he thinned their numbers. He was certain that their behavior wasn't only tied to a stat, but that did nothing to ease his concern over his own low number. To lighten the mood, he struck a confused expression and grunted.

"*Intelligence* good. Me understand."

Shuji kept up his stretched-too-thin smile, and it was then Tilly realized that Shuji might actually think he was an idiot.

"Hey! I'm joking! I get it, alright," Tilly sputtered out in exasperation. "You try getting sent to another world and being immediately thrown into battle again and again!"

Shuji's smile ratcheted down a few notches and he breathed out a sigh. "Apologies, Mr. Tillman. I have just heard many stories over the last few days that lead me to believe that there are good reasons to raise your two lowest stats. Your use of the word 'thrown' is far too apt for me to think otherwise." He grumbled, looking around uncomfortably.

Tilly just fought down a smile in response, mentally assigning two more points to *Endurance* and the three remaining free points to *Intelligence*.

Obviously not trying to change the subject, Shuji harrumphed. "Yes well, you asked about the *Promise*. And it is well you did. For, with the input of *experience* from the refugees who wanted first rights to the longhouses—"

"Wait, you made people pay *experience* for shelter?" Tilly interrupted, his voice hollow in disbelief. At his tone, Shuji's affable expression hardened.

"Mr. Tillman, many are going without sleep, working day and night to get structure and food in place. A queue had to be established somehow, or there would have been riots . . . It was actually Commander Linus's idea, and you can trust that each representative of the council has their people's best interest in mind," he snapped, eyes sharp over dark baggy circles.

Tilly had enough self-awareness to feel the sting of his own assumptions. This wasn't his old world. "Sorry, still wound up from all this," Tilly said, gesturing vaguely around him with a chagrined look plastered on his face. Then he took a deep breath and smiled sardonically.

"How about I suspend any opinions until I actually know what's happening?"

Shuji nodded graciously to Tilly's concession, and continued.

"The Sovereign Crystal is one of the core elements of any faction on Nephesh. With it, you can establish and rule a group, geographical area, or both. It is the chief prize to capture when conquering others and the way power is tracked on a planar scale. It is surely this very thing that drove the Cult to move so quickly on the capital, fearing that it might lose out on so great a prize. When our people were conquered, our own goddess paid dearly to empty and hide ours. This alone is what has allowed us this option generations later."

"So what does it do? I mean, why do we need one? Wouldn't it be better for us to just stay way out here and build up as best we can? I doubt anyone will find us for a while." Even as he said it, Tilly remembered the black veiny growth of **Corruption** emanating from his scarred side. Somewhere out there, the Blue Flower was singing, and he would have to find it sooner rather than later.

"Originally, we had planned to wait some time until we activated it. We wanted to be defensible and well-stocked before declaring our nation on the plane, but now with so many, we need the powers and benefits only the Crystal can provide. What it will do exactly is unpredictable, and a closely guarded secret for many factions. But we do know that the Crystal will provide a means for nation-specific classes, and great boons to any nationality in which it is activated for the first time. We are hoping for some options that will greatly extend our logistical timeline."

"Wait, why defensible? Didn't these woods get cleared out for miles in all directions?"

Shuji opened his mouth to answer and was interrupted by an urgent-sounding staccato drummed out on the sliding door.

"Ah! Time already?" Shuji exclaimed in too loud of a voice for the small room. He got up and moved gracefully to open the door. Behind it, a small paper bird fluttered excitedly.

"Alright! Alright, give me the message, little one," Shuji exclaimed in exasperation, taking the time to look back at Tilly with an abashed shrug as if he wasn't talking to his own spell. The paper bird unfolded itself, and Hiro's voice sounded out as if he was standing in the doorway.

"We have come to an agreement, and are ready to make our way to the temple. If he is willing, I ask you to bring the Deity's Champion to meet us there." The voice came out in oddly formal tones. Not that Hiro was ever not formal, but there was something else going on.

Shuji plucked the paper from the air and tucked it into his robe before turning back to Tilly.

"Well, Mr. Tillman, how would you like to see the genesis of a faction?"

Author's Note

I hope you have enjoyed reading *Son of Flame* as much as I enjoyed writing it! I am still recovering from the mild shock of having real-life readers like you, and it has been an honor to be able to share this story with so many. The dream of dreams would be to support my family with writing income alone, which would mean many more stories like this one. There are so many ways you can help me get there, but by far the most important thing you can do is rate and review this book. You literally have the power to change my life, and it would mean the world to me if you shared your opinion with the rest of the internet.

Regardless, stop by my website: www.jjhutto.com. I would love to hear from you!

About the Author

J. J. Hutto is the author of the Son of Flame series, originally released on Royal Road. He moved often as a kid and became a fixture at various local libraries as a result. There, he studied under fantasy's greatest authors and became obsessed with the hero's journey, which likely inspired his career as a firefighter/first responder. Hutto currently resides in Atlanta, Georgia, and is pursuing writing full-time . . . among a few other dubious professions.